THE WHITE QUEEN

THE WHITE QUEEN

A TALE OF THE YOUTH OF
ST. LOUIS, KING OF FRANCE

BY

WILLIAM STEARNS DAVIS

AUTHOR OF " A FRIEND OF CÆSAR,"
" GOD WILLS IT," ETC., ETC.

"WHO REVERENCED HIS CONSCIENCE AS HIS KING;
WHOSE GLORY WAS REDRESSING HUMAN WRONG;
WHO LOVED ONE ONLY, AND WHO CLAVE TO HER."

Fredonia Books
Amsterdam, The Netherlands

The White Queen:
A Tale of the Youth of St. Louis, King of France

by
William Stearns Davis

ISBN: 1-4101-0800-7

Copyright © 2005 by Fredonia Books

Reprinted from the 1925 edition

Fredonia Books
Amsterdam, The Netherlands
http://www.fredoniabooks.com

PUBLISHER'S NOTE

THIS volume was previously published under the title of "Falaise of the Blessed Voice."

CONTENTS

FALAISE OF THE BLESSED VOICE

FALAISE OF THE BLESSED VOICE

CHAPTER I

THE MASS OF THE ASS

THE mother moved first. When the dawn stole through the chinks beneath the crazy door, she rose, stirred the dying fire, and felt for the hand of her child. It lay warm — too warm — within her own. Then the little one tossed on the trundle-bed, and in a hoarse voice asked for water. She was holding the cup to its lips when Jean the Miller roused from his straw close by, and the mother could guess his question before he uttered it.

"How is the sparrow, Brigite?"

"Hot; very hot."

"Have you slept?"

"Not I."

"What have you been doing, then?"

"Praying. I have vowed to St. Claire twelve tall candles of pure beeswax. She will not hear. The fever has not gone."

"Wet my forehead, sweet mother, — my forehead and my hands; they are like fire," pleaded the girl, — and again she tossed heavily. Then when she turned and saw the bar of light beneath the door, she tried to rise.

"Haste, — make haste, my mother. It is dawn, and soon the town will be waking, and Father Ambroise has promised that I shall march in the procession. For to-day is the 'Mass of the Ass.'"

Now Brigite was so busy cooling the hands and cheeks that she forgot the warmth about her own eyes; but Jean of the Mill arose, coughed gruffly, and gave a great laugh, which almost made the brass plates on the ledge above the fireplace rattle, — a laugh worthy of the licensed miller for the royal city of Pontoise.

"Mass of the Ass! You! — march in the procession, with every idle fool and loose wench for these three leagues trooping at your heels, — fit comrades for the mountebanks, jongleurs, tumblers, and masterless villains, if they list! — But for Nicole of the Mill —"

"But you promised —"

"If I promised, let Satan eat me!"

"Peace, Jean," admonished Brigite, for the child began to weep. Whereupon Jean grew silent. Did St. Michael know his eyes, too, were growing warm?

Nicole sank back on the thin pillow, soothed, as the cool cloth pressed upon her eyes; then of a sudden she started once more, raised her head, and seemed to listen.

"Hark! a voice, a song — it is coming!"

"I hear nothing," said the mother.

"It is nearer; it is very sweet."

"It is only a lark," said Brigite; but the father clapped his mouth close to her ear.

"It is the angel, wife. I always knew I loved the lass too well to have her stay. I have been a sinful man."

But Nicole sat upright, and gladly listened.

"You do hear!" she cried; "and surely it is not a lark."

"The maid is right," said the mother. "A song is coming — it is —"

"Falaise!" called Nicole; and as she called. the door

creaked open. In rushed the pale dawn across the earthen floor; and stencilled against the light in the entrance stood two figures — those of a young woman and of a priest.

"Falaise of the Blessed Voice and Father Ambroise," cried Brigite, and she and Jean went on their knees to the newcomers, whilst all the time Falaise kept on her singing:

"Virgin of noblest fame,
    Earth-born, yet pure in heart,
By Thee is comforted
All human nature!
By Thee is filled with light
Each earth-born creature!"

She ended just in time for the priest to make the sign of the cross above the husband and wife, and to murmur a benediction.

The song ended abruptly, and Father Ambroise's kind voice sounded: —

"And how fares it with Nicole the Sparrow?"

"Alas! father," commenced Brigite, — then her voice stopped; and when she found tongue to go on and thank the curé for coming thus early, he was too busy feeling of Nicole's wrists and temples to give much heed. It was very plain the girl was worse.

"It is little the king's own leech can do for her," Jean was bewailing to himself; "the only leechcraft left for her is for her soul."

But the priest did not listen. He was both heavenly and worldly wise; told the mother not to despair, the father to remember that tears did not become a tall and hulking peasant, and promised Nicole that next year the Mass of the Ass should be celebrated with far more splendor than it would be that day. While he spoke, the young

woman produced a little bag, and drew forth from it dried
leaves, roots, and berries; shook them into a copper pan,
sorting each with quick and skilful fingers. The room
was bright now with the red dawn; but Falaise did all her
work in a corner where the shadows were dense enough to
baffle the eyes of a cat. Light and darkness were alike to
her; all Pontoise knew that she had been born blind.

As Ambroise finished his exhortation, Falaise was com-
pleting her medicine with hot water from the kettle. The
priest explained how to make the poultices, and warned
Brigite that Good Dame Ilsa's invocations to seven kinds
of devils and her charm-stones were on no account to be
set in their stead. Then he said that he would return at
noon, after the procession; and so slipped out with a second blessing almost before Brigite could remember her
thanks. But Falaise — she stayed. She sat by the trundle-
bed, crossing her feet upon the floor, her face close to the
child. As Nicole lay looking upward, the gold of the
morning beat straight into Falaise's unconscious blue eyes,
and made her curling yellow hair one mass of sunbeams.
The blind girl's face was delicately shaped: delicate the
nostrils and lips; the skin very fair, and smooth as the
down of a petal. But dearest to Nicole were Falaise's
hands, for they were white, long, slender, and gentle as
the press of running water. Wherever they touched on
the hot face, there the fever seemed to cool, and all the
time that Falaise smoothed the brow she hummed a crooning little song, — no words, — but as sweet a song as a
brook could murmur gushing over mosses. Brigite and
Jean did not speak. After a long time Falaise rose, drew
the coarse brown cloak about her, and smiled above the
child. She also did not speak, for Nicole was breathing
steadily. Half she heard Brigite blessing her, when she

moved toward the door. At the threshold she picked up a long lithe willow wand; turned back toward the bed and blew a kiss through her fingers. After she was gone Jean found hardihood to whisper to his wife:

"Pluck up heart, Brigite! She will pray to the dear God, — she and Curé Ambroise. Our Father is not likely to listen to knavish dolts such as I; but if *they* two pray, He'll give ear, and there's a chance for our sparrow. . . ."

Up the way went Falaise, and if she lacked sight, hardly it seemed that she missed it. Once or twice she would tap the stones with her willow wand, and that was all her guidance. Yet she had been vastly entertained, could she have seen all the company that trailed before and behind her, up the winding road to the little city. Proudly above the meandering green valley of the Oise rose Pontoise, battlements, roofs red-tiled or thatched, the spires of Notre Dame and of St. Maclou; and higher than them all the donjons and pinnacles of the great château on the crest above the river — the château which four days since had given entrance to its liege lord, — Louis the Ninth of France.

Into the northern Beaumont gate wended the people: unkempt charcoal burners all in leather, peasants from the fields in sombre felt; girls in gaudy kerchiefs; whilst here and there the steel basinet of a man-at-arms, or even the velvet cap of a belted knight; rich and poor, villain and noble, layman and cleric. Early as it was, you could already see the white mule of Madame, the Abbess of Maubuisson, where the omnipotent Queen Mother Blanche had just founded her new Cistercian nunnery; and close beside the white mule clattered its black brother belonging to Monseigneur the Abbot of Le Val, with the prior and sub-prior pattering behind him. The throng jostled, chat-tered, and grew ever thicker, but never too thick to make room for Falaise. So far from pressing her, unseen out-runners seemed smoothing the path as she glided forward. Mothers dragged their noisy boys to one side; and grave farmers stood to gaze at her, as from lip to lip sprang her name, now reverently, now fondly.

"Falaise, Falaise of the Blessed Voice!"

The murmur came even to My Lady Abbess's ears, and she reined the mule, saying to the Abbot—"One must make way for the blind girl;—at Maubuisson the nuns will cease chanting to hear her sing." And so Falaise went forward; for Pontoise and the country-side loved her.

But now within the narrow streets of the town, even with the best of wills, it was hard to clear the way. For just inside the gate, where there was a little square for cattle-troughs, a procession was forming: knights and squires in blazing surcoats, the echevins of the city in their scarlet gowns of office, Maître Bourget and Maître Jourdain syn-dics of the worshipful guilds of woolcombers and fullers in flowing azure mantles; and behind these a vast horde of lesser folk — peasants, burghers, and yeomen of the guard. Horns blew, orders thundered; magnates stormed, and varlets hooted. Fair court ladies leaned from the windows above the square to catch the eye of this or yonder knight. Babel reigned for a few moments, until the dignitaries had fallen into line behind a score of wheezing bagpipes and braying viols. Then the procession started through the crooked, ill-paved streets, climbing toward the upward pointing finger of the tower of St. Maclou.

First the city magnates, then the two syndics, then the knights, and then — the emperor of all this glad array — a comely ass, long-eared, well-fed, sleek, and twined, head, neck, and belly, with May blossoms. Two boys in green doublets led him by a crimson halter. Behind ran all the children of Pontoise; curly heads, laughing eyes, and scampering feet. Great silk banners curiously embroidered with likenesses of Our Lady swung above their flower-crowned army. Cymbals, oboes, and zitherns, horns and kettle-drums, jangled in one unmelodious thunder. You might have looked to see the tiles clatter down from the roofs, as the army swept onward; and all the time — when the music lulled for a twinkling — you could hear the shout of the merrymakers, —

"Stay far away, black Care, to-day!
'Tis the Mass of the Ass: hi ! hé !"

As they came near the church, lo! even the muddy streets were strewn with carpets, that Master the Ass might have a royal passage. Nearer still, and out from St. Maclou came a second army of white-robed choristers, precentors, deacons, and presbyters with candles and swaying censers, who wheeled about and led the way to the central portal. There, under the shadow of the great church, upon the topmost step stood Ambroise the Curé in his most splendid cope and surplice. He held aloft a tall crucifix, and made the sign of the cross, whereat the procession stopped and awaited his proclamation.

"This is a day of mirth. Let all with long faces get far hence. Away with envy, and wrath, and pride; for to-day we commemorate the ever worthy and most pious ass which bore Our Lord and his Blessed Mother from Bethlehem into Egypt. Therefore let all who would join this festival be joyful!"

"Hi! Hé!" bawled a hundred in answer, and they marched, echevins, syndics, knights, ass, and all straight into

the great church and toward the high altar. Falaise was
already there. When the procession began to press on her,
friendly hands guided her through alleys and by-ways, and
while the multitude marched up the aisle, she was under
the safe covert of a pillar. She could not see the scarlet
robes, the flowers, the banners; but the clicking of countless feet, the hum of whispers, the shouting, the lusty
chanting of Monsieur Tabal the arch-precentor — who heard
them better than she? Down the great nave was wafted
the sweet sniff of the incense, as they shook the censers
over the ass, whilst they led him straight up to the high
altar; and then Falaise with two thousand more — for half
Pontoise was in St. Maclou that morn — stood up to swell
the chorus of "The Prose of the Ass."

First, good Monsieur Tabal's voice pealed out in lusty
Latin, and then the chorus reëchoed in French : —

> "Trudged the noble ass along
> Up the rocky way,
> Patient, pious, sturdy, strong ; —
> He did not delay,
> Though all cried,
> From every side

CHORUS.
> *'Hé! sire Ass, ho! hé!*
> *Where do you go to-day?'*

> "Next he Sychar's mountain crossed,
> Reuben's fields cropped quickly,
> Swam across swift Jordan's flood,
> To see the folk swarmed thickly;
> And all did cry
> As he did fly
> Up Bethlehem's streets, —

CHORUS.
> *'Hé! sire Ass! hé! hi!*
> *Better for thee*
> *It could not be,*

For 'neath yon barn
Babe Jesu Christ doth lie!'" . . .

And on through many stanzas.

Falaise had sung forth with full heart and voice. The thunders rising in the vaulted nave, the clapping of the children, the sonorous chanting of the precentor — all these were her life; and if those near stopped their own chorus to hear hers, when knew she? Presently Father Ambroise began the celebration of the Mass. Falaise knelt; and when, at every hallelujah, the congregation answered with a glad "he-haw!" her own was clearest of them all. Only when they all joined in a psalm, as the service was drawing to its close, did she hear voices behind her, — two worshippers kneeling, — a man and a woman; and by that deftness of hearing which is given to the blind, she said "A young man and a maid."

Spoke the man: "When I can rise to heaven, I think St. Gabriel will sing like that."

Spoke the woman: "I know now how St. Cecile sang when the cherubs flew to hear her."

"Do they really think Monsieur Tabal can sing so sweetly?" thought Falaise, and she turned to hear them better. Then the woman spoke again in a pitying whisper: —

"Alas! Poor maid: see, Louis, — blind!"

Falaise ceased to be interested. They were only praising her own voice. She was accustomed to that, and she was sure the precentor's deep and swelling tones were far more worthy of remark than her small part in the chorus. Nevertheless she listened to all the strangers' whisperings, and presently heard the man calling the woman "Margaret." Whereat Falaise smiled to herself. "They have the same name as the king and his young queen. How odd! Yet there is many a Louis and many a Margaret in Pontoise!"

Soon with another and still mightier braying came the benediction; the echevins, syndics, and their train swept down the aisle — this time led by Monsieur Tabal and his acolytes—all bound for a well-spread feast in the guild-house. His ass-ship trudged after, to eat his fill of barley. The church was emptied almost as rapidly as it had been filled. Falaise heard the hundreds of footsteps dying far, far in the distance. Outside, there would be dancing and drinking, juggling and archery, till nightfall, — the city keeping holiday; but within, the great church grew ever more still. Now Falaise heard the click of the gates as old Aimon the sacristan closed the chancel. She stole from her pillar, touched the holy water in its familiar marble, and began her morning round of the little side altars. She began at the left with St. Elizabeth, the mother of John the Baptist; and was just moving on to St. Martin when the wooden shoes of Aimon came clattering nearer, and she arose to hear him.

"Ei! my morning lark, if you could not see, you could at least hear a merry chanting. And Sire the Ass, how sleek, how tame; how sagely he wagged his ears when Father Ambroise upraised the Host! I thought he would kneel too! But how I run on. You are summoned to the sacristy."

"To the sacristy? for what?"

"You will know; great people, I will swear, by St. Maclou himself. But hasten."

"Great people?" spoke Falaise, loath to quit St. Martin; "and send for me?"

"For nothing ill — yet come, I dare not keep them waiting."

Now Falaise was wise enough to know that Aimon was the last man to tell a thing if you teased him. So she followed to the sacristy, and there she heard three voices —of the young man and woman who had knelt behind her, and of old Argot the blind beggar. Argot was talking through his nose, telling how the plague had swept off his four sons these seven years since and left him to Our Lady, and charity; and the woman was interrupting with "Alas!" But when Falaise entered, Argot was left to whine to the four walls, and questions flew at the blind girl.

"What is your name?"

"Falaise."

"Whose child are you?"

"The good God's!"

"You mean, poor girl, you are an orphan?"

"Yes, but I do not grieve: I have two fathers."

"Two fathers?"

"Father Ambroise and Huon of the Castle."

Falaise thought the strangers both gave a little laugh.

Then the woman continued, "They are very good to you?"

"Very good: all Pontoise is good to me. I love every one."

"And you are blind?"

"I can see with my ears, and with my hands."

Falaise's hands floated out in an airy gesture; and again the strangers laughed. But the woman resumed once more.

"You have a very beautiful voice: some day I hope to hear you sing again, and longer than to-day. But now take off your shoes. We desire to wash your feet."

Falaise drew back, blushing; "My feet?—"

"It is a penance. My husband and I have been commanded by our confessor to wash the feet of two poor blind people, — blind, that they may not know who it is that thus summons them; poor, because the poor are very dear to God."

Falaise was reassured. "I understand," said she, though her forehead was still warm; "but first you must let me do one thing."

"What is that?" said the woman.

"You must let me pass my hand across your face, that I may 'see' you." Another little laugh, and then the answer came.

"That you may, right gladly."

Falaise drew near, and did as she wished. She was not mistaken; it was the face of a young woman, younger even than herself, gently moulded, and Falaise's touch dwelt lovingly on the mouth. She withdrew her hand, satisfied.

"You are a lady born. I can feel it by the velvet of your skin; and you have kind lips, without pride. The Saints must love you."

"I would rather hear you say that than have —" here the strangers seemed to hesitate — "than have a purse of forty deniers —"

"Forty deniers!" laughed Falaise; "why, that is a sum for a great seigneur: and all because I said your lips were kind."

But her summoner did not answer. Falaise submitted to be seated on a bench, to have her wooden shoes put off, to have her feet bathed with lavender-scented water. If her strange tire-woman thought those feet as white and shapely as any in the Île-de-France, she did not say it. By another bench the young man whom she addressed as

Louis was ministering in like fashion to old Argot: and will you blame him if he vowed under breath that his wife had the lighter penance of the two? Falaise felt her feet being dried with a fine sweet Flanders towel; then she arose, a coin was pressed in her hand, and she was told that she might go.

"I will hear you soon again, Falaise: and Our Lady bless you!" So spoke the young woman, to which the young man added, "And our Lord Jesus Christ!"

That was all. The blind girl was again in the church, finding her way toward the altar of Saint Martin. But for the fresh coolness of her feet, and the round coin within her hand, Falaise might have thought it half a dream.

"They were great court people," she thought; "a knight and his lady: no, even a count, — who knows? — and their voices were very kind. I wonder if I shall ever meet them again?"

But now she was at the altar and must pray; while Saint Romain was waiting and divers more. She had almost forgotten the strange penance in the sacristy by the time she had completed her round. Then she went to the door and called twice into the street:—

"Boso! Boso!"

CHAPTER II

FALAISE IN THE TOWER

Now in answer to Falaise's call there darted from under a horse shed, a boy. At first you might have thought him ten, but when you had looked twice at the lines on his face, at his drooping jaw, low forehead, and the hard sinews of his limbs, you would have said "fifteen," and known that his was a stunted life. He came to Falaise, pulled off his dirty cap, and stood watching her with pleased reverence, all the while scratching his thatch of yellow tow. Falaise knew his step, and commanded quickly : —

"The folk are thronging in the streets. The jongleurs' viols hurt my ears. I want to go to the tower."

"To the tower it is, and by the shortest way."

Whereupon Boso led her down by street and alley, away from the noisy rout ; until — had Falaise but seen it — over her head upreared the ramparts of the great château. Falaise did not see the huge pile — barbicans, donjons, curtain walls, and baileys — but the cool shadow of the high ramparts told her she was near, and Boso did not need to lead her in.

The castle was Falaise's world. All but born in it, she knew its stony mass from the slimy unsunned oubliettes of the prisons to the storks' nests on the tallest tower. She knew the echo of every stone, she knew how many steps would cross the outer court, how many the smallest chamber. She went on boldly, not heeding all the life that stirred about her. The green-liveried archer at the gate looked once, but did not challenge her, and smiled behind his beard. The two horse-boys, laughing in the court, stilled their coarse jests at the passing of her shadow. The Cistercian monk in white stopped expounding to his Franciscan brother in gray the last error of the hair-splitting schoolmen of Paris, and his shaven face softened. Only four days before, the court had come to Pontoise — ladies, knights, maids, squires, varlets, champing *destriers* and palfreys, velvet caps and "cendal" silk mantles — and yet in four days all seemed to have learned to love the sight of Falaise. She moved across the court as a sunbeam treads; all were brighter when she had passed.

Into a second gate, another courtyard, and then in the tallest tower of all Falaise went, not to the main portal, where well-fed pikemen were on guard, but to a smaller door embedded in the massive masonry. No soldier kept it. Falaise pushed it back, and entered boldly. When the builders of the château had planned for their donjon walls of full sixteen feet thick, there had been ample space for a stair to wind to the summit without communication with the rooms within. The way was narrow, steep, — others would have called it dark. But the blind girl went straight up. So familiar was the climb that she did not count how many stairs she mounted. Once at the top, there burst, on Boso's eyes at least, a noble vision. Here was a round chamber with a few benches, a straw bed, a jar of water; but all the lattices were open, and through them streamed the golden morning light. He could look forth to the May sky and the green Oise Valley. He could look down on the wide castle courts now humming like a hive; and on the red roofs of the clustering town. For an instant he almost wept that Falaise could see nothing. But she did

not need his tears.   She stood by the open lattice breathing the fresh west wind, and holding out her arms as if
bidding the sun come down to her.   She had spoken well.
"She could see with her ears and with her hands."   And
then she turned to Boso with glowing face.

"Oh, Boso, how beautiful is the morning; how I love
Our Blessed Lady for letting me know this day!   How
beautiful to 'hear' the light!"

"Hear the light?" quoth Boso; whereat he did what he
always did in perplexity — began to scratch his head.

"Why, surely; you well know what I say.   Does not the
great wood below the castle whisper differently under the
sunshine than under the night?   Do not the crickets cry,
and a warm hum rise from all the forest?   And in the
night all footfalls crash so loud!   By night I think the
Master Devil is out walking, but by day the angels fly."

As she spoke two doves rustled through the lattice.
They lit upon Falaise's head, and thrust their bills behind
her ears and into her mouth, seeking for corn, and would not
be content until she had opened a little sack, and fed them.
Then she seated herself close to the opening, and leaned
across.   Stout iron bars guarded against a fall, but kept not
the mild west wind from blowing fairly on her face, and
whipping the curls from beneath her hood until no saint
could have hoped for brighter aureole.   Once, while she
leaned, Boso thought he saw a shade of wistfulness cross
her face; the lines of her mouth seemed tightened.   As
long as she was silent, so was he.   But at last she asked a
favor: —

"Tell me all that you can see from here, Boso."

"I have done so twenty times."

"No matter — tell one and twenty."

Boso took a long look outward and downward.

"We are at the top of the high donjon of the castle. If I drop a stone across the ledge, it will look like a pebble before it splashes in the Oise which flows far, far below. It is May, and across the river to eastward all the orchards around Aumône are like a field of snow. You can smell their sweetness. Beyond Aumône, like a great green lake, lies the forest of Maubuisson and Montmorenci. When I look south I can see the towers of Conflans, and a wide steel-blue ribbon. That is the Seine, to which the Oise is hastening. If I point my finger to southward and eastward — so — it is toward Paris. But that is seven leagues away — a great journey — and I can only see the spires of St. Denis."

"You are not telling what I wish to know," interrupted Falaise, almost peevishly. "Pontoise is a town, and Conflans is a town, and Paris is a greater town with more houses, more people, more dogs, more noise. I want to know what is the sun, the sky, the light, the — "

She did not finish, and Boso sighed. His descriptive powers were very small, but he began as bravely as he could.

"The sun is like bright gold."

Falaise shrugged her shoulders.

"Gold is money. Is the sun only a big Tours sou?" But then she stopped, and touched Boso's cheek.

"Ei, lad," she demanded, almost alarmed. "What do I feel — a tear? and what do I hear — a sob?"

"I cannot help it," moaned poor Boso. "How can I tell you what the sun is like when you have never seen it, nor the blue sky. And it has all such beauty, which you can never know."

Whereupon he would have wept outright; but Falaise laughed, and comforted him playfully until kind St. André sent him a thought.

c

"I will tell you what the sky to-day is like. It is like the sweetest brook you ever heard; it is like the great Te Deum they chanted in St. Maclou two years ago when the Breton duke surrendered to the king. It is like the new angelus bell on St. Ouen at Aumône across the river. Put all these in one, and then you know for one thousandth part how beautiful the sky is."

Again Falaise was silent, but Boso saw no wistful lines upon her face. Presently she seemed to wake from her musing, and spoke half playfully: —

"What would you have me do for telling so nicely all about the sky?"

"Sing," commanded Boso.

"One of Monsieur Tabal's hymns?"

"Your own are always finer."

"Roguish boy," cried she; "since the court has come to Pontoise, your tongue trips off flattery like a cavalier. But I will sing to you. I sing best when my face is warmed with the light."

She folded her hands, and lifted her glowing head; after which Boso forgot all about the tower, the orchards, and the sweep of the forest. And perhaps an hundred more in the court below soon were listening; but no bird told it to Falaise.

"Now through all the pleasant greenwood
    Wakes the warm, pure breath of spring;
I hear the glad brooks purling,
    I hear the throstles sing.
I hear the young bee humming
    Above the young sweet flower;
I hear the young roe crashing
    Through the thick young ivy bower.
Oh, joy is in the springtime,
    In beast, and bird, and sky!

But of light hearts in the greenwood
There's none more light than I !

"I'll fall asleep in springtime
Beneath a flowering tree ;
I'll dream till Queen Morgue's faery
Flit down to waken me.
With chains of fragrant posies
They'll bind my neck and hand,
They'll garland me with roses,
They'll lead me to their land
Where it is ever springtime,
Where blossoms never die —
But of light hearts in the faery
Who'll lighter be than I ! "

Falaise sang on, on, making new verses, till fancy failed
and her little throat was weary. Boso had been watching
the sunbeams on her face, as if himself truly ensnared by
the faery. At last she stopped. The doves had flown
away, and their "Coo ! coo !" sounded from the wooden
eaves of the peaked roof of the eyrie. From higher yet
came the clattering of bills around the stork's nest.

"The sun grows hot on my cheeks — the morning
hastens," said Falaise, pouting prettily. "I must go."

"Go where ?"

"Down, out and away again, to Nicole and Brigite.
Nicole is very ill, — more ill, I think Father Ambroise
fears, than he dares to tell Brigite. I must keep all my
other songs to scare the wicked sprites away from the
sparrow."

So she went down the stairs, as steadily as she had
mounted, and Boso, who was faithful as a hound, came
close behind her. But Falaise was not destined to revisit
Jean of the Mill that morn, for as her feet touched the

cobbles of the court she heard a familiar step, and stopped short.

"Ei! Huon?" cried she; and the dapper page who had stopped grooming his baron's barb to squint at her, was grieved to see her arms open to receive a creature very like a walking bear. For Huon the castellan had a great gray beard like a spade, a jerkin of unfleeced sheepskin, a nose like a hawk, and arms that might have crushed Bruin himself. Nevertheless, Falaise gave him not one kiss, but three.

"So late in the day, and I have just seen the Sunbeam," cried Huon, when they unclasped arms; "and whither away just now?"

"Jean of the Mill's Nicole lies sick."

"Leave her to Father Ambroise. You are wanted here."

"Why am I wanted? First Aimon must summon me at the church; then you. I will go."

"You will stay, will you, nill you," asserted Huon, with a mighty paw on her shoulder. "A great lady desires to see you." And something in his manner seemed to show that an august presence was hindering his custom of making every whim of Falaise his law. The blind girl put out her hand and touched a lady standing close beside him.

"Oh!" cried Falaise, "it is you who desire me. Well, I said you seemed kind and good. But you do not wish to wash my feet again?"

"Not at all," said the lady, stepping closer. "I said in the church I hoped to hear you again, and when I heard you singing just above my head in the donjon, I begged the good Huon to bring you. Nor will you refuse to go to my chambers."

"I will go," spoke Falaise, lightly; "for you do not seem proud. And I think your name is Margaret —"

"Margaret!" The words echoed in a horrified whisper from two discreet waiting-women who had been standing at a respectful distance; whereupon Falaise stared with her blind eyes.

"Am I not right?" asked she. "Your husband called you that in the church."

The lady seemed almost laughing. Huon was stifling a chuckle. And then the lady answered her. "Yes, Margaret is my name; they call me Margaret of Provence."

It was a pretty sight to see Falaise's forehead turn to rose, and then to snow, and then to rose again. At last her words came slowly.

"Then — you — are — the — queen."

But Margaret of Provence, queen consort of the very Christian king, only took her by the hand.

"By St. Agatha, I wish I could surprise you twice again to make you blush like that. And because I am the queen of France, have I not two feet, two arms, a head, and a mouth? Do you think I have no ears when you sing? Does the queen of France never grow weary or lonely, nor long for some one of her own age to talk with?"

"Ah!" cried Falaise, perplexed, "but I have had no dealings with courtly folk. How shall I call you? To say 'most gracious queen' sounds very long!"

"Call me 'Margaret,' if you will; but if you fear that, say simply 'Lady.' And now will you go with me?"

"I will; but first I must send off Boso."

Whereupon, to the renewed horror of the worthy waiting damsels, Falaise kept her Grace of France standing till you could have counted fifty, whilst she told the boy to run to Nicole to say that she would come in the afternoon, and tell everything about the queen herself. But if the servants fumed, the mistress tarried smiling, well content.

As she waited, you could have had a fair view of Margaret of Provence. She was barely a woman even yet, and younger than Falaise herself. The court poets sang of "her fair blonde locks, her forehead whiter than lilies, her laughing eyes which changed color with her mood, her fresh face outvying the white and vermilion of flowers, and her chin and throat like the wild rose"; but I think that in truth Margaret was only a tall girl, with blonde hair, clear blue eyes, a gracefully chiselled face, and a gentle mouth that now, as often, was near to laughter, yet seemed sometimes to hide a sob behind the gladness. She was plainly dressed in green,—no gold lace, no ermine, only a few ruby and emerald pins glittered in her hair, and on one long finger was a great topaz. But though so young, she held her head proudly, and looked what she was — the queen of France.

Falaise gave Margaret her hand. The queen thanked Huon, who grinned at seeing his fosterling in such fair company. Margaret walked slowly, but was amazed to find the blind girl leading her.

"You move very fast," said she. "Were you always wholly blind?"

"Always. Boso has just been trying to tell me what the sky was like; he says it is a fine angelus bell, but I know it cannot ring."

"And yet you walk so boldly?"

"Is this not Pontoise château? Do I not know the sound of each stone on which we tread? When the court came, there were so many strange footsteps and voices I was a little confused; but now I grow accustomed."

"I must hear your story." But here the queen

dragged at Falaise's hand, and laughed. "Ah! not so boastful. We are going to my chambers, and this is not the way?"

For the blind girl was nearing a small door that was new to Margaret. Her companion, however, answered laugh with laugh.

"You are queen of France, lady; but you do not know this château. None know it, saving Boso, who is Huon's son, Huon, and I. You would mount to your chambers? Follow — see?"

And leaving the bewildered waiting-women behind, Falaise led up the same winding staircase by which she had just descended from her eyrie. Margaret followed with all the delight of a child in a gay adventure. Thin slits in the massive masonry lighted the turnings at rare intervals. Once the queen slipped, and felt Falaise's arm under her. Once a spider's silk brushed across her face. Once there was a whisk and clatter at her feet. "Only a rat," said Falaise; and was the queen of France to falter where a blind girl led?

But her conductor did not continue to the summit. Suddenly, at one of the darkest turns in the stair, Falaise halted, and tapped with her hand.

"Wood," she announced. "A panel set in the stone."

"This is not my chamber," said Margaret, doubting still.

"Put your finger through this hole. What do you feel now?" questioned Falaise.

It was so dark Margaret had to let the other guide her finger through a small opening. It pushed against heavy arras tapestry upon the inner side. The plank was thin, and Falaise laid her ear against it, and remarked again.

"Listen, — in your own chamber, — you can hear the people talking."

Then she showed how the panels slid easily in grooves, and was about to push and open, when a warning "Hist!" from Margaret stayed her. The queen in turn was listening, — listening so long that Falaise began to wonder. And when Margaret turned away she was glad her companion was blind, for she knew her own lips were twitching and white.

"It is clear that we who are strangers to Pontoise have much to learn," she said, and hoped her voice was steady. "How strange that there is this privy entrance to my chambers. And how I would affright my good women were we to pass in by it. Let us go down and mount by the common way."

They did so; yet all the way down, and all the way up again, Margaret the queen spoke not a word, and Falaise feared lest she was angry.

CHAPTER III

ALITHE, CALLED THE CAT

In Margaret's chamber a lady had been sitting. On her lap lay a blue scarf of Persian silk, and in her hands were the needle and silver thread; but she was not finishing the beak of the embroidered griffin. Her hands lay idle, and her eyes were roving about the room. The court had been four days only in Pontoise, but in that short time much had been done to give splendor to the wonted gloom and grimness of the castle. The floor of black and brown tiles was strewn with peppermint leaves, fresh green twigs, and dried roses, gladioli, and lilies. The dingy red and yellow flowers frescoed on the walls were almost hidden by abundant pictured tapestry from Picardy — here a wedding party, there a hunt, and yonder the whole great battle of Bouvines, with King Philip unhorsing the German emperor. The furniture had likewise been renewed — divans cushioned in yellow brocade, huge silver coffers, and odorous cedar clothes-chests, a graceful prie-dieu, and a luxurious arm-chair. The deep window alcoves were framed between priceless Venetian laces; the crucifix upon the wall was gold; the curtain that separated the room from the queen's sleeping chamber was from the choicest loom in Bruges. The castle, in short, had been transformed into a palace.

But "Alithe of the Bright Face," the noblest born of Margaret's ladies-in-waiting, was not thinking about the Bruges curtains, nor the Venetian laces, nor the Picardy tapestry. She was very handsome, this young lady, and like her mistress had been honored with two long *cansons* by the gallant Count Theobald in praise of her lofty forehead, her tapering hands, her fine hair and eyes, and "the snowdrops of her teeth." Only the good count failed to add that these teeth were just in the least too prominent when she smiled, and that the lines of her face grew a little hard when she was not trying to be gracious. Her teeth and her softly stepping ways gave her another name, that was only spoken behind her back, when "Alithe of the Bright Face" became "Alithe the Cat."

Now at the present moment this lady had very pleasant thoughts. First of all she was thinking how favored she was in her ancestry; how her father Enguerraud, Sire de Coucy, was rising daily in princely honor and might, till no ducal house in France need cause envy to his child. Who did not know the De Coucy motto, and what ample lands, what thousands of vassals, could make it good?

> *" Roi ne suys*
> *Ne prince, ne duc*
> *Ne comte aussi :*
> *Je suys le Sire de Coucy !"*

And Alithe, being in a pious and meditative mood, gave thanks to Our Lady for her high birth. Then again she thought on her own position in the court; how many gallant seigneurs were fawning on her father for her hand, and how the Comte de Neville and the Vicomte de Forgueux had fought in Paris only one week since with her name upon their lips. True, De Neville was dead, — luckless and handsome wight, — and his enemy lay at the Hotel-Dieu, like to follow him; but Alithe had dried all her tears. She was just passing on to consider her third great happiness, when there was a pompous step on the threshold. The hangings parted, and a scarlet-clad usher held up his gilt wand of office.

"Her Grace the queen mother of France!"

Alithe rose, shook her loose black gown about her, and made a studied courtesy. There was a rustling of silks, laces, and ribbons. Alithe meekly studied the rushes, and remained standing until she had to answer a question.

"Is not the queen consort here?"

Alithe courtesied again before replying.

"May it please your Grace, she has been gone some time, taking two maids with her."

"And for what end?"

"She said she wished to summon the blind girl who sings from the top of the tower."

"If that was her errand, she might have sent one of her women."

"Is she not queen? Was I to question her?"

"You understand your station, Alithe; you were *not* to question her."

Through this dialogue Alithe had been looking down. Now she raised her eyes. In the arm-chair sat Blanche of Castile, "The White Queen," actual sovereign of the realm. White she was in name, and white in dress; for since the death of her fondly loved husband, Louis the Eighth, she had never ceased to wear the mourning color of the princesses of France. Her flowing bliaut, her chamois gloves, the veil that floated over her silver hair — all were white. Yet she was no aging woman; her skin was firm and fresh, her dark eyes bright with a masterful fire. Alithe herself might have envied the strong, clear profile and the fine curve of her mouth. She sat erect in the high chair, stripping off her gloves slowly, saying nothing, and so compelling the others to silence. Then she turned to Alithe.

"You say the queen consort is not here?"

"So I have said, your Grace."

Blanche slowly pointed toward the door; the four young women who had followed her vanished noiselessly, and with them the usher. The queen mother pointed again to a divan, and Alithe seated herself. Blanche folded her gloves before she began to question.

"Thus far to-day I presume you have observed nothing, though you have of course been diligent?"

"Nothing," rejoined Alithe, who knew that Blanche detested long answers.

"It is highly unfortunate that this Gui of Avignon should accompany the court to Pontoise."

"Highly unfortunate," reëchoed Alithe.

"I did my best to detain him in Paris. It was largely to shake my children rid of him that I took the court so abruptly to Pontoise, as you well understand. He pretends that his embassy in behalf of his lord, Raymond of Provence, requires his constant attendance upon the king."

"Your Grace has already taken me so far into your confidence," Alithe eyed the queen mother carefully; and then, like a man treading on quicksands, continued, watching each shade of feeling as it crossed Blanche's face, "If I may make so bold, and am not too presuming, your Grace would serve your own cause best if you would tell me clearly what you fear from this Gui, and why you have asked me to keep so close a watch upon the queen consort."

Blanche's first answer was a glance toward the door; then her voice lost half its hardness, and she grew confidential.

"Alithe de Coucy, your fathers have dared and suffered many things for their kings, and I will not distrust their daughter. As you must know, since February, when this Gui of Avignon came up from the South, I have observed his gallantry toward Margaret of Provence. At first I trusted it was mere old-time friendship, seeing that he came straight from her father's court, and the cavaliers of the Languedoc are more given to lip-service and harmless chivalry than those of our colder North. I have watched — I have waited. I fear lest to his friendship and gallantry I must give a yet darker name — "

"Impossible — the queen consort!" If Alithe had expected this declaration, her surprise became her well.

"You may be sure this is an infinite grief to me," went on the queen mother, her speech growing faster. "It was I who arranged the marriage for my son. I considered too much the advantages of alliance with the great court of the South; too little, that I might bring shame and contempt upon the very throne of France. I had trusted that this Margaret, being a mere child, could be pliant to my wiser will; that she would quickly perceive how the king is too young for rule, and gladly leave to me the reins of government. But headstrong, disobedient that she is, does she not daily urge my son to set his wishes against mine, to grasp a sway he is too weak to hold, and plot to set a son against the mother who bore him, nursed him, fought for him, ay, — would die for him?"

Never before had Alithe seen Blanche put by her coldness in such fashion, and she knew that the White Queen was terribly moved, as she ran on hotly: —

"Look on France! When was the kingdom stronger? Are not the rebels crushed? Brittany, Champagne, Boulogne, the rest — all pay their homage. Justice is done,

the roads are safe, the cities thrive, churches and abbeys
rise; and who has done it? I, Blanche, the regent for
my child, whom half the seigneurs of France plotted to
cast down, that they might spoil the royal power. Though
a woman, by St. James's aid I mastered them. And now
victorious, while my son is yet a lad, with the down upon
his lips, this girl, this light Provençal, plots to rob me of
his love, — to thrust me from my power!"

The White Queen's passion ended as abruptly as it had
begun. She sat silent, impassive, — angry, no doubt, with
herself for unveiling her heart to a subject like Alithe.
The young De Coucy turned her thoughts back to their
beginning.

"But your Grace began by speaking of Gui. Surely he
does not remain at court with sinister intent?"

"I would to God I dared think with you. But of the
woman who will come betwixt a mother and a son I
must fear the worst."

Alithe smiled behind the feathered fan she held before
her face. Infidelity and jealousy were strange demons to
possess one wife; but she knew the queen mother had
become unreasonable.

"I will do whatever your Grace commands," suggested
Alithe, and Blanche drew herself up primly.

"My commands are that you speak to no one, not even
to the king, what I have hinted; that you inquire among
the young cavaliers of your acquaintance, and discover
what they think concerning this Gui. My hope is that
he can be found to be infected with the Albigensian
heresy so common in his unhappy country, and may
himself give fair cause for banishment from court. What
ever thing this Margaret says or does, bring straight to me.
If she betray my son —"

"It is no light charge to bring against a queen of France," threw out Alithe; but Blanche caught her up roundly.

"Who said she was the queen of France? All marriages are not valid in Holy Church. Ask the bishop of Beauvais. He was at Sens at the wedding; and if she dare —"

Alithe's fine nostrils had swelled a little as she listened. Once more Blanche was unbridling her tongue. St. Genevieve knew what was on the edge of slipping out, when the queen stopped, like a charger reined in full heat.

"I have said what it is not for you to know. Forget that I have said anything; or I can ruin — even a De Coucy."

For answer Alithe held up a warning hand, and rose as the bowing usher thrust back the curtains.

"Her Grace the queen consort of France."

Alithe stood; Blanche sat stiffly. Margaret entered, leading Falaise by the hand. When the younger queen saw her mother-in-law's unbending presence she faltered, and flushed as if wishing to draw back; but the older lady gathered herself up with dignity and remarked in chilling tones, "that she would not intrude upon her daughter's pastimes;" and so was gone with a great rustle of samite and cendal, to Margaret's plain relief. As for Alithe, she had reseated herself without waiting to be bidden, although at the breach of decorum the Provençal lifted her eyebrows twice. All this time Falaise had been standing near the entrance, and when Margaret bade her draw nearer, she hesitated.

"Some one strange to me is here. I hear her breathing."

"Yes; the Lady Alithe de Coucy, my friend."

"If she is your friend, I will enter; for though you are

the queen, you are not proud, and your friends should not
be proud. Now what do you wish — not to make sport
of one who is poor and blind?"

Alithe had been scanning the blind girl from hair to
sandal. "A pretty doll, with a nightingale's voice," she
had said to herself. Now she was a little alarmed, for
Falaise came straight toward her, and before she knew it
the other's hands were touching her face. Margaret
laughed to see the flush of astonishment upon the lady's
cheeks, and Falaise said simply: —

"Yes, you are a friend of the queen, for, like her, your
skin is soft as flowers, and you are most beautiful; only
your mouth does not feel quite so kind."

Content with her examination, she let Margaret place
her in the great arm-chair just quitted by the queen
mother, while Alithe nursed her wounded pride in silence.

"Now what do you wish?" repeated Falaise.

"What do I wish?" quoth Margaret, leaning easily on
a divan, so that she could watch the pretty bird she was
entreating; "all things — everything. Who are you?
Which angel gave you your voice? Begin at the beginning and tell it all."

Falaise hummed a little catch before she answered.

"Have I not said my father was the good God?"

"The good God is the father of us all; but who was
your earthly father?"

"Well — that I cannot tell, for all save St. Gabriel,
who keeps the great Book of Life, have forgotten, and I
think he will not answer even a queen. Years ago when
the Picards ravaged the Île de France, and the country was
full of landless men and homeless women, Father Ambroise
found my mother lying outside the Beaumont Gate. It
was very cold. She never woke to tell her name; but I

was wrapped up safe and warm upon her breast. I have heard it said that her clothes were of fine Ypres wool, and she had the small feet and hands of a cavalier's lady. That is all I know. Father Ambroise took me to Huon who keeps the castle when you great folk are away. Betwixt the two I have grown up; and because I am blind they love me more. 'You shall never lack eyes, my sunbeam,' says Huon, 'while two stay inside this old head, and you have a song to buy them.'"

"And who taught you to sing?"

"The winds, the rain, the little soft sprites that creep out of the trees, when the breeze falls to sleep, and the forests stand still on a hot day, and sigh, and sigh, and sigh. Then the sprites come out."

"You do not mean you summon devils, girl," thrust in Alithe, addressing Falaise for the first time. "That were rank witchcraft."

The blind girl winced as though suddenly struck with a lash. Her forehead crimsoned; her lips tightened.

"I do not understand; the little soft sprites are not devils — no, no, indeed!"

"The Lady Alithe spoke but in jest, though I think poorly," said Margaret, thrusting a warning glance toward her companion. "Of course they are not devils."

"Oh, not at all," continued Falaise, comforted by her protector. "Sometimes, just as I am falling asleep, I think I feel them all over me. They have gauzy wings like great moths, and tiny hands that touch like down, and they whisper in your ear the loveliest thoughts. And when I wake, I can always sing a new song that Father Ambroise says makes him think he is already in the heavenly city."

"You must be very happy to sing so well?"

"I am only the harp, and the little sprites touch the

D

strings.   I think they are a kind of angel who live on earth for a while, and I can know them because I am blind and do not trust to my eyes."

"Then there are no devils?" said the smiling queen; but Falaise grew sober.

"Do not say that.   In the winter, as I lie in bed, I hear them.   They go through the huge forest boughs, and set them to tumbling and roaring and groaning.   That is when King Satan is calling his liegemen around him and planning 'thus and thus we will plunge Christians into Hell.'   But I know our dear Lord has clipped his claws, and I say a prayer and go to sleep.   In the morning the snow is strewn with broken branches.   'A fierce wind last night,' says George the woodman; but I know better.   King Satan and his imps have flung the branches round in rage because Christ Jesus has brought their plots to naught."

"By Our Lady," cried Alithe, clapping her hands, "your conceits are as charming as a jongleur's tale!"

"I know of no conceits," said Falaise, seriously.   "It is well never to hear the Master Devil.   I deem that you mighty folk have so many confessors, and friars, and bishops around to pray for you, he never dares to pop in his head to plague you; but if you have never felt the little soft sprites, I pity you."

What Alithe would have answered to all this was never written, for Margaret had gestured "silence" in a manner even a child of the De Coucys must obey.   And just as Falaise was running on with more stories — about the music of the millwheel and of the water-maids who hide beneath it, the curtain was parted again to give entrance to a tall, giant knight in a burnished corselet.   A great sword banged at his heels.   He bowed awkwardly, and pulled at his huge grizzled mustachios.   He was Simon de Joinville, commandant of the king's yeomen, the faithful watch-dog ever at the sovereign's side.

"May it please your royal Grace," he began; but Margaret rose instantly.   There was a sudden light in her eyes, a color in her cheek, that made Alithe look at her twice, as she took the words out of the officer's mouth.

"The king is awaiting me below?"

Simon bowed stiffly.

"The queen mother —" Margaret began again, and a shadow of a grin crossed the battered face of the soldier.

"She is not there."

Whereupon Margaret laid her hand on Falaise's shoulder. "You will remain, while I go to the king.   I will not be long.   And the Lady Alithe — the Lady Alithe," repeated the Provençal, "she shall be naught but kind to you."

Then the queen was gone, leaving Falaise and Alithe de Coucy together.

CHAPTER IV

LOUIS OF FRANCE

As Margaret hurried from the chamber, her eyes glanced once at the little steel mirror against the wall, and her hands went up to her hair. She wished there were time for a richer dress, but moments were too golden for that. She followed De Joinville with swift, glad feet that tripped lightly behind his clanging war boots. The ever present ushers, the little herd of scraping varlets and simpering serving-women, all seemed vanished.

"Where are they?" asked the queen; and the commandant only laid a big finger beside his goodly nose, and laughed silently.

"You mean you have withdrawn all the watchers?"

"Yes, please your Grace."

"But there will be a watch below — for *her?*" and Margaret halted at the last word.

"There will be on watch your very humble liegeman, Simon de Joinville; and when you hear the dogs yelping as if he were beating them, that will be a sign that the very Christian king and his dear wife must draw their meeting to a close."

And again his huge frame shook with noiseless laughter. All the time they had been going down the curving staircase, which wound, serpent-like, through the centre of the great donjon. De Joinville flung open a door, and stepped back, bowing from the base of his spine, as if he had a hinge there.

"I wait and watch below — if your Grace will enter."

So Margaret went into a small, bare room. She was face to face with a young man of two and twenty, whose feet were swift to meet her.

"Louis!"

"Margaret!"

Whereat he held her in his arms, their faces very close; and it was a long while before either had their lips ready for speech. Then, after a time, Margaret of Provence could look on her husband's face, and hear him speak.

Now Louis de Poissy was a man in whom any woman might take joy, even had he been other than the grandson of that Philip Augustus who had fretted Cœur de Lion to his death and hounded John Lackland across the Channel. The king was tall, slender, but well knit, and his muscles were like iron. From his grandmother, the great Queen Isabelle, he had inherited the famous beauty of the princes of Hainaut, but most of all "a clear complexion like Flemish carnations, cheeks white and pink, and a very winsome smile." His blonde hair, a little thin, fell over his ears, and was clipped in a straight line at the joining of neck and head. He wore a tight-fitting woollen suit of plain gray color; the only ornament was his belt, the gold clasp whereof was brightly gemmed. When he had first seen Margaret his laugh had rung through the little room. It was a laugh good to hear — so pure, so free, so boyish. And when he spoke in the musical Languedoil, there was another joy in listening.

But after Margaret had fluttered prettily in his arms, she began to look about, as if afraid.

"Are you sure —" twittered she.

"Well, is not Simon watching?"

"Yes, but I cannot help being fearful. You know

that the last time we met alone and she surprised us, she
was so angry! We have scarce been twice alone together
since Easter. Even when this morning we went to the
church was not your confessor there, though the blind girl
might not know it, just to spy on our deeds and words
together?"

"Tush," scoffed the king, not wholly pleased. "Father
Foulque was there because he said he feared lest in the
frailty of our youth we should slight the penance."

Margaret took two steps back, that she might look in
her husband's face.

"Father Foulque may be a holy man," said she, slowly,
"but he has one sin to confess himself."

"Declare it!"

"A lie. He knew that you love nothing better than any
penance, however humbling. And as for me — it was not
for me; he was sent by your mother."

"Margaret," said Louis, — and it gave her pain to see
the other pain that covered his fine face, — "my mother
is my mother." But she gave her head a little toss.

"Ay," spoke she, almost shrilly; "and your wife —
is she not your wife?"

The king lifted his hand, — a shapely, gentle hand, fit to
lie beside the queen's or beside Falaise's, — and made
answer with a soothing gesture.

"Oh, dearest, oh, lady wife, you know I cannot speak
out all I feel. You know what my mother has ever been
to me. I was her first-born, and, unworthy that I am, she
has loved me best. Robert, Alphonso, Charles, — my
brothers, — she has never loved them as she has cared for
me; not because I was king, but because the wise God
has ordered so. And now that we are wed, she has
more grief than we can ever know, to see us drawn to each

other, and, as she dreams, apart from her. Therefore in her excess of love she seems unkind. But we
must bear with her; for we are young and she is old.
And though I know that were you to become tenfold
dearer to me than now — which cannot be — for I love
you with a perfect love, — she can never understand. And
if our pain is great, consider that hers is greater still."

As he spoke the bright tears stood in his eyes; and the
queen grew sad.

"Ah, Louis," she said, "you are wise and right; but
when you say 'her pain is greater still,' speak for yourself, but not for me. You are her son, the king, her only
earthly hope — but what am I? 'The Provençal woman
who has come to thrust myself betwixt her and your love.'
And this is hard to bear."

The king turned pale a little, and set his lips before he
answered slowly : —

"I think you wrong my mother."

"Would God I did!" cried Margaret, her color rising;
"but I have overheard — no matter how! It was her
voice and Alithe de Coucy's. She said that thing of me,
and worse. I could not hear all, nor did I wish to hear;
but I must speak."

"I did not know you were being made so unhappy," said
Louis, twisting his long fingers like a man in bitter doubt.

"Unhappy?" the queen's voice did not betray her feeling by rising. "I presume they call me queen of France,
because I am your wife. In what am I queen save
name? To your mother comes everything; she rules
wide France. Clerks, chancellors, doctors, state papers,
treasurer's scrolls — all go to her. To-day she will give
audience to the abbots protesting against the new tithe;
to-morrow she will arbitrate betwixt the envoys of the

Pope and of the Emperor.   And I — I, your wedded wife
— whose father was not the least of the princes of Christendom — am left to waiting-women, and lute-boys, jugglers
and embroideries, hounds and hawks.   Velvet caps go off
to me, the heralds cry 'God save your Royal Grace';
but that Alithe de Coucy, who is set to spy in my bower,
has mightier sway than I!"

She ended when the king burst into a passionate flood
of tears.

"No more; in Our Lady's name, no more.   I cannot
bear it.   Everything you say is true.   But God has given
me this mother; I love her.   I cannot break her heart.
I am helpless.   Oh! I know I am unworthy to wear the
crown; I have always known it.   I shall be a curse to those
I love, and to my people.   Would that I had not been the
eldest; then I could have been a monk and saved my
soul."

As he stood there, with his hands pressing his face and
his yellow hair falling over them, some stranger might
have said, "Here stands a woman, not a king."   But
Margaret drew near, put her lithe arm about his neck, and
kissed his cheek.

"*Ai!* my lord, my husband, forgive, for it is I who
have caused you pain.   And now that I know we have
this grief together, being shared, it will become for me
most light.   And I will teach your mother to love me, and
all will be glad as on our marriage day."

But Louis only shook his head sadly, though soothed
by her caress.

"No, lady wife," said he at last, "I will not forgive
you, for you have only spoken truth.   It makes the wish
rise stronger in my heart — a wish which I seem all too
weak ever to fulfil: but must — or I am damned."

"O Louis, it is a dreadful word, and you as pure and righteous as St. Bernard's self! What is that wish?"

Louis held her at arm's length, while he answered, measuring each word:—

"*To — be — a — king!*"

"I do not understand. 'To be a king'?"

He dropped his arms, stepped away, spoke rapidly.

"To be a king! For is one king when one is crowned at Reims; when one's name is set on countless parchments, countless coins? I know I am no king. No — though I am the heir of a great name, of Charlemagne, of strong Hugh Capet, of saintly Robert, of Philip Augustus, the bulwark of France. My forehead has been touched by the oil of St. Remi. I have gallant captains and knights for vassals. I could conquer half of Christendom with my lieges. What profit? All that cannot make the paladin arise within me. I am gentle, mild, piteous. I love the ordinances of Holy Church. I love peace and laughter. I love flowers and little children. I could make a saintly woman. But to love war, the spider-web of statecraft, the wearing of the viceregency of God before men — I cannot. I am too weak. I have besought the Blessed Saints for strength. The gift has been denied."

A great wave of sorrow came over the queen. She knew her husband had spoken well. She knew that from their first meeting on the wedding day at Sens there had not dropped from his lips oath or anger; she knew that his heart was guileless as a babe's; but she also knew that never had he set his will against his mother or the ministers who ruled for him; that never had he tossed his head right royally and spoken, "I ordain this — I, the king." The monarch of France was Blanche of Castile.

She stood looking at Louis through her tears, wondering what she might say to comfort him, when he, with changing mood, darted a question.

"Why does this Gui of Avignon linger about Pontoise?"

She was not pleased. Always the same; first the king would bewail his impotence, then speak of something else.

"I do not hear the gossip of the pages," she answered a little coldly. "Of course he is sent here by my father to arrange the payments on my dowry."

"Of course; I had forgotten," said Louis, wearily. "I forget everything except the times for mass. And yet I do not like him."

"And wherefore?"

"Have I not said I was a fool? If you press me, there are stories about — stories it makes my ears burn to hear. They began when we were at Vincennes; they follow us to Pontoise. He is from the Midi, as are you, and seems overgallant. An enemy would say, — "

"Say what?"

"He seems to like you very well, and shows it."

Margaret laughed.

"So you fear lest his *tensos* and *cansons* and *sirventes* are all shot in my face. Fie on you, Louis! Gui of Avignon is no such fool as that; he is but turning his viols against waylaying a dozen ladies when he fares back to Arles."

"Nevertheless," said the king again, nigh testily, "I do not like him. He must be sent away."

I do not know how Margaret would have answered him, for at this moment there was a sound below; the cracking of a whip, the howling of a dog. The queen ran into Louis' arms.

"Your mother! — Simon is warning us. Oh! I must fly or she will find us, and we have been but a moment alone together, and have said so little!"

"To — be — a — king !" repeated Louis, and he kissed
her but did not look after her, only down to the rushes.
Margaret heard feet mounting the long staircase below.
Her own flight was almost breathless. Better a thousand
deaths than the silent anger of the jealous mother.
And as she went up the steps to her own chambers,
she too repeated her husband's words: "To be a king."
Ah! St. Agatha knew whether that prayer would ever
pass beyond a mocking hope.

Alithe had vanished when Margaret reëntered her chamber. Falaise was in the great arm-chair, her lap full of
silken threads, which she was disentangling with marvellous quickness, the white hands flying like shuttles. When
she heard the queen's step she threw all the skeins back
into the basket, and rose instantly.

"The woman you left me with is gone," said she, "and
now I must go also. I must find Boso and hear about
little Nicole."

"You will not — for we had but just begun to talk."

Falaise drew herself up almost haughtily.

"Because you are the queen, I think you will not make
me stay."

"Because I love you, I think that you will stay."

Margaret was very close, when Falaise, as her custom
was, suddenly put out her hand, and touched the lady's
eyes.

"*Ai!* what do I feel? Your lashes are all wet; your
eyelids hot. You have been crying. What has grieved
you? I did not know that queens could weep. What may
I do, or say?"

Now Margaret was on the point of taking the blind girl
in her arms; of doing and saying many things perchance

strange for such short friendship, when there was a step without, and a suave voice inquiring if " His gracious mistress would suffer him to enter?" His mistress, let the truth be told, had no welcome at that instant, even for St. Michael; but she answered " Enter," and the chamberlain, the great Sire Enguerraud de Coucy himself, stood bending and scraping before her. Of the chamberlain, how he looked and how he spoke, shall be told in its own place; enough that now he was come with the most unpleasant tidings imaginable: " That her Grace the queen mother asked her Grace the queen consort, if it was agreeable that she should sit at the king's table that noon, with the very noble seigneur, Gui of Avignon." To which message Margaret answered, " Yes," inly cursing the chamberlain by every imp she could remember, and got him out of the room. No more detaining Falaise now. Margaret's tirewomen had a heavy task before them. The queen was leading the blind girl to the door, when Falaise laughed, turned, ran back nimbly, and pushed through the arras which sundered Margaret's chamber from the inner sleeping room. A little fumbling in the wall-tapestry, and she was thrusting open the sliding panel, revealing the hidden staircase which led to the eyrie. The queen followed her a little way, and when they were at a remote turn of the stairs, Falaise suddenly put her lips close to Margaret's ear.

" I have something to tell you."

" What?"

" Distrust Alithe. I feared her. I was glad when she was gone."

" Distrust Alithe? And for what cause?"

" She is not a good woman. The little soft sprites have whispered it."

And with not a word more Falaise went up to her "wind-tower." But as Margaret stood in the dark passage, down through the gloom floated a snatch of a jongleur's song, borne on the blind girl's bell-like voice:—

> "She is the rose, the lily too,
> The sweetest violet, and through
> Her noble beauty, noble mien,
> I think her now the fairest queen
> Which mortal sight hath ever seen.
>   Simple, though coy,
>   Her eyes flash joy:—
> 'God give thee days without annoy,
> And every bliss whereof I ween!'"

* * * * * * *

Up in the tower Falaise sat for a long time listening to the crooning of the breeze, and catching the slant of the sunbeams on her face. After a while Boso climbed up to her. Nicole was no better. The fever burned hotter than ever. Poor Brigite was at her wits' end.

All this made Falaise very quiet. But at last Boso asked about her visit to royalty; how she had fared with the queen, and how she liked her. Whereupon the shadows on Falaise's face grew yet deeper.

"Boso," said she at last, "I have one thing to tell you, but you must repeat it to no one. I am sure the dear God is angry with those who have eyes and who wear crowns."

"What did you say?" gasped the boy.

"I say," repeated Falaise, "that I have just come away from one who, I know, is very poor and very sad. I know it, although she did not say one word of all her sorrows. Do you know the woman I mean?"

"You are talking in riddles."

"I mean Margaret of Provence, the wife of the king of France."

CHAPTER V

ENGUERRAUD DE COUCY

ALITHE DE COUCY had met the king just as he was passing down the long corridor to his own private chambers. The interview between him and the queen mother had been long, and, Alithe guessed, baneful; for Blanche never spared her tongue when chastening her best-loved child, and Louis' eyes were still red. Alithe had known that the king must pass the yeomen at the door, and had stood gossiping and making smiles at their commandant, the young Sire de Glui, being so kind and gracious that he, poor wight, already was wondering if he dared to ask for her stocking to tie to his lance at the next tourney. In fact, he had the bold wish almost on his lips, and was close to bending his knees to express it, when bang! clatter! his yeomen were holding their pike-staffs "ready," and luckless De Glui had to bend, not to Alithe, but to Louis of France.

Louis came slowly, almost listlessly; and, as has been said, his eyes were red. He did not look up at the clatter of the guardsmen; he gave one nod to De Glui, but stopped short when the lady showed herself courtesying almost across his path. De Glui was one of those gallants who had long since vowed that Alithe de Coucy knew how to courtesy more rarely than Roland's Aude. When she bent her swan-white neck, from the sheen of her dark braids to the curve of the fairest little foot this side of

46

the Loire, every motion, every line spelled its grace. Her black gown half hid, half showed a form to try the virtue of a St. Jerome. The sensuous beauty, the warm life, the witchery that springs from a thousand little things — all were in Alithe de Coucy.

The king saw, stopped, spoke; and something had chased the lack-lustre from his eye.

"You are still in the service of my wife and my mother?" said he, and blushed like the tall boy that he was, bashful at having to speak the first, and not knowing how to begin.

"I am, and may it please you, sire."

Alithe's voice was neither too soft, too timid, nor too bold. Her gaze was always respectful, but she never took it from the king's face.

"My mother is glad to commend your faithfulness. You De Coucys — men and maids — have ever been loyal vassals to our house. I am well pleased to see that your worthy father has so well-favored a child."

If Alithe smiled at this grave compliment from one a year younger than herself, she let that smile be merely one of pleasure.

"I find great joy in the favor of your Grace," and still she kept her black eyes on Louis, and still he looked on her, and spoke as if trying to keep his dignity.

"You must tell your father that we would gladly favor you, both for your own just merits and for his. Tell him it shall be our care to seek out for you a rich and noble marriage, whereon I will consider duly with my lady mother."

Alithe's long lashes quivered for one instant. A second glance reassured her. The king was only speaking because he knew not what else to say. If she could have read hearts, — and she almost read his, — she would have heard him repeating " Here stands the fairest woman in France." But while she was thanking her lord, in the same irreproachable accents, behold, another joined them, a tall, lean man, so soft of voice and step that he was close beside Alithe before either she or the king set eyes on him.

" Thanks, sire. I am proud, nay, puffed up even with sinful pride, at the high favor you have deigned to show to my dear daughter."

Enguerraud de Coucy was making his smoothest bow before his master. Everything about the chamberlain was smooth — his face was smooth, his crown was smooth, his beringed hands were smooth, his motions smooth, his speech was smooth. And you did not have to live at court very long to learn that he loved many things, — namely, his velvet cap, his good dinner, his broad lands, his countless vassals, and his handsome daughter, but chief of all, Enguerraud de Coucy.

The king held out his hand, and the chamberlain kissed it with unction ; yet Louis was not looking on him, but on Alithe.

" Verily," spoke the king, and looked again, " it is not every seigneur who shall lift his eyes to a De Coucy."

" A modest child, your Grace," smiled the baron ; " a very modest and pious girl. I trust I may say so, though I do praise my own. Father Foulque, your reverend confessor — holy man, may St. Martin have pity on his ague ! — Father Foulque, I say, did last St. Philip's day deign to tell me that he did never hear the confession of lad or maid who had fewer sins and frailties to avow than this, mine own."

" I do conceive," said Louis, and now the smile spread

across his handsome mouth, "that were Father Foulque a score years younger, he would say the Lady Alithe had only the sin of having too many virtues. But I will leave the Sire de Glui to speak the rest; for though God crowns me king, He denies me the tongue of a cavalier, and when compliment is the coin to be bartered, I am only an unskilful chapman."

All this, and from royal lips, made the two men and the lady bend very low, as the king swept under the crossed pikes of the yeomen, and into his chamber. But the poor Sire de Glui never saw the moment of opportunity return — no, not though he had vowed Our Lady of Pontoise a very tall candle. For father and daughter passed out of his sight, arm in arm, and the moment they were beyond hearing, each spoke so fast, I think one hardly heard the other.

"Fool!" cried Alithe.

"Woman!" corrected her father.

"Monk!"

"Nun!"

"And this is the king of France!"

"No, my child; have we not been ruled by the Castilian these ten years?"

"Yet we are to crouch at *his* will!"

"My child, are we to despise God's elect?"

"When men say, 'God has elected a mole, smooth fur without, but only sluggishness within,' I think that men err, not God."

"My child, we are nevertheless bidden 'to render unto Cæsar the things that are Cæsar's.'"

"I admit that Cæsar is handsome," confessed the lady.

"Though simple."

"And harmless for good or ill."

E

"Again, dear child, you are wholly wrong."

"And how wrong?"

"A king is never powerless and harmless; if powerless for good, he is, by the nature of kingship, all powerful for ill."

Alithe shrugged her shapely shoulders, and De Coucy continued : —

"I have watched the king. He is now at full manhood. He is pious enough to be canonized by the Holy Father; but he is no lord for France."

"But we have the Castilian?"

"Ay," spoke De Coucy, bitterly, "the Castilian! I have heard jongleurs sing of Sire Theseus, the great count of Athens, and how he fought the Lady Hippolyte, duchess of the Amazons. I think her Grace, the queen mother, one of her brats. A fairer chance for us seigneurs to gain our rights and spread our lands there never seemed, than when the late king died at the siege of Avignon. We, who had lain so close since Philip Augustus began to rage abroad, thought our hour was surely come; but no, by the heart of St. Germain, the fetters of France were never tighter than to-day!"

Alithe did not answer him, and her father regarded her sharply.

"So the king promised you a great baron? Of course he was speaking only for his mother. How do you like the thought?"

"I would like something better," and Alithe gave the chamberlain one of her most pregnant smiles, a little incurving of the lips; and by experience he knew she had something worth telling.

"No one listens; what is it?" and he drew nearer.

"The end of our plots."

"And what end?"

Alithe's hands rose to her head, and seemed to press something upon it.

"A crown," spoke she, and her eyes flashed fire, while her whisper trembled, "a crown — set here."

Whereupon De Coucy talked with his daughter a great while, and then sent scampering varlets to call to his rooms Theobald, Count of Champagne, Peter, Count of Brittany, and Godfrey, Bishop of Beauvais.

* * * * * * *

It was not the first meeting of these five; it did not promise to be the last. All through the regency of the redoubtable Blanche of Castile had the seigneurs of France spun their intrigues, plotted, conspired, revolted — and been crushed. The arm of the queen mother had been too heavy. Two years since, Peter of Brittany, most defiant of the barons, had come to Paris, a halter about his neck, to make submission to the victorious suzerain. He had knelt before the young monarch, laid his hands in Louis', had become "the king's man." Louis had raised him up, bidden him to disgorge his pleasant castles in Anjou and Maine, but handed back the rule of Brittany on condition of good behavior.

That had been the end of the conspiring and the fighting. France had peace. No more ravaged fields around the village, nor burning roofs in the city. The land had prospered. Peasant, burgher, petty noble, blessed God and the strong queen mother. But the great seigneurs who idled at the court, who saw their men-at-arms disbanding, their dear blood-feuds growing cold in these dull days of the king's peace, and the royal provosts usurping the "high and low justice" which they had loved to dispense from their castle halls — the seigneurs, I say, gnawed their tongues and were thoughtful. And the most thoughtful of them all was Enguerraud de Coucy.

The chamberlain was taking counsel with his friends. Peter of Brittany, whose lip-loyalty of late had been the loudest in the court, sat on the long couch, bent almost double as he traced the joints in the tiled floor with the tip of his short sword. He was a broad, beefy man, red both in hair and face, and dressed in a taste the politer cavaliers swore was execrable — too much scarlet, white ermine, and gold lace. He was very taciturn, and only looked up when asked to reply to something. Beside him spread his one-time arch-enemy, Theobald the great Count of Champagne. Theobald was perennially young. He wore a sharp little beard, dyed to a fiery yellow; his thin hair was quite as golden. Two squires that morning had painted the ruddy "bloom of spring" upon his cheeks. The surest way to win his wrath was to hint that he was not young enough to steal the hearts of all the ladies. He was politely mourning a cousin whose lands he had inherited, and his bliaut, cape, furs, bonnet, and scented gloves, all were correctly black. He also was studying one thing only — the face of Alithe. As for the Very Reverend Bishop of Beauvais in the chair, he was in the prime of strength and health, a robust, rosy man on the nearer side of forty, pleasant to his peers, haughty to his servants, and a mighty hunter. He wore still his green cassock, because he had come in with the hounds clear from Montmorenci just as De Coucy summoned him. He again was looking chiefly at Alithe.

Now all that was said — hopes, fears, plot, and counter-plot — will tell itself in due time and place. But toward the end, the speech between the chamberlain and the

bishop became so warm that even the sullen Breton was
fain to raise his head.

"We must promptly remove the Provençal." It was
De Coucy who said it; and the bishop replied, while
stroking his growing under-chin, that

"The matter was certainly of importance. As he had
remarked, the case of the queen consort's marriage at
Sens would certainly smell very strangely to good canonists, were the matter presented before the Roman curia.
He would not say, however, that an absolute annulment
could be granted; at least, not speedily. The king could
indeed cut off his wife *a mensâ et toro;* but a complete
annulment without contributing cause —" His wisdom
ended in a second stroking of the chin.

Theobald, however, had wisely pricked up his ears.
"You mean, *eminentissime*, that unless the Provençal
gives fair color for such proceedings, we shall have our
pains as quittance for our labor?"

"Your Lordship is a very 'sage' man," assented the
bishop. "You are aware our Father in God, the ninth
Gregory, and his Imperial Majesty, Frederick, have, in
their brotherly love for each other, passed now from bans
and excommunications to open war, crossbows, and
battle-axes. An hundred thousand livres rightly bestowed
at Rome would be a weighty argument with his Holiness,
whilst he is in such need of carnal wealth to secure the
purer riches of his spiritual kingdom." One of the
bishop's pale blue eyes went up in his head, and he
laughed silently. But De Coucy, who sat beside his
daughter, facing the three, was knitting his forehead.

"You say well. A little 'largesse' at Rome, — to this
vice-chancellor and to that is good; but do not deceive yourselves, Raymond Bérenger of Provence is a

great prince. He will not sit quietly and see his daughter clapped into a nunnery, because a few words in the marriage service were mumbled. Nor is the deed we will to do so slight that we dare raise up new foes to either side."

"Ay," thrust in Peter for the first time, snarling through his nose, "if the king is a whimpering girl, the queen mother is a paladin."

"Were she Roland, Oliver, and Bishop Turpin too," darted De Coucy, darkly, "she'll bow her head at last."

"No threats," flung out Theobald, snatching at his little beard. "The queen mother gave me her gage the year the old king died. You promised — when I entered this last plot — no violence to her, a quiet removal from court, ample revenues, a princely establishment."

"We will not harm your lady," sneered Peter, showing his teeth, and the bishop's lips curled. Court gossip had long since buzzed how Theobald had waited on Blanche with more than passing gallantry, and been soundly rebuffed by that pure and prudish dame.

"No bickerings, fair lords, in St. Germain's name, no bickerings," urged De Coucy. "We act not for our own weal and profit, which God forbid! but for the good of every seigneur in France who is ground down by the tyrannous sway of this Castilian."

"*Salus populi suprema lex*," threw in the bishop sardonically, and rolled his eye again. "We all know the pious devotion of you De Coucys."

"I am not here to have it questioned," shot back the chamberlain tartly, forgetting his own admonitions. "If I pray for a broader fief, will Godfrey of Beauvais refuse a new presentation when Our Lady sends it?"

"Much talking, much strife," growled the Breton, toss-

ing in a jongleur's proverb. "Whither is this ship drifting ?"

"To the rule of France."

The speaker was one who had been silent a long time, —
Alithe de Coucy, and even the sullen Peter gazed hard at
her as she arose from her father's side. Her white neck
was no longer bent in courtly courtesy, but carried her
splendid head high, and she sent the "puissance of the
stars of her eyes" into the eyes of each of the four who
gazed on her.

"The king," she spoke, " is the king. You, fair sirs,
when you plot of setting another on the throne of Hugh
Capet, know that your schemes are folly. Were my Lord
of Champagne crowned to-day, my Lord of Brittany would
conspire against him to-morrow. And France is wedded
to the present house. But what this Louis of Poissy is, I
need not tell ; and France calls not for a mendicant friar
with a crown on his head, but for one whose arm is strong.
You have never sworn liege-homage to the Castilian. Let
us sweep her away to exile. But first " — she paused, with
her white teeth open, and let every man hang on her breath :

"What first ? " cried out Theobald.

"First strike the Provençal down. Make her weave her
own shroud. Let the queen mother sew it. Would your
Eminence say the canonists can untie no loops when the
wife of the king of France is unfaithful to her vows ?"

" Do not boast that, lady," interposed the sly Breton. "I
watch men, I watch women. And I know — despite flying
gossip — that the Provençal has one patron saint — the king."

" And I answer you," returned Alithe, haughtily, "that
Gui of Avignon shall be proven the lover of Margaret the
queen of France — proven, if all goes well, ere Pontoise
chateau is one day older ! "

"By God's eyes!" rang Theobald's oath, and all were on their feet saving the silent De Coucy.

"I did not know the virtue of her Grace was so highly prized," said Alithe with the least sneer. "I repeat that this can be proven. Only do you to-day, my Lord Bishop, repeat in the presence, first of Gui, then of the queen consort, if Gui ask it, all that you have told us this hour concerning the strange manner you celebrated the wedding at Sens. Had you revealed this earlier, monseigneur, we had been saved many days of counselling."

"Woman, woman!" burst in the bishop, turning very red; "this is a fearful thing. It lies upon my conscience. A great indulgence, viaticum from the Holy Father, pilgrimage to Jerusalem — I fear lest all these can never purge it away. How may I tell this tale you wish?"

"Yet you *will* tell," was her firm answer, "and tell to-day."

"No, not to-day, not to-day. When was ever a plot sprung so quickly; like a bolt from a crossbow?"

Theobald too had flushed. You could see his hot blood shining through the rouge.

"Monseigneur is right," he hinted. "It is incredible that your Ladyship proposes any final steps to-day. Our friends have not been warned, nor our vassals mustered. De Joinville has the royal yeomen in his grip, and all his fealty is for the king. We shall get our heads too near the block to rush in lightly and without aid —"

"Save from the 'Free-Captain' Henri de Ormoy!"

"Ah! I understand!" and the count's jaw fell, while he smiled uneasily, and looked at Alithe. She put her hand in her bosom, and pulled forth a dirty vellum written in an awkward hand.

"This is from De Ormoy, and within one hour come

privately to my father.   It tells itself why there is need of
haste.

"Here I am at Conflans with the band I led out of Aragon
— all sturdy villains, very fit to serve your purpose.   I shall lie
here to-day and to-morrow, and if you still hold to the gallant
design you last had when we talked at Bordeaux, use me.   I
am your man to follow to victory or to the devil.   I cannot
remain here longer, or her Grace the Castilian, whom we both
hold in such loyal reverence, will move against me.   So prove
your brave words were not wind."

"And you dare undertake — ?"   The three spoke all
together to the De Coucys.

"I dare undertake," answered the chamberlain calmly,
"to keep all knowledge of the presence of De Ormoy's
band at Conflans for the rest of this day from the Castilian,
the king, and from De Joinville.   To-morrow the news will
leak in to them, the yeomen guard will be doubled, and we
undone.   To-day we have what we have always needed —
an armed force, to strike one blow, and that enough."

"And you propose — " cried the three as one; but
Alithe beckoned to her father "silence," and herself
answered them, looking each in the eye and laughing
gently.

"No, my fair sirs, we will not tell it yet.   For while
my father and I are silent, you can lay your hands on the
true cross and swear you know nothing.   And every man
who hears a plot becomes sometimes a traitor, even against
his will.   I only ask your patience till this afternoon and
night."

"And then?"

"I have said that you will see: only have your ears
open, your swords sharp, your wits sharper, be prepared
for all things, be surprised at nothing."

"And you De Coucys will attempt this now?" spoke Theobald.

"Will execute this now," retorted the lady; and as they gazed on her, still bound by the spell of her glance and presence, they all thought, "She boasts aright."

"But your reward?" cried the Breton.

Alithe seemed to grow taller by three fingers, when she whispered across the still chamber:—

"The crown of France."

The men stood silent, looking first at each other, then back at her glowing face.

"You deserve it," vowed Theobald; and he bent the knee, and raised to his lips her ivory fingers.

The others had no more questions. They went out with never another word, glancing about them furtively, as if dreading to fall again beneath her fell influence. When they were gone, De Coucy barred the door and talked again with Alithe, but in tones so low no eavesdropper, even with the ears of Falaise, could have stolen anything. Then he called in his squires, had them bring him a more handsome bliaut, and hastened away to another part of the rambling castle, seeking the knight, Gui of Avignon.

CHAPTER VI

GUI OF PROVENCE

THE wise jongleur, Ugo of Arques, I believe, has sung
of the great labyrinth of "Minos, the most sage Duke of
Crete," with ten thousand and five fair chambers, and
courts, towers, and donjons innumerable; but the castle of
Pontoise had nearly as many. The first keep had been
gray when they crowned Charlemagne. Louis the Pious
had added an outwork here, Hugh Capet a turret there,
and Louis the Fat had built the barbican, the lower fort
thrown out against Pontoise. The castle was not a palace
but a city, with hovel and throne-room under one rambling
roof. The centre was the massy donjon, above which blew
the royal standard of the fleur-de-lis, and where Falaise
had her eyrie, the king and the queens their chambers;
but the château wandered away — courts, banquet halls,
and little gardens, — till on one side it crowded down
against the town, on the other hung perilously above the
swollen Oise. Enguerraud de Coucy, whose rooms were
close to his master's, was on his way to a distant tower of
the castle. Through narrow passages, where the watchful
yeomen saluted him, across dirty courts, where he could
hear the stamping and snorting of the great stallions in
the stables; across other courts, where grave monks were
gossipping — Cistercians in white, black Dominicans, and
gray Franciscans, the pious queen mother's ghostly establishment. Through all these walked De Coucy, never so
fast as to seem in haste, never so slow as to seem idling.

59

He had a courtly smile for my lady, the Countess of St. Pol, a friendly nod for my lord, the Vicomte of Melun; he politely craved the benediction of monseigneur, the Bishop of Caen. De Coucy was a general favorite, for despite his high station and his many lieges, he seemed anxious only to serve his king and his good friends.

The chamberlain continued until, at the remotest tower of all, he found two pages sitting in the open doorway, busy over a dice-box; so busy, that when they looked up, and beheld how great a lord they had kept waiting, their knees knocked together, and their legs began to smart with the strapping sure to come. De Coucy, however, only pulled his blandest smile, addressed them as "my right handsome lads," and asked if their master, "that most admirable and redoubtable Seigneur Gui," were enjoying a few moments of leisure? For answer, the bolder of the youths pointed to a grated window above the entrance.

"Hearken, lord, he is playing, and would not be disturbed."

Then De Coucy heard the strumming of a viol, and a thin voice singing softly from on high.

"Ah! I am charmed to find your valiant knight is now wooing the 'gay science.' Yet tell him I cry his mercy; but if he will only suffer me to listen to his sweet and witty songs, I will be at his service forever."

All this, very graciously spoken, and followed up by a silver sou, made the page go up and return speedily, bidding the chamberlain to follow, and De Coucy was in the presence of the cavalier he sought.

The envoy of the Count of Provence had been given chambers furnished in a manner worthy of his noble master, — fine arras, sweet herbs on the tiling, silver-plated couches and chairs, and burnished brass chests and coffers.

But Gui had adorned the room with ornaments all his own, to wit: some scores of silken girdles, purple fillets, ribbons, bracelets, clasps, rings, and sachet bags of musk, which he had pinned upon the tapestry; each favor the gift of a sighing dame in the Midi, whose heart he vowed he had stolen. Upon the chairs and couches were spread some dozen viols of every shape and manner, and the largest of these lay in its owner's lap, and gave him excuse for failing to rise when De Coucy entered.

Gui of Avignon was a small man, so small that the great viol almost overpowered him. He was near his thirtieth year, and, unlike the young cavaliers of the North, had never shaved, so that his black beard fell in silky down around his bright, clear face, making him a loadstone for the eyes of the younger ladies. He was, as ever, well groomed and combed. His hands had been washed five times that day in scented water, and the finger nails genteelly tinted. His close-fitting dress, from the bliaut that floated over his shoulders to his leathern shoes, was of a single color, pale blue. He wore more rings than he had fingers. There was the price of a seigneury in the gems of his sword hilt. In short, if Gui of Avignon was not a paragon among cavaliers, it was no fault of his varlets, his tailor, and his barber.

The knight, I have said, did not arise. He continued strumming the viol until De Coucy had found an empty seat, and then, with a muttered curse to St. Genevieve, flung the instrument down upon the soft pillows; yet notwithstanding them, a string snapped.

"Immaculate Mother of God! Where are my wits? Where is that immortal fire of poesy, that indestructible spark, that unquenchable heat, that undying power of song which thou, O Love, hast planted in my breast? The

morning! the morning lost! when I had vowed to com-
pose, execute, complete, a most sage, entertaining, and irre-
sistible *canson*, — one to shame Benart de Ventadorn's best
— and lo! I accomplish nothing!"

All this speech was delivered in shrill Provençal, almost
to the wall it seemed, but De Coucy chose to feel called
upon to answer.

"Ah, my fair lord, I cry your pardon, but do not do
yourself this wrong. What did I not hear as I came up
the stair? 'Eyes like two moons,' 'lips that part as roses
blush'? We of the colder North, brave sir, must think
you the very paladin of song."

"You flatter, you flatter," and the knight reddened to
his little ears, in pleased vanity. "I make my feeble effort.
Perchance it was my viol's fault, not mine; for, by my
hope of heaven, there lies a deal in that! I had the
Flemish viol with the silver frets and oaken bridge. A
goodly comrade when the moon is bright, and one would
bewail the coldness of one's mistress; but by day it fits
ill with my gladder humors. See, I will take this smaller
Portuguese, made of walnut wood, and with gold frets. As
a rider curbs his steed, so will I curb its strings to the
commandments of my fancy. Hear! Does not that rich
and golden sound set all my head a-dance with May
blossoms and dark eyes and soft caresses? Do not
eleven rhymes for that blessed word 'love' spring upward
in my ravished soul? Is there no wise, discreet, and ever
beautiful dame, my lord, whose honors I may praise in
your behalf?"

All this time the chamberlain had been watching like
a cat his chance to thrust in a word, so now he said that
he knew of no such dame. But quick as a hawk Gui was
off again, faster than ever.

"Alas! I cannot serve you; yet command my art. For am I not a slave? Yes; though the least of the myriad servitors of the 'gay science' of that divinely honorable mystery which raised the immortal Pierre Vidal from the son of a petty huckster to be peer of princes, companion of five kings, husband of an Empress of Greece, and saint adored by every tuneful troubadour. And since you will not have a *canson*, that is to say, a song of love, I fall on my knees, and humbly beg that you signify which you desire — an *estampida*, after the fashion of the Midi — a tale in verse of gallant deeds and knightly courtesy, or shall I bewail the errors and follies of these evil times in a *sirvente;* or are you, too — as I dare scarce doubt — likewise a neophyte in this noble brotherhood, and will hold with me a debate in verse, a *tenso;* which *tenso*, if you take it not amiss, I would desire to be 'whom ought a lady to prefer, the knight who confesses his love, or him who dares not avow it?' But in this, as in every other matter, I fall on my knees, I kiss your hands, and wait your most gentle and ever courtly pleasure."

The troubadour ended, not because he had no more to say, but because his breath was ended, and De Coucy, who had kept his temper, knew that his time was come.

"Most gallant and serene Seigneur of Avignon," he began, with a due cocking of the eye, to add to his weighty accents, "it is my misfortune that I cannot vie with you in your wholly admirable pleasures, nor did I now — dare I confess it — come wholly to hear your excellent viols and far more excellent poesy and songs. May I proceed to quite another matter?"

Gui nodded, being still short of breath, and the chamberlain went on in his smooth, passionless voice.

"What I shall say, is, I will not repeat, only for the ears

of a cavalier of unblemished honor, like your most valiant self. If it is painful to you, rest assured it is more painful to me, for we De Coucys have ever poured out blood and service for the royal house. In short, I wish to speak concerning his Grace the king, and his most noble wife."

"The queen?" The troubadour almost let the viol crash from his hands as he leaned forward.

"You understand, fair sir," said De Coucy, his voice growing ever softer, "that what I say touches not the policy of the realm, — for that I, a poor vassal, should thrust my hand into such high matters, God and St. Germain forbid! but of our royal lord's more personal estate."

"I attend you, sir," and Gui laid down the viol.

"I must ask you, noble knight, to answer me without dissimulation, and remember your avowals to me are made unto a man of honor. Was it your fair fortune while you served at Count Raymond Bérenger's court, to know our Lady Margaret before her marriage?"

"Know? know?" flew off the troubadour, whose breath was now recovered. "I cry your mercy, 'know' is but a harsh, a clownish word. By St. Tropheme! 'worship,' 'adore,' 'fall prostrate,' 'kiss her footsteps,' 'crave the sight of her from three score fathoms off,' or any other mild and gentle term like these, more truly may depict how absolutely, completely, and utterly was my enslavement to that peerless, incomparable, and almost divine princess. Indeed, as most wittily says Raimon de Miraval, in his eighth *tenso* with Rogier, his rival —"

"I accept your oath," cut short De Coucy, the least flush mounting to his forehead, and leaving the *tenso* hanging in thin air; "enough that you loved the princess well, that you would, like a true knight and liegeman, serve her,

that she could command your most valiant service. But
now that she is wedded to the king —"

"Wedded? wedded?" flared forth Gui, twisting his
mustachios upwards threateningly; "and are you all, sir
chamberlain, such untaught knights here amongst the
Languedoil, that simply because a lady marries she is forbidden to have seven courtly worshippers? Look you, look
on these gay trophies here — crowns, ribbons, bracelets, all
— were they not given me in fair affection by so many
wedded dames? Nay, as again so rightly says Raimon
in his fifth *tenso* with Bernart de Tarascon, concerning the
love of married and unmarried ladies that —"

"It is plain then, worthy knight," charged in the chamberlain, who was bound never to raise the sluice too long
for such a torrent, "that because your one-time *inamorata*
has become the wedded wife, yes, even of a king of France,
you do not hold yourself indifferent to her happiness."

"Indifferent! no, by Christ's own wounds!" and here
the troubadour forgot his wind, banged his scabbard upon
the floor, and the flash of his eyes showed that De Coucy
had struck home. The chamberlain saw his chance, rose,
put his hands on his hips.

"My lord," said he, "you have now been in our French
court many days. The affairs of state which brought you
from your master are close to ending. You have seen
much of his Grace the king. What think you of him — of
his person, his piety, his manners?"

The troubadour did a strange thing for him — he coughed,
hesitated, and answered slowly: —

"You ask a hard question, fair sir. I have hardly seen
his Grace except in high audiences, or now perchance at
a hunt, now perchance at a dinner, as to-day, when he
has graciously deigned to command that I sit with him.

F

As for his person, it is passing well; only the leathern girdles which he wears are by two fingers over-broad. As for his piety, he is a little more watchful of fast days and vigils than certain godly bishops. As for his manners, his speech lacks the many quaint and admirable conceits wherewith we of the softer Midi are wont to embellish our talk; but yet — "

"And what of the king's treatment of the most gracious queen, his wife?"

De Coucy spoke softly, and Gui waited while you could have counted ten, before he began to reply.

"I pray St. Tropheme I am wrong; and yet — I dare not on mine knightly honor swear that I have seen the king show over much passion for her most beauteous grace. True, perchance the queen mother's presence did abate the natural flow of love."

The chamberlain drew his hand slowly across his lips.

"My lord, it is not a pleasant thing to say, but I must tell you straitly — you do not know the king, or how he treats his wife."

"Treats his wife!" The little knight's fingers closed over his jewelled hilt.

"I will not dissemble, Sir Gui. I owe Louis de Poissy liege-homage — may it never be wanting from a De Coucy! — but as a man of knightly honor, my gorge rises in me when I behold his faithlessness to the queen."

"Faithlessness! Is he not an austere monk? Are your wits addled, or are you in wine?"

Gui's sword moved in its sheath.

"I would I were! I say, you do not know the king. But I who watch and serve him hour by hour grow every day more sad. His piety is one of masses and of fasts, while from one light love he turns how swiftly to another!

I will not name the many noble ladies whose honor he has dared besiege."

"His mother? her Grace, Blanche?" Gui's voice was a bated whisper now.

"Her Grace the queen mother is too content to let her son squander his health and honor in such dalliance, so long as he leaves the reins of power within her hands. It is in vain you look for any reproof from her. And for his wife — alas!"

"Yes. Does she know this? Oh, let him be cursed!"

"I pray she does not dream the worst, or how gross is his unfaithfulness, though all her ladies buzz the foul gossip at her very ears. Yet she grows every day more sad. The king neglects her. Long days pass without a look, a word. She is as much a prisoner as if in the well beneath the tower."

"God's death!" swore the little knight, tearing out his sword. "Well that you came to me! My arm thrills, my head reels, my heart burns. I feel the might of twelve paladins. I will have your foul monarch's life."

"Peace!" commanded the chamberlain, with a hand on the upraised sword-arm. "I still owe homage to the king, and you must do no violence. But the queen — beautiful, piteous, forsaken, for whom my soul must bleed — think first of her. Last night my daughter, Alithe, overheard her at her prayers, beseeching Our Lady's mercy, praying for return to Arles and to her father, lamenting her husband's coldness and her mother-in-law's disdain, and repeating twice and thrice the name of the knight on whom she had long since set her love."

"Aha! aha!" and Gui made his sword dance in his hands, while sparks shot out of his eyes.

"I will not dissemble, sir knight; her Grace was repeat-

ing your name. I dare not counsel you. God forbid that
you should do anything contrary to honor or Holy Church!
Yet, if you wish, I will, through my daughter, a discreet
child, arrange for you this night a private meeting with the
queen. You can then best discover what the vows you
swore when dubbed a knight demand. At the table, when
you meet the king and the queens, I entreat you to dissemble if you may."

De Coucy was fain to leap back ten feet, for the troubadour was making valiant passes with his sword against
some ghostly foe.

"By the thumb-bone of St. Hilaire, set now in this fair
hilt," he was declaiming, "he who denies the peerless
beauty of the Lady Margaret of Provence, with my good
sword will I smite him down, thus, and thus, and thus,"
and the blade flashed and whistled.

"Not so loud," warned the chamberlain. "But will you
bid me scheme the meeting?"

"Yes — as I hope in heaven."

"And you will conceal your just wrath and passions till
that hour?"

"Upon mine honor as a knight."

"Then, my Lord of Avignon," said De Coucy, with his
most courtly bow, "I wish you a very good day." And
without another word he went out of the tower. His arrow
had shot home.

*   *   *   *   *   *   *

He traced his way back through the maze of courts,
turrets, and stables, till again he was close to the great
donjon where the king's white standard flew. In a ring
beneath it were standing a multitude — squires, grooms,
men-at-arms, seigneurs — all wedged together; all looking
upward; and De Coucy was fain to join them, whilst

down, as if from the clear vault of the azure, drifted a
song.

> *" Veni, Sancte Spiritus,*
> *Et emitte coelitus*
> *Lucis tuae radium.*
> *Veni, pater pauperum,*
> *Veni, dator munerum,*
> *Veni, lumen cordium. . . ."*

A human voice? or that of some soaring spirit pealing
heavenward the great hymn of Robert the King? De
Coucy heard a little murmur, one young knight whispering
in his comrade's ear, "They call her Falaise, and say that
she is blind."

The chamberlain stood and listened. Listened till every
plot and scheme and other hope had vanished from his
ken. His soul seemed lifted upward to the crest of the
gray tower, and beyond. When at last the voice died, his
impenetrable face wore an unwonted smile — a smile not
wholly evil, not wholly good. He was standing in a kind
of trance, when a touch on his mantle roused him. The
crowd had scattered. At his elbow stood Alithe, with no
intruder near.

"The fish has bitten?" asked she.

"Has taken barb and all."

"He loves the Provençal?"

"He is storming great oaths about her. I had to pacify
him by promising to arrange a meeting."

Alithe rewarded him with her most snaring smile.

"You throw your dice well, sweet father," answered
she, and laughed; "while I — I will talk with the queen
mother." Then she turned and looked in his face
sharply, adding, "But are you now bewitched? Who is
it now?"

"The blind girl: the lark, the nightingale of the tower. You have surely listened. Her songs have been running in my head since we came to Pontoise, and her form and face —"

"Are almost as dangerous as those of the last one — of the little Jewess you saw at Mayenne, and who cost you enough deniers to ruin any seigneury save Coucy. Fie on you, my father, you are too old for more of this! And to-day, when ten thousand things rush together and all is at stake —"

"If 'all' is at stake, another matter more or less can do no harm. I am resolved. Did you see the young knights prick up their ears while she sang? I must forestall them. I trust she has no parents I must bribe to stop their squealing?"

"Oh, none at all. I have talked with her. She is a pretty, harmless linnet, with a sweet enough voice. Only the queen consort seems utterly in love with her, and might make you trouble for her sake, — if she could." Here Alithe opened her mouth wide and showed her beautiful teeth.

"If she could, if she could!" her father laughed, as if at an admirable jest. "A valiant protectress! Then there is nothing to prevent my speaking to Pons. He is a discreet rascal, and managed the affair of the Jewess well. We will send her off to Coucy if needs be."

He was moving away, but Alithe still followed with her hand upon his arm.

"Promise one thing," she commanded.

"Promise what?"

"That you will not let this folly trip up the prospering of our plot."

He gave her the pledge readily with his wonted good-nature. She glanced around slyly. No one was looking. She kissed her father on the forehead.

"Farewell, farewell for an hour," cried she, with a wave of her lovely hands; "and let all saints favor me as I go to her Grace the Castilian!"

CHAPTER VII

AT THE KING'S TABLE

ALL his servants loved Louis of Poissy, from little Rolf the page who kept the royal bliauts, to Martin the giant sergeant-at-arms, in whose fingers an iron bar bent like lithe willow. The king was never known to speak a word in anger, never cursed, never swore, even by a blessed saint, never laid his riding whip around a clumsy groom's shins — and where was there another seigneur who did not that? True, he was rigorous in requiring every wight to be at an unmercifully early mass, no matter how cold the morning; and his quiet frown hurt more than all my Lord of Champagne's storming. Be that as it may, his body-servants worshipped him, and thought, as Simon de Joinville put it, that "Father Foulque had far better ask absolution of the king than the king of Father Foulque." Such being their feelings, you may be sure they were not pleased that morning to find their royal master passing sad.

There was no reason for it. The queen mother had not reproved him more harshly than usual; no messenger had come steaming in from Arras to say that Flemish communes were in an uproar; none from Rennes to tell of a fresh Breton rising; neither had a Knight Templar ridden to the court to relate a new victory of the infidels in the East, nor had a deputation of burghers appeared to protest against an extortionate bailiff. Nevertheless Louis the king seemed sad. Of all the "fifteen joyful diversions" told over by the wise Antoine de La Salle, for the delighting of a seigneur in days of peace, not one — from playing chess to watching bears fight — could remove the prince's black mood. All the time that the seven odd barbers, grooms, and pages needful for such high mysteries had been dressing their master for his dinner with the Provençal envoy, he had been almost silent. "A very bad sign," as a wiseacre observed to Simon de Joinville, who was keeping the door of the "royal closet."

"A very bad sign," assented the commandant, and he pulled his great mustachios.

"And what is oppressing his Grace?" slyly urged the master of the wardrobe, who had passed off duty upon seeing the last brooch duly fastened. "The queen mother —"

"I am not favored with their Graces' confidence, Maître le Greve," returned the soldier, bluntly. "It is enough for subjects to obey orders, and leave the wherefores to their betters."

"But this unwonted silence — never a laugh, never a smile, — so unusual. Why, when Maître Bernave, the high barber, was curling the royal hair, he passed the most admirable jest, so aptly, neatly, and precisely turned, that we who stood by in the closet held our sides, awaiting the king's laugh, to laugh ourselves. But lo! his Grace was silent as a sculptured saint, and we perforce were silent too. Alas! poor Bernave — and I knew he had treasured that rare jest since St. Mark's Day."

"And therein his Grace proclaimed himself no fool. That Bernave's brains are smaller than a fowl's; and as for the jest, I swear Father Foulque made it and sold it to Bernave for a couple of sous." The commandant was further delivering himself, when the sudden dispersal of the half-score of lackeys outside the closet door made him bow his courtliest, while the master-usher's high voice sounded,

"Messieurs — the king!"

Louis, as ever, was soberly dressed, and De Joinville's glance told him that Le Greve was right. The king's face was no gayer than his doublet. Since the dinner horns were not yet blaring in the hall below, Louis came beside his officer and stood waiting, his hands hanging awkwardly, his whole bearing saying, " I want a word alone." De Joinville contrived to edge up close beside his master, despite Maître le Greve's envious scowl, and the king's question was not long in coming.

"Will you tell me why Gui of Avignon is to sit with my mother and my wife at my table?"

"Has not your Grace commanded it?" asked the soldier, with well-feigned innocence.

"My mother has commanded it," answered Louis, half obediently, half helplessly; "but wherefore?"

"I have not been reckoned worthy of sharing her Grace's councils," returned De Joinville, coldly, and thought that the subject was closed; but the king drew nearer.

"Simon de Joinville, you are a true friend of mine, if friend I have in the world. Do you know, there is something about the palace to-day that delights me little."

"I do not understand, sire."

"Nor I. It is in the air I breathe, the ground I touch, the sounds I hear. Something ill is brewing. God is about to bring upon me some great sorrow; to try me with some great temptation, some direful peril to me and to France."

The commandant shrugged his burly shoulders. " I am no leech from Montpellier, fair sire, and cannot stop the headache; but while I rule the yeomen of the guard —"

The king laughed; the same good laugh it gave such joy to hear, and De Joinville was well pleased.

"It will be about foes crossing your slain body next," cried the king, his face very merry. "No, it will not be so bad as that. I think there must be art-magic in this Pontoise castle — a task for my good mother's holy men, to find the wizard. Yet I would — " here the smile faded a little — "I would that Gui of Avignon was not to dine with us."

"As your Grace commands," hinted De Joinville.

"As madame, my mother, commands," corrected the king, frankly; "for in all the universe I fear two things — the good God and my wise mother."

To which perfectly frank avowal the officer did not answer, muttering under his breath, "To fear God is well — to fear one's mother — "

But now the great horns began to jar through all the château. Ten pikemen in burnished corselets fell in before the king. De Joinville drew his sword, and stalked proudly at their head down into the banqueting hall.

It was not a great feast — merely the ordinary entertainment set before the royal household every day; yet the king of France could not feed an hundred gentlemen and as many dames without a deal of clatter and glitter and state. A long, high hall — small painted windows, a wealth of arras, gaudy banners trailing from the timbered ceiling, sweet herbs on the floor, rows of white tables and of benches, another table on a dais at the end of the chamber — that was the picture. The king sat facing the feasters in a great arm-chair with a canopy, and before him were arrayed his three companions, their backs upon the hall — his mother at his right, Margaret at his left, Gui, the guest of honor, between them. There was

indefinite courtesying, scraping, doubling, a long delay
while my Lord of Vendome quarrelled with my Lord of
La Marche as to the right to a seat at the table next to the
dais — a dispute tactfully settled by the omnipresent chamberlain. The royal party was seated, then the rest. Father
Foulque pronounced grace, and the high server knelt before
Louis with the first silver plate. The dinner was begun.

*   *   *   *   *   *   *

I think it was Enguerraud de Coucy who enjoyed that
feast the most, although he ate and drank up nothing but
talk. His duty set him beside his master's chair, to
summon or dismiss the pages by a nod or upraised finger.
As he stood, he could study the four at the table as a
spider studies four overdaring flies who are buzzing near
his stronghold. The king was clearly ill at ease, and
showed it by long lapses of silence, broken by sudden out-
bursts of forced merriment. Blanche, white as ever, in
face and dress, also spoke rarely, and then with a chilly
authority that defied all lighter counter-thrusts. Margaret
strove desperately to be gay; she smiled, laughed, praised
all her husband's commonplaces. Only when the queen
mother's cold eyes lit on her she would seem to draw into
herself and shiver, then crawl out again, and laugh once
more. But Gui of Avignon made good the silence of the
rest. Indeed, had the king wished to say more, he would
have had small chance. The little knight waxed eloquent
over the food. The peacock centrepiece he vowed was
worthy of three *cansons;* he ran short of words in praising
the great pie of roe-deer and capons; he harangued so
long about the roasted leveret that the page took the plate
away before he tasted it; and as for the sturgeon served
in parsley, he wished himself gifted with the lyre of Ber-
trand de Born to do it justice.

De Coucy, however, had something better for his eyes than the agile gestures of the troubadour. Right behind Margaret of Provence stood the gentlewoman who served her — the Lady Alithe. And the chamberlain saw how the king's eyes were always going over toward his wife's face, then rising as to something above it, where they would rest long. Perhaps De Coucy blessed St. Germain in his heart, thinking, " One has but to look to see which of these twain should be the queen of France, and if — " But the meditation went no further; for at this moment Gui, who had given three words for the queen consort, to one for the king, leaned visibly toward Margaret, and began rattling on in Provençal with a lower voice. De Coucy saw Louis' face cloud. The queen mother raised her eyebrows a very little; but Margaret was answering the knight in the northern Languedoil which all might hear.

"I fear, brave sir, my husband's people of the North have too little experience in our knightly lore and gallantry not to take some things therein amiss."

Her color showed that she was vexed at what he had just said; but the queen mother's eyebrows rose again, and De Coucy saw Alithe lift her hand to him in signal. The troubadour seemed never to hear his countrywoman's warning.

"I did affirm," quoth he, still louder, while his hands flew around his head in protestation, "and will make good, whether by lance or viol or voice, according to the fair pleasure of mine adversary, that he who is truly devoted to a noble dame, be she wedded or unwedded, should account all dangers joys, all rebuffs as new incitements, all coldness as spurs to greater faithfulness. And as says the immortal Pierre Vidal, he shall find his reward in the pleasures of beholding his lady's eyes, whence 'shoot arrows of delight, wrought in the fire of love, and tempered with pure sweetness.'"

The speech again ended with Gui's face close to Margaret's, and her color was yet higher. De Coucy quaked, lest she reprove the troubadour to his face, but his terrors ended when the queen mother spoke in her cold irony.

"Assuredly, fair sir, you of the South do learn to blaze up with love, like to a very haystack."

"A haystack, madam!" cried he, gesturing harder than ever; "say rather our hearts are become as the burning fiery furnace, after it had been heated seven times by the commandment of the Babylonish emperor, the tyrant Nebuchadnezzar. And by St. Tropheme! are we without the meed of bright reward? Not that such as I dare to claim the high recompense of a great master in the mystery of love, and make bold, as did Pierre d'Alverhoe, to demand a kiss from the fairest lady present, after each of my *cansons*. Nevertheless, I may — "

His speech had been aimed at the queen mother, but now he was staring into her daughter-in-law's face. A very loud cough from Blanche ended his sally.

"We do not doubt your gallantries find due reward," said she, pregnantly. "I did but think we of the North had much to learn from our Provençal kinsfolk. My son," and her glance went across to Louis, "if you will meet me in my cabinet, before we go out into the garden, you will greatly prove your love."

Louis nodded. The troubadour ceased staring at Margaret. All the royal party seemed trying to forget the one thing uppermost in every mind. De Coucy had heard enough. He raised his hand the first instant the queen mother's eyes were away from him, and Alithe obeyed his signal. Another young noblewoman stepped forward to serve Margaret, and Alithe drew back with her father, from the royal table to a second table, also on the dais, piled with discarded plates, and covered with a heavy white linen that fell to the floor.

The chamberlain stood against this table, and was not sorry to see the king's glance follow Alithe all through her brief journey to his side. When she stopped, the eyes of Louis stopped; and the king gazed and gazed, until a word from his mother called him back. There was no mistaking. Never had the king looked on any woman, save his mother, as he had then looked on Alithe de Coucy. Her father was sure of that.

Alithe stood beside the chamberlain, and for a moment the two kept silence. They were passing the wine now, and Gui was exhibiting his fine breeding by never drinking save when his mouth was empty, nor lifting a morsel from the trencher with anything save his thumb and two fingers. Louis' face had grown more troubled than ever. He seemed darting little fitful glances across the table at the troubadour, while his mother sat forward on her chair, as though alert against any new sally from the indiscreet ambassador. Only Margaret talked desperately about everything, which was the same as about nothing.

"You did right, my child," purred De Coucy, in his smoothest whisper, "very right, when you called his Grace 'a mole.'"

"Yes," answered the daughter, "moles are blind."

"Heart of St. Germain!" avowed the chamberlain, never taking his sight from his royal charges. "Has not the king two eyes, can he not hear, see, think, feel? No sense of honor, dignity, or shame? His wife is wooed beneath his eyes, and he — the chair beneath him is far more stirred."

Louis had, in fact, lapsed into perfect silence. The queen consort and the troubadour were doing all the talking, doubtless on less perilous themes, for Blanche was settling back on her cushions. Alithe cocked her head that it might be at its archest curve, should the king look about at her, before she answered the chamberlain.

"His Grace was very clearly made to have another think and feel for him, that other, no doubt, to be a woman — until this hour my Lady Blanche of Castile."

"And, St. Martin willing, my Lady Alithe —"

"Hush!" commanded she, and clapped her hand upon his mouth. "Not to your own soul dare to breathe it! Ah! the king looks at us."

Whether it was to sign to the cupbearers, or for something else, Louis looked again toward Alithe, again let his eyes stay long. When they went back, it was to the sight of Margaret and Gui of Avignon side by side. Was the king comparing the twain — setting the queen consort beside her waiting-lady, and asking which was the nobler, wiser, and more fair? Surely he had caught Alithe's rarest smile, though cast only at her father. The face of Margaret was so clouded! And faces sombre are so much less enchanting than faces gay!

"You have spoken to the queen mother?" asked De Coucy, when the royal gaze lifted again.

"I have. *She* is not silent because she does not know or feel."

"Our Lady have pity on the Provençal then," was the pious wish of the chamberlain, "for Blanche of Castile will have none! The more I scheme against the queen mother, the more I would doff my cap to her. Were she a man, we could see a second Charlemagne!"

"So you pity the Provençal?" Alithe's question was

neither serious nor wanton, but only skimmed off the sur-
face of her thoughts.

"So I do, my child, so I do," repeated the chamberlain,
soberly. "It is a grievous thing we have plotted against
her. It will cost me dear. I shall not rest easy for my
soul until our monks at Coucy have added two more farms
to their glebe, and rebuilt the abbey church at my charge.
Even then — but I will do my best. St. Germain will in-
tercede for me, and Our Father will prove merciful —"

"How fortunate," retorted Alithe, a little contempt
curving her lips, "we De Coucys are so passing rich!
Were we born poorer, how little we could dare!"

"And for this, our wealth," replied her father, "we
should the more thank the good Lord God, for making
open to us the kingdom of heaven, as well as of this present
world. Nevertheless," and here his voice grew unctuous,
"we do meditate a weighty sin. Have you considered,
daughter, considered well the stakes, the risk, the cost?
There will be no lands left at Coucy if we fail to buy
indulgence and viaticum before the scaffold, none to buy
masses for our souls thereafter. To blind the queen
mother to our plots, to dash down the queen consort to
dishonor, or speed her to her death, to turn then against
the Castilian, and thrust her into a monastery, to force
another bride and preceptor upon this weakling king —"

His wisdom was ended by a sudden sneeze from beneath the low-hanging table cloth. I think that even
Alithe's forehead was a little white, when, quick as
thought, her father thrust under an arm, and dragged
forth a lad who was snapping, snarling, whining, like a
puppy. De Coucy gripped his captive by the nape of the
neck, and cast one glance over him.

"Who are you?" was his ungentle question.

G

"Boso!" The boy thrust his fists into his eyes, and wept.

"Wounds of Our Lord!" swore the nobleman, "and what were you doing?"

"Hiding."

"Could you hear our talk?"

But Boso only twisted and groaned. To tell plain truth, he had stolen into the hall whilst the tables were being set, to see the grand array of plate; had feared to slip out past the yeomen, and had taken himself to what he deemed to be a safe refuge. With the chamberlain's hand upon his collar, his wits almost forsook him.

"Could you hear our talk?" stormed De Coucy.

"I'm a poor lad," chattered the culprit, answering, of course, exactly what he ought not to. "Who am I to say your Lordship nay? I humbly beg—"

"You confess, then!" shouted the chamberlain, when a touch of Alithe upon his arm recalled him to time and place.

"Out with him, father," she was whispering. "Will you stand here on the dais and clutch at a varlet? People are tittering. What if the queen mother sees?"

Alithe was right, and her father knew it. With long strides he haled his captive through a side door, and into an empty anteroom. Then he blew out his rage. "Off to Coucy you shall go, and I will see if tearing asunder by wild horses can silence that tongue of yours. You overheard!— then tell your story to the devil!"

"As it may pleasure your Excellency," whimpered Boso, shaking all over, but watching his chance, as a rat in the cat's claws. My lord's grip had relaxed in the least, when a lightning twist and turn set the prisoner loose and his noble captor sprawling upon the rushes. Half stunned, it was an instant before De Coucy could rise to stare and to curse. The outer door had banged; frightened feet were scampering across the courtyard. Boso was beyond all present pursuit, unless the guard were roused, and the chamberlain had no wish for such publicity. Whilst he was rubbing his bruised shins, the noise from the hall told that the feast was ended, and a host of duties claimed the nobleman. The interloper therefore went scot-free, "for no such churl could understand anything." Nevertheless, in sage prudence, the chamberlain added to the fields he had vowed to the abbey of St. Germain de Coucy yet a third, thus making trebly sure the most helpful favor of the blessed saints in heaven. And after that, as he thought of the things likely to happen when Gui of Avignon met his royal hosts again in the château gardens, Enguerraud de Coucy forgot all about Boso.

CHAPTER VIII

HOW FALAISE WORE A CROWN

IF only my Lord de Coucy had never heard poor Boso
sneeze, I am sure that Boso, for his part, would never have
remembered a word that had been spoken by my Lord de
Coucy. The boy had made rather less out of Alithe's and
her father's talk than out of so much monk's Latin, and
thanks to the clattering of trenchers and table knives, it
had been nothing easy to hear. But now, whilst he ran
like a rabbit through one court, down a dark alley into a
second court, and so into a third, and all the time deemed
the chamberlain thundering after him, there was time for
the last utterance of the nobleman to sink well into his
victim's head. "To blind the queen mother to our plots,
to dash down the queen consort to dishonor or speed her
to her death; to turn then against the Castilian and thrust
her into a monastery; to force another bride and preceptor
upon this weakling king," — what did it all mean? Boso
ran and ran, the words he remembered frightening him,
just because it was so plain he ought never to remember
them. "Tearing by wild horses" — Boso knew what
that meant. So they had treated Jacques the bandit, and
already he felt his own young legs stretching asunder.
Then of a sudden he stopped, gazed about him. No one
was pursuing. No shouts were rising from the guard.
All seemed safe. Boso rubbed his eyes, panted, and like
a pious lad, said a little prayer to good Archangel Michael,

"who saves from the peril." After a while it grew upon him that he was standing in the court before the great donjon tower, and it did not take him long to clamber to the eyrie at the summit, to make confession to his patron saint — Falaise.

    *   *   *   *   *   *   *

When Margaret had risen from the king's table she had gone straight back to her chamber. She was angry with Gui of Avignon. Only the sincere faith that Louis could never distrust her, let the giddy troubadour do what he might, had prevented her from giving no soft answers to his wordy gallantry. And despite his lightly tripping tongue and the tinsel of the Southerner's compliment, she knew there was something in his eye, and tone, and touch, that spoke out "danger," and danger for her. Yet what to say and do she did not know. "He who excuses himself, accuses himself," is an old proverb, and no woman will declare her honor in danger unless sorely pushed to bay. Besides, Gui of Avignon was no unproven friend. In those happy days in dear Provence, before the least cloud had blown across her youth, they had been play-fellows together in the gay castle at Arles. In the fêtes and tourneys it was Gui who had won the princess's ribbons. His first *cansons* had been in her praise. She had even repaid him verse for verse with her own. It had meant nothing. It had harmed no one. Margaret had fared away to the North with never a tear for Gui; but she had missed his merry comradeship. For beneath his viols, his love-gazes, his *tensos*, and his high-winging talk, Margaret knew that he was, as valor and honor went, a passing brave and knightly man, who was less wayward than his speech might seem. So she had welcomed him when he came on the embassy. There had been Maying-parties at Vincennes, boats upon the Seine, hunts at Fontainebleau, and always Gui had been near the queen consort. Herself from the South, Margaret had understood him better than the rest. He had brought news from home, of father and of mother. How could she dismiss him now, by any public chiding? And yet — and yet despite all this, a voice was speaking to her very loudly, "Distrust the knight, for there is danger."

There was to be a simple fête of the court in the palace gardens before evening fell, and at it Margaret must at least show herself; but till then her time was her own. She ordered her ladies to lay out her dresses and jewels, that all might be ready, then begged to be alone. "Her confessor," quoth she, "had enjoined some prayers as penance, and there was no better time for them than this." If Margaret told a white lie, I am sure the Blessed Mother forgave her. The queen sat on a low stool, her elbows on her knees, her chin upon her hands. She was resolving to call Gui apart at the fête, to tell him that gossip was bandying her name and his about, and that he must quit the court. It would mortify the knight, but there would be no public disgrace, and what was a better way? She would have given all her jewels for one hour with her mother — but wishing never answers a prayer.

Whilst the queen sat in deep revery, she caught, as it were, a rustling of the curtains of her bedchamber, the tapping of the tassels of the arras, then a foot, soft as a spirit's treading, across the rushes. Ere she knew it Falaise was beside her, and touching her with her hands.

"Lady, gracious lady, it is you. Yes! I am sure. I had been listening, to see if it was the sound of your breath. I cannot always tell, even when it is still, unless I have known one very long."

What the queen did was to slip her hand about the blind girl's waist and draw her down upon a seat.

"Did the little soft sprites send you down to me," asked Margaret, in half playful mood, "because they knew I was alone and very lonely?"

"I do not think it was the sprites," said Falaise, seriously. "I am sure it was not the Master Devil; but whether it was a holy saint I cannot tell. I have come because Boso is frightened."

"Is frightened?"

"Yes, surely. It was very wrong of him. He ought never to have done it. So I told him, and you, dear lady, will not be too angry. But of a truth, he meant no ill, and such dreadful things they were he overheard."

Now, after such a beginning, Margaret could do only two things, vow that she would forgive Boso, even if he had stabbed a duchess, and ask Falaise to tell her story. And the blind girl answered with a tale over which the queen shivered much, but out of which she gathered little. First of all, Boso was not sure who had been the persons talking, save that they were "great folk," or they would not have been so near the royal table. In the second place, he could remember almost nothing of what they had said, except that they had expressed contempt for the king and hatred for his wife. Only the words last spoken had burned themselves into Boso's mind, and Falaise could repeat them all. She told them over three times, while the queen sat and wondered and wondered. A plot — a plot that would shake all France, and of which the keystone was her own ruin! If Boso's tale meant anything, it meant that. And who had stood on the king's dais and chattered treason? Who, but — Margaret smiled as she spoke the names — Enguerraud de Coucy and the Lady

Alithe? Surely they had stood against the side table
just as Boso had said. But to distrust the chamberlain,
the shadow of the queen mother and of the young
king, passed belief in human frailty. At last Margaret
lifted her head with a merry laugh. She drew Falaise
closer and kissed both cheeks. "O dearest flower,—
and by which dare I name you?—I think the little soft
sprites have been playing your Boso's ears a knavish trick.
Do you know, he would make a traitor of my Lord de
Coucy himself, and though I love him little, and his
daughter less, I try to love them,—they are so faithful to
the king. And as you sometimes dream of angels, so
Boso has dreamed of imps. Who knows but that he fell
asleep, and was found out by his loud snoring?"

Falaise could only shake her head, and vow that Boso
was the most truthful of Eve's race; but the queen would
take no denial. And when Falaise arose to go away,
Margaret with gentle force constrained her.

"You have come by the sliding door, from the secret
stair, and entered unbidden the queen of France's chamber. High treason—and you must pay the traitor's price."

"What price?"

"You must stay with me until I dress for the fête. You
shall sit—thus, where the light through this window can
slant across your face—thus, and you must answer all my
questions."

Falaise folded her hands in meek obedience. It was a
great relief to find that Margaret did not take Boso's tale
too seriously, and did not fear some horrid treason.

"First," commanded the queen, "you must tell me why
you seem never sad."

"And how dare I be ungrateful to the good God by
being sad, when I have no cause, save the sickness of

Nicole? Have I not Father Ambroise, Huon, Boso, old
Martine who keeps the manse, Jean of the Mill, and
Brigite for friends? Do I lack good food? Do not the
doves come to me, and the dear talking winds, and at night
the little soft sprites? Do not the trees sing in my ears, and
the brooks? Have I not May-flowers to-day? and June
flowers to-morrow? How dare I wish for more than that?
Only," here Falaise sighed almost anxiously, "I am afraid
Our Father loves Nicole so much he needs her up in
heaven. Yet that should not make me sad!"

"But your blindness never frets you?"

Falaise answered with her brightest smile.

"It used to once; but one day Father Ambroise said
'the kind God has loved you very much, Falaise, above
all common folk; for you shall never see all the pain and
ugliness of this world, and when you awake in heaven,
even heaven will be more beautiful because you have
never seen before.' Since then I have been most content."

"Father Ambroise is an exceeding wise man," said
the queen; then for a while she sat in silence, until her
eyes fell on the gay dress laid out for the fête.

"Tell me, Falaise of the Blessed Voice," spoke Margaret, "have you never wished for what we other women
love — for silks and velvets, for jewels and scents, and for
all the things that make life beautiful and gay?"

The blind girl seemed a little puzzled, and held her
head first at this pretty angle, then at that, before she
ventured an answer.

"Dear lady, once I felt a piece of velvet ribbon; it was
given Father Ambroise by some great dame to bind
around his missal. It was very soft to touch, but not so
pleasant as a rose petal, which I like better. Once the

Abbess of Maubuisson put in my hand what she said was
a diamond. It was only a hard tiny stone, with points
that pricked. Once at a fair, old Martine brought me a
scent bag of musk. I did not tell her, but I like the wild
flowers better. Therefore I fear I do not understand."

The queen kissed her eyes, but would not turn her from
a conceit of her own.

"Rise up, Falaise," said she, "that I may look at
you and your dress."

The blind girl obeyed unhesitatingly. And Margaret
took pains that her own smiles should not pass into
laughter, for in truth Falaise was most strangely dressed.
She wore a long, tight-fitting sleeveless apron of dark
brown cloth embroidered plentifully with fantastic figures
in bright red, a master-work by good Martine; but one to
have made my Lady Countesses raise their delicate eyebrows high. Margaret looked toward the door with the
sly glance of a girl at forbidden pleasures: safe closed,
and she grew bold.

"Forget that I am queen!" cried the Provençal, talking now in her own Languedoc, which Falaise might
scarcely follow; "forget that you are the maid of the
tower! Watch — I will make you a great lady. I am your
waiting-woman, and my fingers are swift and skilled. I
will put on you the dress which I must wear before the
court at the fête." And before the blind girl knew aught
that was happening, lo! the queen was laying smooth
samite and *cendal* over her; Falaise's fingers brushed
downy ermine. Then a heavy chain dropped round her
neck, and she felt Margaret's hands setting something
heavier upon her hair.

"O gracious lady, what is this you do?" cried the
blind girl, wondering; while the queen, forgetting every-

thing, in her own delight, flashed the steel mirror before
the other's eyes, then clapped her hands.

"Look, my Falaise! look, look! I always knew you
were a lovely queen for France. How well the blue
samite falls about you, and the red cendal and white
ermine shows against your throat, and the gold beads over
them. And the tiara—how its gold blends with the gold
of your hair; and the light which springs from its pearls
and diamonds adds to your beauty twenty fold. *Ai!* I
must not let Louis the king see you thus, or he will learn
to love you all too well for me!"

"Dear lady, what is this you do?" so cried again
Falaise. And Margaret dropped the mirror.

"Oh! cruel, thoughtless have I been, for you can never
see. You cannot know how beautiful you are. You
cannot know how, had your eyes the light, all France
from Guienne to Calais would run to you, would worship
you; and you would be countess, queen, empress, anything you wish, because of your beautiful face and voice.
And I—I would begin to fear you, and then to hate you.
Woe is me!"

Falaise's voice trembled now with a kind of fear.
"Dear lady, you frighten me. You forget who I am. I
am only the blind maid of Pontoise, and I only know two
things—that I love God and that He loves me. I cannot
follow all you say."

"And well you do not," cried the queen. "Haste, forget it all." Then, as she looked on Falaise and her angell-
like beauty, a great wave of sorrow and helplessness
swept over Margaret. Before she knew what she was
doing, she had knelt at the blind girl's side, pressing her
hands about the other's waist.

"Oh! Falaise of the Blessed Voice, O Falaise, from

whom God has taken the sight of this world, that you may, even now, behold His heaven, pity me, pray for me, succor me, for I am desolate, and sick for love, and very sad."

Strangely enough, Falaise did not start at this strange turn of the queen.

"Rise up, dear lady," answered she, "for I am not St. Elizabeth, that you should kneel to me. I know that you are sad. What may I do?"

"Be my friend, Falaise, my friend! For I have none in all wide France."

The queen sobbed bitterly. The blind girl waited for the first burst of grief to pass before urging a question, — then at last she spoke.

"And wherefore none, dear lady? The king — does not his Grace love you?"

"Does Louis love me?" echoed Margaret, rising, and in her tone were blended joy and pain. "Does Louis love me? Yes, if the Blessed Mother loves me, so does he! But you cannot understand, Falaise, his love is not all of love. *Ei*, woe."

"You love another," and at the thought the blind girl's face turned white. Who was she, to be confessor to the first lady of France? But the queen sprang back, as if struck by an arrow.

"It is not so, as I hope for heaven. No man's name is on my heart save his, and I would die for him! I cannot teach you why I have such pain. Yet every day the burden grows. Yesterday I saw an old woman bearing a great load of sticks. Her back was so bent it seemed the poor thing's bones would break. My ladies and I were all moved to pity. 'See her distress,' we cried, and pelted her with deniers. But I think the hardest loads are not upon our backs, but in our breasts. And every day they grow, and every day we are a little less strong to bear. But because they are all within, and seen only by God — and surely He forgets — we get no pity. What must I do this afternoon at the fête? Smile, laugh, answer gay words with gayer still; for I am the queen of France. The world has no place for a frowning lord or mistress. All women envy me. 'As happy as a queen,' the girls sing in their play; but perhaps to bear the heavy sticks is far less hard."

Margaret had spoken bitterly, almost shrilly, and Falaise twice had raised a hand to stay her, in vain. When she ended, the blind girl drew again close to the queen, put out her arms, and let her wonderful fingers touch the Provençal's forehead gently, gently. Under the charm of their caress, Margaret's passions calmed silently, and only after a long time did Falaise say a word.

"Dear lady," said she at last, and her speech was itself like the music of the lulling wind, sighing, melodious, "dear lady, I do not know why you have chosen one so weak and ignorant as I to hark to all your grief. You have but known me since this morn."

"Morn," echoed the queen; "yes, that is true. What matter? for your heart is pure. That makes me think I have known you always."

"Dear lady, I will not pry into the causes of your sorrow. I only know if you say, 'the good God can forget,' you do Him grievous wrong. It cannot be; and yet what do you wish that I, who have nothing, shall give to you who have all the world?"

"Pray for me," cried the queen; "pray that I may be strong. I dread to-day, to-night, to-morrow. I feel some creeping weakness. I may not be able to battle against

some direful sin. Oh! I have besought every saint, the
Blessed Mother, and even Our Dear Lord, but I am only
a feeble girl. I know I shall be sorely pressed. Too
likely I shall give way, and bring on my soul a load of
shame and sin. But I shall be purer, stronger to suffer
and withstand, if I know that you, Falaise of the Blessed
Voice, will pray for me, for your sister Margaret of Provence, who craves the compassion of God."

I do not remember all that they said, all that Falaise
promised, or how often the queen wept for her mother, or
how the blind girl stilled her. I only know that at last, when
the sunbeams began to slant lower through the windows,
Margaret took off Falaise's diadem and the ermine and
the silks. The queen was calm again. You would have
thought, to hear her laugh, that she had been whiling away
a merry hour. Falaise wished to glide away through the
hidden panel, but Margaret forbade her.

"You shall go down in sight of all my women and leave
them to puzzle their wise brains with marvelling how I let
you in."

So the queen had her way, and was rewarded by the
wide stares of the worthy waiting-ladies when the blind
girl went down the great staircase of the donjon. Then,
having dismissed Falaise, she called in the attendants to
dress her for the fête, and with them was so busy that
she did not see what happened in the court below. For
Falaise had no sooner reached it than a sprucely arrayed
squire plucked the edge of her cape.

"What do you desire?" said the blind girl, and halted,
at which the squire, with perfect gentleness, but equal
firmness, took her by the hand.

"My fair mistress," spoke he, "I am commanded to
lead you to my good lord, the Sire Enguerraud de Coucy."

CHAPTER IX

THE SPIDER BECOMES THE FLY

FALAISE made no resistance to the squire. So far as
her life experience had taught her anything, it taught that
all men and women were good to her. Even the hag
Justine, whom half Pontoise said was cross-tongued enough
to be Sir Satan's grandmother, would not fail to cry " Our
Lady prosper you, Falaise," as often as they met. Father
Ambroise had indeed spoken well; thanks to her blindness, Falaise had dwelt on the earth these twenty years,
being in the world, but not of it. That any real evil could
befall her at the hands of this strange guide she did not
take time to believe. Thrown wholly upon herself, shut
up within herself, creating for herself a new world of
fancies, wonderful, and brighter than sun could ever gild,
Falaise was in worldly wisdom but a little child, though
in heavenly knowledge I think a meet sister for the angels.
Therefore, I say, she went forward without hesitance, without fear.

But not so the squire. He was Pons de Rosay, a small-
ish, smooth-cheeked young man, the son of a noble vassal
of the Coucys, who had learned in his lord's service to
hawk well, to sing well, to make speeches to ladies well,
but especially to hold a discreet tongue as to all the
chamberlain's doings. This was not the first time he had
done his master a service very like this, and his conscience

had never troubled him. But now,—well, he looked at
the lithe form tripping at his side, at the forehead un-
dimmed by sin or by worldly knowledge or fear, at the
bright eyes which could never see. And once he thought
of his mother, ten years dead; and once he thought of the
saints; then his hand within Falaise's began to slacken
its hold and his own feet grew slow. St. Gabriel knows
what would have happened next, if a horse-laugh at his
other elbow had not made him look away from Falaise
to a burly pikeman off duty, another follower of De
Coucy.

"Ei, my merry Pons, so that was the roebuck I have
seen you so stealthily stalking at the foot of the tower.
My lord's commands, no doubt. But in with her quickly,
or we'll have half the castle banging round our ears for
stealing off their song-bird."

"The devil catch you, Robert," quoth Pons, uncivilly.
"How do you know I'm hunting for my lord?"

"Well," flung back the archer, "if for only yourself,
I've a mind to have the venison for mine own!"

And Falaise, who had made nothing of all this ungodly
thrust and parry, felt a great hand clap upon her shoulder.
She stood still, shivered all over, and her face seemed
white as snow. Danger was so strange a thing to her
that she hardly knew how to be afraid.

"What are you doing? Your fingers are rough. You
hurt!" said she, in a shrill voice, still standing.

Pons bade the pikeman take himself off to the lowest
cupboard in hell, and tried to pacify her.

"Come with me, little mistress; he shall not touch you
again," he said with blandest accents; but Falaise, once
scared, was not to be quieted with a word.

"I must know what you wish, or I will not go with

you," she said, and a little tightening about her lips showed that her fears were rising.

" To my Lord de Coucy," soothed the squire. " Surely you have heard of the great Sire de Coucy. It is a passing honor for a pretty maid, if she catch his eye — "

" I will not go with you," and Falaise's little foot rang down upon the stones. There was something in her glance which told Pons " what you must do, do quickly." The fear of his master's wrath made him forget all about his mother and the blessed saints. He gave a wink to Robert, who understood. Falaise felt a cloth drawn firmly across her mouth to gag all cries. Four hands lifted her, as one might lift a kitten. It was all so swiftly done she had no time to think to struggle. Had she had sight, she would have known the court they stood in was for the moment empty, with no friendly eye to follow her. The strange hands bore her up stairs, down corridors, and at last into a room, for she could hear the rushes cracking under their feet. Then the cloth was whipped from her mouth. She was planted on deep cushions; two pairs of feet retired; a door-latch clicked. For a time even Falaise's keen ears caught only silence. She sat motionless, while her heart throbbed, throbbed, and seemed like to fly up into her throat. What had happened? What was about to happen? She was too affrighted even to pray.

Falaise's ideas of evil were very vague, therefore doubly dreadful. Half of the reason you fear the devil is because his ugliness is so unwonted. And she — when had she ever been touched by force before? For the first time in her life, her blindness rose up to madden her, for out of its black penthouse sprang shapeless goblins manifold to heighten every pain. At first she was too scared to weep. Then at last, when the first great terror passed, came a

H

hard sob, another, another, and the comforting of tears.
I do not know how long she cried, when of a sudden she
raised her head and listened.   A delicate step was ap-
proaching her; then came a voice.

"Now, by St. Germain! what am I hearing?   And what
do I see — tears?   My cruel rascals, to bring your pretty
eyes to that!   They'll feel the whip across their legs ere
they grow an hour older."

It was a smooth, appeasing voice.   Falaise stopped sobbing, but still she did not answer.

"*Hé!* that is better.   We will soon put an end to tears.
The good God made those eyes of yours only to shine like
twin stars.   Alas, that though all the world can worship
them, you cannot see their light!   Still silent?   Well, I
will hear that voice trill like a nightingale soon.   I will sit
myself close, thus; and I will do the talking."

Falaise knew that an unknown man was sitting down
beside her.   Nothing that he said was in itself alarming, but
she was so frightened now that everything was dreadful.

"You must not think, dear child," went on the newcomer, "that you are strange to me, though I am strange
to you.   Since the first day the court came to Pontoise, I
have listened to your singing from the tower; yes, and
though you knew it not, I have watched you come in and
out, have caught the light of your charming face, have
vowed to possess myself of your friendship."

"Who are you, sir?" spoke Falaise, simply, with her
hand across her eyes.

"I," was the answer, "am the Sire Enguerraud de Coucy,
chamberlain to his Grace the king."

Falaise was springing from the cushion.

"Let me go — go instantly!   You are the lord of the
evil men who dragged me hither!" she cried.

She fluttered about the room like a bird, and almost beat herself against the wall, when the other caught her gently by the wrists and led her back.

"Hush!" he admonished in the same smooth voice. "Have I not cursed my clumsy varlets? Be quiet, dear child, and let me speak. I sent for you this day because I have desired your friendship, and I desired to summon you upon a lucky day. Therefore, being mindful of God, and desiring to do only His will, I commanded my chaplain to consult the Holy Scriptures, as being our infallible guide both in this world and the world to come. Doing as he was bid, he closed the book, prayed over it, and then, shutting his eyes, opened it. The first words he beheld on looking were even these, 'and the *fourth* beast was like a flying eagle.' Then I knew that if I would win your love, I must seek you on this *fourth* day that the court has come to Pontoise. For we should never disobey the manifest will of God, my child, or we may miss His blessing."

How much Falaise understood of all this I do not know. At least it served its end. She grew quieter, and her heart half ceased from pounding. Finally she had another question.

"Do you truly desire to be my friend?"

"Ah, yes, dear child, more than I can ever tell! If you only knew how many and great things I have on foot this day — things touching the welfare of all France — and have put them all by for an hour, just for your own sake, you would not again ask that."

He sat close beside Falaise, and she held out her hands, saying: "Then I must do to you as to all who would be my friends. I must touch your face."

"Willingly, dear child — such beautiful hands!"

Falaise touched forehead, cheeks, mouth, chin, with the

careful press of the honey-bee that treads upon the flower; but when she finished she did not smile.

"Lord," she said at last, "you are a handsome man, but I feel upon your face that which I do not like. I cannot trust you." And he felt her move away from him.

"Peace, peace," spoke the chamberlain, putting an arm about her waist to press her nearer. "You do not trust me because my face is strange, yet by each and every saint you love the best, — St. Martin, St. Hilaire, St. Michael, or Our Blessed Lady herself, — I swear to you undying friendship."

He ended, for he saw the whiteness coming again across the face of Falaise.

"Do not hold me, sir," commanded the blind girl, putting on a kind of dignity through very weakness, "and tell me why a great lord such as you should talk of 'friendship' to such a one as I. The great to the great, and the little to the little. If you are a seigneur, are there no noble ladies to hear your pretty words and vows? Leave me to Boso, to Huon, and Jean of the Mill. They may praise me, but never such as you."

De Coucy felt her gliding out of his hold despite himself. His voice sank to a softer purr than ever.

"Eh! my dearest child, but what are those rough uncouth names I hear — Boso, Huon, Jean? Who are those *canaille* to so much as speak to one who might be the queen of the gayest tourney in all France, and have a hundred knights break lances for her smile?"

He stopped, because he saw that Falaise was becoming whiter still.

"You do not answer my question, sir," said she. "Why do you bring me here? What will you do to me?"

De Coucy put on his most winsome smile, forgetting that his companion was blind.

"Alas! I have not the tripping tongue of my Lord of Champagne, nor of that blithe Provençal, the Knight Gui, or I would tell you in most beautiful words. What I wish to tell you is that to-day is a day of great good fortune unto you; more than ever you dreamed."

"Yes," broke in Falaise; "for to-day I have won the favor of the queen."

"Which queen?" darted the chamberlain, so abruptly that he forgot his benignant part.

"How sharp your voice is! Why are you angry? Surely I mean her Grace Margaret, the queen consort."

"Then, my lovely maid," warned De Coucy, with paternal gravity, "I must tell you to count her friendship no part of your good fortune. This Margaret of Provence is a most sinful woman, soon, by the finger of God, to receive her just deserts, and stand exposed and chastened before wide France."

"The queen sinful?"

"I grieve to say it, yes."

Falaise rose from beside him, slowly, almost proudly. He had never admired her more than now. "What a marvel if she had sight!" he was thinking.

"Sir," said Falaise, and her wonderful voice seemed to ring hard like iron, "what you say is untrue; Margaret of Provence is a sister to the saints. I will not sit and hear her slandered, for she is my friend."

The Sire de Coucy knew a strange thing was befalling him. He was being pushed to bay by a woman who was utterly in his power. He came very near to cursing outright. For power to conquer this sin of blasphemy he duly thanked St. Germain.

"I would not talk of her, but of your lovely self," he said, with vain cajolery.

"And I will ask again," said Falaise, "wherefore am I here, and what thing will you do? For now I fear you."

"Here? Because I desire you. Do? I will take you away to Coucy. Fear? I will teach you to love me."

But now he trembled at the gusts of anguish and passion that swept across the blind girl's face. First white, then dark, then white again, and her sightless eyes shone brighter, brighter.

"I know your name now," she said, in a creeping whisper, more dreadful than her cry. "You are the devil."

"Not so; be quiet, hearken, stay," commanded the chamberlain, repenting his rash candor. Falaise answered him slowly, moving her hands hither and thither, as though beckoning every sprite from her own dark world to wing down to her aid.

"Lord," said she, "you are a mighty man, and I know by your face your ways are high and hard. And what you will, you do, and what you hate, you crush; but what you love, is more cursed than what you hate. Oh, spare me from that love and I will bear the hate!"

"The hate?" swore the chamberlain. "Have I not turned aside on this day of all others to summon you? Shall not your wish be law in Coucy? Shall I not cover you with *cendals*, with *samites*, and with *cisclatons*? Shall not twenty maidens run by night, by day, at your least whim? Shall you not sleep on rose-leaves, and wake amid fair music? Shall not fifty jongleurs sing the live-long year the praises of 'Falaise of the Blessed Voice,' beloved of the Sire de Coucy?"

"Gone, gone, gone," spoke Falaise, in infinite bitterness, — "my dream that all men were good unto me, that all the tales I heard of sin and wrath were but as fancies of the night. I can never put trust in men again. Oh, the winds shall sing, and the birds and the brooks and the rivers; but never so sweet as before; for once I thought the wide world loved me, but now — I know some love is born in hell!"

Her words broke into a sob, and at that sob I think Enguerraud de Coucy for the first time in twoscore years felt an arrow of true shame. For the devil is not so strong that he can crush the spark of heaven's fire out of our souls. Though many the ashes that cover it, and dim the flickering, still it burns, and in unguarded moments, when guile and guilt seem running freest course, it will awake. And I think for one short instant my Lord de Coucy thought on his tale of sins, and doubted whether even the glebe lands for St. Germain could blot them out of God's Book of Life. He was as pale as Falaise, whilst the blind girl moved toward him slowly.

"Lord," she said, her voice rising steadily, "lord, my hands are weak, and yours are very strong. My friends are poor, and you are a high seigneur. You have the Master Devil for your friend, and great is his power. But I am stronger than you; and that you know full well. For on the dreadful day when we both stand before Our Father's throne, I know He will remember that my heart has been always pure, and ask how pure is yours. And then if He finds that in your lust and might you have done great evil against a weak maid who loved Him, will your oath — or will mine — avail the most in His all-holy sight?"

All the time she spoke she went forward, and he retreated. Insensibly he moved toward the door, she following the sound of his footsteps. She did not seem to fear him now. Facing the worst, she held it back with queenly disdain. Blanche of Castile was never haughtier than she. Then again she was speaking, whilst the Sire de Coucy felt his knees beat together under his fur-lined bliaut.

"Lord, — at God's judgment bar I will accuse you of this sin; so do not do it. Do not dash your soul to hell because of a flitting fancy for my face; for I am one of Christ's little ones, and because I am so weak, therefore I say I am so strong. And he who does wrong to me had been wiser to wrong the king. For when I say to the just God, 'Enguerraud de Coucy did this sin to me,' then the Lord Christ will rise from the Father's own right hand and say, 'Be of good cheer, Falaise, for I will be your advocate.' And who will be your advocate, great sir; who save the Master Devil, and will God hark to *him*?"

The chamberlain had been pressing against the door. He feared Falaise with a dread unspeakable; every word had been a hot brand upon his soul, enkindling the old ashes of remorse. He had one hope, one thought — to get away from her. Why had he summoned this angel of light to reprove him for his sin? As she drew closer he watched her with a wild, almost animal, terror. Then when she was near enough to lay a hand on him, he felt the latch pressing against his back. Praised be Our Lady, here was deliverance! Scarcely knowing what he did, he drew the bolts, opened, leaped aside, and Falaise swept out with the noiseless tread of one in a dream.

"Go, go, go!" cried the chamberlain. "May I never set eyes on you again!"

He did not look after Falaise. All the fountains of his superstition were opened. He was sure the blind girl was an angel or a saint, making a brief sojourn on earth. Woe to him who offended! For the moment he was ready to renounce every hope, every plot he had spent years in spinning. He knelt on the floor, tore a little gold crucifix from his breast, kissed it passionately, and shook all over with cold fear, whilst praying aloud:—

"*Mea culpa, mea culpa, mea maxima culpa! Sancta Maria beata mater Dei, ora pro nobis! Sancte Michael Angele, salvator ex periculis, ora pro nobis! Sancte Petre, custos portarum cœli, ora pro nobis!*"

His piety was at full heat, when a touch on his shoulder made him cut short just as he came to St. Raphael. He looked up to see Alithe gazing down on him. Her voice was as water dashed on his glowing embers.

"Pious as always, my father. I see you are praying; and what is the sorrow now? So you had an unlucky passage-at-arms with the blind linnet? I saw her glide out with her face like snow, and knew you had met misfortune. Be consoled; there are more such birds—"

"I am a sinful man," mumbled the chamberlain, beating his breast. "I was considering—"

"Whether we could pull the Provençal and queen mother down. Well, we will not, unless you leap up, change your mantle, and get you quickly to the king. For it is only to-day that we have De Ormoy."

"Of course; I am very forgetful," muttered De Coucy; and as he rose he forgot that a moment before he had been wishing every project of Alithe in the bottom of the sea. He obeyed his daughter meekly, put on the garments he was bid, and hasted away to the king.

It was not the first time that the hand of Alithe had plucked my Lord Enguerraud back from a deed very good for his soul.

*   *   *   *   *   *   *

As for Falaise, she was already going down the way to the cottage of Jean of the Mill. She was with Brigite and Nicole until the edge of evening, when once more she set forth for the castle. What had passed between her and the chamberlain she told to no one. In returning she took her way through a postern near to the tower where Gui of Avignon had his chambers, and it was near here that something in the touch and sniff of the evening breeze pleased her so that she began to sing.

CHAPTER X

THE MOTHER AND THE SON

THE chamberlain had made many mistakes in his life, but few greater than when he said that the king was blind to what passed between Gui and the queen consort. Louis was sadly perplexed and tormented. Ever since they had knelt together at the wedding mass in the cathedral at Sens and had risen up man and wife, his love for Margaret had burned as his guiding star. He adored his mother, as men bow before an angel; he loved his wife. He had loved her more because of the jealousy of Blanche; more because that jealousy had forced him so often to keep his love pent up within himself. And now — what dared he think, hope, dread?

One thing was plain. Gui of Avignon was desperately in love with the queen. Every word, look, gesture, uttered that. And Louis cursed — so far as his mild lips cursed anything — the hour the dapper ambassador had first met him at Vincennes. It was clear, too, that Margaret had left an old flame behind her in Provence, and that Gui's sight of her had blown everything again to a fine heat. The only question for Louis was — did Margaret care for Gui?

For her sake Louis had been silent; for her sake he had done nothing at the dinner to proclaim his distrust of the envoy. What a sin against his wife, were he to rebuke her, and learn that she had counted all the giddy Pro-

vençal's chatterings only frippery ! Nevertheless, the king
went from the great hall silent and sad. The humblest of
men, he did not ask himself, "Who is this petty Seigneur
of Avignon to be loved before the lord of France ?" He
had dreamed that Margaret desired him because he was
Louis de Poissy, not because he wore the crown of Hugh
Capet. And he asked himself whether there were no
actions of his, done and undone, which might have cost
him his wife's love ? He was ignorant, childish, the tool of
his mother. Who was he for a noble woman to trust and
honor ? Could Margaret cast all her love upon a weakling
boy ?

Amid such communings he left the hall, face bowed, and
scarce knowing whither the usher was leading him, until
that functionary coughed loudly to attract the royal
attention.

"May it please his Grace to order whither he should be
conducted ? " And Louis, not caring what he said, answered
listlessly, "The scriptorium."

The usher pattered on ahead. A staircase, a great
creaking door, and Louis was in the library of the château.
The king motioned. The usher and the attendant yeomen
vanished, leaving their master alone.

The library was a musty, dusty, high-ceiled room, in-
habited commonly by spiders, bats, and the old monk Benno,
who kept the moths out of the parchments during the ten
months of the year that the court was away from Pontoise.
The smell of scaling leather and bleaching ink made the
air heavy and drowsy. The rushes were very dry and
almost falling into powder. Nevertheless, Louis loved the
place, where were the long shelves and cupboards loaded
with a treasure above gold ; tall books bound in wood and
leather, with a gilt clasp here, and there a plaque of ivory.

At the end, against the dimly glazed window, was a broad
oaken table and two heavy chairs. The table was piled
with books, besides an inkhorn or two, quills, and sheets
of cotton paper.

The king cast himself into a chair, seized a book, opened,
and tried to read. It was Huges de St. Victor's *Treatise on
Beasts and Other Things;* but Louis found no pleasure in
discovering that the stag lived nine hundred years, and that
the dove with her right eye looked on herself, with her left
contemplated God.

Another trial. He dragged forth Abbess Herrat's
Garden of Delight. But he liked it less, though it told
how falling stars were bright sparks struck out by the wind,
which disturbs the ether betwixt the moon and the upper
firmament of heaven, and although every page was beautifully initialled in gold-leaf and color, and written in the
fairest round minuscule.

"This is because I turn to books of worldly learning, and
not to the true wisdom of God," muttered the king, and
snatched again at a well-conned friend, Augustine's *Civitas
Dei*, when the door grated, and Louis glanced up angrily.
Old Benno no doubt was returning from the buttery, when
the king would fain be alone. But a second glance
brought Louis to his feet. His mother was entering the
library.

The White Queen closed the door carefully, and came
across the floor with a rustle of her flowing garments. He
ran to her, and they kissed; then he put his hand to her
throat, and frowned.

"It is well to belong to the lay sisterhood of the blessed
St. Francis, my mother," said he, "but must you always
wear their coarse dress beneath your own?"

"It is for your father's soul, Louis," she answered

calmly, "and God is well pleased with my mortification. Say nothing of it. And why are you here?"

Louis did not answer. Truly he did not know why he was in the library at all, and to his mother he could tell not even the palest lie.

"I see," said she, ironically, "the king of France owes nothing more to his own honor than the fumbling of these pleasant books — St. Victor, Herrat — and yonder lies a troubadour's song-book from the South. From the South," she repeated meaningly.

"I have scarcely touched them," he confessed, blushing, and the queen without another word sat down in a chair and beckoned for him to take the other facing her.

"Are we quite alone, Louis?" she asked.

"So I believe, unless old Benno enters."

"Then this is better than your cabinet, where are often too many other ears than ours. For what I have come to ask is wherefore the king of France has no eyes and ears himself for the strange deeds of his wife and of some one else?"

"My mother!"

"I know you, Louis," went on the White Queen, slowly, coldly. "I have seen your love toward me grow chill. Toward me — who bore you, fought the battles of a man for you, who live only for you and your fair glory. And to-day you draw away from me, my son. I pity you; you know not what you trust and love."

"My mother!"

"Oh, I have reared you in blindness and girlish piety; I have my reward! It is my sin, and I will bear it. You do not hear the gossip of the court. You do not see even when your wife allows a stranger from her South to set desirous eyes on her before your face. The tale will run from Artois to Navarre and stir all France before you know you have sacrificed your mother for a——" Louis had leaped to his feet; his face was crimson. Then he fell on his knees before Blanche, holding forth his hands.

"Not that, not that! I cannot bear it. I have seen, heard, feared,—but I will not distrust Margaret. She is innocent. Gui of Avignon is a fool. I will send him away. She shall never chill our love. I am yours, my mother, utterly. I will die at your least bidding,—but not distrust my wife."

"Rise up," commanded Blanche, with fine sarcasm, "it ill becomes his Grace of France to kneel. Well, you have, you say, seen and heard. I ask another question. What will you *do?*"

"Do?" and Louis clutched his head.

"Ay, do; for it is castle gossip now, and it will be chattered over by the fish and apple women of Paris to-morrow. I brought these two Provençals face to face at your table this day, that the scales might fall from your eyes at seeing their wantonness. I will not tell now all the dark tales which that discreet maid Alithe de Coucy has reported to my ears. She is a proven friend, and does not lie. Enough. If one tenth part of all she says be true, expect the worst."

"Do what?" groaned Louis again, almost tearing his hair; but Blanche sat immovable, and spoke with quiet sadness.

"I will not blame you, my son. The sins of the parents are visited on the children. In my excess of love for you, I taught you to be virtuous, not how to be strong. For this I must answer to God. To God I must answer for having arranged this marriage with the Provençal. I hoped for the best, but I cannot be pardoned."

"All men make errors, my mother," spoke Louis.

"With princes all errors are great crimes," corrected she, icily. "But you I do not blame. The woman was bad. She has insnared you, and now drags your honor down with hers."

"I say it cannot be!" and again the king clutched at his hair.

"There is enough to be sifted thoroughly," answered the unmoved queen. "The honor of France will clamor for that."

"What do you wish?" cried Louis, stopping his pacing.

"Wish?" returned she. "Have I borne a fool? Are you a helpless clown? Are there no dungeons for the Seigneur of Avignon, no yeomen to guard before the door of his paramour?"

Louis cast himself at her knees again, and she could not make him rise.

"Oh, mother!" cried he, in anguish, "mother, with heart as clear as crystal, and as crystal hard, have pity! Margaret must be innocent. Be not so swift to condemn! I cannot think this evil of my wife. I cannot do this fearful thing you ask."

A strange thing happened then. In the hard blue eyes of Blanche there stood tears. She touched his neck gently, lovingly, and answered in a low voice: —

"You are a good son, Louis, mine own. I feel for you more than word may utter, yet be strong and dare."

"I cannot," and the king shook with a great sob.

"I say the honor of France demands it, and the case is proved. Show that you are worthy of your father's and Philip Augustus's crown."

"The case is nowise proved. I will not hear slander of my wife. Oh, do not press me thus!"

The White Queen smiled with a kind of mingled scorn and pity, and stroked his neck again.

"Then suffer me to act for you, for I see you are yet young, and this Provençal has proved to you a Countess Circe. Say only that you will suffer me to do the deed, order the yeomen, arrest, examine, spare the innocent, requite the guilty. Do you fear *your mother* can be unjust to her son's own wife?"

"What do you demand?" and Louis sprang once more to his feet. The queen pointed to the great beryl signet on his finger.

"Let me have your seal ring; that will be sufficient warrant to De Joinville, and will give me the use of the guards. Go to your chamber, lock yourself in, and know that I will be merciful, but just."

Her tone again was like steel; but it rang too hard even on the anvil of Louis of Poissy. He met Blanche's command with a sweeping gesture.

"Madame — mother," spoke he, rapidly, "know that this ring is a gift to me from mine own true wife the queen of France. The wise tell how the beryl has potence to hold husband and wife in love. I will not belie the power by giving it to you. As for Margaret of Provence, if judged at all, she shall be judged by only one — by her wedded lord, the king."

It was the first time Louis had ever set his will against her own. Perhaps her proud Spanish heart was not wholly ill pleased to find her son had yet a high glance and her own unbending will. But to be crossed thus hotly sent the red into the forehead of even Blanche of Castile.

"And you defy your mother, Louis?" said she, softly.

He turned and looked out of the window, that his eyes might not meet hers. He knew that he was passing

I

through a crisis. One false step now, and he was again in the old bondage, never more utterly her tool.

"And you defy your mother?" repeated Blanche. "You are the king. What then will you do?"

"I will wait till Margaret and I are alone this night. Then I will tell her all the gossip, all the lies, that flit about; will tell her all I have seen, and how I distrust my sight. I will tell her that I know she is still true to me, but bid her tell the truth about Gui of Avignon, whether she once loved him, and then say that he must return with speed to Provence."

"And you will believe all that she swears, as though a blessed saint were speaking?" But Louis did not turn to see how his mother's lip was curled, nor did he answer her next taunt.

"They will of course meet in the garden; a troubadour would sing of them as a 'beauteous pair of lovers.'"

Then he knew that Blanche was rising. He did not trust himself to look at her. She gave him no farewell. The door jarred; the White Queen was gone. He cast himself into the chair, seized the *Civitas Dei*, and scanned page after page, remembering nothing of the Latin, but seeing above every black letter two heads — Gui's, Margaret's, — and very close together. He read on desperately, fighting against thought. He had defied his mother. He knew her love was wounded. And God knew his own heart held nothing glad.

Suddenly the calls of the sentinels, as they changed the watch below the window, told him that the afternoon was well sped. The fête in the gardens! He wished it were in Egypt! But he must be present to stand betwixt his mother and Margaret. He left the *scriptorium* and hastened toward his chambers for another change of dress.

It was while he was crossing a court that there came a rustle of bright silks and ribbons, a delicate step, and before he knew it, Alithe de Coucy was courtesying to him more gracefully than ever. Why did a manner of fire seem to leap out of her eyes and through his own being? Why did he look twice, thrice, at those curves of blooming life, that symmetry of form, motion, color? "She is the most beautiful woman I have ever seen!" said the king in his breast. Then another thrill came over him; he passed on without a word. Was he looking with desire upon a woman not his wife? How then dared he judge Margaret, be her sins as scarlet? Why could he not chase the chamberlain's daughter from his mind? She had been long at court, yet had never before so tempted him.

"Let me once get this Gui of Avignon hence," he vowed, "and I must wed her to some distant seigneur, and never see her more." Meantime he had only one prayer, "Lord, I grow weak. Deliver me from temptation."

But at his chambers the king met old De Coucy himself. Whereupon the chamberlain most humbly craved permission to speak on a highly delicate matter, and having of course got it, hinted — albeit in terms so refined and vague that none could take amiss — "how certain of his Grace's most faithful servants were not a little amazed at the favor showed by the queen consort to one of her fellow-countrymen." De Coucy took a great while in saying very little, and his master thanked him very kindly, praised his circumspectness, and promised to be watchful.

The king's servants noticed that their lord was more than commonly gentle and courteous to them when they dressed him for the fête, though poor Maître Bernave, the high barber, tried three more of his rarest jests with never a smile to reward him. After that the king went to his private chapel and heard service, following the worship even more piously than was his wont. He likewise ordered his almoner to give a double dole to all the beggars who might come near the castle gate that evening. But those who watched carefully saw that he was pale and nervous. De Joinville shrugged his big shoulders as he regarded the king in the chapel.

"A three-pound taper to St. Mark," vowed the veteran, "if the watch cry 'midnight,' and no evil has lit on my good lord or his lady!"

*   *   *   *   *   *   *

Now whilst Louis was at chapel these were the letters which De Coucy's trustiest valets were carrying three different ways.

Thus ran the first: —

"To my Lord Theobald of Champagne: — Challenge Gui of Avignon to match you with a song, when you meet him with the king and the queens at the fête in the gardens. And send to me forthwith your sage *jongleur* Jacques of Auray. I have an arrow that he can best shoot from my crossbow."

And the second was this: —

"To my Lord Peter of Brittany: — Do not fail to remain near the king and the queens at the fête. Do not let Gui of Avignon wander from their company, and be present to see and hear everything when Count Theobald challenges Gui to sing."

But the third went out of the castle in the belt of a dis creet and trusty squire, upon the chamberlain's fastest Arab *destrier*. The rider cantered carelessly across the bridge to Aumône, but once in the open country spurred like mad, never drawing rein till he rattled into Conflans, five good miles to the south of Pontoise. There he gave the letter to the commander of the band of *routiers*, free-lance cavalrymen, who had been addling their heads at the town ale-houses since the morning.

The third letter ran thus : —

" To the right gallant captain, the Sire Henri de Ormoy : greeting : — We know you can be trusted to beard the very devil and the devil's wife to boot, and will not fail.   Ride for Aumône as though the fiends were pillioned up behind you.   The time long awaited comes to-night — praised be St. Germain and Our Lady ever Virgin !   Bring every man or knave who can bend bow or swing axe, for we shall need them all to do the deed before the wind blows anything to La Girard who commands for the king at Beaumont.   His men are ugly wolves ; beware their teeth.   Come then with speed.   I have made great vows to Heaven, and we can but prosper.   The messenger will tell you all the rest.   Your knightly and loving friend,

" ENGUERRAUD DE COUCY."

After the Sire de Ormoy had read this, and passed ten words with the squire, a prodigious clattering, buckling, stamping, and jangling, like to the marshalling of Charlemagne's host, stirred all the quiet town of Conflans.

CHAPTER XI

UNDER THE TREES

THERE is no need to say that Gui of Avignon seldom had to present "unseemliness of dress" amongst the sins he told over to his confessor; but that afternoon he surpassed himself in all his pains. So many oaths, such carefulness, such fretting, such fidgeting, not to mention cuffs on the ear, and even kicks, his hard-pressed squires had never tasted. He must needs try on five fur-lined *pelisons*, before he found just the sable that matched his mood. Seven pairs of fine Flemish hose were cast aside before the eighth fitted his calves so as to display their full shapeliness. The civet he touched upon his beard was selected after long and sober deliberation, and the bliaut — Holy Mother of Sorrows! when had the squires known him to hang so long between the white, the sad color, and the blue one? At last he seemed ready — praised be St. Tropheme! — and yet he lingered, not going down to the gardens.

"And what is my lord awaiting?" asked the oldest of his dressers, only to be told to fetch out all the Provençal's viols, for he "would go arrayed in the time and knightly armor of a 'Pilgrim of Love,' and perchance that most puissant prince his Grace King Cupid would send him a gallant *tenso* with some courteous and worthy antagonist."

So, after infinite more sighs and hems and haltings, the

viol was chosen, hung about its owner's neck by a silver chain, and away he went to the fête.

"Anselm," quoth the first squire, "his Lordship has either the devil or a lady perched upon his eyebrow, or he would not act thus."

"Bernart," quoth the second, "I think he has both a lady and a devil sitting together; but the angels forbid that she be the one my fears tell me. There are things too high even for our master."

Gui, however, never heard this wisdom. Probably he would not have cared if he had. Out of the castle courts was already pouring a gay host — knights, ladies, pages, and here and there the more sombre robe of some prelate. "To the gardens" was the word from lip to lip, and to the gardens they were going.

The little city was holding its festival of the "Mass of the Ass." You could hear the shrill shouts of the peasant champions around the archery butts, and the deep roars as an oaf slid down the greased pole, after a vain attempt to clamber. But the château also had its festival after a milder and more courtly fashion. South of the fortifications, yet themselves guarded by walls from vulgar ken, ran the gardens — laurel thickets, black pines, ivy bowers, locust trees, rose bushes, growing half wild in all the bright luxury of May in France. Over the greensward were spread portable tables covered with snowy linen and scattered with silver plates. Pages offered wine to those who asked it; but not to profusion, for there was no drunkenness or gluttony where Blanche of Castile bore wise sway. And in and out under the whispering trees, while the bird songs answered the crooning river down beneath them, walked the young seigneurs and their ladies. Light of head, light of heart, and light of foot seemed they all that afternoon; and I cannot tell all the vows that were made, or the words spoken lightly, but not so lightly forgotten, or how many bright eyes flashed, or how, when the throb and sob of the music began to echo through the wood, sweet thoughts hummed about like bees.

It was in such company that Gui of Avignon found himself, and what wonder that he discovered the rhymes for a score of most excellent and moving *cansons* leaping into his brain together, and that his fingers fairly itched to strum the strings of his viol! Since he did not see the lady of his choice, he was just puckering his lips for a gallant speech to the blonde little Countess de la Hove, when the Chamberlain de Coucy himself touched his elbow.

"You are notably arrayed, Sir Troubadour."

"As in the lists, I would to-day wear my brightest armor under the eyes of my chosen damosel."

"You will doubtless find the opportunity you desire to proclaim your devotion to her; yet you must have courage."

"I lack courage!" The knight clapped his hand on his hilt in a twinkling.

"A thousand pardons; it was but a clumsy manner of jest. I would merely hint that perhaps the Count of Champagne will challenge you to sing the praise of your lady, and that her Grace the queen consort will assuredly hear you — likewise the king."

Gui held up his little nose like a charger sniffing battle.

"No fear, no fear; I am discreet. I can speak with a word, a look, a sigh, a turning of the little finger, a drooping of the ear. And as most truly says that learned troubadour, Raimbant de Vagueiras — "

"Your pardon," and De Coucy cut him short. "The

king and queen come now. Do not be amazed if the
queen consort seem exceeding cold to you, nay, chide
you to your face. She must dissemble. Her life is hard;
such jealousy! such unfaithfulness!"

"Hail, hail, your Grace!"

De Coucy bowed. Gui knelt and rose again at the royal
greeting with such a pretty bending of his small body that
the Countess would have lost her heart to him, if she had not
lost it already. The king and the queens were dressed for
the fête, but the smiles on their faces were a little too rigid.
Margaret wore the crown and robes with which she had
covered Falaise. She was very beautiful — too beautiful,
the chamberlain thought, and he frowned and looked away.
Blanche was in her wonted white, but her dress was rip-
pling samite, and on her hair were pearls set in silver.
The king wore a red velvet cap trimmed with gold lace,
a long blue cloak lined with gray squirrel skin, and above
this a gray surcoat trimmed with white ermine. There was
mother-of-pearl over his belt; he wore an Eastern dagger
in a gilt sheath. The loose robes gave his boyish figure
a majesty that it sometimes lacked, and there was a grave
courtesy in all his words and deeds that afternoon which
made him seem an older man.

Gui rose at Louis' bidding and followed his royal hosts
as they advanced through the garden. The groups of
courtiers made way for them, but the king took pains to
thrust himself upon nobody. Presently he was joined by
the Count of Champagne, Peter of Brittany, and one or
two other high nobles, whereupon the chamberlain with
scrapes and excuses begged of his master a boon.

Would he deign to listen to the merry songs of a most
incomparable *jongleur*, Jacques of Auray, who had come
to Pontoise in the service of my Lord of Champagne?

The king frowned. He did not enjoy jongleurs and gleemen. Why did not De Coucy remember that? But there was a large company to entertain; promenading under the trees would be tedious; the chamberlain no doubt had done his best to provide amusement. Being a king, Louis dared not be discourteous.

"Lead the way, then," was his decision.

Under two noble oaks, monarchs themselves, were arranged bright couches in an irregular circle; in the centre, a low table. The king was seated; then, in due precedence, such of the rest as cared to quit their chatter to listen. Across the circle, facing the king, Louis noticed one empty seat, and once when a knight made to sit thereon, he saw De Coucy touch the gallant's shoulder and he took another place. One other thing Louis noted, and rejoiced, — that Margaret and Gui had many chairs between them. Then after due bustling, dallying, twanging of psalteries, and small talk, the jongleur, Jacques of Auray, came forward. He was a fat, red-faced man, with a tripping tongue and a shifting blue eye, and Louis did not like him. The right half of his gown and hose was flaming orange, the left of sober gray. He gave the king a nimble bow, clambered upon the table, bowed again to the company, pressed his harp against his breast, rang out a few chords, then looked about with a smile which told that he was ready to sing. He did not begin instantly, however, for there was a faint rustle and motion behind him. Louis looked straight toward the jongleur, and beyond him saw Alithe de Coucy sitting down in the vacant seat. She was in black — black cloak, bliaut, and furs. All these heightened the color of her face and bare neck, as well as the lustre of her eyes. Louis' own eyes dropped. He dared not look on her. And at this moment he caught a rustle nearer at hand. Peter of Brittany, who sat near to Margaret, had arisen. Without bidding, Gui of Avignon had glided into his place. The king still looked down, but winked hard. He was almost grinding his teeth.

"Do they think me so blind, do they think me so much a saint, that the demon can never rise up to master me? O Lord Jesus Christ, keep me strong to abide in silence until I can speak privily with my wife!"

The jongleur hesitated; then at a nod from the chamberlain began his "lay." And all the time he sang, Louis dared not take his gaze from the greensward, for the varlet's chant went through the king's soul like a blade of Granada.

For Jacques of Auray sang the tale of Tristan and Isolde. He sang how Isolde, fairest of women, was the princess of Ireland; how Mark, the king of Cornwall, sent to her, seeking her in marriage, how he won her, but how, thanks to the misreading of a love-draught, the valiant knight Tristan and she drank the fateful potion together, and then all her faithfulness to the unloved king was at an end. Then he chanted how, by the aid of the clever waiting-woman Brenguain, the lovers for years hoodwinked the guileless Mark, who all the time thought his wife worshipped him, whereas he was her ogre and tyrant. So at the end came discovery, vengeance, and a sorrowful death for all three.

Louis had heard the "lay" before; but now it took all his power of will to sit silent before that company. He would have given two baronies to walk away, and set no tongues to wagging. And twice he looked up, and twice he saw — Alithe de Coucy. Blessed Mother of Pity, how beautiful she was! but why must he still behold her whether he shut his eyes or stared at the grass! He was in a kind of daze, and was shaken out of it by the sudden clapping of hands, while the jongleur took off his cap and bawled : —

"*Largesse*, fair lords, *largesse !* "

The others threw copper deniers into the cap; Louis added one of silver. "Wherein was the villain to blame!" mused the king, bitterly. And he trusted that the ordeal was ended, when my Lord Theobald arose.

The count pressed his hands upon his hips and stood up jauntily before the little knight of Provence.

"Gallantly sung, was it not, Sir Gui?" quoth Theobald, a bit too loudly. "You are a master of this fair art of song and poesy, and praise from you will be praise indeed. Say that this worthy jongleur of mine would meet well-won applause, even at the court of Arles."

Something in the count's tone, more than the words themselves, made the Provençal's forehead begin to redden.

"For a *canson de gest*, a 'lay' by an unknighted varlet, I do like it well," he assented, with a patronizing smile toward the simpering jongleur; "but we in the South Country rejoice more in singing ourselves than in listening to others, more in outpouring our own loves and their sweet woes than in hearing of the ill-starred passions of a Tristan and an Isolde."

"Ah!" smiled Theobald, with the blandest accent, "I forget my Lord Gui is a very prince of troubadours, and that all the gay dames at Arles count one *canson* from him as dearer than their wedded husbands' heads."

The count glanced about him, now to one lady, now to another, twirled his little yellow beard, and everybody leaned forward, everybody save Louis, his wife, and his mother. Theobald turned to the nearest countess-in-waiting.

"O very beautiful, chaste, and discreet mistress, succor me, your knight, and you other ladies, — flowers, let me call you, — hearken, join with me, for I will crave of the Lord Gui a boon. Let him teach us of the colder North one of his troubadour songs. Let him sing it even as if under his own bright mistress's eye, and how dare he lack passion when you all gaze upon him! Speak with me, pray with me. He will hear you. See! his viol is about his neck. He will not refuse to sing."

I will say this for Gui of Avignon: he would not have deliberately chosen to sing before that company. But was a Pilgrim of Love to blench, and with those eyes upon him! So when Alithe de Coucy spoke, whilst the other women chimed "Yes! yes!" begging him to begin, the silver chain of the viol was unclasped how quickly! And I cannot tell with what bows and reverences he stood forth to begin his song. Just as he was touching the first strings, Alithe's red lips shot at him a question.

"Sir knight, what are you to sing to us?"

"A *canson* of love."

"Your own or another's?"

"My powers are too weak for so courtly and fair a company. I will sing the spring song of the never-to-be-overpraised troubadour Arnaud de Marveil."

"Not that," darted she, "but the love, — is it your own, or the troubadour's also?"

Gui struck the viol, and all its strings rang loud.

"No, by St. Tropheme, the love is my own, and I sing the praise of my mistress, my queen, the fairest and wisest of women."

"Happy lady," smiled Alithe; "yet you will not confess who is that fortunate dame who sighs for you at Arles, or Nismes, or Avignon?"

"Most beauteous mistress," quoth the troubadour, with a sweeping bow, "the clear flame that burns my heart burns not in the Languedoc, but in France."

His speech was to Alithe; his bow, his glance — no lady had it but Margaret the queen. Louis felt his forehead growing hotter, hotter. He knew that his wife was stirring in her seat, and how red was her brow also! One last thought comforted the king. "If that Provençal is a knave, he is still more a fool. Let me keep silence now, but he shall never sing again."

But Gui, who never ceased to tell himself that Gui of Avignon did all things excellently well, laid the viol to his shoulder, sawed the strings once or twice with his bow, then began the song, first warbling gently, then letting his little cheeks puff, his throat swell, and his eyes burn big, as he looked on Margaret. The queen consort sat stock-still, and all the color had left her cheeks. She knew the song and how it would end.

> "Oh, how sweet the breeze of April,
>   Breathing soft as May draws near;
> While, through nights serene and gentle,
>   Songs of gladness meet the ear;
> Every bird his well-known language
>   Warbling in the morning's pride,
> Revelling on in joy and gladness
>   By his happy partner's side!

> "When around me all is smiling,
>   When to life the young birds spring,
> Thoughts of love I cannot hinder
>   Come, my heart inspiriting.
> Nature, habit, both incline me
>   In such joys to bear my part;
> With such sounds of bliss around me
>   Who could wear a saddened heart?"

And then the little knight smote the viol until it fairly sobbed with his passion; and all the time he stared at Margaret the queen.

> "Fairer than the far-famed Helen,
> Lovelier than the flowerets gay:
> Snow-white teeth, and lips truth telling,
> Heart as open as the day,
> Golden hair, and fresh, bright roses;—
> Heaven, that formed all things so fair,
> *Knows that never yet another*
> *Lived, who could with her compare.*"

The last lines had been sung straight into Margaret's face. A power almost overmastering was driving Louis out of his seat, to leap upon the hardy troubadour and throttle him. True, the king knew that in Provence a married lady might accept the praises of a knight and her husband take no just anger; but Gui had gone beyond all this. The song had been in the Languedoc, but every soul present had understood. The singer was looking about him, half pleased, half defiant, as if expecting thanks from the queen herself. Margaret sat like a white stone image, and seemed never to breathe. It was so still for an instant that you could hear the least whispers of the upper branches. Then Count Theobald clapped his hands.

"Nobly sung; a knightly song by a knightly singer! Notre Dame! but we must learn from the South Country if we would fitly praise fair women."

"A noble song!" So cried Alithe de Coucy; and twenty others joined. Two of the younger ladies cast the little knight ribbons from their hair, which he received with profound bows, kissed, and folded in his bosom, vowing loudly that he would esteem it high privilege to drink the water wherein they washed their "ever-adorable hands." Louis thought he saw Gui glancing again toward Margaret, vainly hoping for a like guerdon from the queen, but her face was stony. Then without warning Peter of Brittany thrust in his word.

"I am an uncourtly man, Sir Gui; but, as I hope in God's mercy, my desire is roused to know who is this wondrous dame you praise. You say she is in France. Happy the lady who wins the knight of Avignon. Some stout baron's daughter, I take oath. Happy father, happy bride —"

"Sir," returned Gui, bristling formidably, "I do warn you there is no baron's daughter in France who has my love. The lady I desire, worship, sing, is raised so high — though not too high for her most just desert — that the Emperor himself might justly stoop to woo her hand."

The Breton's lips drew into a slight sneer.

"Then my brave knight of Provence, unless the flowers of your speech do somewhat overlay the truth, take care lest your mistress be too high for even you. Be wise; remember the fox, the cherries, and how betimes he called them sour."

If Peter was seeking a quarrel, he succeeded as well as he dared wish. The Provençal almost tore the viol from his neck, and began tugging at his sword. Then his speech came thickly.

"Death of Our Lord! I will answer you with *tensons* of hard steel. Is there a dame too high for me — me, Gui, Lord of Avignon, Viscomte of Toulay, advocate of the Abbey of Creseil, heir to the county of —"

"I need no pursuivant to tell of your Excellency's titles," darted back the unmoved Breton, and all the others were pressing up around, when suddenly the king's voice sounded. Louis was standing. He held his head high, he spoke with a ring and command unwonted, and obedience was quick.

"Sirs, I will have no more brawling before my face. The fête has lasted long enough. I will return to the castle with their Graces, my mother and my wife."

Majesty had spoken. It was time for black looks to end, for Gui's sword to slip back into the sheath, for Peter of Brittany to glide out of sight behind a laurel thicket. Some of the party lingered to taste the pasties and fruits piled on the tables; most followed the king and the queens. The troubadour gathered up his dear viol and returned to his tower. To his own mind he had sung excellently, had displayed his passion most delicately, had met the Breton's haughty front in a manner worthy of a Pilgrim of Love. True, once or twice he feared he had glanced a little too openly at the queen. What if the king were not so faithless as De Coucy had hinted? what if he truly loved his wife? But had not Mark of Cornwall been blind for fourteen years, whilst Tristan and Isolde made love beneath his eyes? And if Gui of Avignon had any doubts as to the righteousness or wisdom of his course, they died speedily when the chamberlain came to him with a letter, written on white vellum, delicately perfumed, and in a fine feminine hand.

"To the knight of Avignon, from one in great distress! To-night I shall be alone. Come to me at the hour the good De Coucy will tell you, and all will be safe. I am in great sorrow, as you know, and if you would prove yourself no faithless troubadour, the test is now.

"MARGARET, REGINA."

"Tell her Grace the queen consort," the knight had said to De Coucy, "that in all things I am her slave. I am in your hands. I will come."

K

After the chamberlain was gone, however, Bernart the squire came to Gui with a complaint.

"Lord, one of your fawn-skin gloves, embroidered with gold, also your silken scarf, dyed with the scarlet of Montpellier and with your arms in needle-work, are both missing."

"You have searched for them?"

"Floor, chests, cupboards, and beds."

"Strange," said his master; "then there are thieves in the castle. But praised be St. Tropheme, I have many more!" And thanks to his thousand other cares, the knight did not even storm at Bernart for the loss.

CHAPTER XII

THE SCARF OF GUI

LOUIS OF POISSY said not one word to either his mother or his wife until they were reëntering the great donjon of the castle. Blanche and Margaret were silent as he. Louis looked at his mother, and the hard smile about her mouth made him tremble. He knew that she would drive him to do a harsh deed in the harshest way. As for Margaret, she neither smiled nor frowned, only pressed her lips together and was still. The bearing of both of the women reminded Louis of the calm before the thunderclap. He was weak, faint, pale, and thought that he knew now how the luckless bandit felt whom three weeks before he had with his own tongue doomed to hanging. "I would as lief walk to the gallows than to the things I must see this night." So thought the king.

The royal train was in the wide lower hall of the donjon before Louis came out of his black revery. Blanche was addressing her daughter-in-law with ominous gentleness.

" You will retire to your own chamber, Margaret? "

The queen consort bowed her head silently, was gone, and Blanche turned to the king.

" A few words alone? " asked she.

" You shall have them; " but Louis' tongue moved painfully, and one of the ushers made bold to take his arm.

" Your Grace is pale and unwell. Spiced wine? I will summon the physician? "

Louis straightened himself, and his eyes flashed. "I know when I am ill; unhand me!"

So sharp a word from so mild a prince sent the usher away quaking. The next thing the king knew he was in his mother's rooms. Blanche was standing with her back against the door, and speaking in a tense whisper. Her face was almost black with wrath, and Louis wondered if he himself were going wild.

"You see. You know. Or must an angel come down from heaven to open your blind eyes?"

"I see. O dear Lord Christ, I would that I were blind! What shall I do?"

"Do? Do? Have I borne a babbling idiot, whom fools call 'King of France'? Give me the ring!"

Louis pressed his fingers to his breast, though Blanche stretched out her hand. He knew for what end his mother desired the ring.

"*Ai!*" he groaned, "do not doubt me! I will act. I will strike hard."

"There spoke the son of the eighth Louis, the grandson of Philip Augustus," and the Castilian's eyes burned brighter. "You will not spare. You will expose, punish, clear the fair honor of France, and show yourself a king?"

"Yes, I will clear my honor — so help me God!"

There was a silver box standing against the wall. Two candles burned before it, a gold crucifix hung above. In it the queen mother kept her precious volumes of the Vulgate. Louis went across, laid his hand on the box, and then took his oath: —

"If I find not the truth in this matter, reward the guilty, and cleanse my honor, let the good God burn my soul with fire through the ages of ages. Amen."

"You speak well, my son; be strong." There was fond

pride in the voice of Blanche. The king was of her own
hard stock, and was coming to his own at last. And then
she pitied him, for she knew he was only a youth, and her
love for him was great.

"Trust God, and purge your honor, Louis, my own, my
joy, my all. For now I know that you do truly love me.
Do not spare. Often the deepest wounds give but the
least of pain. The Provençal has yielded herself to that
foul troubadour. Remember that justice is mercy, for she
destroys her soul unhindered now, and what matters the
ruin of her poor body, if her soul be dragged back from
perdition's brink?"

"Do not doubt me!" cried the king again. "I will dare
all, will do all. To-night this thing shall end."

He started toward the door, then stopped, looked around
frighted, halting. He pressed his hands against his face,
and his body shook.

"O my mother, is there no other way? How can I do
this fearful thing against my wife? Can I not dash that
horrid song from out my ears, or forget her guilty silence?
Alithe is wrong, the court gossip is wrong, my senses
wrong. I will wake from it all as from a dream, and take
back Margaret's love."

"Gui has flaunted his passion before all the court,"
Blanche's voice was cold, biting like a frosty wind, "and I
will not name the devil that made her meet his vile mad-
rigals without one blush. But if you doubt, we will summon Alithe. You saw how she drew the troubadour on.
She hears all; she will tell."

"Not Alithe, but my wife shall tell," flashed Louis,
haughtily. "I am strong enough. I will go to Margaret."

"And I with you," cried Blanche, making to follow.
But Louis faced his mother almost sternly.

"Do not fear me, madame mother. But this battle must be won by me alone."

When he came out of the room he was so pale that the pages and yeomen stared, almost looking to see him fall; but his step was firm, his mien proud.

"I would go at once to my wife," said he to the usher in waiting. The worthy man bowed low, and begged permission to say that her Grace the queen consort was closeted with her maids, doubtless changing her dress after the fête. He turned pale himself when Louis threw back his head.

"I am the king, and I will see my wife!"

What had happened? The king of France was bearing himself as loftily as a baron! There would be something to chatter about the next three days. Louis led the way with long strides. He mounted the stairs, two at a step. He entered his wife's chamber without a knock at the door. Margaret was surrounded by her maids. She had just laid off the blue samite surcoat; but her dress of red silk still clung about her; the gold beads shone on her neck, the pearls and diamonds in her hair. I do not know which was the whiter, — Louis, Margaret, — as they stood face to face. And even as he looked, Louis was saying in his heart, "She is as beautiful as Alithe de Coucy." But her beauty was like the beauty of snow and had no power to move him.

"Go!" the king pointed. The frightened maids scattered at the royal frown. Louis thrust a heavy stool against the door to hinder opening. Margaret looked on, dumb, shivering. She had never seen her husband in wrath before, and his silent anger terrified her far more than noisy rage.

"Are we alone, your Grace?" said the king, sweeping the room with his glance.

"'Your Grace!' Must you say this to me? Oh Louis!"
Margaret clasped her hands upon her breast.

The king stood before her, his own hands behind his
back. He spoke slowly, and now and then with the least
hiss, as his teeth came together.

"We will do well to remember who we are. I am the
king of France, and saving his Holiness the Pope, a Vicegerent of Christ on earth. You are my wife and share
my royal state, its honors and its trials. We are born a
man and woman; the decree of heaven has made us something more. That we are not able to sink our manhood
and womanhood in our kingship is a cross laid on us by
heaven. We must bear it."

Part of Margaret's color returned. She unclasped her
hands. Into her voice crept scorn.

"I am not standing here to hark to a quibbling homily
from a Nominalist or Realist of the Paris schools," said
she, and moved toward a divan.

"What I say will be much to the purpose, your Grace,"
said Louis, with terrible gravity, and Margaret watched
him steadfastly.

"Lady," he continued, "it has been our misfortune to
be born to parents who considered quite as much the welfare of their lands as our own happiness. In childhood
we were betrothed, with no meeting, and scarce hearing
one of another. When we met at Sens to be joined in
marriage, older and stronger wills than ours taught us to
repeat words and vows that perchance in after days were
to cost us dear. My mother and your father saw in our
marriage a noble alliance for France and for Provence —
they thought of little else. The deed was theirs, but ours
the burden."

Margaret fell back three steps; and motioned piteously, as if bidding her husband blaze into more merciful heat.

"I do not understand. I do not understand." She repeated it in little tearless sobs.

"I hope you speak the truth," said Louis, bitterly, but with no hastening. "I fear you do not. You must hear me to the end, and then I will hear you. The church declares marriage an inviolate sacrament, but I am a king, the Pope is open to reason; if you unite with me in a petition —"

"Holy Mother! For what?" Margaret's soul seemed burning in her eyes, and Louis' lit up, too.

"To dissolve our marriage!"

He had not known how hard the blow would strike her, or he would have never said that word. She fell upon the couch; her body quivered with agony. The king could not see the working of her face. He wished that she would cry aloud; then he would have known she had less pain. But those smooth lips of Louis of Poissy were pitiless as his mother's now.

"We were better unyoked," he continued. "At present your name and Gui's and mine are too often linked in base report."

But the blood of proud princes was Margaret's, too. She leaped up, and anger began to stifle her grief. Her cheeks flushed crimson.

"A base report — lies, calumny, devil's slander. Who repeats it? Tell me, or I shall think I am wedded to the fiend himself. Show the accuser!"

Louis was glad to see her flint strike fire on his steel. His task was easier now.

"My mother says the castle prates of you."

"Your mother is my foe."

"But a just foe," quoth Louis, calmly. "She does not love you, but she will not lie."

"And who else pours poison into your ears?"

"That loyal soul, De Coucy, told me even before the fête that your conduct with Gui caused more than whispers."

"De Coucy is a snake. I have loathed him. Who else accuses me?"

"My own eyes and ears."

"For the love of Christ, what have you seen me do?"

"Nothing. Would to God I had! Gui of Avignon played the fool with you at table; he all but swore his love for you in the garden, with fifty swallowing all the chatterings of his sinful tongue. And you — you sat there silent, when silence was a sin!"

Margaret fell on her knees, caught the fringe of the king's ermine, clung to it, kissed it. At last came the tears. As she wept, Louis spoke on in the same cold voice.

"Do not think I fail to pity you. I can understand you well. You have loved this knight of Avignon in Provence. It grieved you both to part. He followed you hither, persuading your father to trust him on the embassy. You had tried to be my faithful wife. Gui came. The temptation was strong. You are human, and unto you I will be most merciful."

"Louis, Louis, husband, lord, king, for whom, by whom, I live," — and now in agony she was fain to kiss his feet, — "it is not so! Oh, as I trust to see Our Dear Lord's face in heaven, it is not so! Gui was never more to me in Provence than a passing friend. Perchance I have been unwise since his coming; we were too much together. He is a very foolish troubadour, but worships me no more than he does twoscore other women. You do not know the custom of the South, — a wedded dame may

be praised by the *cansons* of twenty knights, and her husband take no wrath.   How could I know this telling of
vile tongues?   I have enemies, they seek my ruin, — to
pluck from me my dearest crown, not that of France, but
that of my husband's love.   Gui is a fool, I own it.   I was
angry with him, terribly angry.   I had resolved to meet
him once, alone, and bid him begone from France.   For
though I heard no gossip, some angel whispered his stay
brought no good for me or him."

"And your silence when that song ended, — that song
meant all for you."   Louis' voice was still hard, but it was
trembling.   Margaret held up her arms.

"How did I know the calumny?   How did I know you
had been taught to mistrust me?   I had resolved to send
Gui away.   Would it have beseemed the queen of France
to meet a song like his with open reproaches?   But all the
time my heart shook with rage and with the angry chid-
ings I stored up till we two were alone."

"This is an easy thing to say.   May I believe you,
Margaret?"   The words were harsh; but the name Margaret — it was not spoken as before.   Then she saw her
husband's eyes were wet, and still she clung about his feet.

"Louis, Louis, slay if you will, yours the power.   But
do not doubt me.   Have we not pledged troth together?
This morning were we not in one another's arms?   Could
I look in your eyes, as now, if my heart was not as pure
to you as yours to me?   They have lied to your mother.
They have lied to De Coucy, or he is false.   Gui is a fool,
but never a knave.   He must be sent away.   The slanders
will all die.   I would lay down my life for you, but to cease
from your love, that were a living hell!"

Louis knew that all the fell resolve with which he had
entered that chamber was passing out of him.

Margaret had cleared herself in his sight; what cared he for his mother? Their gaze had met. From the queen's eyes her power passed over him. She was rising from her knees; one moment and they would have clasped, and after that — But in that moment Louis' glance went by her to the divan. He seemed fading out of her arms as might a ghost. His face bore horror. He pointed at the divan.

"Look! look! look!"

In silence he lifted a fawn-skin glove and a scarlet scarf; then dropped them like two coals, and once more clutched at his head.

"Margaret," said he, at last, his face gray, "how did these come here?"

"I do not know."

"Whose are they?"

"I do not know. Why do you stare? You are ill?"

"Because I know. I know this glove. I know this scarf dyed in the scarlet of Montpellier, this azure unicorn on sable wrought upon its ends, — the arms of Gui of Avignon. And shall I trust you *now*?"

"Lord, Louis, this cannot be! Not Gui's!"

"Ask any herald at Paris," quoth the king, retreating toward the door; "ask any squire here what are the arms of the house of Avignon, and do you, mistress, as you fear aught in this world or the next, think well before you lie."

"Yes, they are Gui's. Oh, God! I know not how they came here! What shall I say? A devil brought them."

Louis strode across, seized her wrist fiercely. "A devil indeed, arrayed not as an angel of light, but a troubadour. This afternoon you have seen Gui in this chamber privily."

"I have not."

"Confess, and I will think of mercy."

"I have naught to confess."

"Do not mock me."   Louis was at white heat now, and in her anguish Margaret turned at bay, striking with every weapon.

"Then you dare doubt my word?"

"Yes!"

"My oath?"

"Yes, you have lied to cover your foulness and your lover's."

Margaret tore away her wrist and drew back, that she might fling the words in his face.

"Then if you must dash revilings over me, take this. For now I do doubt you — I, who did not doubt an hour before, though not without fair cause.   Why do your eyes ever rest so long on that Alithe de Coucy?   Be I ever so guilty, is your own soul white?"

"The devil seize you!"

It was the first curse of Louis' life.   His lips were darkening.   His dagger was out of its sheath, and he leaped upon her like a beast.   Had she flinched, St. André knows there might have been murder.   But she rent back the gown at her throat as if to take the stroke.

"Slay quick," cried she; "then learn that I am guiltless."

The king stood like a steed reined in mid-charge and the dagger went into the sheath.

"I go," he flung out, whilst his eyes wandered here, there, everywhere, and the blackness never left him.

"Go where?"

He had turned so swiftly that he almost spurned her, as he shouted the answer over his shoulder: —

"To kill your lover!"

He flung the stool aside, clashed the door behind him, never stopping to wonder whether he left Margaret to live or die. Only one thought possessed him, "Gui of Avignon had ruined his happiness, his honor, the soul of his wife." The beast in Louis of Poissy was roused for the first time. He would have the Provençal's blood. Yet all the while, as if at the summons of the Master Devil, the form of Alithe de Coucy was floating before his eyes, snaring, beckoning straight down to the deathless death; but he seemed fain to follow her. Margaret was lost! He felt only that. What matter how many thousand fiends thereafter waited him?

When next he knew aught, he was in the great black armory, had dragged from the racks two keen swords, and was testing their equal length, when a sly step behind startled him. It was the chamberlain himself.

"Can I assist your Grace? Your Grace is selecting foils for fencing?"

The smooth voice of De Coucy seemed to his lord as harsh as a dragon's. Louis almost smote him with the hilt, and the vaulted chambers rang with the king's oath.

"Back, and let no man halt me. For let God do so to me and more also, if in one hour I have not Gui of Avignon's life!"

Louis was gone. The chamberlain stood quaking.

"Lucifer is roused," ran his troubled thoughts, "and our schemes nigh blasted. For if Gui kill him, and Monseigneur Robert take the kingdom, our game is done, and if he kill Gui before Gui sees the queen, our game is done, too. It is clearly time to make new vows to heaven, to stay the shedding of blood."

CHAPTER XIII

THE SONG OF FALAISE

In all the webs which those industrious spiders, Enguerraud and Alithe de Coucy, had been weaving for more
months than a few, one thread at the centre of the whole
wide net they had never changed or retraced — that Louis
the king could be treated as a block of wood, inert, harmless, usable. When therefore the block of wood became
a raging lion, I will not tell how many fears and wonders
raced through the good chamberlain's head. If De Coucy
had not been rightly reputed a most sage man, he
would have sat down in the armory to groan and ponder.
As it was, before you could have counted twenty after
the king left him, he was running down into the court,
and glancing slyly to either side. Gui was in fearful
danger, Gui or the king. And the life of the king was
precious to this loyal seigneur, as was Gui's, for that
night.

It was now on the edge of evening. The long shadows
from turret and battlement were veiling the courtyards;
but the blazoned banners overhead yet whipped against
a sky of deepening blue and gold. Young knights and
ladies were still promenading hither, thither. Great
puncheons of beer and sack stood near the gates for the
pleasures of the men-at-arms, and grooms were drinking the king's health in deep horn bumpers. Even with

a forty stone weight upon his mind, Enguerraud de Coucy did not forget to greet this and that friend graciously, but all the time kept a catlike watch out of the corners of his eyes. Soon he saw his quest and pounced upon it.

"My most reverend prelate of Beauvais!"

The bishop, who was walking with a viscountess on his arm, stopped and smiled blandly. The bishop had not been in the circle that heard Gui sing; for truth to tell, he was not in favor with Blanche of Castile, who had small love for frocked worshippers of St. Hubert. He mingled little with the grave churchmen who commanded her confidence, and the viscountess — I must add — moved on the very fringe of the court, and strange tales buzzed forth about her. The bishop's smile ended on a second look at De Coucy's face.

"St. Mary and all angels — what has happened? betrayed?"

The chamberlain plucked the prelate unceremoniously away from his companion, and led forward feverishly.

"Not betrayed; oh, no! But undone! Haste, or all is over. The king is roused!"

"Roused? Impossible! Then the dumb speak and the dead are raised! What do you mean?"

"He is in a black rage. He has rushed from the armory swearing he will kill Gui."

"You yourself are raving. Whither are you dragging me? What will you do?"

"Separate the twain if we can. You know where Gui is lodged? In this tower."

"*Ai, ai*, hold!" puffed the bishop; "not so fast. I perish; the blood surges up. The seven humors of my system are aroused. What have I, a man of prayer and quiet, to do with the brawls of kings?"

"Wait, and follow as Beelzebub lets you!" flung the chamberlain. "I'll do what I may."

At the entrance to the tower, the two squires of the Provençal almost ran out to meet him.

"Haste, fair sir; up, up, quick, or there'll be murder done!" And they raced before him up the winding stairs, to stop suddenly at a heavy door, firmly barred, as a few thrusts told them.

"Who is within?" demanded the chamberlain.

"By our Lady of Arles I dare not lie," whimpered Anselm; "it is the king."

"And what does he here?"

"Ask yourself, lord. His face is like a thunder cloud. He foams up to us like an unbitted stallion, cries out, 'Is your master above?' 'Yes, sire,' I answer, all quaking. 'Then aside, as you love your heads!' shouts he, and up he goes, with two long swords in his hands. Next, the door clashed, and was bolted. You can hear them now inside."

The door was thick; when De Coucy clapped his ear to the crack he could only discover the jangle of two voices, both high, angry; he distinguished the tones of the king and of the Provençal, but could catch no word. Vainly the three dashed their weight against the wood. It would take a heavy timber to shiver that oak and those bars. And now the panting bishop joined them; whereupon the chamberlain upraised his voice.

"Your Grace! noble Gui! unbar and do no violence! Unbar for the love of Our Lady!"

Another storm of threats within was the sole answer.

"Unbar! Oh, shed no blood!"

As an echo came two fierce howls and the clash of steel. Then the chamberlain's knees beat together, and he turned pale.

"Either Gui kills the king, or the king kills Gui. They are fighting desperately. Is your master a good swordsman, sirrah?"

"The best in the Languedoc, though small of body," quoth Bernart; "it will not be his Grace who comes out of this room alive, if our master's blood be roused."

"Then there is no hope save in God. Monseigneur Robert has the kingdom! And we are undone!"

So cried De Coucy; and he and the bishop fell together on their knees, on the dusty boards before the door.

"Let us pray," spoke the prelate; whereupon the chamberlain began to beat his breast, saying: —

"*Sancte Germane Conciensis, ora pro nobis!*"

* * * * * * *

I do not know what unseen devil led Louis straight through the mazes of the castle courts to the tower of Gui, or how that same sprite spread over him the famous 'cloak of darkness' and hid his going from the two hundred pairs of eyes that swarmed those courts, so that none stopped him with untimely salutation; but to the tower of Gui he went, with long strides mounted, and thrust himself into the presence of the Provençal.

The knight of Avignon was just smiling over the little vellum bearing the name of Margaret, and bethinking himself of the thousand and seven comforting, courtly, and discreet things he would say to that 'divinest lady' when he met her in secret. Cowardice was the very least of his sins; yet I think a little of the blood quitted his cheek when, without knock or word, lo! before him stood Louis the king! And such a king! For this was no mild and merry-mouthed boy who stared him in the face. He saw a strong, proud man, eyes like coals, and a brow like

L

night. The king had torn off his fur-trimmed bliaut and
his cap. His long, yellow hair blew in disorder. He
grasped two swords, one in either hand, and they shook
as he held them, for he himself was trembling with his
passion. As for Gui, he staggered to his feet, and tried to
remember his bow. Then the two men glared at each
other, silent, the Provençal with wonder, the king for lack
of breath.

"Sire, sire, the unexpected delight, the joy it gives
to welcome you to this humble lodging of a Pilgrim of
Love —" So began Gui, but Louis charged in madly.

"To the devil with hypocrisies! I am merciful, for I do
not bid the yeomen hang you like a dog. But you shall
only answer to me as man to man."

"Sire, sire," gasped the Provençal, at his wits' end.

"My wife, the purest soul in France — an angel sent
from heaven to lift me thither — you have ruined her."

"That very noble lady, the queen consort, is, I trust, still
well —" faltered Gui, grasping at the first commonplace
that entered his head.

"Too well, the black fiends take her! Would she
were dead before your foul face had ever showed itself at
my court. Now, though she live a thousand years, she
is eternally undone. It is such as you, vipers arrayed as
braying asses, that pluck white saints down from heaven,
and slay both the body and the soul. But you shall not
escape. You shall answer at the throne of God."

"Sire," cried the Provençal, "you do impugn my
knightly honor."

"Honor," laughed the king, horribly, "and can you
speak that word? Prepare!" He held out one of the
swords by the tip. "Take one of these swords."

"What is your wish, sire?"

"To kill you," cried the king; "for the wrong unto Margaret, queen of France."

Gui put his hands behind his back. He was a brave man, and though swift to anger in small things, in real danger took fire somewhat slowly.

"I do not understand you, sire. You do not intend to murder me unarmed, and you know I cannot fight with the heir of Hugh Capet."

The king flung the swords across a chair. Parchment and ink lay on a table, where the troubadour had been copying a music-score. Louis wrote very rapidly:—

"The Knight Gui of Avignon has fought me in fair battle, upon my own challenge, and if I am slain, is to go safe and scathless out of France, with all his company.

"LUDOVICUS REX."

"Let this content you," cried the king, casting his enemy the parchment, but Gui stood fast.

"I cannot fight your Grace. I have not wronged your wife. You have no just quarrel."

"Sir," answered Louis, "I do not ask you to confess the truth, being already dead to honor. Your villany is known, and must be paid. Yet, if you would make your peace with God—"

"Your Grace," flung back the Provençal, "my foes need make their peace with God, not I. This is not my first duel. The Count of Pamiers, Sir Rudel of Bordeaux, the Marquis Berthold—"

"You have killed them. I know it. I know, too, that you have robbed me of my wife. Now, will you fight?" Whereat Louis stepped up lightly, and smote the other's cheek.

"Now by Christ's wounds!" raged the knight, "be you

king, be you villain, no man shall do that to Gui of Avignon and live."

"An you will!" rang the answer; "these swords are of equal length and weight. Take which you will."

"I will take this," flared the troubadour, flinging prudence to every wind, "and now hear, vile prince, the truth. You, not your slandered wife nor I, are the one untrue. Your infidelities and amours are known to me. I fight as the knightly Pilgrim of Love, to defend the fair name of Margaret of France against her faithless husband!"

"Liar!"

I do not know which man was the more angry. De Coucy's pleadings at the door they never heard. To strip to their shirts, to fling chairs and stools one side, this was a moment's work. One instant they measured distance, felt the hot veins swelling in their temples, watched the whites of each other's eyes. Then the swords met.

The fury of a hasty man is terrible. The fury of a mild man, roused, is terrific. And Louis de Poissy was roused. He had never struck a blow in anger before. He had watched afar a few skirmishes, when Blanche had led the royal troops against the English at Nantes. At the siege of a Breton castle he had heard a dozen arrows whiz. But Simon de Joinville had taught him to fence well: he had a firm wrist, a quick eye, and a devil within him, — that was enough. He thirsted for Gui of Avignon's blood, and Gui, to speak truth, for his. Neither had stopped to pray, to breathe one "Our Father" or "Ave," though the next instant were, perchance, their last, and death was dancing very close to those two sinful hearts of theirs.

Having rushed together like wild bulls, discovered that

neither could pound down the enemy's guard, their blood
cooled enough to send them back to a slow and steady
fence and foil, each watching the other's eye, and never
caring how close the hostile point flashed to his own
throat, if his own point flashed close at the foe's throat
also. Breath was too precious for curses; they did not
waste it. Once, twice, Louis felt pricks on arm and neck;
then he forgot them. Yet after a while he saw by a kind
of half-vision that his shirt was strangely red. As for
Gui, the little knight's sword leaped like a shuttle; he had
expected to master the king in a trice. Now pride made
him press faster and faster. In one rush he nearly drove
the king against the wall; but Louis charged back, and
the Provençal needed all his art to ward off a like disaster.
And as Louis fought, the angels who watched and loved
him must have grieved to see all the coarse beast passion
hardening his face, its fine lines fading, and leaving there
only dark purpose to strike, strike, strike, until he had his
evil will.

Now Gui lunged again. A body stroke this time, but
the king avoided it. The blow shot past, tearing the
shirt, fraying the skin, saved by a finger. And Louis felt
his heart turning to a ball of fire and rising in his throat,
while his soul cried, not his lips: —

"I will avenge my honor, I will, I can, I will speed to
hell this evil knight!"

It must have been the Master Devil surely that taught
the king to hold his own against the best sword of the
South. Gui used his arts; Louis his fury. And fury
proved the better champion; for fury never thinks of
fending, but only strikes. After a time there was a red spot
on the Provençal's sleeve also; then another, — scratches,
but they told how the fight swayed.

Then Louis gathered up his wrath as does the bristling boar at bay. Gui had his back against the wall before either knew it. Twice, thrice, four times, the king's stroke beat on him as the smith's sledge on the iron. He parried. But at the fifth, his guard swept down. Louis' blade dashed on his head just above the ear, and the Provençal dropped upon the rushes.

Not dead; not wounded even; for in sweeping down Gui's guard Louis' edge had turned. The blow was only with the flat; yet for that moment the knight lay on his face and never groaned nor stirred.

The king had leaped back four paces, at his triumph. He looked about him craftily, wickedly, as does a boy at guilty pleasure. How still the room was! How hot he was! How his heart was leaping, leaping! He did not realize all that he had done. He looked at his sword, and felt sorry there was no blood on it. Yes, he had avenged his honor. He had slain the ruiner of his happiness, of his wife. The devils must be bearing off Gui of Avignon's soul to his Satanic Grace, King Lucifer, and Louis was glad. He even smiled, which was the most evil deed of all his life. He watched the prostrate body with the joy of the demoniacal cat above the helpless mouse. His handiwork! Fit handiwork for a king of France!

Then, whilst he gazed, fascinated, lo! there was a little loosening of the hands, a sigh, a moan. Not dead? Gui's soul was not yet in the claws of my Lords Apollin, Mahom, Cahun, Berzebuth, and the rest! "Up, Louis of Poissy, there remains work still to clear your honor!"

Whereat the king's veins became molten fire. He had dropped his sword. He knelt beside the knight. He turned the body that the face might look straight upward. To revive, restore? From his belt he dragged the little dagger, and held its sharp point at the Provençal's breast.

"Hear now, Gui of Avignon!" Louis' voice rang like hard brass, and he was frightened at hearing himself. "Your sin is proved. God has judged our quarrel. You have lost. Confess now, before I kill you, and so gain mercy for your soul. Confess that it was you who sought Margaret my wife, not she that first sought you!"

No answer. A little rattling in Gui's throat. He did not yet know anything. His eyes were blank and filmy.

"Speak, speak, for now you die!"

Louis raised the dagger, and lowered it again to repeat the summons. "Confess!" But still there were only groans and rattlings. And whether he would have summoned a fourth time I do not know.

What was the sound floating in at the grated window? Was it an angel or only a bird? Why did a cool hand seem laid on Louis of Poissy's brow, calming as his mother's touch had been that night he burned up with fever? Why did his heart cease springing in his throat? Why did his blood run slower? It was coming into the window, in clear melody at last. Then all the bells of the Golden City seemed ringing in Louis' ears. He was forgetting Gui, his wrath, the dagger.

"Falaise!" the king whispered in his heart, and listened while below on her way the singer passed unseen.

"West wind, west wind, wing to the heavens with me.
  Fly to the far, far plains in the sky, where God's fair gardens be:
  Fly to the flowers that are more sweet than any blossoming tree
  Then take me up in thine arms, dear wind, and bear me thither with
      thee!

"West wind, west wind, fly where the sun may be:
  The sun which is like ten echoing harps, played by wise minstrelsy,

Which when they play make every care to fall and fade and flee.
Then take me up in thine arms, dear wind, and bear me thither with
    thee !

" West wind, west wind, fly where the angels be :
The angels whose hearts are as pure as the snow, when it falls on the
    open lea,
When I learn their laugh, and their song and dance, ah! well will it
    be with me !
Then take me up in thine arms, dear wind, and bear me thither with
    thee !

" West wind, west wind, fly where dear God may be ;
To view his face I have no fear, for the love he bears towards me.
*And when first I look, in that blessed hour, I know that I then shall
    see!*
*Haste! take me up in thine arms, dear wind, and bear me thither with
    thee ! . . ."*

Falaise was gone. Her song was gone. The king
was rising to his feet. He was shivering, cold, weak.
His teeth chattered. He flung the dagger against the wall.
Gui was still stirring, groaning, coming slowly to life.
Louis leaned against a table and closed his eyes, for the
room seemed wheeling around him.

"Only by the mercy of God and the voice of His angel
have I been plucked back from that sin against the Holy
Ghost which may not be forgiven." And again a voice
spoke to him. "I have reviled my brother and desired
murder. I am one of those whereof it is written, '*He shall
be in danger of hell fire!*'" Then in terror he looked
again at Gui. The knight was reviving, was beginning to
curse between his teeth. He was not hurt. Soon he
would stir and speak; but Louis would sooner have stayed
and talked with the Father of Lies than with that troubadour. He unbolted the door, and saw the frightened
four kneeling on the landing. They leaped up as one

whilst he opened, and the bishop pointed at him in horror.

"Your Grace — wounded! Blood is on your arm and shirt."

"Scratches," darted the king. "I am unhurt. Go in to Gui. He also is safe, but needs more aid."

"*Ai!* woe! what's befallen?" screamed the chamberlain. But Louis never gave him a moment for howling.

"Give me your bliaut to cast over my shirt. I will go to my mother alone, and do you care for the knight. But not a word of this, or even the head of a De Coucy feels the block."

The king snatched the cloak from the chamberlain's shoulders, hurried down the tower, and across the courts. De Coucy stood for an instant like a man half mad, staring, gesturing; then he rushed in with the others to Gui. The squires were already lifting their master to a couch. Two bloody scratches and a ringing head — that was all. The chamberlain made sure of this blessed truth, and almost fell into the bishop's arms.

"Safe! Both are safe! Our prayers are answered. Our schemes shall prosper. *Laus et gloria tibi, O Domine!*"

CHAPTER XIV

ALITHE IS OVERKIND

Louis went straight to his refuge, the room of his mother. Already the shadows of the spring day were grown so deep, the maids had lighted the gilt lamps which swung on silver chains from the great beams of the ceiling. Blanche was at her *prie-dieu*, and her white veil floated over her bended shoulders like a mist of snow. Louis feared to touch her. Who was he — man of passion, blood, and sin — to look upon this saintly author of his being? But Blanche had known the step; the prayer ended quickly. Up she rose; and as the king cast back the borrowed cloak, she exclaimed: —

"Louis! What have you done? Blood!"

"I have fought Gui of Avignon, my mother;" and still his eyes wandered, and his words came half as a sob, half as a laugh more terrible than sob.

"Holy Virgin of Pity, you have fought him? He has wounded you: your shirt is red! And does he live?"

"He lives: — praised be all saints!"

But here the mother rose up strongest in the White Queen's heart. I cannot tell the tenderness with which Blanche tore the stained linen asunder and took from her chests the lint and unguents to dress the cuts. All the time her skilled hands worked, she never asked a question, spoke a word. The wounds were trifles. She had chanced to be alone, and did not call the wise doctor with his lore of Salerno, Padua, and Montpellier. Louis suffered her to work, rejoicing in her silence. The scratches smarted a little. He did not mind that. It took his thoughts from that dread instant when he went down into hell above the body of Gui, and learned how it feels to become a devil. Out of the tall Majolica ewer Blanche poured water scented with rose and lavender into a silver bowl, and bathed his face, brow, hands, he submitting gratefully as a little child. When this was finished, she led him by the hand, and made him sit by her upon the cushioned couch, resting her own arm about his neck, and her head close to his. Only then she spoke, very slowly.

"So you have fought Gui of Avignon? That was rash. He was a trained swordsman. And how did the fight end? Did he fear to harm the king of France?"

"He fought for his life or mine. We were both in black anger. I dashed down his guard and smote him. Had not my edge turned, he were now dead."

"Your deed was headstrong," returned Blanche, quietly; "the king of France can cross swords only with a king. The yeomen should have dragged the troubadour to a dungeon. Where is he now?"

"In his own tower, coming, please God, to life. I left him in De Coucy's hands, and straightway ran to you."

The White Queen at this last word smiled calmly. Perhaps the press of her arm tightened a little.

"You have avenged your honor," said she; "you have proved yourself a knight as well as king. Now let justice be done. Simon de Joinville shall go with his guard. But what —" and here the low voice hardened, "what have you done — to *her?*"

"To my wife?" and Louis' tone grew three shades more bitter.

"To Margaret of Provence, the dishonor of your crown."

"I left her with my curse. Christ pity me!"

"It is she that deserves the pity — she, the guilty!" and Blanche's hand was no longer on his neck.

"Do not revile her now. I cannot bear it. Have I not suffered enough this direful day? When they break traitors on the wheel, do the wretches feel greater pain than is mine?"

"Are you a boy again, and weeping? Has all your strength burned out in one mad fury at the knight? What will you do to her?"

"I do not know."

They were no longer side by side. Blanche had risen up before him. She stood in her white majesty, out-stretching hands that rained at once command and scorn upon her son. He trembled, but not with anger now; he was about to match his will against his mother's. Her questions hailed on him fast.

"And do you still lack proof?" — this with fearful irony.

"Dear God, no; I see all that you see. And more besides — enough to damn an angel."

"What more?"

At which Louis truthfully told of the finding of the glove and scarf of Gui, for the presence whereof Margaret could give no account whatever. He did not like the all but glee which burned in the White Queen's eyes when he had finished.

"God reveals all sin. 'There is nothing hid that shall not be made manifest,' says Our Lord."

"My mother," Louis was speaking calmly now, and cutting every word off short, "do you believe in devils?"

"In devils, yes; and human devils, too, whereof the name of one is Margaret, one is Gui."

"My mother, I believe in devils also. I believe a devil has come to ruin my wife, Gui of Avignon, and my own heart's joy. An hour ago that devil held me also, and drove me to all but murder. Let my eyes say 'Margaret is guilty,' my ears, your lips, the lips of all wide France. Yet I answer, 'There is no proof, not till her own tongue confess it.'"

"Proof," shrieked Blanche, scanning the king's face line by line, to see if he were an idiot; "you prate of proof, when your own mouth tells the foulest proof of all."

Louis stood up; he was tranquil. He did not clutch at his hair. Blanche was wilder than he. She saw behind his eyes a steady gleam never there before.

"Madame mother, God sets a wiser thing within our bodies than even our heads, — our hearts. I know my wife. I know that till these last few weeks, when you have pelted flying scandal in my ears, no doubt of her had ever crossed my soul. And even now my soul cries out against belief. She has denied, Gui has denied. Gui has flung the charge of faithless wantonness back into my teeth. How dare I cry 'The charge is false concerning me, but true concerning you?' Let me judge not swiftly, lest I too be swiftly judged."

"Be a king!" cried the mother; "arrest, expose, avenge — or take the tonsure. Hide inside a convent, and let Robert take the kingdom. *He* at least would dare to purge his name."

Step by step, Louis drew toward the door; twice his lips moved without answer. Blanche beckoned. Her power seemed sweeping on him like a flood; but he was growing strong. When close to the door, he spoke to her.

"Madame mother, you say well, the proof against my wife is great; but my love is likewise great. For that cause I will take heed to do naught rashly. I will take three days. There is a shrine of St. Romain in the depths of the forest of Montmorenci. I will go thither, pray, meditate, and again pray. Then God perchance will shed over me His wisdom. It shall be said that I have ridden a-hunting, or on a private pilgrimage with a few companions; any tale will do. My wife and Gui are not to be molested. If innocent, who would harm them? If guilty, let them think of repentance."

He put his hand on the latch, lifted it, looked his mother fairly in the face, and saw that she was bursting into tears.

"Be strong, be a king, Louis; be a king."

"Mother mine," said he, with perfect sweetness, "I am strong. I will prove myself a king by daring to take my will in place of yours."

She opened her arms wide. Ten wild horses seemed dragging the king back into them, yet he knew that he must not yield, if he loved his soul's liberty.

"Come back," she called; "we must not part thus!"

But Louis only answered her, "Farewell."

The latch clicked behind him. He had turned his back on his mother. He knew that he had turned his back on all his old life. Henceforth must he reign a king of men, or serve a slave of devils.

*   *   *   *   *   *   *

The king went at once to his own rooms; if his valets dropped their jaws a little at the strange bliaut and the blood-stained dressings, there was something on their lord's forehead that made them slow with questions. Louis asked for strong wine. They brought him a great goblet of red Saintonge, and marvelled to see him turn down its

fire at one draught. Then he sent two pages, one for
Simon de Joinville, master of the guard, one for the chamberlain De Coucy. Those two great men came quickly,
and communed with their master behind a barred door, to
the infinite discomfort of some score of curious dressers,
grooms, ushers, and valets, whose meat and drink was the
least whisper of their royal lord. When the door unbolted,
De Coucy was carrying in his hands a parchment stamped
with the signet-royal, and the ubiquitous Maître Bernave
was rewarded by catching these words from the king, as
he passed with the chamberlain at his elbow.

"You will of course have control of the watch of the
castle in De Joinville's absence. That scroll is your full
warrant."

Whereupon De Coucy gave his most courtly bow, and
kissed his Grace's hands. After that he and De Joinville
vanished below stairs, whilst in the dimly lighted corridor
the king paced up and down, tapping with his thumbs
upon the brass plates of his belt, clearly killing time and
waiting. Next, as he waited, behold! there was a soft
rustle of smooth silks and ribbons, then every courtier fell
back dutifully to give place for a lady to pass. And for
the last time on that day of wonder and of wrath the king
was greeting Alithe of the Bright Face.

She was still in her black. What with the wavering
cressets that half lit the dim corridor, her face and hands
seemed self-illumined with rosy light. Her eyes flashed
like twin stars. The fall and rustle of her dress was like the
gentle music of rain. From her face the king could look
away, but the sound of those silks, those footfalls — why
had God made lids for eyes yet not for ears?

Now she was close. Now she was courtesying; he
knew it though he did not see. And for the first time

there sprang across his soul a flash of anger against her Why must she ever be crossing his path to-day? Was she always ambushed to meet him? Had Satan come down and taken on angel's raiment — her form? Was he to escape from the chaste love of his mother, of Margaret, to fall into the meshes of this? But at last he looked on her. She was standing by him in her rich, high beauty, her head a little bowed, as beseemed the presence of a king, but even humility can well be proud. As the light flickered over her he could see her crimson lips, and her cheeks bright as a monk's vermilion. Then whilst he wondered what safe and courteous thing he might say, her sensitive nostrils swelled, her lips opened, letting the pearls flash out beneath them.

"Lord," came the whisper, which none of the rest might hear, "my father has told me all, — your wife — "

"Yes." That was all that the king dared say.

"Lord," a throb was in that voice, but to Louis' mind the tone did not ring true, "Lord, — I am bold, but I will speak. I pity you. I weep for you."

It was as if a wizard's wand had snapped a spell. Louis lifted his head.

"The king of France is above all pity."

Whereat, to the infinite amazement of all who saw, the king gathered his cloak about him, and went swiftly down the stairs, summoning none, speaking to none. Soon he was in the castle court. Above him was the span of the night. He stood alone against a stone horse-post, and whispered twice, thrice.

"She has no power over me! *gratias Deo!*"

For hate he could have borne, and wrath he could have borne, but pity — from Alithe! He was a king. He could not bear that! And now up before his eyes a woman's form was rising, but not the young De Coucy's. He saw Margaret. Margaret's last image, when she stood with bared neck, unshrinking breast, to take his stroke, as he in his fiend's mood threatened her, "Slay quick, then learn that I am guiltless!" Could the guilty do that? Could Alithe do that? Would not a sinful woman have shrieked for life, for the priest, for absolution, for any little bribe to God to make His punishments less fierce than man's? But Margaret had been strong. She had pleaded not to keep life, but her own husband's love. And he had met her courage with a curse; had all but slain her as she stood; he had felt the influence of Alithe come over him. But that power now was broken forever. Only a word, softly spoken, but Alithe of the Bright Face had done herself more harm than all the years could wipe away. "I love you:" her power might have dragged his soul to hell with hers. "I pity you:" his soul soared away from her to Margaret. As if an angel had trumpeted it from heaven, Louis of Poissy knew that the De Coucy was evil, and that he must shrink from her forever.

"Lord," some one was saying at his side, "all is ready, the hoods, the dresses. Will you come?"

"Yes," answered the king, shaking off his vision. And he let Simon de Joinville lead him from the castle.

At the gates the yeomen crossed their pikes, saluting the commandant, but not knowing, thanks to the dark, the young man who followed. Once without the fortress Simon led to the shadow of a bastion, where stood a trusted squire with a torch. The king exchanged his silks and morocco slippers for a hood, cloak, and shoes of sombre brown baize. De Joinville laid off his armor, and dressed likewise. No one spoke. The squire gathered their garments, blew out the torch, and vanished into the dark.

M

"What do you wish?" quoth the guardsman, whose business commonly was to obey orders, not to advise.

"I would see a priest — an honest priest whom God loves, and who will not know who I am."

De Joinville scratched his head with his great fingers.

"They say the curé of St. Maclou is a very pious man."

"Good, let us go to his manse."

"It will take us through the village."

"All the better; we will hasten."

But De Joinville for the first time in his life did not do as bidden; he stopped to question his lord.

"*Damoiseau*, little master," quoth he ruggedly yet boldly, "you are the king; but you know that Simon de Joinville loves you as Jongleur Daurel did his prince, when he stood by silent and saw his own babe butchered by those who thought they were slaying the royal heir. Therefore answer me. Why do you have it said in the castle 'The king has gone to St. Romain's shrine,' and yet we steal out here alone, and in this dress? What will you do?"

Louis took the great hard hand of the soldier and pressed it with all his might.

"Dearest Simon, it is written, 'When thy father and thy mother forsake thee, then the Lord will take thee up.' God has called my father long since unto His heaven. My mother — she has forsaken now," the grasp on the hand tightened yet, "and I have only myself, unless I may find God. And God dwells not in this tall château, I am too sure of that. Therefore I will seek Him somewhere else, and see if He will remember me with mercy." Simon was wiser than Alithe. He did not say a word; only girded his cloak about his big frame and led down the winding way from the castle. Yet I think Louis would

not have been angry, had he known all the things that
went through the good soldier's heart.

Soon the ramparts were behind them. The night was
kind and balmy, one of those clear warm nights that are
the joy of the bursting spring. The thin evening haze
bore a fresh earthy smell, which made the foot trip light.
All the trees, as the twain passed under them, were rocking,
every young leaf gossiping to every other. In and out of
the thickets darted the sparks of the fireflies. The cry of
the crickets, the trembling of the last thrush before he
drowsed, — all these came like a soothing balm to Louis
the king.

Next they were in the little town, between the tall black
houses. At first the streets were still, but presently they
met merrymakers, here, there ; young men ragged and
merry ; and girls who trailed no samite and cendal, but
whom a countess might have envied for the laugh and
the light of their eyes. These all were hovering about
great bonfires that crackled to heaven, spreading a wide
ring of ruddy light, and painting all outside with blackness, so that those who entered the bright circle seemed
sudden apparitions springing forward from the night.
Torches ran hither and thither, as Georges chased Joéta,
and Philippa fluttered away from Pierre. Much scream-
ing; much laughter; much singing. It was the aftermath
of the little festival.

> " *Stay far away, black Care, to-day!*
> '*Tis the Mass of the Ass, hi! hé!* "

A swarm of unkempt urchins dinned their chorus into
Louis' ears, hovering about him like kites around the eagle,
and one gave his cloak a naughty twitch. But he was not
angry. And presently a pretty girl caught sight of him

as he crossed a ring of light.   She tore the crown of apple blossoms from her head, calling, "Catch this, you handsome man!" and flung it at the king.   Then De Joinville showed his mighty shoulders and clattered his dreadful sword, at which there was a shrill cry, "Court people," a scampering of feet, and giggles and merry gibes out of the safe covert of the dark.   Louis stopped for nothing; though once when he saw the maids and young men dancing hand in hand about a crackling fire to the bray of a broken viol, a great wish came into his heart.   "Oh! to join hands with Margaret, and to dance around that fire, too."   But at the name of Margaret, all lesser wishes died.   He was back in a revery deeper, blacker than the night.   The next thing he knew, they were before a little thatched house in a narrow side street.

"This is the manse of St. Maclou, your Grace," announced the soldier.

"The manse?   The curé dwells in this?" quoth Louis, wondering.

"The house of a parish priest is not a bishop's palace," said De Joinville, laughing; "there is no light.   Let us see if there is a cat or mouse that we can rouse."

Twice the guardsman thumped upon the door, and gained no reply.   A tap with his scabbard made a lattice by the door open a scant two fingers, and a cracked female voice demanded, "Your business?"

"Is the curé of St. Maclou within?"

"He is not."

"When will he return?"

"God knows; do not rouse honest Christians from their straw by your pounding.   Go back to the streets and bonfires with your roistering."

"We are no roisterers, beldame," said De Joinville, none

too mildly, "but from the château; we will await the curé.
Let us in!"

"From the château," — Louis could hear the worthy
woman sniff as she spoke it; — "escaped from the stocks
more likely! But you'll not enter here, were you the
Count of Brittany himself. So be quiet, or I'll cry out
'watch.'"

The lattice closed with a slam. A double bolt rattled
behind the door, but De Joinville put his knee against it.

"A push, and we're inside. Then Lucifer catch the
termagant!"

But the king dragged him back, and ordered him, "Keep
silent; let us tarry on the porch." Whereupon the guardsman grumbled behind his mustachios and obeyed: whilst
his companion — the King of France, Count of Paris,
Over-Lord of Gascony and the Languedoc, and heir of
Philip Augustus, Hugh Capet, and Charlemagne, gathered
his cloak about him, sat himself upon the cold, stone doorstep beneath the stars, and waited the coming of the curé.

CHAPTER XV

A DAY of mirth it had been in Pontoise, but not for Ambroise the curé. People must keep on falling sick, sinful, and heavy hearted even on the day of the Mass of the Ass. Ambroise had done his part in the church that morning. In the afternoon he had been across the river with the Host to poor old dame Garsendis, who had lain on her bed these six years, and now the kind God had appointed that she should cease to be a burden to herself and her grandchildren. But after he had supped, Ambroise had gone forth again to the house of Jean the Miller, for he carried Nicole on his heart. And the curé saw, with a dread he dared not tell to the father and mother, how the battle with the fever was proving exceeding hard, and that this night the little life would be mending or ending. He could not stay now. There might be another summons at the manse; but when he left the mill Brigite clung to his hand so long that he promised, "I will return before midnight," and went away, all the time trying to chase the haunting face of the mother from his vision.

Ambroise was gray, and tonsured by age. But his eyes and mouth were wise and kind. Little enough of his tithes went for fat capons and white Beaune. Had monseigneur, the bishop of Beauvais, been forced to sit at his board, I doubt not monseigneur would have preferred a house in purgatory. But the tithes were paid willingly in Pontoise, so much of them went to Ambroise's poor. He was a peasant, the son of a peasant; he knew a little Latin, and read his breviary. Once, having gone to the Abbey of Le Val, he had seen the outside of a wonderful book. The subprior had told him, "Here is the whole of God's word done into Latin by St. Jerome;" and Ambroise had crossed himself, as before a rare and holy relic. Perhaps, however, one may read the Bible with the heart as well as the eyes, in which case Ambroise knew his Scriptures well. And whenever the good folk of Pontoise railed at the greedy monks and clutching priests, as laymen always did, they never failed to add, however fierce the scolding, "always saving the Curé of St. Maclou, whose heart is made of gold."

Ambroise went up the steep to the town and into the gate, slowly, for he was weary; likewise because he had great joy in watching the young men and maidens dance about the bonfires. They were his flock, and he their more than shepherd. He had christened the fathers and mothers of most of them. He knew the little woes and secrets of them all. Childless himself, all Pontoise were his children, who dropped the "Reverence," and always called him "Father." There had scarce been a love-match in all the little city for many a year, whereof the priest had not known, sooner perchance than the pair themselves, for he was very sage. And even now as he stood following the ring that whirled in the red glow, out to him ran a girl and a shamefaced stripling, who waited hand in hand before the curé, each desiring the other to begin. Neither would speak, until Ambroise did it for them: —

"What have you said to Angalette this night, Aimeri, that makes her blush and hold down her head?"

"*Ai*, father, but we thought you ought to know. I have such joy, and yet it is so hard to tell. You gave me such courage when last I confessed, — and as we danced — "

Here Aimeri's present confession ended in mumbling, and Angalette's cheeks were like the flame, but she spoke never a word. The curé held his hands over them.

"*Dominus vobiscum*, and there shall be a merry wedding in St. Maclou. My heart is very glad for you, dear children ; I have always wished it."

And all the rest of the way to the manse Ambroise forgot a little about sick Nicole, and came to his own door smiling.

The moon had not yet risen. In the darkness, he did not see the two figures sitting on the doorstep, until he almost trod upon them.

"What is it ? Who is ill ? "

The voice of a young man assured him that no one was ill in body, but that a stranger had come to desire his ghostly counsel. The door was unbolted now ; old Martine, the housekeeper, brought a torch and set it sputtering into a wall cresset. The living room of the manse was bare, but so clean you could have dined off the floor. Three heavy wooden chairs, a heavier oaken chest, a brass crucifix upon one wall, a cavernous brick fireplace where a few red embers smouldered, sunk into the other, — that was the whole picture.

Ambroise looked twice at his guests after the torch was ready, and gave a little sigh of surprise.

"You are from the château ? "

"Yes," assented the young man, who already warmed the curé's heart by his pure and handsome face, his mild and reverent bearing.

"Why do you come to me ? The château is full of holy monks and bishops."

"Your pardon, father, — they are not all holy, — but they all know me ; for that cause I cannot go to them."

"What is your name ?"

"I will not tell my name, father ; yet I will not conceal from you I am of knightly birth. Call me Sir Roland of Poissy if you will."

Ambroise had looked at the stranger shrewdly and kindly before he pressed again.

"You will not tell your name, yet why do you seek for me ? It is not well to seek for strange confessors, save when one would deceive himself, and gain absolution by an imperfect confession of the sin. But such confessions are of the devil. 'God is not mocked,' and the absolution is turned to damnation."

"You say well, father ; you shall hear all things, — all save my true name, and the names of those I shall mention. After you have heard me — judge !"

De Joinville, who had all this time been standing like a dumb post, turned his back and went out of the door. It was part of his honor never to pry into the deeds or words of his masters.

The young man knelt on the bare floor before Ambroise and bowed his head.

"This is my sin, good father ; I fear I have set at naught the holy sacrament of matrimony, by wedding a woman who is unable to love me."

At which avowal, you will not wonder if the good curé looked a little blank.

"I suffered myself to wed at the wish of my mother, never considering, in my youth, whether my bride could come to me with any other name upon her heart than mine. I have thus led her into great temptation, for she was bargained away to me by her father for temporal gain, and we had never met."

"You mean your marriage was made not for love, but for the advantage of your two noble houses. Tell me the rest."

Whereupon Louis finished all his tale, concealing nothing but the names and the qualities of the actors, and veiling a few things lest Ambroise should catch a truth which, spread abroad, might rack wide France. When he had ended, there were drops of sweat on the brow of the king, and he was breathing hard. Ambroise, looking down on him, was moved toward him, for he saw that all he said came from the depths of his soul, and that his pain was great.

"And your wife is still dear to you?"

"As our Lady in heaven!"

"Poor lad." He touched Louis' shoulder gently, and a warm thrill seemed to spring all through the king. He almost kissed that comforting hand. Margaret and his mother had touched him thus, but never a man. He had never known a father's love.

"You have no guilt upon your soul," spoke Ambroise, slowly. "If you love your wife with a pure heart, you are blameless before God and man, save for those harsh words flung at her, those murderous blows against your rival. But now rise up, for wisdom, human and from on high, you need — and I will give you all I can."

Then step by step he went over all that Louis had told him, making his strange guest fill in every nook and cranny, searching here and feeling there, yet never pressing from the king the truth about his name. Full soon Louis saw that he was dealing with a man exceeding worldly as well

as heavenly wise, a prime counsellor who set each thing
in its place and weighed it justly.

"And you say," quoth the priest at last, "your wife and
your rival both denied the charge?"

"Yes, both, and my wife had almost persuaded me.
Then my eyes fell upon the scarf and glove, and she
could only cry, 'The devil put them there.'"

"And, perchance, rightly, my dear son!"

"*Ai*, would to God I were sure," groaned Louis.

"You did not question more thereof, but rushed off
straightway to kill your enemy?"

"Too true, alas! for the fiends were in me. I knew
the scarf so well — his arms were embroidered on it. How
came it there, unless he had been secretly to her this afternoon, and left it by some chance?"

"Yet had he worn it at that time he sang in the garden,
and, as you vow, made love to her before your face?"

"No, he had not."

"So it was doubtless either in your wife's chamber or in
his, whilst you were all in the garden?"

"Right."

"And if he had been to your wife it must have been
before the fête, and early in the afternoon?"

"Again right."

Ambroise looked at his penitent shrewdly and his smile
was enigmatic.

"Now, my dear son, answer this question truly, for much
hangs thereon. Your wife may be never so guilty, yet
did God create her mad or quite a fool?"

"No! no! she is the sagest lady in the world, saving
always my mother."

"And, again I ask, was she alone when you burst in on
her, or did you say she was with her maids?"

"Her maids were undressing her."

"And where was the scarf lying?"

"In plain sight upon the divan."

"Then, my dear son, if your wife is not an utter fool, she would never have left that scarf there in manifest view all the time her chambers were empty, whilst she was in the garden.   Neither could she have dared to bring it forth whilst her maids were undressing her.   She had, you say, been but a little time come from the garden before you ran to her?"

"Yes, I recall now, she stopped to speak with the Countess of Roche, while I went in with my mother. She had been in her chamber only a few moments."

"Dear son," said Ambroise, his voice trembling a little, "now do your eyes see anything?"

"See what?   I do not dare to hope."

"See that the glove and scarf you set such store by were doubtless in the chambers of him whom you call your rival; that whilst you all were at the fête, an enemy stole them thence, and laid them in plain view in the chambers of your wife, trusting you would come to her so swiftly that she or her maids could have no time to notice them, and that you would be the first to discover them."

"My God, and can this be!"   Louis pressed his hands across his face, and his body swayed, until Ambroise held him firm to keep him steadfast.

"I do not say this is proved.   I do say this is possible.   And if your wife has an enemy in this, why not in all things else; in the blackening rumors you say have blown into your ears, making you think the darkest of your rival's minstrelsy and its follies?"

"But my mother, — she has not lied to me?   No angel of heaven can persuade me that!"

"No doubt your mother is a saint on earth, but who is all-righteous save God? If she were jealous of the love you bore your wife, no doubt she caught too eagerly everything that an enemy prattled to her."

"An enemy, — ah! that is where my hopes are breaking down. I have none, — none in the world, — unless it be the troubadour knight."

"Are you sure? Has your wife never spoken of fearing this or that? Think well —"

"I know not what to think."

Louis winked hard. Had he known Ambroise longer he would have wept there in the little cottage; that morning he would surely have wept; but since that morning when he knelt beside Margaret in St. Maclou and heard Falaise sing, the king thought that he had lived out twenty years. He was growing strong, and fought the tears of helplessness away. As for Ambroise, he stood silent, pitiful, by mere presence comforting.

"Dear son," said he at last, "you have a tangled skein to unroll; be not too hasty in the untwining. Trust in Our Father, and hope in His great mercy."

"Yes," cried the other, opening his arms, "I will wait, hope, wait. But for to-night, — what shall I do? I have all but committed foul murder. I have cursed my wife. I have nursed demons in my heart. What is the penance to wipe away God's wrath? I have said I was knightly. Now I confess that I am passing rich. By what alms may I be forgiven?"

"Not all the golden deniers of his Grace the King can win one jot of God's least mercy," said Ambroise, smiling solemnly.

"What then? — prayer, fast, pilgrimage? I will go to St. Martin of Tours, to St. James of Compostella. Alas!

though I fain would, my affairs are such I cannot go yet to the East, to war for Our Dear Lord's tomb."

Now all this time Ambroise had looked on his penitent, and had been meditating wisely. He knew that the youth had been pent up within himself, and in his doubts and griefs, and had great need of thinking less on them but more on the griefs of another. Therefore the priest said at last : —

"I will tell you a penance pleasing to God; but I do not know that you will accept it."

"Anything at your hand, O holy father!"

"To-night I must go to the bed of the child of a poor miller. She lies sick, — I fear to death. Come and watch with me till dawn. In the morning go with me on my rounds amongst the stricken and sorrowful; and see what chance Our Lady sends for you to do deeds of mercy."

Louis bent and kissed the tattered cassock of the priest; then he went out to the doorstep, where De Joinville sat mutely.

"Good Simon," said the king, "this kind priest has assigned me a penance that will take me away in secret till next nightfall. You are to leave me, but at to-morrow's sunset you will be here to guide me whithersoever seems best."

Simon's long scabbard rattled. Even in the dark Louis knew he was twisting his mustachios, as he demurred —

"You alone? all night and all day? remember who you are, *damoiseau!*" But the king put on his dignity. "I do remember. Therefore I command you — go!"

De Joinville rose stiffly and gave a military salute. Soon Louis heard him clanking down the streets. Where the commandant went the king neither knew nor cared.

"Will you go to the sick child now, father?" he asked of Ambroise, turning again toward the house; but the priest shook his head.

"Not now, fair son. I must take this mortar, pound these dry herbs, then steep them on the fire, before I go back to the little one. It will needs be until this candle burns down to there," and he pointed to the rim cut in the tallow dip to mark the time.

"Very good! I will go out and watch the village sports, but I will return."

"*Benedicite meum filium!*" quoth Ambroise, busy already over the mortar; and Louis wandered back into the town.

Close by the cottage two streets met in a little square; and hither the chief part of the revellers had drifted. Fifty great torches made a glare as clear as day. Two or three well-to-do burghers had opened their shutters and were passing out deep leathern mugs of *cervoise*, — the strong barley beer of the countryside. Little children scampered in and out of the crowd, and many lean, black pigs, the scavengers of the streets, routed to-night out of their dens in the alleys. On a stone cross against one house stood a girl with a tambourine. She tossed her flying dark curls, smote the tambourine, and tried to sing, beginning: —

"I have a pretty chaplet
I love it very well — "

But from the opposite corner a mountebank jongleur made shift to bawl her down.

"Give ear, good folk! Hear now the most marvellous and vastly entertaining romance of the stout knight Girart of Rousillon — "

Louis never heard more, for, once on the skirts of the crowd, a sudden pushing and rushing swept him into the

midst of it.   He was elbowed and jostled more in that one
moment than before in all his life.   The swirl of strange,
rough faces about him ; the clamor of easy oaths and rail-
lery, the hustling hither, thither, against his will — the
king knew not whether to be angry or to rejoice.   He was
like a man first tasting an untried dish which he doubts
whether to call bitter or sweet.   Now the cause of this
jostling was the zeal and authority of the two worshipful
syndics, who, appearing in their robes of office, cleared a
wide circle in the square, while another dignitary proclaimed that,

"Four of the choicest of the youth of Pontoise would
now ride at the quintain, and he who excelled in this most
noble sport should receive the silver arrow awarded annually
by the right honorable corporation of the echevins."

Whereupon there was set in the midst of the little square,
full under the torch-light, a kind of gibbet, from the arm
whereof dangled a hideous straw-stuffed manikin about the
size of a boy, with a large hole pierced through the spot
for the heart.   I need not tell the "oh-ing!" "ah-ing!"
cheers, wagers, chaffering, that went on, while the first
noble champion came forward in the lists.   Alas! for the
pampered ass of the morning : he wore flowers then, but
a bit and saddle now!   A square-shouldered young varlet,
"Conon Chase-the-Devil" everybody called him, bestrode
his back.   Conon brandished a long, slim pole, and poised
it like a lance.   His purpose was to run the weapon through
the hole in the quintain's heart and snap it short.   His
steed winced, but two kicks in the ribs sent him flying.
A noble charge — a swelling cheer!   But "Conon Chase-
the-Devil" never bore off the silver arrow!   He missed
the hole, the lance glided from the slippery manikin, then
whack!   the swinging bag of straw smote the luckless

cavalier on the pate as he rushed under, and the champion went clattering down upon the stones.

Louis joined in the howl and laugh which three hundred throats sent up. He was thinking that these hard-handed, low-browed folk were sucking infinitely more joy out of these coarse sports than all his white-fingered court friends from their polite tourneys and jongleur's tinklings, when right at his elbow he heard words that sent all the blood to his ears. A young man and his wife were talking.

"What a lout Conon is! I always knew it!" quoth she.

"Right, by St. Maclou. He is as idle, reckless, and doltish — as — well, as his Grace the king!"

"As the king? Hush, Sicard, don't talk treason!"

"Why, we're all friends and neighbors here, and there's no fear of the gallows. You know the stories that buzz. Once the king was young, and it was well enough that petticoats and kirtles should govern him; yet now he is a man they say his mother and two or three great lords still carry his power around in the bags at their girdles. Aimer who sells eggs at the château says he has heard a squire whisper — "

"Well — what?" urged the wife.

"That the king was very pious and chaste, but, like Conon just now, somewhat ailing here!"

And Sicard gave a tap on his forehead. Louis thought the veins in his head would burst. He had his dagger halfway from the sheath, before he knew what he was doing, to silence that clappering tongue with one sure stab. Then the king bent his head. "Murder is still in my heart. I am still hot with wrath and passion. How know I that this stranger is not a better man than I? that he spoke not truly? If I may not rule myself, God forbid that I bear sway over wide France!"

N

Another champion was mounting the ass, but Louis did not tarry. Drawing his cloak tightly about him, he forced his way out of the crowd, and returned to the manse. Ambroise had stirred up the fire, and put his herbs into a kettle where they were simmering, filling the room with a sweet odor. Louis fell into one of the heavy chairs and sat, silently, patiently, his head upon his hands, his elbows on his knees, until the priest took the pot from the fire, and poured off the liquor into a pitcher.

"Come," commanded Ambroise, and Louis followed him eagerly out into the night.

CHAPTER XVI

MARGARET AT BAY

IF you will read the learned history of the Monk of Corbie you will not fail to discover that ever and again Providence has been singularly pleased to use the most humble instruments for the advancement of His own high ends — to wit, a serpent beguiled our first parent Eve; a raven fed the man of God Elijah in the wilderness; a gnat devoured the brain of the cruel emperor Titus, and so avenged the captive Jews. This being so, you will not think it strange if the great angels who have as their care to watch over their dear sons, the kings of France, made use neither of a count nor a seigneur, nor even an honest burgess to cast confusion upon much of the plot which the Father of Lies had taught to Enguerraud de Coucy. And heaven ordained the thing to fall in this wise.

When Louis and De Joinville left the castle, if they had looked back they might have seen a gliding shadow following them. Looking harder they would have known that this shadow was a man, and that he had his cloak pulled carefully about his face, so carefully, that the king must have come very close to recognize Pons the squire of the chamberlain. I cannot tell all that De Coucy had commanded Pons; enough that the squire had been ordered to follow the king, never to lose track of him, to find which way he went, and to bring back full word before midnight. To all of which Pons had answered: —

"I will do so, sir, or you may break me on the wheel, if you list."

Pons had no fears of the vigilance of Louis, but a wholesome awe of De Joinville made him keep a safe distance behind his quarry, until they came to the manse. There he wished the guardsman would go inside, in order that he himself might clamber up and try a lattice to find if he could overhear what passed betwixt the king and the curé. But Joinville sat stolidly upon the step, and Pons had to gnaw his fingers and wait in the dark. Then of a sudden the commandant stalked away, but, to the infinite amazement of the squire, the king was not with him. Then the king went out of the manse alone, and watched the little throng in the square. Louis never knew how close to him the squire stood in the crowd, and how the excellent Pons was puzzled at his movements. When Louis went back to the manse, the watcher went after him ; when Louis followed Ambroise forth on his errand, Pons was only twenty paces behind, and still was racking his brains as to what it all might mean. But as they passed away from the throng in the square into the darker streets, it would have been well for the squire had he too sent a few glances backward. So intent was he on his quest that he never heard the stealthy footfalls behind him. In fact, he hardly heard the whistle of the bludgeon, that dashed upon his head, and made his eyes dance with bright stars swiftly followed by blackness. He knew he had fallen. He felt hands tugging at his pouch and rummaging his pockets, and that was all he knew for a long time. His fate was simple enough. Eblé the footpad, who had been hunting all the evening for a lonely wayfarer on a lonely street, had found his chance. He had stunned his man before there was any outcry, and so did not think it needful to kill him.

"Two silver sous of Tours, one Paris denier, and a gold Venetian zecchin — not a bad haul, praised be St. Anne!" thus, safe in his cellar, he told his wife; "but we must go without flesh on next Wednesday, or my conscience will smite me." . . .

As for Pons, in the morning Aimon the sacristan found him more dead than alive. He took him to the little hospice close to the Hôtel de Ville, where old Claire the midwife so bandaged and poulticed him that by the morning following he was able to tell everything that he remembered; but by that time what he remembered had little interest to Enguerraud de Coucy.

Thus it came to pass that Eblé, the greatest rogue in Pontoise, was used of God for a most wonderful purpose; but the full import of his deed is best told hereafter.

* * * * * * *

Louis went his way, the chamberlain his, but Margaret of Provence went no way at all. She had none to go. The saints seemed to have appointed that she only suffer and wait. After Louis left her, she had lain on the divan, face downward, sobbing, — she thought, for an eternity; more likely it was only an hour. All her worst forebodings were realized; everything seemed gone, — everything but life, and with that she would have parted gladly. Yet so fierce was her tempest of grief that even self-destruction never entered her head. She had lost Louis! Lost his love forever — forever! The crown of France, her fame among good women — all this for the moment weighed as nothing. "I go to kill your lover!" The threat rang in her ears like the roar of waves in a seashell. Nothing could hush them. Margaret knew that her husband was roused, that from the gentlest of men he had become the fiend incarnate. She knew how Gui could fight. "By this time they are crossing swords. By this time one is dead. By this time there is an unshriven soul in the presence of God uttering my name. Yet I am innocent! Why must I suffer thus?"

Her thoughts raced like the wind. She caught up the tell-tale scarf and rent it to fine bits, taking a kind of joy in destroying this engine of calamity. "A devil had placed it there!" No other thought was possible.

She did not faint, though she almost wished it. Her brain remained clear. Her head did not reel. The room had grown dark; she thought it surely midnight, when lo! the calls of the sentries in the court below told that they were just changing the watch on the end of evening. Her maids, warned by some good angel, did not come to trouble her. She would have given anything to learn the issue of the duel, but whom dared she summon? She might ring her silver bell, but very likely the hateful beauty Alithe would answer her. Still there was no scampering, no shouting, in the castle court — none of the breathless tumult that would surely rise, if ill had befallen the king of France. For mortal harm to Louis could not have been covered long. "Then it is Gui that is slain." And though Margaret held down her head, and tried to say a prayer for the troubadour, she knew that a great weight of ice had been lifted from her heart. Let Louis hate her, spurn her, torture her. He was living. That was peace enough!

But she could not endure to be alone any longer. The room was very dark now, and the gloom frightened her. But the darkness itself brought a thought. "The night has no terror for Falaise." Was the blind girl in her eyrie? Margaret made clumsy work with her unaccustomed hands in thrusting back the tapestry and the sliding

panel, before she was able to stand on the hidden stair
of the great black donjon.   All around pressed the sightless gloom, but Margaret was too desperate to balk at
imps and kobolds now.

"Falaise!"   She sent her voice up into the darkness,
and there was no reply.   "Falaise!" again.   Still none.
But at a third summons, "Who calls?" came from far
above in thin answer.

"It is I — Margaret.   I am in direful trouble.   God
has forsaken me.   Ah! have pity on me and come down
to me quickly."

A rustle floated down the turns of the stairway; at last
Margaret saw even in that midnight a kind of whiteness
drawing toward her.   The next moment she was kissing
the blind girl, and sobbing in her arms.

"Oh, Falaise of the Blessed Voice, it has all happened
as I feared, — worse than as I feared.   I am undone forever."

"*Ai!* dear lady," spoke Falaise's sweet voice, "what is
this you say?"

And they were back in the chamber together, where
amid I know not how many moans Margaret told the
story of all that had happened as far as she understood
anything thereof at all.   As for Falaise, she for once could
think of not one thing to say, not even of the dear God
and the little soft sprites, but the mere touch of her hand
on the queen's forehead was priceless comfort.   They sat
together a long time in the deepening darkness.

"Have you supped?" quoth Margaret at last.   "On
the table are, I think, some Chailly buns and a pitcher of
wine."

"I have supped," said the blind maid; "you see, I
had to stay close in my tower most of the afternoon"

(she would not burden the queen with De Coucy's ill deed now); "but toward evening I went forth again to Jean of the Mill to find Nicole, who is still so sick. Brigite gave me a nice soft crust and some fresh strawberries, and I was just going to sleep in my tower when you called."

"Are you never lonely in that tower?"

"Why should I be? The winds come every night to talk to me and bring me the breath of the flowers."

Margaret's grasp on the girl's hand tightened.

"Dear Falaise, do you know what I wish?"

"What?"

"That the good God would make me blind like you, and make me forget all things save that I were your sister."

"Dear Margaret," spoke the other, "you need not be blind to be my sister, for I love you as one already, and I will forget that you are a queen."

They drew nearer one to the other, sitting again in long silence, and the Provençal was a little comforted. She was again losing count of time when at last came the long awaited knocking at the door. Margaret rose, crossed herself, and seemed summoning courage for a dread ordeal.

"I dare not refuse them entrance," she said; "but do not you leave me. Wait behind the curtains of the inner chamber. There you will be quite safe."

Falaise hid herself. Margaret unbolted. As the first glare of an upraised lamp flickered round the room, the queen stood gazing stupidly, then recoiled as if in horror. She was face to face with Gui of Avignon! . . .

The troubadour wore a white bandage tied about his head; his face was somewhat pale, otherwise he seemed as sound and bold as ever. Not marking the lady's terror, he bent in courtly obeisance; then in long-winded terms desired the honor of entering her chamber.

"The king! the king!" was all her answer, to which Gui replied a little dryly that he understood that his Grace had just left the castle on a pilgrimage to a forest shrine, and that he was enjoying excellent health.

"Then you have not killed him?"

The troubadour set down his lamp and gazed about shrewdly.

"Not killed him? To St. Tropheme of Arles, fair mistress, I owe it that he has not killed me. Cursed be my skill! my head still rings like an anvil! But enough of this. You have summoned me. I come. Behold your knight, your cavalier, your paladin, ready, by St. Cupido's grace, to make good your wish, your least whim, against all contemners, even as is provided, commanded, and most properly enjoined in that most excellent book, the wise Rogier's *Lover's Credo*."

Gui had by this time begun to gesture furiously with both hands, and Margaret, who knew him all too well, stopped him instantly.

"*I* have summoned you, and therefore *you* come? Explain yourself; I do not understand."

Gui's little body shut up like a clasp-knife yet again. When it opened he had one hand in his bosom, and drew out a perfumed note of white vellum.

"Oh, dame of incomparable sagacity and virtue — lady whom I, your unworthy knight, would try to praise even as the illustrious Pierre Vidal sang the charms of his Alazais de Roca, or Guirant de Borneil his Escarontra — "

"This is no *tenson* of wits, sir knight," darted Margaret, fiercely; "we play to-day with life and death. Why have you come, you who of all men should never meet me? For we have met too much."

Even Gui of Avignon's wagging tongue moved haltingly

at this rebuke. Ladies, he sadly knew, were fickle, but this blank incredulity on Margaret's part was not to be ascribed to any caprice taught by Duchess Venus. He could only thrust into her hands the letter. But when she had read it the queen looked even paler than before.

" I have not written it," was all she said, and felt herself turning cold all over. Here was another sign the devils were working her ruin.

" Not written it ? Does my mistress say that ? "

" Gui of Avignon," said the queen, slowly, " if I have written that letter, may God cut me off from the joys of heaven as utterly as He has from the joys of earth ! "

Then at last the hot Provençal blew his passion out. No more in troubadour gallantry, but with words keen and swift from the heart. " He had always loved her ! " that was the burden. But it were needless to tell how he knelt, groaned, beat his breast, swore fidelity, devotion undying, and anything else the maddest lover can swear. And as he blazed, Margaret almost against her will knew herself to be answering him, telling him all that the king had said and done ; all the queen mother had done ; and of all the pains that made her own heart's agony. At hearing which, I promise you, Gui's own fires did not burn one whit the less. Then before she knew it the troubadour was kissing her hands, though she would not let him touch her lips, much as he wished it. At last he passed from bows and ecstasy to saner questions.

" Ah, but the letter ! You did not write it ? "

" And the scarf and the glove. You were never here — you never sent them — they were stolen ? "

" By the queen mother ? " the knight threw out darkly.

" No, not by the queen mother. She would kill me, but

face to face. And where have I another enemy in the world?"

"An enemy it was, or perchance —" here the trouba-dour crossed himself, "the very living fiend has done this for your pain. What matter? We will fetch good out of Beelzebub! I am here. The riddle will wait to-night. For to-night I must deliver you from this purgatory!"

"Alas! what can you do?"

"You must flee from Pontoise."

"Ah, yes — I understand; the convent is always open to the wretched. They say the Abbess of Maubuisson is very kind. She will receive me."

"No, no; I have friends and helpers in the castle as have you. We will flee together. To the South Country — Arles — lovely Provence, the home of poets and of roses — your father, your mother!"

Whereupon Margaret knew what it was to be tempted of the devil, but she tried to put the tempter by.

"How dare you speak the word?" and now her cheeks were hot. "I am innocent now, however blackly men may accuse me. I were guilty before God, if I fled thus from my lord and husband."

"Your lord and husband?" There was a strange tone in Gui's voice that made Margaret shudder again. A fear-ful instinct told her that another great blow was about to fall.

"Yes; have you never suspected? Has it never been hinted? Are you beyond doubt sure that your marriage to the king is without flaw in the sight of Holy Church?"

Margaret clapped her hands to her ears, as if she would not hear him.

"Gui," she said desperately, "one of us is mad; it is you or I? Or are we both mad?"

"Would to Our Lady we were! It is that which sent me
hither with my blood boiling. *Ai!* If I had but known
the truth before I fought that caitiff king, my arm would
not have failed, and one less sinner would run upon this
earth."

"The truth? the truth? what is the truth?"

"That there was a flaw in your marriage at Sens, ex-
pressly interposed by order of Queen Blanche, so that the
bond might be dissolved if at any time it seemed incon-
venient."

Margaret took two deep breaths and stood facing him,
raised to full height.

"I do not believe this," she said with a coldness more
dangerous than a passion.

"But I will prove it by the mouth of the Bishop of
Beauvais, who performed the marriage. And then will
you believe?"

"When I have spoken to the bishop face to face, not
sooner. And then — may God have mercy upon me!"

"And if I prove it, will you fly with me?"

"To Provence or to the infidels, — whither you list: for
I shall be better dead than living."

Gui bowed again very humbly.

"Most gracious lady, since you suffer me, I will depart and bring to you the Bishop of Beauvais. You
shall hear with your own ears what he has just said in
mine."

"Bring him — and then shall I know how he lies!"

Her boast sounded after him, as he vanished, but there
was no pride left in Margaret of Provence. She was past
tears, past moaning. Forth from her hiding glided Falaise
to caress and kiss her forehead.

"I only knew you this morning," said the queen, "and

to-night you are the only friend I have in the world. Have you heard all that this knight said to me?"

" Ah, yes, and my heart burns with pity!"

" Go back, then! Hear the rest. Then to all that I say or do, I shall have one witness. Hist — there are the footsteps. So pray for me, Falaise; pray, for God and Our Lady must love your prayers better than all of mine."

The curtains of the inner chamber had scarcely ceased swaying, before Gui reëntered, and at his heels was another that Margaret knew well — Godfrey, Prince-bishop of Beauvais.

CHAPTER XVII

WHAT THE BISHOP TOLD

My lord, the prince-bishop, had exchanged the gayer dress he wore at the fête for such a sedate and sad-colored cassock as became a man of the church. He had likewise hung about his neck a small, but heavy, silver crucifix. It was plain that he came not as courtier but as cleric, and Margaret received him as such, kneeling, and hardly raising her eyes whilst he lifted his two fingers and muttered his *benedicite*. Gui flung himself to and fro with quick, impatient steps, and all three waited an instant, each desiring the other to begin. The bishop clearly did not enjoy his task, and found it easier to look down at his crucifix than at the queen; but Gui at last jerked out angrily:—

"Well, *reverendissime*, you had better commence!"

"Ei! so you may say, fair son; but heart and flesh alike cry out. It is no light thing that you ask!"

"It is no light thing that Sir Gui has told me," shot Margaret, whose hands clasped and unclasped nervously. "I cried it was a lie; he swore he had the tale from you. Good, then,—it is a lie! I throw it in your teeth. Who dares to say I am not wife to Louis of France?"

The prelate shrugged his shoulders and gave a long cough.

"Be calm and patient, *delecta filia*. It is a grievous matter to tell of; likewise it touches upon high concerns of state. '*Eloquar an sileam?*' as says Master Virgil. Shall I speak out or be silent? I am in sore doubt."

"Cruel!" and now the tears rushed to her eyes; "you have told Gui already. Are you the Paris torturer? Speak out, for the love of Christ!"

The bishop gave another deeper cough, and moved sluggishly toward a seat.

"My beloved daughter in God," he began, with a peculiar oiliness of tone that cut through Margaret more horribly than curses, "you must understand that I was the unwilling partner, on the day of your so-called marriage at Sens, in a deed which at that time afflicted my conscience not a little, and which since I have had sore cause to dread will be laid up against me upon that Great Day."

"Proceed, father." Margaret had seated herself also; she was fearfully calm, for her mind had been racing fast. She more than guessed what was coming, and the iron had entered deep into her soul.

"You will recall that when you came to Sens, to be joined in marriage to his Grace the king, it was intended that the ceremony should be solemnized by none other than the eminent primate the Archbishop of Reims. But it pleased God at that time to send upon him a sickness, whereby he was unable to be present, and the queen mother deigned — for I was more in her kind favor then than, alas! at present — to invite me to unite you to the king, and to set the crown-royal upon your head."

"I remember." Margaret's lips seemed never to move as she said it.

"You know it was upon the Saturday before Ascension, in the year of our redemption twelve hundred and thirty-four, that you entered the Cathedral of St. Stephen of Sens to be wedded and crowned. You were accompanied by a noble following of seigneurs and prelates from your father's

court in the South, your uncle William, Bishop of Valence
at their head. I was in the sacristy of the cathedral array-
ing myself in cope and mitre to go forth and do my part,
when her Grace the queen mother came in to me, and bade
me put forth all the lesser clergy. Then she opened it
to me, that though she trusted she had chosen for the best,
and had sought her son a worthy marriage, nevertheless
your dowry was only ten thousand marks, and that, too, by
no means paid; and for many reasons poor human wisdom
could not then foresee, it might be needful to have the
marriage dissolved."

"A—h!" The word came out of Margaret as a long
whisper; then she was silent once more.

"I did not fail to present to her Grace that the easiest
manner of dissolving a marriage was to prove some affinity
or consanguinity between the contracting parties; but she
replied that she had already spoken to learned canonists,
and these answered her that by the decree of the late
Lateran Council the forbidden degrees had been so
widely abolished, — all marriage outside of third cousins
being declared lawful, — that no such impediment could
arise in your case, and some other ground must be necessary."

The bishop paused, expecting an outbreak from the lady,
but she only twitched her hands again, and he continued : —

"I then inquired of her Grace what I could do to serve
her, to which she replied, 'You must do as I know well is
often done in like cases : you must mutter the marriage
ceremony in a low voice, saying some of it beneath your
breath ; and what you thus say you must pervert, so that
you can, if needful, declare upon your oath, "I did not join
Louis of France and Margaret of Provence in lawful wedlock."'"

"Bishop of Beauvais," spoke Margaret, uprising, "I knew you were an evil man; I never knew you were the devil. Go on — and say you consented."

"*Ai*, daughter! your tongue is sharp; like a sword it cleaves even to the dividing of my bones and marrow." My Lord Bishop twisted on his seat, and I truly think half pitied her : "Do not blame. I am only a sinful man, though by the world styled 'God's anointed.' You know the queen mother, — the flash of her eye, the turn of her voice, and how was I to say her nay? '*Quidquid principi placuit legis habet vigorem,*' so says the jurist, declaring the whim of the prince to have the force of law."

"You consented?" repeated Margaret, simply.

"Alas! how could I otherwise? When you stood with his Grace the king before me, do you remember how I spoke the words of the service?"

"Very haltingly, and ever and anon your voice would drop. Many mentioned it afterward, saying, 'The reverend bishop was so overcome by his emotions that he scarce could finish the service.'"

"And rightly said. *O meum maximum peccatum!* Then when I came to the solemn words, *Ego jungo vos*, did you hear what it was I said?"

"I did not. Speak! oh, speak!"

"*Ego non jungo vos.*"

After that the silence was long, and Margaret felt her heart beating, beating; and something above her eyes seemed ready to burst. But still she did not go mad. Still the bishop sat, rubbed his smooth hands, and waited for her to answer him. Then Margaret flung her last javelin, though her forehead blushed. "You have lied. The queen mother would never have dared this. God has not yet blessed me with children, but even she in her madness

o

cannot have wished to have a taint cast upon an heir to France."

"You are wrong, daughter," returned the prelate, more oily than ever; "you forget that Holy Church declares that though such irregular marriages are too often void, nevertheless where the parties are of tender age, and at the time ignorant, they are exempt from the pains and penances of what were otherwise mortal sin. The children of 'putative marriages' are legitimate, though not born in undoubted wedlock. But as for such marriages themselves, as any doctor of Padua, Salerno, or Bologna will confess, — "

"They are void. You need not tell me that. Now, how many then knew this thing saving you yourself?"

"Two — the queen mother and the Primate of Reims. I had trusted that it could die with me, and God would pardon the guilt — " Margaret had clasped her hands behind her head, and moved to and fro, to and fro, rapidly. She was marvellously beautiful, as the red lamp-light now hid the alabaster of her face, now shone upon its whiteness. So the bishop thought; but still she hurled her questions at him.

"And why have you told this to Gui?"

"Because I saw too well that the king and the queen mother planned your mischief — that the queen mother would soon cast you down into shame. That it was right you should know everything, and fly before it was too late, and you were undone."

"And has the king learned this, too?"

"Yes, surely," cast in Gui, "or by the seven wounds of God he would not have dared to outrage your honor and mine as he has dared this day, save as he knew he could cast you off with impunity."

"You speak well, sir knight," quoth the bishop, nodding.

Margaret stood rigid before the prelate, and made his eyes meet hers.

"Now lay your hand upon this crucifix, my lord bishop, — so; grasp it well. I have not time to ask, to sift, to let the wise 'legists' fight my battle in the law. But you who say all this shall answer truly on your soul. Repeat what I command you; or be silent, then I shall know that you have lied."

"I am waiting, daughter."

"Your hand quakes; you turn pale."

"You press me hard; but I am waiting."

"Then repeat this after me: 'I swear, as I hope in salvation, that Margaret is not the lawful wife of Louis of France — in the name of the Father, and of the Son, and of the Holy Ghost, Amen.'"

The bishop's brow grew white, then red. If only she had not commanded him to set his hand upon the crucifix! Why had he forgotten to take it off?

"Will you not swear? Have you come to play with me?"

"*Ai*, Monseigneur," darted the knight, going as ever for his hilt; "swear, and swear quickly, or I brand you liar, and cram this good steel down your throat."

Then the Bishop of Beauvais grasped the crucifix tightly, for having resolved upon the deed, he must see it through, and swore in a passing steady voice that the queen mother had said to him even what he related, and that he had performed the marriage according to her commandment. And in less steady voice, — not grasping so tightly, — he swore that Margaret of Provence was no wife of Louis of France. After that he arose, puffed, wiped his forehead, and desired his "beloved children in God to suffer him to leave them.

and he would not fail to beseech Our Lady's and St. Bernard's help upon their sore extremity."

When next Margaret knew anything she and Gui were alone, and the troubadour was again kneeling at her feet, holding both her hands.

" You will fly with me — to Provence! to Provence!"

Margaret brushed her hands across her eyes as if to break some clinging cobweb.

" I am not his wife! am not his wife! am not his wife!" She might have repeated it longer, but Gui rushed on with his passion.

" You know I have always loved you. You know that whether I sang the praise of a dame of Avignon or Grenoble, of Valence or Narbonne, it was you that danced before my sight. I have friends in the castle; they will aid me. God has removed the king hence, making him blind in his sins. Trust me, follow me, wait for me."

" Louis! Louis! Louis!" that was all she cried.

" Yes, I know the pain is great, but I will teach you to forget it. *Ai!* By the splendor of God will it not be an adventure! France will ring of my deed: how I took you from the king's own castle. I shall be praised as a paladin, an Olivier, an Ogier, a Roland! Jongleurs shall sing of my exploit a thousand years."

" Louis! Louis!" cried Margaret.

" Do not fear. My squires are skilful and brave. We will have swift horses. If a hundred oppose, my good arm shall dash them down."

The lady did not answer him. She was not thinking of brave adventures or deeds of valor. Then all the power seemed to pass out of her. She did not know whether what she said was right or wrong. She was very sure the Master Devil himself had been working her woe since morning.

"I — I will go with you."

As she said it, she dragged her hand away from his lips and put five steps between herself and the troubadour.

"Gui — I have known and trusted you. Unwittingly you have done me the greatest hurt that man can do to woman. But you are innocent. I do not blame you. As for the king, it is not he, but some fiend that wears his shape to-day, so do not curse him. But the queen mother — author and finisher of all this woe — I curse, and may God do to her as she has done to me! Now, how and when will you fly?"

"To-night — two hours suffice. I have told you I have friends whose duty to the king does not blind them to his faithlessness. I will find everything; do you but be dressed and ready when I come."

"I will be ready."

A few words more and he went, leaving Margaret staring round the empty room. Then she called Falaise.

* * * * * * *

Gui went into the castle court, walking as they say men walk on air. A noble adventure! An hypocritical, faithless, unknightly king to be requited! A lady, fair as Countess Helen, Cleopatra, or the incomparable Princess Dido — not to mention more recent dames — to be delivered from outrage and infamy! The name of Gui of Avignon would peal down the lists of chivalric song. Had ever a "Pilgrim of Love" more cause to thank Sir Cupido?

As he descended the donjon he saw with pleasure that there was no yeoman on watch at the lower entrance, and as he crossed the court the castle seemed to him strangely empty and still. No doubt the king had led away a considerable train on his pilgrimage. The more cause to bless the saints! Gui grew truly reckless in his vows of gratitude.

Then as he was passing under a dark gate on his way to his own tower, a quick step following made him turn. He was confronting the chamberlain.

"And did the reverend bishop tell her all?" quoth De Coucy, in a voice that was almost piteous.

"All, my fair lord; I need not beg your mercy upon her sorrow when she heard it. Yet it was for the best."

"For the best; so on my honor I assured you. For the Castilian was resolved on using her secret power to depose her enemy: likewise the king, grown weary of his marriage, would gladly end it. I have that from my daughter."

"We are much beholden to your courtesy."

"In no wise. I am myself a knight, and will aid you so far as I may in conscience to my king. So you have persuaded her to flee with you?"

"Yes — by Our Lady's grace!"

"Draw closer, then, under this shadow. For my own sake I must not seem to commune with you. You have, I gather, sturdy and discreet squires, who will conduct your horses privily from the castle and across the bridge. Tether them under the wall of the chapel of St. Lucie, and bring the lady to them. You will of course flee toward Poissy?"

"So I had desired."

"Very good. I will direct the keenest pursuit then toward Meulan. It has pleased the king to intrust to me the control of the guard to-night, and I will so dispose the sentries that you can pass from the royal donjon and through the southernmost sally-port without molestation. Doubtless I imperil my head in this, but my love and pity for your poor mistress is so great —"

"You are a Christian and courtly seigneur," protested Gui, snatching at the chamberlain's hands, and ready to undam a torrent of fire words, but De Coucy put him aside gently, vowed he was only doing what became him as a cavalier, and vanished by a quick turn down the next gateway. The Provençal made his way to his own tower, and again he noted how solitary the great black castle seemed. The night, too, was overcast, though without rain, and a murky south wind blew, piling the clouds thicker. " Never a more suitable hour for the deed," he meditated. He roused his yawning squires, and made their eyes grow big when he declared to them the coming adventure. They knew their lord, and had risked their necks for him before; but to aid to bear away a queen of France? — Anselm, the stoutest of the squires, pulled a long face.

" Sir," said he, "we have followed you, leal and true, through many a foray, many a tourney, but do you well to enter upon this thing, which may bring us nearer to Purgatory than to Provence, unless indeed your honor is engaged ? "

" Mine honor *is* engaged, sirrah," rejoined his master, sternly, "and were it not, you do betray a woful ignorance of the eleventh precept in *The Sage Knight's True Missal*, to wit, 'The perfect squire shall ask no questions of his lord.' Go and prepare the horses as commanded."

Anselm went out, holding down his head, while Bernart his companion whistled a little tune and followed. Neither was too old to remember his sins and wonder if he would ever again see his mother, but both knew it was far better to be drawn and quartered than for a squire to haggle over the commandment of his seigneur. As for Gui himself, he duly prepared for his adventure on his knees, forgetting not to invoke Our Blessed Lady, his patron St. Tropheme, nor, I must add, that most puissant dame Queen Venus. He arose steadfast in mind and body. Only one thing irked him — to leave his dear viols amongst these uncourtly

Frenchmen; hostages almost in the hands of a wanton
and deceitful king. But even the "Pilgrim of Love" must
pay his price, and there were more viols waiting him in
that pleasant château at Avignon, for which his soul was
pining. He had no great fears for the adventure. Let
him gain a fair start of one night and by dawn be well on
his way out of the Île de France. Then once clear of the
king's personal dominions he was friend to many dis-
affected barons who would speed him on his way southward, even if they dared not long harbor him.

Bernart presently came back to assure his master that
Anselm had led their four best horses out of the southernmost sally-port, which was unlocked and unguarded, even
as De Coucy had promised. Provisions and clothing were
in the saddle-bags. Gui put a light mail shirt under his
doublet, and girded on his best sword. Now was the time
when he had promised to return to Margaret, and he summoned Bernart to follow him. Yet again they crossed the
court, and as before it was solitary and still, the tall towers
looming gloomily over them, hardly a window pierced by
a light. Only once, as they were passing, Bernart stopped.

" Hearken, lord ! " said he.

"What do you hear ? "

"A great body of horsemen seem to be crossing the
bridge from Aumône."

"What matter, we do not stay for trifles ? " And Gui
went with longer strides toward the door of the great
donjon.

CHAPTER XVIII

DE COUCY STRIKES

WHEN Enguerraud de Coucy quitted Gui in the castle court, quick steps took him down a narrow vaulted passage lit by a few cressets and which led to the heart of the castle. When he came to a pikeman of the guard, who saluted mechanically, the chamberlain answered with a condescending smile, and put his hand into his belt.

" Why are you here on sentry ? " asked the nobleman.

" Because the captain De Joinville set me here," was the fellow's answer; but he gave a broad grin when the chamberlain held out a bright denier.

"Ah! your good captain is always looking for the enemy, as if Pontoise lay on the wild Guyenne marches. Well, I command the guard to-night, and proclaim a truce. Go to your quarters, and take this silver to drink the health of his Grace the king."

The soldier put down his pikestaff with a clatter, but De Coucy never waited for his awkward thanks. A few steps brought him into a square room lighted by a score of flaring copper lamps swung from the arched ceiling. The stone floor was very smooth, and the dozen or more gentlemen in the room were either the players or the watchers of a hard-fought game of billiards. The rattling of the hooked sticks, which sent the wooden balls skimming across the flagging, drowned the chamberlain's voice when he called for the first time to the Counts of Brittany and

Champagne. But at the second summons their sticks
dropped quickly, and the Breton sent one sly question.

"Is he here?"

"He is here," spoke De Coucy, in a half whisper.

"Good; then we follow you."

And despite a few protests and a little wonder from the
courtiers whose game was spoiled, the three kindred spirits
went off together toward the chamberlain's own rooms,
where they were soon behind door and bolt, and deep in
talk with Alithe, his Reverence of Beauvais, and a stranger
whom De Coucy presented as his friend, the right gallant
captain the Sire Henri de Ormoy.

A sight to behold was this captain.   There were more
scars on his face than one has fingers.   One ear was gone
and half of the other.   His arms and feet were a mass
of sinews.   When he smiled, as he did often and evilly,
you could see that all the front teeth were gone.   His
hair was black as a crow.   In short, De Ormoy was one
of those landless and masterless roving spirits who had
fought, plundered, slaughtered, changed sides, and fled
out of every land from Scotland to Palestine.   He had
more strange deeds on his soul than he could ever remember to confess.   And just now he had withdrawn himself
with his band of free lances from Aragon, because King
James had ordered him to suffer the loss of that small neces-
sity—his head.   Only that dawn had his band come to Conflans, very likely brought thither by a hint from De Coucy.
Be that as it may, if Gui of Avignon stood at the zenith
of knightly courtesy, this "seigneur sans terre" lay very
close to its nadir.   Even Peter of Brittany, not a man over-
nice in such matters, looked twice before he took this
ally's hooked hand, and Theobald of Champagne held his
own behind his back.

"Faugh, the old he-goat!" the bishop bewailed in De Coucy's ear. "*Homo atrox asper indecor!* I am fain to grasp my nose! How can I abide him?"

"Hush, hush, *reverendissime*," soothed the chamberlain, "you forget the habits of many saintly monks and anchorites, who cleanse not their bodies but their souls. Besides, this knight has been a notable champion against the Infidels."

"I will perforce endure him. 'He that is filthy, let him be filthy still;' so says the scripture."

"Come then to the point," urged De Coucy, "and you, good friends, give ear. The holy bishop has been to Margaret of Provence. I understand, even as I urged, at last that brave and gallant simpleton of Avignon will take her off in two hours in flight."

"The fish bite," thrust in De Ormoy, grinning more hideously than ever.

"And we are prepared," continued the chamberlain, not raising his eyebrows. "I have promised yet a new altar — besides my former vows to St. Germain in Coucy — for that signal favor which took De Joinville, our chief danger, out of the way, and gave me the ordering of the yeomen. I have withdrawn them from many points, weakened the watch at others, plied those in the guard-room with wine. De Glui, De Joinville's lieutenant, is a thin-headed wight, and will give us no trouble; nor will any other, if you, De Ormoy, are ready on your part with your men close by. How many have you?"

"Three hundred of the toughest wolves that ever ran together in a pack. Scarce a knave of them but has fled the gallows, and dances at my pipe just to escape dancing at the hangman's."

"Brisk boys for our purpose. I will give them work;

but you must keep an iron glove on them. No plundering, slaughtering, or touching women. You understand, and only I to give them the signal."

"I understand."

"Eh! my dear friends," quoth the chamberlain, rubbing his hands, "our game is rushing marvellously, swiftly, to a happy end. As for the king — "

"Ay, there will be some trouble," spoke Theobald.

"Pons will bring word whence to fetch him, when all else is righted. Would to God we had only the king to quake about. But I mistrust lest we have trouble with the rest. The city will rise, our enemies gather. Henry of England[1] is engaged to us, but his Grace is a most slippery Grace. We must make no misstep."

"Well said," hinted the Breton, darkly; "this is not the first conspiracy that has failed. Let us understand one another. Your daughter marries the king, once the Provençal disgraces herself."

"Foul business," muttered Theobald, frowning, but Peter did not notice him.

"You, my fair sire, of course, become the omnipotent father-in-law; the king in all but crown and name. The queen mother vanishes in a convent. But my Lord Champagne and myself — what is ours? We should know plainly."

"It was provided clearly," rejoined the chamberlain, not wholly pleased, "that to Brittany should be restored all of Maine."

"And Anjou, may it pleasure your Mightiness," shot back Peter, scowling.

"And to Champagne, Vermandois and Brie," hinted Theobald, while the bishop added, half insolently, —

[1] Henry III.

"And to myself the reversion of the Archbishopric of Reims when it shall please God to remove the present prelate; whilst my excellent nephew Sir Roger must not miss a fair county, Ponthieu or Dreux."

"Your nephew?" sneered De Ormoy, who had been watching the wrangle with open scorn.

"Yes, my sister's son, a noble youth, *puer fortis, ingenuus et piissimus.*"

"Holy Mother!" swore the freebooter, striking his thigh and bursting into a horse-laugh; "how many 'nephews' you surpliced gentry have! So 'your sister' was his mother."

"Be silent, man of sin," ordered the bishop, turning grave. And I think then and there they would have quarrelled, had not Alithe, who had been speechless since her father's coming, suddenly thrown up her white arms and burst into a trilling laugh.

"Oh, wise, wise old story—of the hunters who divided the bearskin before they first had killed the bear!" cried she.

"Your ladyship is right," asserted Peter, almost sheepishly; "we can parcel the hide later. We cry your pardon. Noble chamberlain, direct us."

"First of all, there is the Provençal," began De Coucy, pragmatically; "on her hangs everything. We must make her guilt patent before France, so that no one dare point the finger at us when the king takes another wife. The crime of her flight with an avowed lover, coupled with the irregularity of her marriage, will silence the most scrupulous canonist."

"And do with her—what?" queried the Breton, at which De Ormoy tapped his hand against his dagger. Alithe showed her white teeth, but said nothing. Theobald, however, thrust out angrily:—

"Hark you, my lords. If this is your chess game, I'm

a pawn in it no longer. I would we could crush the king down knightly wise, as man to man. If we cannot, let us dip no hand in the innocent blood of women "

"While the Provençal lives it will be awkward. Taken red-handed in flight, a flagrant crime, dishonor to the majesty of France — there'll not want extenuation." The chamberlain's smile was insinuating, but Theobald pulled at his little yellow beard fiercely.

"I have said it. Neither the lady nor Gui of Provence whom you have baited into this trap must lose a hair. The thing lies on my soul."

"This is an ill business, my dear Count, for tender souls," said De Coucy, still smiling; "yet I see that we must humor you. It shall be as you wish. But time is pressing us hard. You and my Lord Peter understand your task — the chapel of St. Lucie in Aumône."

"I understand," retorted Theobald, still very sour, "and understand too well that when one strikes hands with Enguerraud de Coucy, one must brave it through with the very devil."

"The devil, fair sir, is an exceeding sage and unfathomable counsellor; you do overpraise my humble skill and wisdom." And with this passing of thrusts the two counts went out, to be followed shortly by De Ormoy, bearing the chamberlain's orders to bring his men over the bridge as swiftly and quietly as he could, and to be ready for three bright torches waved from above the postern. When the twain were alone, De Coucy turned to his daughter, and she ran into his arms.

"My father, my noble father, you have planned everything! I am proud of you!"

"It was all for you, daughter, all for you." But they both knew he lied, and Alithe gave a charming laugh.

"No, it was not for that. Yet it is you that deserves to wear the crown, not I. For we shall conquer. We shall raise the De Coucys above all the great houses of France — Anjou, Aquitaine, Burgundy, Artois. Where will be the power like to ours?"

He held her away from his face, that he might look on all her beauty.

"*Sancte Spiritus*, how handsome you are! And you are my child! Ah, if I could only give you a fairer husband than this *fainéant* king!"

"But a fairer husband would not be a king, sweet father," said she, smiling still more bewitchingly.

"You are very right; after all, there must be flies in every pot of honey. Besides, it is not the crown that makes the monarch, though that will befit you rarely."

Alithe laughed again, then grew graver.

"There's one thing I little like."

"What is it?"

"You have promised no harm shall befall the Provençal. This will breed trouble."

"You saw how Theobald insisted. Lucifer catch the count! He is not a reasonable man. If his conscience troubles, let him double his vow to his St. Isodore of Troyes, as we have done. That is the best physic. But I dared not quarrel with him."

Alithe made a gesture with both arms.

"Ah, yes, quite good; but to hold the Provençal prisoner means letters to Rome and storms from Count Raymond, while canonists and legists wag their heads and turn over books. The Papal legate asks questions. The provosts of Paris ask questions. The Holy Father, the Pope, may take up her cause. There is long delay."

Two candles stood on the table close by the chamberlain.

"Let me have Blanche of Castile in a convent, and your king in my hands, I will puff that Provençal out like this." And he blew one of the candles out as he said it. Whereat Alithe clapped her hands.

"There spoke the Sire of Coucy," cried she, and would have praised him more, had not a tapping at the door forced them to open to one of the queen mother's waiting women, who told Alithe that her mistress desired her company. The young lady was not pleased, but she could only obey.

"Do not suffer her out of your presence," was her father's whispered warning; "remember our deer all rush into one net to-night." And then when she came close again, he kissed her. "One year, or less, far less — one month, perchance, and I kiss the queen of France."

⁕   ⁕   ⁕   ⁕   ⁕   ⁕   ⁕

Never had Alithe found her mistress so exacting, so unlike her coldly placid self. The struggle with Louis, his defiance, the violent parting, had shaken the White Queen to the foundations of her soul. "I have never seen her so aged and haggard before," thought the young De Coucy; "and yet men still say she is one of the loveliest women of France."

Blanche's pride kept her silent — her high Spanish pride which locked her out from friendly touch or sympathy. Yet Alithe had not been two moments with the queen ere she knew something was not well. She guessed the king's strange departure was perhaps a cause; yet even she, — as she looked on the cold, inscrutable face of the woman whose iron will and unerring wit had crushed down every rebel lord, — even she shuddered as a fearful thought crossed her. "Can it be that she knows the plot? Can it be that she will ruin all?"

But a few moments more were reassuring. Blanche was plainly in some great distress and denied herself all comfort. Alithe sought vainly to divert her.

"Will your Grace have me play to you on the zithern?"

"There were enough ungodly melodies twanged by the jongleurs at the fête. There is no need for more."

"Or shall I read from that new and diverting romance of Flamenca, which Father Foulque brought from Paris? The king has praised it."

"The king! the king!" Alithe trembled at the storm that she had raised. "So he praised it, mistress, and who were you to hang upon his folly? The king, my son, is but a stubborn fool in all such matters, I would now tell you. He has the judgment of a bat, a crow! I will not hear your empty romance of Flamenca."

"Or does it please your Grace," said Alithe, with dove-like glances of submission, "that I read from some good and holy book which you have often praised as edifying? A homily of St. Bernard, or of Peter Damiani"—again she was ended by an outburst scarcely less violent.

"When I desire holy books, a holy man shall read them. You are not my chaplain, girl, though you make some boasts of Latin."

"Or would your Grace try my poor skill at chess?"

The White Queen nodded sullenly. She had learned the hard lesson of royalty, that princes dare not make themselves too absurd. Chess was a game frowned on by the sterner churchmen, as first cousin to dicing; but Blanche that night was in no mood for such nice scruples. Alithe drew forth a splendid chess-board of gold and rock crystals. Saladin had given it to Philip Augustus. The men were of gold and silver; but alas! gold and silver did not make the White Queen's play the more skilful.

P

Alithe won piece after piece without the least exertion, and the game ended abruptly.

"I cannot play to-night, my head is giddy," spoke Blanche, thrusting back the board when Alithe offered a second battle.

"Your Grace is unwell, and would best retire."

She never had an answer. The door of the queen mother's chambers opened suddenly, to give entrance to a woman, pale and excited. Alithe recognized her as Alienor, one of the waiting maids of Margaret. She did not stop even to courtesy, but spoke by gasps and jerks.

"*Ai, ai*, something has happened! Oh, my mistress! Very terrible, I am sure! What must be done?"

All Blanche's cold majesty returned in an instant.

"Speak plainly, girl; what are you raving about? If the queen consort is ill, send for the physician."

"She is not ill, but ah, madam, how can I begin to tell? We, her women, do not know what to hope or what to fear. She had but just returned from the fête when the king came to us, as we unrobed her, and sent us from the room."

"Yes; but be calm and do not wring your hands. Tell the truth, and you will not be hurt."

Alienor only wrung her hands the harder.

"Surely, merciful madam, surely! But what is the truth? The king flies out with a terrible face like thunder-clouds, and never looks at us, but clashes the door. We are not summoned back. Presently, after a very long time, we are thinking it best to go and knock, when my Lord Gui of Avignon comes up the stair."

"Gui of Avignon!" Even the White Queen took a long breath and leaned forward.

"Surely it was he, and with him Monseigneur, the

Bishop of Beauvais. Sir Gui goes in; the bishop waits
without. We watch him through a crack in the door to
the antechamber. Voices are raised high. Sir Gui's
voice, and our mistress's. Sir Gui comes out, and stands
talking with the bishop a moment. They both go in together. More voices. Her Grace seems very much dis-
tressed. Then Monseigneur comes out alone and goes
away, then Sir Gui goes out, by great leaps, looking not
to right or left. We start for the door. It is bolted from
within. We knock. Her Grace's voice bids us to go away.
We hear her running swiftly to and fro, to and fro, and
opening presses. Then Gisla, who serves with me, sets
her eye to the keyhole, and swears she saw her Grace
putting on a coarse bliaut and riding-hood, likewise taking
her jewels from her casket and hiding them in a little bag
in her bosom."

"Do not lie, wench!" commanded Blanche, sternly.

"*Ai!* pity, sweet madam. Gisla tells me all this, not
myself. But still the door is shut. We are in terror.
Something strange is about to happen. So I come to
you."

Blanche was drawing on her gloves with swift energy.

"You have done right, Alienor. Come, Alithe, we go
to my daughter instantly."

For once the young De Coucy winced. She had reason
enough for not wishing the White Queen to stand between
Gui of Avignon and his purpose. Others could best do
that.

"Your Grace is very unwell," she began; "I will go
alone — or my father —"

"Where the honor of France is staked, as is now manifest," spoke the Castilian, arising in her pride, "it is *I* who
will guard the fair name of my son."

"But you said you were unwell."

"I am very well. Take the lamp, Alithe, and follow."

One flash of those compelling eyes, and the younger woman knew resistance was worse than vain.

"Must I go alone!" cried Blanche, upon the threshold.

"I obey your Grace," said Alithe. She lifted the lamp, and went after, thanking Our Lady that Blanche had not at least summoned a guard of yeomen. Was all to be ruined now, by two peering, overcurious girls? Avert it, saints! Yet Alithe could only trust to chance.

The queen mother went down the darkened corridors and up the winding stairs with swift, almost manly strides. But as she went she kept her head bowed, and Alithe heard her speaking, as if to herself.

"Oh, Louis! A king of France brought to this! Would God that I had reared you up to be a man! Oh, Louis, my son! oh, my son!"

CHAPTER XIX

THE MEETING OF THE QUEENS

MARGARET was almost ready. She had not swooned. Her head was going round and round. She wondered at her own calmness. She had asked Gui few questions as to the hows and wherefores of their flight; she knew that she must trust to him or trust to none at all. The thought of leaving Pontoise and the French court cost her never a pang now. No doubt they would be blazoning her infamy abroad in a week; her good name would be sold by all the Paris and Orleans hucksters, along with their Flanders woollens and Chaillot cheeses. What matter? She would be out of the clutches of them that hated her. Her father, her mother, at Arles, would believe her word. "I am white and innocent." She did not care for all the rest of the world just now.

Very carefully she had dressed herself and chosen a sombre bliaut, not too dainty, not too thin. As the prudent Gisla had noted, she took her jewels from their casket and hid them in her breast. Only one jewel she did not take. The wedding ring with its huge ruby, which Louis had set on her finger that fatal day at Sens, she tore off, and striding to the window, flung it far into the night. Blackness it had brought her; to blackness let it return. Yet she hoped it would be found and brought to Louis; then might he know how utterly she had spurned him.

She had bidden the maids cease knocking and go away, and trusted they had obeyed her. Once or twice before, she had thus barred them out, and she did not see why their curiosity should waken; but she did not reflect that the king's, the bishop's, and Gui's strange comings and goings would make Gisla's and Alienor's ears prick high.

One real sorrow alone fastened on Margaret now when she thought of departure. She must leave Falaise. The blind girl sat dumbly in her hiding place, giving the same kind of mute sympathy that one gets from the presence of a faithful though silent dog. Only at last, when Margaret ran in behind the curtains, to the little inner room, Falaise clasped her tightly.

"*Ai!* but you have put off all your soft and beautiful dress, and are in this coarse stuff. It cannot be I heard aright. You will not fly —"

"And why not fly?" said Margaret, almost wondering.

"Oh, is it not a mortal sin?"

"A sin to quit this den of vipers? this man who is not my husband? this cruel woman who is not my mother-in-law? No, no, Falaise! God is most angry with me; but He is not so angry as to forbid that I fly back to those that love me."

"And do you love this Gui?"

"Have I not said I do not? He is only a friend, and plays the part of a knight."

"The world will not say that, dear Margaret," said the blind girl, soberly, and fixing her bright though sightless eyes upon the Provençal.

"I care not what the world says, for I know what my heart says. I have been tricked, outraged in that which a woman holds most dear. I cannot suffer it. I wish I could go mad. Since I may not, I must therefore fly."

Falaise took both the other's hands within her own, and stroked them tenderly, lovingly.

"How hot they are! You are burning up like poor little Nicole. So you think you are not the king's own wedded wife? You are quite sure?"

"You heard. The bishop swore it. The bishop who joined us in that mock marriage. Oh, Holy Mother! if I could dare to doubt!"

"Yes,—but I did not like Monseigneur's voice. Boso has brought me a story of late, how he is a most evil man, even though he wears a mitre."

"I know it; but he swore—"

"Hark!" interrupted Falaise; "footsteps on the stair!"

"Gui and his squires—alas! and we must part. God keep you—" But Falaise shook her head.

"No feet of men: it is the step of women."

"I have sent my maids away. Who dares to come?" And Margaret started toward the door.

Falaise rose, and almost dragged her friend away. "You will be taken. Fly through the sliding panel and by the winding stairs."

But Margaret waited, alert, high-strung, poised like a deer ready to spring this way or that.

"Wait—if only women, I will know their purpose."

Then a loud knock shook the room, and Falaise begged still harder. "Come, come, or all is lost."

But Margaret, guided by some prescience, went straight to the door, and Falaise was wise enough to shrink back noiselessly into her hiding.

"Open. I command you open!" And Margaret, who knew that voice, did not tremble but opened instantly. A flash of another lamp, and into the room swept three women, the White Queen and two more. Margaret fell back before she faced them, then stood drawn to full height, with her hands hid in the folds of her dark cloak. She seemed one figure of gloom in that dimly lighted chamber, save as her face shone out with an unearthly brightness from beneath her close-drawn hood. Blanche let a moment pass in silence, while her swift eye roved through the room as if in quest of some intruding lover. The search failing, she came back to the Provençal.

"You are dressed, mistress?" said she, coldly.

"It is not late, please your Grace," replied Margaret, with a mildness fit harbinger for a storm.

"I presume Father Foulque assigned as a penance," continued Blanche, her lips curling in scorn, "that the queen of France spend the evening in this sad-colored riding-cloak."

"I dare not contradict your Grace," said the Provençal.

"Let us have an end to prattling," darted the White Queen, growing warmer as she saw the boldness of the sinner. "Why are you dressed in this strange fashion? Why have you thus barred out your maids? The king, the bishop, that Gui of Avignon — why have they all come to you? Speak — I bid you — speak!"

Margaret made one gesture toward the door, which Alienor understood. "Go," she directed, but Alithe stood still, and the Provençal's color rose.

"Madam," said she to Blanche, "I answer you nothing, — nothing until that woman," with a glance at the De Coucy, "gets herself hence."

Alithe was angry. She would have liked to twist her fingers about Margaret's slender neck; but she could only courtesy meekly and obey when Blanche turned on her with —

"Her Grace is right. A queen is answerable only to a queen. Shut the door fast, Alithe."

But when the door was shut, a great change came upon

Margaret. She seemed to shake all over, then held out her hands.

"Why have you come to torture me? Have you not wrought woe enough? Will you not gain back your son? Will he not set his love to you above his love to me? Oh, let me go in peace!"

Blanche of Castile was as hard of soul — I need not say it again — as ever a woman might be, and yet be good. But in that voice, that gesture, there was something that stirred her deep within. She knew she was in the presence of a sister woman in infinite distress, and her answer was tinged perchance with unwilling softness.

"I would not torture you. I do not understand! What have I done?"

"Done!" echoed Margaret, with a kind of laugh; "you have had your will. I know it, and therefore I go away."

Whereat for one of the first times in her life the White Queen was puzzled.

"You know — know what? That you do not love Louis my son?"

The Provençal's face seemed to twitch all over. "Dear Lord Christ, not that! I have seen the bishop. He has told everything — Sens — your orders to him — how he obeyed you. No — do not start. I will not curse you for your sin, for I have cursed you already. You have taken my husband from me; you have taught him his wife is not his wife. So, let me speed back to the pleasant South, and see if God can heal my pure heart and forgive your dark one."

But here the wrath of the White Queen arose, when Margaret praised herself.

"Your heart is pure? And will you fly alone? or in

what gallant cavalier's brave company? A courtly, innocent, and diverting tale to spread through the châteaux of
France."

"I have considered all of that, your Grace," said Margaret, with a chill earnestness that told Blanche how useless
was her own grim banter.

"Then you are sunken indeed. I do rejoice my Lord
Bishop told you. I was long mindful to tell my son that
he was not bound by fetters which Holy Church could
never cut asunder. But now—"

"Blanche of Castile," spoke the Provençal, in so strange
a tone that the older woman grew more amazed than ever,
"do you swear to me that Louis did not know there was a
flaw in the bond that made us man and wife?"

"He did not; well for him if he had. Your snares about
him had been quicker snapped."

"O Mother of God, have mercy on me!" said Margaret, not aloud, but in a low whisper, that made Blanche's
wonderment deeper still; but her righteous pride was rising, and she was not too saintly a woman to refrain from
meting out admonitions to the wicked.

"Well for him, I say, if he had. But I have perchance
been culpable. Ah! even you, evil-hearted woman of the
wanton South, would have pity on his guileless innocency,
could you have seen my son. This moment, no doubt, he
beseeches God to prove you guiltless, little knowing that
whilst he prays his well-loved wife makes ready to fly with
her old paramour."

"Speak it again, ah, again, that still he loves me!"

"Such is his folly, sinful girl. Your stony heart is too
hard ever to think on his grief when his last dim hope is
fled and the world points the finger at your shame—"

Margaret interrupted with a cry,—not a sob, or groan,

or laugh, but all in one. She came closer to the White Queen, stretching out her hands, and groping after the fashion of the blind. And then she repeated in one tone, each word by itself : —

"And — you — say — he — still — has — hope ? "

"That you are innocent. *Ai*, what is happening to your eyes ? Surely you are not turned mad ? "

For perchance the first time in her life, Blanche was truly frightened, by the look on Margaret's face.

"I think I am turned mad ! I know I am ! I feel it ! Oh, your Grace, oh, you are not too hard to pity me ! My husband still trusts me ! Am I waking from a hideous dream ? No, do not thrust me by ! I am strong ! I can bear up ! But what am I saying ? "

"Plainly, you are unwell." Blanche began to look about her. She did not know whether to rain curses or tears on the Provençal. The White Queen moved toward the door, Margaret following step by step.

"Alithe," Blanche was about to call ; but before the call the door flew wide and through it, booted and girded, strode Gui of Avignon.

I know not which stared the more blankly, the White Queen or he. Gui sent his hand to his sword as by second nature, but dropped the hilt after a curse. One cannot draw on a woman. But the sight of Margaret, darkly wrapped, with her white, outpeering face, sent him past Blanche, and upon his knees before his countrywoman.

"Away, away, all is ready ! Then, ho, for the red spur and the race to merry Provence ! "

Gui had never overmuch discretion. The crisis stole all that he ever had. He held Margaret's hands so tight she might not tear them away, while once more he pressed burning kisses, and swore a score of times in a breath that he was prepared to hew their flight through five hundred paladins. Only at last could Margaret make him listen.

"I do not love you."

"Ah, all the better; I will conquer your heart as I conquer those who halt us! The nobler victory!"

"I will not fly."

"I know better again! You will be in Chartres tomorrow, the next in Orleans, the next in Bourges."

"Hearken, Gui, hearken, or indeed I think you are possessed of a devil." And she strove piteously to free her hands.

"I am possessed of a devil. A right noble and courtly devil, for whom my house is swept and garnished, the demon of love! Oh, at last! at last!"

"Hearken. Do not rage. There is a frightful mistake. The king does not know there is a flaw in our marriage. He loves me still. I will prove to him that you and I were only friends, and that I am innocent."

All this time Blanche stood stock still and said not one word. Margaret looked from her to Gui, from Gui back again. She did not know from which face she drew less comfort — the stony one or the one on fire with passion. And Gui flew on : —

"He loves you still? After his deeds and words to you and me? His cruelty has crazed you; you know not what you say. But you shall be saved. Away now, no tarrying! The horses wait."

His hands were about Margaret's waist. She struggled and moaned feebly. And still Blanche was silent, wonderstruck. She was a wise woman, but her wisdom gave no key to this wild scene. Should she cry, "Rescue," or bid god-speed to this strange pair who were trailing the fair

fame of France in the dust? Then, at last, Margaret did
what was to Blanche the strangest of all.

"Oh, save me! I will not go with this man. He is
beside himself. He must not take me."

And Margaret stretched out her hands to the White
Queen for help. But Gui was past reason now; the fires
of his Southern blood were raging at white heat. With
marvellous strength he dragged his captive toward the
door. Blanche stood across it, but Gui, with one sweep of
his frantic arm, had dashed her aside.

"Alithe! help! rescue!" Blanche found her voice
at last. It echoed down the dark windings of the great
donjon stair; but echoes were all the answer.

"Alithe, guardsmen, up! A crime against the king!
Are you all turned traitors?"

Gui, with his victim, was vanishing from sight. Blanche
started down the stairs. Another man ran up to greet the
lovers. A yeoman? But the stranger was too young. He
was aiding Gui in bearing down the lady, — Bernart the
squire, clearly, and the three vanished together.

"Alithe!" cried Blanche again; but the tall donjon
seemed to have opened its massy depths and taken the
De Coucy and Alienor into them.

The queen mother ran to the deep recessed window;
the château courts seemed broad pits of blackness, the
sky moonless, overcast. No outcry, no alarm, told the
arrest of the fugitives. A frightful crime had been committed against the honor of France. And where was
Louis to avenge what his mother had failed to forestall?
Why was the castle so still? What meant this conspiracy
of darkness and silence? Was Margaret guilty or an
innocent victim? What had withdrawn the yeomen of
the guard? A numbing sense of impotency smote the

Castilian. All through her widowhood she had struggled with one hope, "Louis will bear the burden worthily at last." Now in this sore test he had turned his back upon her utterly. And the reward for all her love and nurture was but this!

"Alithe!" cried Blanche again. She knew that she was fainting. She clung to the curtain, then blackness came, and for that night the queen mother knew nothing more.

*   *   *   *   *   *   *

But Margaret had not fainted. As Gui and Bernart half bore, half led, her from the donjon, she thought she knew at last how the sparrow felt in the jaws of the remorseless cat: not in great pain, but wholly helpless, motionless, dumb. And with a returning surge it came to her how mad was Gui's project; how mad was she to place her all within the wild troubadour's keeping. "Honor" he might have, but "honor" may suffer strange deeds at times, and Gui of Avignon was the man to do them. And all the time they went she saw Louis' face, and, as if she were drowning, the last scene betwixt them passed before her twenty times. She knew now that his voice was hard because his love was great. She knew now that he had stood betwixt her and his wrathful mother. And she was repaying this love, this championship, by headlong flight. The bishop had lied. The king had never dreamed of a flaw in the marriage. His mother had not told him. Why had she not believed Falaise?

"I will not go! Let me go back, but fly yourselves!"

Margaret pleaded with her guardian a dozen times, and only felt his pace grow longer. She besought him by prayers, she invoked each and every saint, to get one answer.

"I have no saint but St. Margaret! Mother of God, how beautiful you are! Will you, nill you, we fly together, and are never parted!"

Then he did what no man had ever done to Margaret of Provence before, save only her father and her husband: he kissed her face; and a terrible fire seemed to leap from his lips and all over her, the fire of torment.

She never knew how they passed out of the château, while their strong hands hurried her onward. Once she looked up; the tall towers were above their heads, dimly traced against a murky sky. A second time, and the castle was not so near. She heard their feet upon a bridge. Bernart let go her arm, and turned to listen.

"No one follows," declared he; whereat his master slapped his hand upon his sword, and swore by the soul of the incomparable and unconquerable Pierre Vidal that this adventure should be celebrated in the noblest *canson* ever sung in the South Country.

Next they mounted a little hillock. A tiny village sleeping under the hazy night, the faint outline of white houses, the rustling of shadowy poplars, the crowing of a wakeful cock — that seemed all. A churchyard next, gravestones, and a little chapel. Out of the gloom came a figure leading horses, then a swift dialogue.

"You have the horses, Anselm?"

"Yes, and you have the lady, my master?"

"She is here. Lead up the palfrey with the side-saddle. Make sure of the girths."

"Back, back! I will not go with you!" appealed Margaret for the last time. She wished she had been silent, for again Gui kissed her.

"You will go with me to the ends of the earth!" he

cried, and grasped her in his arms to swing her into the
saddle, when a cry from Bernart palsied him. The door
of the chapel was grating, opening; torches waved, and
their red radiance shot over the helmets and cuirasses of
many men.

CHAPTER XX

ALITHE VICTRIX

WHEN Alithe de Coucy went out of the queen consort's chamber, I cannot begin to tell all the evil sprites she was wishing would make away with both Margaret and Blanche. Everything — she knew full well — stood on the edge of ruin, and all because two silly maids must needs eavesdrop! Her first thought was to hasten to her father; her second was to stay. For St. Gabriel himself might well wonder what would happen next; and she might still do something to fend off disaster. When the White Queen sent the De Coucy forth she still carried her head high, as if her heart was not beating overloudly. In the darkened antechamber outside the door stood Alienor and Gisla, pale and almost whimpering. Alithe pointed down the stair.

" Of what you have just seen or heard, say nothing, not even in your prayers to Our Lady, unless my father or I command you. Disobey, and your tongues are cut out of your heads. Now go — instantly."

"Yes, yes," mumbled the shivering maids, and away they went. Alithe was at least a little happier to be alone. She could hear the rush of words inside the door — now high and distinct, now falling and hidden. She could guess well that neither queen was sparing the other. Though the moments crept slowly, Alithe realized that the end was coming near. How soon before the White Queen

would be calling for the yeomen ?   But, praised be Our
Mother of Consolations, the chamberlain had seen to that.
She would call for them in vain.   In a like case Alithe's
father would have begun to pray ; but Alithe did not.   She
liked to invoke the saints, but life was so warm, real, de-
lightful, that help from tatter-clad martyrs and anchorites,
who had mouldered in the cold ground these thousand
years, did not seem very real.   Once or twice the smallest
ray of something akin to pity for the Provençal touched
Alithe.   She was never wantonly cruel.   If only the Al-
mighty had not made it necessary to brush Margaret from
her path !   The world was strangely made; and Alithe was
so sure that she could have fashioned everything much
better.   Yet here she checked herself with a start.   One
must not have blasphemous thoughts to offend God at a
crisis like this, when so much depended on His good
humor.

And then of a sudden came the expected step of Gui.
Close by the door was a niche — unlighted, deep.   Alithe
shrank into it to let the Provençal pass.   There was just
light enough for her to catch the glance and passion of his
face and eye, and she took courage.   More fierce words ;
and then Alithe realized that Margaret was appealing to
Blanche to defend her from Gui.   The lady shivered all
over.   Never — never must those two women be suffered
to meet again.   Next followed the hurried opening of the
door — Gui half dragging, half bearing, his countrywoman; the White Queen following to the stair; the
coming of Bernart; the vanishing of Gui and his victim.
Alithe saw everything, and, when Blanche called her
name, shrank deeper into her niche and kept silence.   If
the White Queen had really striven to quit the donjon the
De Coucy would have stayed her flight by force.   But

Blanche sped back into the chamber. Alithe heard her running to and fro, as from window to window; then another call, thin, quavering — "Alithe!" — followed by a heavy fall. The younger woman did not falter now, but entered quickly. The queen mother lay on a heavy rug above the rushes, silent, motionless.

Dead? But as Alithe knelt and felt for the heart, there answered a fluttering, and the De Coucy was glad. She did not require the queen mother's death, and yet this swoon would be very useful. She dragged a silk pillow from the divan and thrust it under Blanche's head; then sent one glance about the chamber. Empty! Whereat Alithe arose, and took the key of the door.

"She will revive of herself presently, and by that time all will be well," she reflected, as she locked the door from the outside, and with nimble feet ran down from the donjon. In the shadow of the entrance a man sprang out to meet her — her own father, who had been watching Gui's happy flight, and who swore big vows of gratitude to his favorite saints when he learned how close the queen mother came to wrecking all.

"De Ormoy is ready?" asked Alithe, in his ear.

"Ready with three hundred lurking just outside. Besides, all the gentlemen and knights in Peter's and Theobald's suites are with us if needs be; but they need not draw a sword, only cry 'quarter!' when the blows begin banging."

"And the yeomen?"

"I have withdrawn them from both sally-ports, and there are only two at the postern. De Glui is Joinville's lieutenant —" Alithe grasped her father's wrist.

"Hist! Who are those two coming deep in talk?"

"De Glui himself and their Graces' worthy confessor,

Father Foulque, to be sure. Let me glide off and do you hold them busy. It will not be long."

There was a lantern swinging above the spot where Alithe stood, and she let its rays fall over her upturned face, well knowing what would happen. As two dogs run toward a bone, so the man of God and the man of weapons came toward her. De Glui was in an elegant gilt cuirass of Milan armor, too precious ever to be dinted in battle, and was toying with his little leathern baton, sign that he was officer of the night watch. As for Father Foulque, he was a guileless, learned, and soft-spoken churchman, pious enough, who owed his confidential position solely to the fact that he cried "*Ancilla Domini,*" or "*Verba Dei,*" to everything the queen mother said in his hearing. Having a taste for such matters, he had just been expounding to the guardsman the last disputation at the Paris University as to "what happened if a mouse chanced to nibble the consecrated wafer," when the sight of Alithe sent their wits far away from the Doctors and the Realists.

"Your ladyship chooses a gloomy night for walking abroad," began de Glui, with his courtliest flourish. "Moon, stars, a nightingale's song, the harp of a loyal cavalier — those are the fittest companions for my Lady de Coucy."

"The harp of a loyal cavalier!" cried she, with a radiant beam that made the officer's heart grow warm, "fie! fie! my dear Captain, you will keep those fine speeches for me when we are alone; and do not scandalize this holy father."

"Tut, tut, dear chiid," quoth Father Foulque, grinning from one kindly ear to the other, "we are human, we are men. Though cut off ourselves from the gentle passion, we can rejoice when Prince Cupido —"

"Prince Cupido!" cried Alithe, merrily; "what a name on holy lips."

"Oh, do not marvel," charged De Glui; "yesterday I saw your ladyship walking with Monseigneur of Beauvais, and he said — "

"Hush!" admonished the cleric, holding up a hand; "Monseigneur of Beauvais is a canonical bishop; therefore, let his follies pass in silence; but our saintly and venerable queen mother deigned to tell me only to-day that she should request his Holiness at Rome to consider the many grave charges against him. But as for ourselves, '*Touch not mine anointed*,' enjoins the Scripture."

De Glui held down his head, to show that he took the rebuke dutifully. But Alithe soon made him look at her again.

"So you command the watch to-night, fair sir?"

"Under the noble chamberlain's orders; and I fear I am the only watch there is. For your father, with his usual goodness of heart, has sent half my men to the guard-house, where they lie drunk as fishes. 'A summer's night,' said he, 'and Christians are best in bed.' If there were a foe abroad — "

"Well, there is none."

De Glui bowed very low. "You are right; no foe is abroad; and the only arrows flying are those my Milan mail cannot stay."

"And those are?"

"Shot from the bright eyes of my mistress, Alithe de Coucy." Whereupon the lady could only put her hand to her throat, untie a ribbon, and pass it to the officer.

"For so well turned an answer, dear friend, will you not take this?"

"As more than gold!"

"And wear it on the great tourney Corpus Christi day."

"You entrance me."

"And write my name on your shield."

"I am the proudest knight in France!"

She let him take the ends of two of her long fingers and just touch them with his lips. As for poor De Glui, he was thinking about the seventh paradise, when Foulque caught his arm.

"Hark, what is this?"

The officer drew his sword in a twinkling.

"By the splendor of God! Horsemen approach the castle at fierce gallop!"

"There is some alarm," advised Alithe; "I dare not keep you."

"To the great gate, men," thundered De Glui. "Fiends take you rascals! are you all drunk? Well, come down, then, you sentries, from the walls. And now, warders, do you stand by to raise the portcullis and lower the drawbridge."

His zeal was furious; thanks to stripping all the rest of the castle of its watch, he had speedily a score of pikemen presenting arms inside the gate, when the massy doors swung inward. Alithe stood distantly regarding the scene revealed by many torches. Two dozen horsemen entered, all armed but three, and these with their hands bound behind their backs. Across the saddle of the leader was borne a woman. Alithe was sure of it. Some one uplifted a flambeau, and the light shone fair on Peter of Brittany bearing Margaret of Provence.

*   *   *   *   *   *   *

Lights, shouts, and the hasting of an hundred feet. With one shock and cry the castle woke. They ran from their chambers full clad, half clad, scarce clad at all. Knights jostled grooms, countesses the scullion maids; some cried, " Treason ;" some, " The plague has broken out ;" and each and all stared in fright at his neighbor. The bell above the gate clanged furiously, six frantic hands upon its rope. In the dark court all stood for a time, — quarrelled, trembled, shouted ; and then one impulse caught the bewildered host. "To the great hall!" And there the wild devil that lashes mobs sent them. Ready torches lit all the dangling lamps, which sent a shivering glare across the floor of excited men and women. " The king is deathly ill!" " The Flemish count takes arms!" " The emperor is invading!" One rumor was as likely as the other. Then through the midst came De Glui, with his score of pikemen drawn in a hollow wedge; and within it walked Gui of Avignon, sullen, his hands roped behind his back. Then Monseigneur of Beauvais and Theobald of Champagne, and then — how the necks did crane, and the titter of horror rise! — Peter of Brittany and Enguerraud de Coucy, leading between them, held fast, Margaret, queen consort of France.

She was pale, with the pallor of a corpse, not of snow. She was speaking. They could not hear what she spoke in her guardians' ears, but her face was torn with pain. And when the three came to the dais and the two lords would have her mount thereon, all could see her stand and struggle a little before she was lifted by sheer force. All this went on before three hundred pairs of eyes, and you may guess how the silence was deepening whilst De Glui's yeomen formed a line across the dais, making a solid barrier with their crossed pikestaffs.

" The queen consort ! The queen consort with Gui of Avignon !" The names flashed from eye to eye, rather than

from lip to lip.   And ere De Coucy or his fellows had
spoken a word, I think Margaret's name was writ black in
the minds of half the men there present, and — God pity
them — more than half the women.

Had any looked for Alithe, they would not have found
her.   Across the rear of the high hall, above the dais, ran
a narrow balcony, its parapet nigh hidden by the folds of
half a score of mouldering banners of ancient blazonry.
Behind these stood Alithe, seeing everything, but seen of
none.   Yet she almost wished to be seen.   She was so
proud — of herself, of her father, of this night, when every
seigneur and varlet there should learn to know themselves
mere pawns on her great chess-board.

And now at last there was a dead hush.   Enguerraud
de Coucy, first minister of the realm, and, in the king's
absence, master of the court, let go the queen consort's
hand.   Alithe saw her lips move as in one last entreaty,
saw her try to kneel, saw the Bishop of Beauvais step
beside her swiftly and force her to her feet.   The chamberlain came to the edge of the dais and waited till every
eye was answering his, before he spoke in tones that rang
through that deep, crowded hall.

" Give ear, lieges and subjects of the most Christian king
of France ; " and then he told his story, while all looked
from him to Margaret, from Margaret back to him.   De
Coucy's spare form had never swelled to fairer height ;
his smooth voice never rang so close to ringing true.   It
was his moment of triumph.   He enjoyed it to the full.
First he told the court that it was notorious how for days
past the faithful vassals who watched about the king had
been sorely disturbed at the strange and most unchristian
familiarity accorded the knight of Avignon by the presumed queen consort.   And at that word " presumed " one

should have heard the women flutter. He declared that
the favor Margaret of Provence deigned to pay to that
young countryman was flaunted before her husband's very
eyes, and to that fact many who were at the fête would
rise up as witness. The king, pious and stricken with
sorrow in this sore strait, had withdrawn himself to a
pilgrimage chapel in the forest, to beseech the wisdom of
God how to deal with his erring spouse, whilst the queen
mother, also smitten with grief, was at this instant lying
sorely ill.

"One would think," and my lord wrung his smooth and
unctuous hands, "even a woman abandoned to shame would
draw back in such an hour. But Margaret of Provence,
blinded by Satan and her own lusts, would have heaped
crime on crime and defiled the honor of France, had not
her intent been revealed — by a manifest act of God and
St. Germain — to certain of his Grace's loyal vassals. For
since the devil had willed her destruction, he had suffered
Gui of Avignon to carry her away that self-same night in
flight from Pontoise; when, moved by the Holy Ghost to
a Christian and sacred zeal for their suzerain's honor, my
Lords of Champagne and Brittany had laid a trap for the
guilty lovers, and seized them red-handed in their sins."

By this time, I need not tell it, every woman, every
man, had forgotten they were breathing. Gossip indeed
had fastened little on the queen consort till a few days
of late. But charges like these — and vouched for by the
first minister of the realm — you could hear a gown rustle
across that crowded hall! As Alithe leaned from her
balcony, she saw Margaret's face glow like hot iron. She
was trying to speak, but Monseigneur of Beauvais pressed
a silk handkerchief against her mouth. Then like the
crack of a lash rang Gui's voice.

"Cowards! Cowards all! A sword, a sword, fair gentlemen, that I may thrust it down these false lords' throats. Let me fight all at once, and yonder bishop, too. Is there less honor here in France than among Paynims? A sword, I say!"

He struggled so that four pikemen, despite his small stature and the cords, had hard shift to hold him back; but De Coucy only leered at him complacently.

"Peace, my brave 'Pilgrim of Love,' and keep your defiance for the king's high chamber at Paris." Then he turned to Peter of Brittany. "And now, my lord, give your testimony, that all the gentlefolk of France may know the manner of woman we have called 'queen consort' of our king."

The Breton held up his hand to make oath.

"Hear, then, and Our Mother of Rennes be the witness. I took Margaret of Provence out of the arms of Gui of Avignon at the Chapel of St. Lucie at Aumône, even as he was lifting her upon a palfrey ready for flight."

"And you, my Lord of Champagne?" demanded De Coucy. Theobald had not looked up all the time he stood upon the dais. Now he raised his hand, but not so high as Peter's, and his tone too was clear.

"I swear I was with the Count of Brittany, and saw all that he has said."

"And you, Monseigneur of Beauvais?" spoke Enguerraud.

The bishop's face was crimson as Margaret's. Perhaps it was only too much old Montargis. The silence was deeper yet when he began, his voice like harsh metal.

"Hear then, Christians and true lieges of France. For what I tell now has been on my conscience long, yet would not be uttered save as this woman has cast off every right to mercy by her sin. Know, therefore, what she truly is. For I confess to you that at Sens, by the commandment of the queen mother, at the wedding of our lord the king, I did make such errors in the service of marriage that there may well be grievous doubts whether she be canonical wife of his Grace the king, or lawful queen of France." Then turning upon the prisoners, and stretching forth his hands, "And now may God, Our Blessed Lady, and Peter, Prince of the Apostles, have mercy upon your guilty souls, for man dares to have none. Amen."

But the pikemen who had taken the place of Peter and his Reverence in holding Margaret were less hardened to their task. Being only peasant born, not courtly knights and gentle seigneurs, they pitied her. The handkerchief fell from her mouth. She glided from their hands. She ran to the edge of the dais, and Alithe trembled lest she leap down into the pressing throng. Then with the cry of some harmless hunted thing dying at bay, Margaret called clearly : —

"Oh, people, friends, dear friends who hope in God, rally, stand by me, and do not hear these lies. Wait till the king returns. Let him judge all. The chamberlain has lied. The bishop thrust me on. It was he who drove me mad ! De Coucy is my enemy."

So far the chamberlain had suffered her ; now with a strong hand he seized her shoulder, and strove to force her back. She struggled there in the sight of all, desperately at first, trusting a few at least would spring forward with their aid. She did not know that scarce a pitying eye was on her. And as De Coucy thrust her back she sent a despairing curse at the bishop.

"Remember this night's work, when I rise up to blast your soul on God's great judgment day !"

A raving woman's threat; but it sent all the blood out of Monseigneur's cheeks, and being a cowardly man, he did a coward's deed. He beckoned to the silent people.

"Away with this vile woman from the earth!" He used worse names than that. "What need of courts, of judges? Her guilt is manifest. Avenge your king and the polluted honor of France. Away with her and with her paramour!"

It was the word to snap the cord long strained too near to breaking. Instantly the hall seemed rising as one man. One shout rang up against the shadow-hung rafters.

"*Mort! Mort!* Death to the vile Provençal! Death to the troubadour! Avenge the king! Hack both in pieces!"

So many rushed toward the dais now that they strove with one another, halting their own progress. Then the swords came out — ten, twenty, fifty, all flashing red in the lamp-light, waving, clashing together. And the shout pealed louder till the trailing pennons shook — "*Mort! Mort!* Avenge the king!"

Alithe leaned from her balcony. She saw Margaret standing facing the raging multitude. The Provençal was saying nothing — who could have heard her? Her head was bowed. She had drawn a little gold cross from her bosom, and her lips moved. Alithe guessed she was praying. The barrier of the handful of pikemen was almost swept away. Knights, barons, a wild-beast fury driving them, were leaping on the dais. Alithe looked away. She was delicate — the young De Coucy. She did not wish to see Margaret falling under those swinging swords. Then a voice — Theobald's voice — rang even above the din.

"Hold, seigneurs of France! We are no assize to judge this man and woman. God and the law have not spoken the final word. Our king can avenge himself —"

"*Mort! Mort!* Stay, who dares — we will do the avenging!"

The swords danced closer; but Theobald, who held his place manfully as became a peer of France and a famous cavalier, swept his own blade out.

"Fair sirs!" cried he, "I swear to you, you shall touch these prisoners only across my body."

It was one will against an hundred, but the hundred paused. Men looked in the great count's eyes and knew he would keep his oath. Yet, I know not whether the next surge would have been forward or back. But in that instant of silence a rending crash shook the great hall, and some of the lamps jarred out. Then at the door pealed a shout of terror.

"Arm! For the love of God, arm! Pontoise is attacked!" And after that, few there were who gave two thoughts to Gui or to Margaret.

CHAPTER XXI

MARGARET IN PROFUNDIS

How De Ormoy took Pontoise as he had been commanded, without slaughter or rapine, almost without spilling of blood, I will not tell. De Glui's luckless yeomen — for the most part snoring — scarcely woke to strike ten blows before they found all lost, and bawled out "Quarter!" Half the court was ready to cry "Amen!" to any deed in which De Coucy and the great Counts of Brittany and Champagne led the way; and these seigneurs had been the first to join the attackers. It was about midnight when the chamberlain reëntered the great hall, empty now, the last lights flickering dimly in their sockets. With him were De Ormoy, Peter, Theobald, Monseigneur, and Alithe, and their tongues were going fast.

The triumph was complete, yes, complete, so De Coucy was saying, "though to be sure Pons had not yet come in to tell which way the king and De Joinville had taken. But that was a small matter. They could send out and fetch his Grace in the morning."

"Only the king," cried Alithe, clapping her pretty hands. "Poor, simple, guileless, pious king. Yet I am to make him my husband —"

"And *your* husband, dear lady," quoth Peter, with his finest flourish, "is in no wise to be pitied, for he will have France and will have you."

Nevertheless Alithe liked to repeat it all again, "Only the king is left, only the king!"

But here one of De Ormoy's lieutenants, who had taken over the guard of the two prisoners from the now disarmed pikemen, came up and saluted stiffly.

"The lady and the knight —"

"What about them?" demanded his commander.

"They are still here. The knight has a devil in him, and we have had to double-rope him. As for the lady, she is as quiet as a scared fowl. But we cannot keep them in the hall all night."

"This is for you to order," said the free-lance, looking on De Coucy, who in turn looked on Theobald.

"You still persist in your scruples, my lord?"

The count shrugged his shoulders. "Have I not just shielded these people with my life?"

"Very good, then," said the chamberlain, with the least frown. "Separate them, and clap them both in the oubliettes."

"The lady?" asked the free-lance, raising his eyebrows.

"Yes, by God's death, — the lady!"

The trooper saluted again and tramped away, muttering in his mustachios that "orders were orders; but these he did not like." His disliking, however, did not make him in any wise disobedient. Margaret, who had sat for two mortal hours upon a hard oaken bench, not faint, not sleeping, only utterly stunned and numb, was roused of a sudden by rude shaking.

"Wake quickly, mistress!" She rubbed her eyes. A man in battered armor, himself of grim and brutish countenance, was standing over her. She did not even groan, but rose up to go with him. Three other such men were grasping Gui. The troubadour was making a last struggle. Alas, for that poor thing — his pride! If only knightly hands had conquered him, his cup of woe would have been

not half so bitter. But for the " Pilgrim of Love," the
sagest and wittiest cavalier in the South Country, to be
haled away by three ignoble churls scarce better than
bandits — breaking on the wheel was not worse than this!
Vainly he writhed, kicked, swore. It was Margaret's
voice that recalled him partly to his senses.

"Do you not see, fair sir, that all your struggles give
merriment to these hounds? We can at least prove our
gentle blood by patient suffering."

Gui stopped cursing, and looked on her. He knew that
however shamefully they two had been betrayed, he himself was the prime author of Margaret's calamity, and, so
far as his proud, passionate little soul suffered him, he was
sorry.

"Alas! noble, incomparably beautiful mistress, into
what disasters have I dragged you? Not the sorrows
of Roland's Aude, nor of Berte espoused to that gallant
though unfortunate cavalier Girart of Roussillon —"

"This is no 'court of love,'" cried Margaret, sternly,
and with her head high, "and telling of other sorrows can
make our own no less. These creatures are come to part
us. Whether we shall meet in this world again, I know
not. You have wrought me great ill; but much of the
folly was mine, and God has ordered that we both suffer.
I forgive you."

"Permit me, varlets!" Gui ordered the troopers, and
they, not being wholly stone-hearted, let him draw near to
the lady, bend, and kiss her hand.

"Farewell, peerless though ill-fated star of my life!"

"Farewell!" answered she, very coldly, and stood, dry-
eyed and steadfast, looking after him as he was led away.
Then a hard hand clasped her wrist also.

"Come. it is commanded —"

"Where are you taking me?"

"To the oubliettes, surely."

She twitched once to tear away, but the grasp on her wrist was like iron. Useless! The trooper heard one little sobbing cry, and then both went on together in perfect silence. The soldier, I say, did not love his task, but as the eyes of a cart-horse are guided by his blinders, so obedience to the will of a captain was the screen that held this trooper secure against all distractions of pity, or, had Margaret tried it, persuasion. But she, like Gui, was proud, and even as they walked she never forgot that the blood of a sovereign prince was hers, and that she had been yoked in marriage, lawful or unlawful, to a king of France. Where she could not command, she would not supplicate.

Out of the hall and into the open court, where through a rift now in the clouds were peeping a few stars, they went; into the castle again and through chambers and guard-rooms, where De Ormoy's vagabond troopers were disporting themselves after their easy victory, opening great butts of Gascon or of hard Normandy cider. And Margaret heard foul words and foul songs, and craved to shudder, but could not. Nothing could seem to make her tremble now. Then she was being led downward, and her keeper was calling a deaf old turnkey, who was just returned from despatching Gui. After long shouting in his ear he took a great bunch of keys and a lamp and led their way. Downward and downward yet, the stairs narrow, steep, and hewn in the rock, while blackness closed in before, behind, and the little lamp spread only a narrow circle of wan light. Then a long corridor, so low that the trooper could scarce stretch his tall height upright. Margaret saw a line of little doors let into the wall of virgin

R

limestone. The turnkey set down his lamp, fumbled for a key, and opened. A little chamber — floor, walls, ceiling, all of living rock, no window visible. The turnkey was a man with eyes and ears, but no heart — else he would never have kept his office in Pontoise; yet even he looked twice at the prisoner.

"My Lord de Coucy commands the castle, but has he commanded *this?*" he asked the trooper.

"Ay, by the Trinity, and do not gape and question!" The jailer twisted his clawlike fingers like little writhing snakes.

"I trust this lady is not to be kept here long."

"That is no business of yours or of mine. I only know, if you let her slip through your meshes, it is the worst day's fishing of your life."

"Oh, as it pleases your worship," whimpered the fellow. And Margaret felt a hand thrusting her inward, while in a twinkling the door clattered behind her, and instantly down shut the night.

She stood a moment or two, listening as the barrier was locked and bolted, and the muffled footsteps died away outside. Then in one wave the horror of her condition smote her. She flung herself against the door, struggled, strove, shrieked in abject fear, and fell back only to strive and groan again. The silence and the dark were plunging her in torment. She was in utter blackness. She ran about the narrow circuit of her cell, — stone, stone, always cold hard stone, and she was back at the door again, and there was no end to the blackness. Ever since Peter of Brittany took her, she had been ready for death. She did not fear that. Her heart was pure. Our Blessed Lady and her Dear Son would receive her to their heaven, which was fairer than all the joyous South Country, and where the angels were kinder than her sisters. But for this death-in-life — by what prayer, the intercession of what saint, might she make ready? She only had one question now — "How long does it take to die?" And the answer brought small comfort.

The oubliettes of Pontoise were not damp, being high above the river. A hidden shaft dispelled the foulness of the air. And Margaret had not lived in this world without hearing tales of how one could last five, ten, twenty years in such a tomb, and yet keep living after memory and reason had long sped. Once in her father's court at Arles they had taken from the oubliettes a woman. The jailer said that the grandfather of the present count had cast her in. Her crime was forgotten, but she was a fair young maid when she entered the prison; — when she came forth — Margaret did not let her wild brain drag her further. Tired of wrestling with the hopeless door, she tried in vain to think how she might pray. Could saint or angel hear a prayer with a mountain of stone betwixt the suppliant and their bright unbounded heavens? Margaret scarcely dared to answer "Yes!" But she was calm enough at last to feel for her little cross, to fold her hands, and think of what she must say. "Our Lady of Pity," — yes, she must hear, as pity was not in sky or earth. But Margaret never began. Steps in the gallery brought down her thoughts to earth. Nearer, nearer, — then the door opened. A flash of red light, something pushed inside, the light gone, the door clashing and being bolted. But Margaret knew her prison held another, and spoke.

"Who is this?"

A cry, part joy, part anguish, answered her, "Margaret!"

"Falaise!" she cried, and no darkness hindered when they both embraced.

They sat together hand in hand on the dry floor, while Margaret rained her questions eagerly.

"You tell how you went out to the queen mother, after some one, you think Alithe, had left her?"

"Yes, — I said that."

"And that you did what you could to revive her, and that she is not dead?"

"She is not dead, though when she woke she seemed sadly stricken, moaned, 'Louis! Louis!' and was too weak and dazed to rise."

"Bless God she is not dead. It would have been I that had killed her. — So you say you stayed by her a long time, while the uproar told how the castle was being taken, and then Alithe and the chamberlain came up to seek the queen, but did not find you at first?"

"Just as you repeat."

"But why did you not fly through the hidden panel and to your eyrie?"

"Why? — because I was listening to their talk. I know not whether father or daughter is the worse. They have learned the tricks of the Master Devil."

"Yes, yes, what did they say?" and Margaret pressed closer.

"Why tell? You have pain enough already."

"So great, it can never be more; therefore, tell me. Speak, dear Falaise."

"Boso heard aright; you remember him. And I have very good ears and wits if I have no eyes. It is all Alithe's and her father's doing. They have put hatred between you and the king and his mother. Gui has been their dupe, the bishop their ally. Now they have seized the castle, they will fling the queen mother into a convent.

At dawn they will send out and seize the king. De Coucy will be regent. And Alithe —"

"Ah! what will Alithe be? Go on, Falaise, I guess the truth. You cannot hurt me now."

"Alithe will soon be the queen of France, for, thanks to your flight, and the flaw in your marriage, it cannot stand."

Margaret laid her head on the blind girl's lap, and at last came the rush of tears, while Falaise stroked her neck and cheeks with her wonderful hands. Presently the Provençal went on with her questions.

"So as you listened Alithe found you behind the curtain. I wonder she did not kill you."

"I think she wished it. But her father would not suffer her."

"Her father? show pity? *he?*"

"No pity, dear Margaret, but fear. For I will soon tell you how he sought to do me wrong, and then drew back when I threatened Heaven's anger. He called me witch, sorceress, whose blind eyes could see better than a cat's, yet vowed that 'killing me would breed ill-luck.' Then he cried out, 'Away to the oubliette with her; we will give her to her Grace the queen consort for waiting lady.' At which Alithe gave a little laugh, that sounded not at all wicked, saying, 'If they both go out together, father, that will be safe enough and soon enough for all our ends!'"

"I see her meaning. We shall be in heaven soon! Ah, sweetest Falaise, can you ever forgive me for bringing you to this? It was I who summoned you to my chamber after Louis fled."

Again Falaise began comforting with her hands. "Forgive you? When they said I was to go to you, full half my terror fled. And I am more sure than ever no truly evil thing can happen to those who love God as do you and I."

"Oh, yes, 'Our Lord will wipe away all tears,' it is promised! But not now. And even with you here the dark is terrible. It is like a great weight on my eyes. To be so far beneath the ground! it drives one mad!"

Falaise rose and began tracing her way around the cell, tapping the wall gently and reaching up. Presently she proclaimed, "I have found it."

"What?"

"The air-shaft. Come beside me, and feel the cool draft on your face. By its touch and smell, I think it is halfway between dawn and midnight. Also I think I know where we are in the oubliettes; it is not very far to a gate, nor are we in the deepest tier of dungeons."

"What does it matter?" groaned Margaret, hopelessly; "we shall never go from this cell except to heaven."

"Did not an angel come to St. Peter when Herod the king made ready to destroy him, and save him not merely out of the oubliette, but out of the hands of sixteen fierce men-at-arms?" said Falaise, naïvely.

"But we are not saints, at least not I. Though, I doubt not, God will pity you, Falaise of the Blessed Voice."

"God will pity us both," said the blind girl. "But I am sure it is close to morning, and you must sleep."

"Sleep! my head is on fire, and bright lights dance before my eyes just because it is so dark."

"Nevertheless," said Falaise, with quiet authority, "you must sleep. Wrap your cloak about you, so; and lay your head upon my lap, and I will smooth your face and sing."

And Margaret, obedient as a child, lay down. The floor was hard, but the touch of Falaise made her think of the angels, while the blind girl sang over her one after another of the grand Latin hymns she had learned from Priest Ambroise in St. Maclou.

> "Rising by night we unite in our vigil;
> Joining in psalms will we ever continue,
> And with glad voice unto God sing we clearly
> Our hymns melodious.

> "Thus to the Holy King lift we our chorus,
> Praying that we with his saints be deemed worthy
> Into the high halls of heaven to enter
> And life eternal.

> "Praise then the Godhead, the Triune and blessed;
> Praise then the Father, the Son, and the Spirit,
> Whose glory spreadeth, unbounded and timeless,
> Through wide creation!" [1]

One hymn followed another, and slowly Margaret's waves of sorrow and dread grew quieter. The face of Louis ceased haunting her out of the oppressing dark. Sleep came indeed, dreamless, pangless, and Falaise's head also sank at last. I will not tell of the waking, and the return of the old agony, not so keen as before. At least the darkness had ceased to terrify Margaret. Falaise went to the air-shaft and declared, by the warm balmy breeze that greeted her, that it was quite past noon. As Margaret came beside her, far up the dark inlet there spread out something white and wonderful. One ray of God's pure sunlight, and Margaret looked on it as on a jewel dearer than all that burned in the crown of France. Why had she never thought what a marvellously beautiful thing a sunbeam was? She pitied Falaise; the blind girl could not join her ecstasies over this one unpriced treasure. An hour perhaps she stood looking upward watching it

---

[1] A hymn of Gregory the Great.

creep, creep, slowly along the sides of the air-shaft; and poignant fear possessed her, as she was thinking, "So soon it will go!" She was still watching when the door was unbolted, and opened far enough for the jailer to thrust in his arm and his head, while a lantern flashed.

"Here is a jug of water, my mistresses, and a basket of soft bread. Likewise I have made bold, though perchance exceeding orders, to add this little bottle of wine. It is good wine and will hearten you."

"You are very kind," said the prisoners together, and looked to see the door close instantly. The sudden inrush of light was almost painful to Margaret; but the turnkey stood a moment on the threshold.

"I will tell you something;" and his voice grew confidential.

"What is it? The king is taken?" cried the Provençal, catching at her chief dread.

The turnkey drawled slowly when he made his answer.

"The king is not taken."

"Not taken; the good God bless the word! Are you sure?"

"My Lord de Coucy's men have just returned to the château with their noses down like the tails of whipped hounds. They have searched the forest, have scoured all the pilgrimage chapels in the wood where his Grace may be praying. The king and De Joinville have vanished. If they are not found soon, my Lord Chamberlain will begin to scratch his head."

"Oh, bless you, bless you!" Whereupon the fellow took off his cap.

"Your noble ladyship, I am treating you as my betters command. If I did less than I do, you would in no wise profit, but I should lose my head. But in case it becomes

another time of day with our noble seigneurs in the great
hall yonder, do not forget that I gave you the wine and a
scrap of news."

He was gone before Margaret could throw another word
after him, but he had left a lamp, not lit with oil, but with
something better — hope.   Margaret shook as she grasped
Falaise's hands.

"Oh, the king is not found.   He may still be warned.
If we were free we could tell him all, and could save him.
Oh, we must be free!   His honor, crown, the woe and
weal of France is staked; we cannot let this little bit of
iron and stone undo us all!"

And not knowing what she did, she began to hurl herself again against the door.   But Falaise led her back.

"We must indeed save France, but not by useless blows
and groans.   There is a better way than that."

"Ah, yes, we must pray.   It is not so hard to pray even
in this sepulchre, while you are here.   But you know best
which is the strongest saint in such an hour, St. Laurent,
my own St. Tropheme, St. Denis, who loves the kings of
France, or the Holy Mother."

"Pray to the Lord Christ, for He *must* hear, since only
He is strong enough to save.   And He is not so busy with
His great heavenly kingdom as not to hear our cry in
straits like these."

Then Falaise drew the other down upon her knees, and
I will not repeat all that each said.   Only I think that if
the pure in heart shall see God, they must also be heard by
Him; wherefore two mightier prayers there never rose, not
from the Holy Father at Rome, than from that dungeon.
Yet the first answer seemed perhaps as no answer at all,
for it was this.   Even as they knelt and prayed they heard
feet in the corridor, and thought, "again the jailer," but

when the door opened, and she had finished blinking at the smoking lamp, Margaret saw standing beside the turn-key some one else, a woman, who thrust now the hood back from her face, and Margaret felt herself turning cold and then hot.   Her visitor was Alithe de Coucy.

CHAPTER XXII

THE HAND OF A CHILD

LOUIS the king followed Ambroise the priest out of the manse into the dark street, and I have told how neither saw Pons the squire following them, nor Eblé the footpad following Pons. In the little square, where the torches and bonfires were still blazing, the sport had changed; a contortionist was going through his feats standing on an empty hogshead, and the boys and lasses danced about singing the old song : —

> " He folds himself,
> He unfolds himself,
> And unfolding himself
> He folds himself."

" Stay and watch, dear father," cried many to Ambroise, but he only smiled and shook his head. " I must go to Jean's Nicole; she is very sick, but the good God double all your joy, my children."

So he led Louis away, and as the dark streets closed again around them, the darkness closed about the king also. All Pontoise was glad, was making merry, save he, the lord of Pontoise and of a hundred cities fairer. And out of the dark, turned he right, left, before, behind him, he was seeing one face—Margaret's. The impulse almost came to quit Ambroise then and there — to fly back to the château and his wife's arms, to cry, " I believe all you say. I believe nothing else. Forgive ! " But Ambroise was wise, and had bidden him to follow, and Louis had learned on this fateful day to be humble and obedient.

Down the dusty shadow-veiled streets, and through the Beaumont gate, they went; then in vague tracery Louis saw the spires of Notre Dame and St. Maclou and the remoter donjons of the château lifting above his head. Still downward, and the king heard the rushing of the river nearer, as over a mill-dam. Then a low little house on the margin of the gurgling water, and a thin ray of light creeping out under the door. Ambroise went forward and knocked, to be answered by a man's voice.

"Ah! it is you, father, so kind to come again!"

"I said I would watch with you. How is the little bird?"

"Lord Christ pity us, she does not know us now. She grows worse and worse. You must make haste and anoint her before she goes to heaven."

"Hush; be a man, Jean," admonished the curé; "it is not at that pass yet, praise St. Maclou! Let me in. I have an herb poultice that will do good."

The door opened wide; but the man looked hard at the priest's companion.

"Who is your friend, father?" quoth Jean, scanning Louis from head to toe doubtfully. "This is no place for great knights from the castle."

"This," said Ambroise, taking Louis almost affectionately by the hand, "is the kind knight Sir Roland of Poissy, who, being bent on good works, has consented to share my vigil to-night. Believe me, he will only bless you."

Jean came close to Louis, and the king caught the garlic of the other's breath, as the miller looked him fairly in the eyes.

"I like your face," said the miller, bluntly; "you are not a haughty gallant doing a penance. Come in, sir."

So Louis entered — the first peasant's hut he had ever entered in all his life. Straw beds, a dying fire in a cavernous chimney where a black pot dangled, thick thatch over smoky rafters, a few chests, one bench, a hard earthen floor. The king saw little else. As Jean came back with the lantern, Brigite rose up to greet her guests, and Louis looked on the father and mother, a pair with hard hands, hard bodies, hard faces, — thanks to toil, — yet the last were not unkindly. Their hair was gray; but Louis guessed it was more from labor than from age. Also the king soon saw that they were honest Christian folk, who treated him with that high courtesy which is born in a true man and a true woman, though not as taught by Gui of Avignon. And, almost before he knew it, Louis' first strangeness in the hut was gone, and he was standing beside the smaller bed with Ambroise, who bent over the little maid.

When the priest looked up, he pressed his lips together and said nothing, whereat Brigite and Jean said nothing, but the hard lines about their eyes grew deeper yet; Brigite turned her back on the bed and stood a long time. Ambroise, without a word, began disposing his poultices, his pitcher of herb water, and opening a little hamper of medicines. He did not talk learnedly like the court physician from the school of Montpellier, whose speech was one jargon of "the natural spirits, animal spirits, and logistics of the body," but Louis saw clearly that he knew his craft as clearly as that worthy, and that Nicole was in good keeping.

The little one would toss on the straw, tear away the tattered blanket, and hold out her hands.

"I am so hot! so hot!" she would moan. "Oh, let me

rise up, and bathe in the cool water by the dam! I must run to the fête of the Mass of the Ass."

The mother forced her back with gentle violence, but Louis knelt quickly by the bed.

"How long has she been thus?" he whispered, and Brigite answered dolefully : —

"Since noon she has not known me — not the voice of her own mother!"

"Then you are very weary," said the king, "and I can do as well. Rest for a while, and I will keep the coverings upon your child."

"And who are you, sir," quoth Brigite, flaring up a little, but Ambroise wisely turned his head.

"You will do as the knight says, Brigite," and that order ended her scruples. Louis sat on the earthen floor behind the straw bed, and took Nicole's hand within his own. It almost burned him; but it was a soft, shapely little hand, such as Margaret's might have been — he thought — when Margaret was only a little maid. The dim lantern sent a vague halo over the child's face, now revealing, now concealing its red flush and its lines of sinless mobile beauty. She was an unblown flower still. The hard toil stamped on the father and mother had not yet begun to blight her loveliness. Give back health, take her to the château, let her live her life in cendals and samites, and she would bloom as bright as Alithe de Coucy. "Who maketh thee to differ?" Louis had often heard Father Foulque drone it off in a prosing homily. He never had thought so much on it as now. Presently the child tugged at his hand, and would rise.

"Let go, you hurt, the streets are full of children, the jongleurs' viols are sounding. They are leading out Monsieur the Ass. Let me go, let me run to them!" And then she wandered on about the blue ribbons and orange hand-kerchief she was to buy of Etienne the chapman, a whole "round sou's worth," which sou her aunt in Heronville had given her. But Louis only held fast, and put his face near to hers to comfort her, bidding her —

"Be quiet, like a good maid, and when Our Lady makes you well, you shall have, not a little sou, but a great gold bezant to do with as you list!"

I cannot tell what else he would have promised, had not Brigite recalled him by clapping her hands.

"Ah, fine sir!" cried she, her outraged frugality making her speak loud. "What is this to promise a wee maid though in mere jest? A golden bezant! It is three months' wage for Jean himself. Not even the king dare toss red gold like that!"

I doubt if Louis knew whether to smile or frown at the rebuke. And now came Ambroise to the bed with the cool poultice and a cordial in a little silver cup. After that father, mother, and priest all settled themselves on the bench or in a corner and waited; waited till Louis was sure the night must end and red dawn be breaking, though it had been only one scant hour. Then Brigite crept back to the bed, touched the child's face twice, then gave a little hopeless cry.

"No better, hot, — still hot!"

And Ambroise, stealing beside her, did the same, and shook his kind old head, whereat Louis let go the hand and crept beside the priest.

"Is there no hope?" he whispered softly.

"Yes — in God."

"And in nothing else? No power of man?"

"Were I king of France, I could not save her; nor could you. But yet —"

"What is it?"

Ambroise took Louis by the arm and led him across the room, where the shadows hid from them the haunting faces of the father and the mother.

"Fair sir," said the priest, "you have represented yourself as passing rich. Do you know Jew Haggai who dwells in upper Pontoise?"

"I do not."

"No matter. The Jew is an honest man for one of his creed. Some years since he brought from Cordova a wondrous collection of elixirs of incomparable merit, and, I must say, equally marvellous price. Among others he has one —"

"That may save this child? Oh, fetch it, in Our Lord's name."

"I do not say that. I say if his vial of the elixir of Kairowan will not stem this fever, no earthly power may. Yet I am not sure it can avail, let that be plain to you, and the price is very great."

"How great?"

"Great even to a seigneur. I dared not mention this to Jean. It is folly to approach Haggai with less than ten bezants."

Louis was feeling for his pouch. Then he almost cursed. In the haste of the moment of leaving he had not thought of taking money; De Joinville had enough. When did the king himself need money? And next his fingers touched something on his hand that made him feel a thrill. The ring with the great beryl, which Margaret had given him! The one link which bound him to his wife. He pressed his hand around the treasure, and voices rose up in him, all crying out, "Not so."

"It is a great price, as you say, father," said Louis.

"A great sum. Let it not be on your conscience if you cannot pay it. For, as I said, the elixir is not certain."

Yet now the mother spoke across the dim, bare room.

"Oh, dear father, tell us quick. Must the child die? For it is best to know the worst, and to try to bow to God's will if He must have it so —"

But before she ended Louis had put the ring in the hands of Ambroise, telling him, "Here is a gem-stone of price. If the Jew is an honest man, he will confess its worth is much more than ten bezants. Take it — and let God prosper the elixir!"

Ambroise looked twice at the young man, kindly, wisely, for he knew the words came less lightly than they were spoken. Then he set his hand on Louis' shoulder softly, saying, "Dear sir, I know not whether Nicole will be saved to-night; but this I know, a gracious deed will be recorded up in heaven."

Then he took Jean aside, gave him the ring, and made plain to him all that he must say. The miller took his great iron-headed staff, vowing he would have the elixir or brain the Jew. Soon he went out into the night, leaving the three to watch beside the maid.

Nicole lay silent for a time: then again she began to turn, toss, and moan peevishly.

"Falaise, I want Falaise to put her hands upon my head, and take away the fire."

Louis, as he knelt, stroked the burning forehead, and felt love and great pity flow out with every touch, till presently the little one grew quieter.

"You are not Falaise," spoke Nicole, half awaking from her delirium, "but you are very kind, you are very good, and I will love you —"

"Ah, bless you, sweet child, for that!" said the king, and

then she fell into a sort of wakeful drowsiness, in which Ambroise said she would doubtless continue till after Jean returned.

"We can do nothing," declared the priest, and drew apart into a shadowy corner where, Louis guessed, he was at prayer. But the king himself felt in no mood for prayer, though when was hour for it more meet? He sat himself on the hard earth floor at one side of the low, straw bed, and Brigite sat on the other. Since it was clear that much noise or little was all the same to Nicole, the two fought back their thoughts by talking. He listened to the desperate chatter of Brigite, who plied him with questions for the sake of making conversation.

"So you are a cavalier? Your name is Sir Roland of Poissy, Father Ambroise said?"

"I am called so."

"Poissy is the town of his Grace the king?"

"He was born there."

"And I think he must be a young man of about your age?"

"That is likely," assented Louis.

"Have you ever met the king?" asked Brigite.

Louis raised his eyes and gazed at her truthfully.

"I have never looked on him," he said.

"Not looked on him, and yet you are a cavalier! Well, that's strange, seeing he is in Pontoise château. But I presume he only shows himself to his greatest lords."

"How do you know I am not a great lord?"

"Ah!" cried Brigite, lifting her hands, "you are only a simple knight, I am right sure. No count or baron or Monseigneur ever follows a curé round to his sick. But you are a right noble gentleman, fair sir — that's more than plain, and may St. Maclou bless you as you bless us!

And yet I hoped you had met the king, and could tell about him."

"Why the king? Has he ever wronged you?"

"No, no, but he must be a kind of archangel! I am slow of speech and know not how to say it; yet were kings but common sinful men, I am sure the Lord Christ would never set them up so high above us common folk, who toil and sometimes starve, while that young Louis has all the earth, and sleeps on silken pillows, and wakes with never a care."

"With never a care!" His echo came so fast, that Brigite looked at him quickly, but still spoke out.

"Yes, and why not? What is it to be king save to have every good thing God can send you. A round Auvergne cheese, whenever you like cheese; a Harfleur herring, whenever herring; the brightest bliaut, — ay, and have the loveliest wife in France. And what is beyond that?"

"The loveliest wife?"

"Why, yes; I've heard her Grace Margaret is an angel born. And as for the queen mother, she is wise as a man; and if the king likes best to sit at home, or hunt, or feast, or kiss his pretty wife, and know that, being king, no man can steal her from him,   what is it to him, I say, if his mother rules the realm, and people mutter 'girlling'? He is king; he can do as he will."

"It is a great and terrible thing to be a king," said Louis, so solemnly that Brigite looked again at him.

"Well, I do not think his present Grace finds it very terrible," quoth she, sharply; "yet sometimes — "

"Sometimes what?"

"I wish that kings could cease being kings for an hour, could put the armor off their hearts, and understand how hearts can break. Then we folk would get more pity."

I do not think Louis answered her; and Brigite, fearing he deemed her a most disloyal miller's wife, grew silent. For a long time the only sound in the room was the labored breathing of Nicole. At last came the thumping steps of Jean, and the father fairly burst in the door to come to them.

"Here! here! I dragged the Jew from bed! I crammed the ring nigh down his stingy throat! Here is the elixir! The sparrow is saved — saved!"

"Quiet, fool!" ordered Ambroise, a little roughly. "Would you kill her by sheer bawling? Give me the vial."

There was silence again while the precious glass flask was emptied into the silver cup. The liquor shone in the lantern-light like a green emerald. Ambroise dipped his finger in the cup, and put one drop on his tongue.

"The elixir of Kairowan!" he said simply. Then turning to the father and mother: "Dear children, there is no greater help in man than this, but the help of man is weak. Let us pray, but not hope too fondly. Let us bow to the will of God!"

"Amen!" said Brigite, the tears on either cheek, but the miller only turned away his head, and did not watch when Ambroise raised the child and set the cup to her lips.

"Dear Lord," he said softly, so that Louis could just hear, "grant that thou mayest say unto this maid as to that other, 'Damsel, arise,' *sed non sicut ego volo, sed sicut Tu.*"

The medicine was drunk. Nicole lay as before, now motionless, now tossing a little, now giving the same weak moan.

"What can we do now?" asked the mother.

And Ambroise answered her, "Now we can turn to God."

Each was again in his place — Ambroise in the dark corner, Louis on one side of the bed, Brigite at the other.

But her husband sat with her now, and Louis guessed they would face their bitter hour together, their pain and love drawing them closer than before. The lamp was burning low, the shadows deepened. Ever and again Louis looked at the face of Nicole. No change — the burning brightness of the fever, the tossing, the hard breath — and as Louis looked, he felt a kind of indignation even against great God for suffering a thing so fair to shed light upon an evil world, and then pass out of it amid such pain. Next it seemed as if the king's eyes were opening, and the little cottage became a thousand such, strewn up and down wide France, each with its burden of sorrow and sore woe, which only God could heal; while with one surge it came to Louis as not before that these were all his people, small and great; that their griefs were his griefs, and in some strange manner he must try to bear them all, and lighten them all. And Margaret was forgotten. His own pain was forgotten. His mother was forgotten. France, wide, noble, yet sorrowing, tear-stained France, seemed opening her arms to him and crying, "You are my king, and with God's aid be swift to succor me;" or, "Have I crowned you only to be cursed?" But next all his thoughts rushed back to the one sick child. The last scene stood out before him. The dead form, the little bier, the coffin, the pale face of Brigite, the stony face of Jean, and two souls questioning, "Is it true that God is good?" Then Nicole stirred, — moaned. He knew she still was living. The battle was not quite lost. All was silence; but the king held her hand tightly, knelt, and prayed in his own soul.

"Lord, Lord, if these prayers from me in my sins can pass up to Thy holy sight, spare now this little one's life. Oh, take it not unto Thyself! Thou hast enough bright holy ones in heaven. I ask but this, dear Lord, I ask only this!" And when he would have prayed otherwise, invoking every healing saint, St. Martin and St. Luc, he could not do it. His plea always came back to "I ask only this!"

Now Jean was rising. He went across to an earthen water-pot, and filled a huge pewter cup, which he held out to Louis.

"Will you drink, Sir Knight?" said he, and the king took a long draught, for his throat was strangely dry, after which Jean gave to Ambroise and Brigite. The miller drank himself, and was picking up the lamp when a cry hissed from the mother.

"Hark!" and they heard Nicole turning on her side, and all her sore breathing seemed stilled.

"The end!" groaned Brigite, and she sank into her husband's arms, but Ambroise held up his hand for silence, and crossed the room on tiptoe. He touched the little maid's forehead and her breast, then beckoned "Come," and each drew near. The forehead no more burned them. They put their ears close to her, and heard her breathing gently, sweetly.

"She is asleep," said Ambroise, in a faint whisper, "and when she awakes the fever will be gone." . . .

After a time Louis prevailed on the father and mother and on the priest to lie down. This had not been their first vigil, and he would wake them if Nicole so much as stirred. Ambroise had rolled up a meal sack for a pillow and lay upon the bench. Jean and Brigite were on the floor by the bed; their heavy eyes had made their hard couch into down. Soon Louis heard their drowsy breathing. He himself would watch. Nicole lay with her face toward him. He could see the beauty of its curves, the fair texture of its skin, under the halo of the lamp, as the sickly crimson was vanishing. What a wonderful thing was a little child!

More wonderful than the huge Louvre castle at Paris, more wonderful than all the wise books in the great library at Clugny — that treasure house of human wit. How much the works of God exceeded the works of man! Louis found his head drooping twice, and twice he roused. "I have promised to watch!" He drew closer to the child. Next, as he looked, he wondered that he had not seen before how much Nicole's face was like to Margaret's. Now he was sure she was Margaret. Yet a kind of veil lay over her. He could not come to his wife. Then the whole scene changed; the hut seemed growing full of people, there was a strange shouting. The thatch vanished over his head. Sunlight streamed, and the king saw this: —

* * * * * * *

Reims: the morning of the coronation. Louis knew it without being told. All night long, he remembered, he had watched before the high altar in the tall minster at his *veillée des armes* — the darkness spent in prayer. And now, the vigil ended, he was in the great square of the city. Above him whipped five hundred flags and tossed a thousand glittering lances. From the windows of all the high houses leaned the people in festive array; east, west, north, south, he saw only the heads and helmets, and all the eyes he knew went out to one man — to him. Around him gathered the high officers of state — the six lay peers of France, the twelve spiritual peers, the prince-bishops, every one in blazing pelisson and surcoat, cope and mitre. Around him, too, stood the knighted chivalry of France, their burnished casques like suns, with the arms of not one great house lacking from Flanders to Navarre. Then came the goodly company of the barons of France, and at their head, in his proud vestments, the Lord Abbot of St. Remi bearing aloft the crystal vial of the sacred oil — the vial

which the angel had brought down from high heaven to
Clovis, founder of the kingdom. At his side went the Abbot
of St. Denis, bearing the chasuble of Charlemagne, the
mantle which only the king of France might wear. They
bowed the knee to the king, and then stood forth the Toison
d'Or and Guienne heralds, and all the royal pursuivants,
their tabards one sheen of silver, lace, and gold. They
clapped their gilded trumpets to their lips. The keen
blasts blew, all the lances tossed and flashed like fire, and
Louis knew himself moving forward, forward, while a
great cry pealed from the thronging, rejoicing people.

"Hail, Louis! Hail, Louis, *servant of the least of men* —
advance to take thy crown!"

"Servant of the least of men." Why that? But still the
king went on, wondering and growing humble in his heart.
Still onward, and out of the square, until in the clear blue before them he saw the springing heights of the Cathedral, the
gray minster of Reims, the symmetry of sculptured stone,
the bible of God written in pinnacle, tower, and fair carving.
Now the people thronged him closer. A thousand trumpets
blared. Would they ever cease to fling down flowers —
flowers still? Now in the belfries up against the sun, shrill
Jacquilline, loud Carolus, and deep voiced Holy Trinity,
began their brazen rumblings and tumblings. And again
the people were shouting : —

"Hail, Louis! Advance, Louis, servant of the least of
men — advance to take thy crown!"

At the high gates : and the Toison d'Or herald led the
acclamation, hailing the king in a clear voice, as —

"*Ludovicus, Magnus Rex Francorum, Franciæ totiæ
Dominus ; universis Dominis, universis Principibus et
Populis semper venerandus !*" Then, turning to the doors,
he gave the loud summons : —

"Lift up your heads, O ye gates, and be ye lifted up, ye everlasting doors, for Louis, vicegerent of God, now enters in!"

Whereat, as by unseen hands, the great bronze valves unclosed, and Louis saw in the inner gloom the height and length of the vast nave, the array of lights on the altar far away. As by some magic all the shouting died, and the shadow of the royal church fell over him as he passed within.

But as he passed he looked behind, and saw neither bishop nor baron, knight nor herald. With never a sound the doors were closed behind him. The king stood wondering, with all the church before. Then as he looked he knew he met some miracle, wrought as by apostle or prophet seer of old. For up and down the light-bathed nave, up and down transept and choir, spread out a host in white, — white robes, white wings, and faces glistering, — angels innumerable who stretched out to him green palms. And Louis knew that he was all alone; all human help was impotent and gone. Alone he must tread that path up to the high altar. This is not Reims; no man has built this minster, so high, so vast. He looks up, and snow-clouds hide the soaring arches, and fear comes on him. He would gladly flee. Then all the radiant heads are bowed, the palms all beckon him onward. The light from the windows — red, orange, azure — burns as with a brightness not found on land or sea. The throb and sob of the organ rocks the long nave with a chord from no human touch. And yet again comes the shout.

"Hail, Louis! Advance, Louis, servant of the least of men — advance to take thy crown!"

Then the king went on, though the high altar glowed so that it dazzled him. He could not look. Before it. burned.

he thought, one pearl, ever brightening, till the sun was but a star beside it. Out of the pearl sprang fire which covered the king. He felt the flames and the pain thereof, but after a manner this pain itself was sweet. And as he went he saw that the pearl was a form, an angel, taller, stronger, than the rest. He knew that this was "Michael-who-saves-from-the-Peril," the spirit closest to God. And all the time music swelled till it seemed to lift the massy church toward heaven. And still the angels shouted.

The king walked, he thought, through a mist of flame, but it had ceased to burn him. When he touched the altar steps, lo! his gay samite and jewels fell away. He was dressed in pure white, the robes of Christ's elect. He was kneeling before the archangel. Then all the music and shouting died, while Michael spoke through the spreading calm.

"Welcome, Louis; for God hath chosen thee to show His face unto His people of France. Therefore receive thy crown."

Yet the king answered, not lifting up his eyes:—

"How may I show His face, being myself in sin, requiring His mercy? Am I not weak and all but a child?"

But Michael answered him:—

"Behold, it was spoken, 'My Grace is sufficient for thee,' and, 'Thou shalt go to all that I shall send thee.' God's strength is thine, therefore receive thy crown."

So the king looked up, and saw the archangel hold over him, not the diadem of France, but a crown of lilies, every one of which seemed kissed with fire. And again great Michael spoke:—

"Because thou hast forgotten thine own griefs for the griefs of one of Christ's little ones; because thou hast prayed for her and not for thyself; therefore shall His peace come upon thee, and His joy pass into thy heart, and none shall take them away. And thou shalt rule many years, and do and suffer great things for Him. And men shall call thee blessed, and thy Lord shall receive thee at the end."

Then he set the lilies on Louis' head, and his voice rang down the nave : —

> " Rise, Louis, servant of all and therefore king of all !
> Rise, Louis, crowned of God the king of France!"

Whereat all the myriad angels clapped their wings, and a shout went up such as never rose in Reims : —

" *God save Louis the king !* "

Then all the cathedral throbbed with the heavenly chanting, as Louis stood crowned with the lilies before the high altar : —

> " A king shall reign in righteousness
> And princes shall rule in judgment.
> And a man shall be for a hiding place from the wind,
> As rivers of water in a dry place,
> As the shadow of a great rock in a weary land.
> He shall spare the poor and needy,
> And precious shall their blood be in his sight.
> His name shall endure forever,
> And men shall be blessed in him,
> All nations shall call him blessed."

*   *   *   *   *   *   *

Louis looked around him. Vanished the cathedral, the rainbow lights from the windows, the sniff of incense, the chant and shouting, the beating surges of the music, the innumerable, glistering host. The lamp had burned low. He saw the dingy walls of the cottage. He saw the sleeping father and mother, and the little child whose hand was

yet clasped in his.   Nicole stirred, whispered something:
" You are kind and good," then faded deeper into healthful
sleep.

"Lo! God is in this place, and the spot whereon I rest
is holy ground," said Louis, softly, yet aloud; " here is a
room of heaven."

Then he put Nicole's hand gently aside.   He trod across
the earthen floor reverently.   Was this not a shrine more
sacred than St. Martin's at Tours, St. James' at Compostella?   Again he thought of the sorrows of France, of the
myriad hearts with burdens heavy to be borne, and how
they were all his people, of the sin, the groping for
God's peace, the ceaseless toil and moil and travail.   He
was their king.   He would help them all he might.

" My grace is sufficient for thee," a voice again was saying, though within.   "Thou shalt drink of the cup that I
drink of, and be baptized with the baptism that I am baptized with," and yet again, " My grace is sufficient for
thee."

Louis opened the door; the clouds had broken; two
pale silver stars gleamed just over a dark elm tree, and
in the east hung a line of gray light.   Louis knelt down.

"*I am a king!*" he repeated.   " I am a king!"

God had given his wish.   He knew that a strange
power had come to him, that he had a will of iron, to
grapple with men's wickedness, to dare, to do.   He was
sure that Margaret was innocent, that he would re-
gain her love, and that he would continue in love with
his mother, yet be no more ruled by her.   He belonged
to France.   His past life of careful prayer and heedless
almsgiving had been scarce better than hypocrisy.   In his
desire to win heaven for himself by selfish deeds such
as these he had been all but damned.   And now he saw

strength was come to him for long, glad years of toil and high emprise, to lift the burdens from his people.

He looked back into the little hut. The four were calmly sleeping. Then a third time he spoke it:—

"I am a king!"

CHAPTER XXIII

IN THE FOREST

WHAT Louis said, what Ambroise said, what Jean and Brigite said, what Nicole said, when they all woke in the morning, there is no place here to tell. Nicole's fever was almost gone, her skin was moist. She was still very worn, but, please God, in two weeks she would be as sound as the big black kettle which her mother was hanging above the fire. Jean had brought a bag of fine white flour from the mill behind the cottage, and when Louis waked, for he waked last of all, he found ready a noble feast — cakes which Brigite had baked in the embers, a slice of the ham which dangled from the rafter, and a great turnip — all served up to him on a wooden platter, with a knife at hand huge enough to serve for a short sword; whilst to wash all down, Jean had dived into the hole in the bank beside the mill, and had tapped his one treasure, — a cask of rare Orléanais, which his uncle the vintner had left him two years since by will, and which had been hoarded up like so much gold. Assuredly, the mug was only pewter, but that did not lessen Jean's pride. He stood by while his guest ate and drank up everything, and when "Sir Roland" praised Brigite's flour cakes, the miller's smile spanned from ear to ear.

"Ah, yes, he knew that his little wife had a handy way ten years before the knight did — begging his worship's pardon."

But after Ambroise and Louis had had their fill, and
Louis at least had begun to fear that by not slighting the
good wine of Jean, he had gotten himself an aching head,
there were long adieus, especially with Nicole, who was
not content until "the good knight" had promised to
come to her again right speedily, and, if possible, bring
Falaise. They still stood in the cottage door talking, and
the king imagined that Ambroise was about to lead him
out on a long pilgrimage among the poor of Pontoise,
when there came running from the town a strange manner of man, who made straight for the priest. "A forester,"
thought Louis at first; but no royal forester ever wore
such unkempt, shaggy beard and locks, or let his green
livery fall in such tattered array. The stranger carried
a boar-spear and a dagger. But the sheath of this was
set with gems, which shone like a marvel among the
tatters. The man had pulled the hood of his jerkin up,
and it was long before he looked Louis in the eye, while
he talked with Ambroise in a kind of jargon that the king
but half understood.

"Renart sends for you. I ran to the manse — they said
you were here. Pfu! but I have run all the way!"

Ambroise frowned.

"Renart sends for me? He has not been so careful of
late in confession and keeping fast days as to be over-
familiar with my counsel — not to mention greater things."

"Ah, yes; but, father, it was not, you see, anything on
the road, — no Paris caravan, no fat abbot's party, — but a
stag. He will never hunt another. He is sadly gored.
He vows he would not himself fear the going to hell, but
for his mother up in heaven. When she hears of it, he
swears her heart will break, even there."

"I will go to him, my son," announced Ambroise,

beginning to gird up his well-worn cassock; and then he looked on Louis. "But you, sir knight, will you go with me? You were to follow me all this day. There is no peril."

"Who are these men? bandits?" said Louis, but not in hearing of the stranger.

"Say rather they are men who think God has forsaken them."

"And their hold is in the forest? Very good. If they will suffer me, I will go with you."

The newcomer in green stared at Louis when he strode out at the priest's side, and was about to say something, when Jean, who saw his black looks, whispered in his ear.

"No scowls, Ogier; this young knight is a saint of God, if there ever walked one. If you doubt my word, ask Brigite." But Ogier was satisfied, and the three trudged off together, while all around them spread the beauties of the morning.

A morning that Louis would never forget. No clouds, and a fresh, south wind that bowed the new grass and set the new leaves whispering. They crossed the Oise on a foot-bridge, shunned Maubuisson — where, I think, Ogier had no wish to go near the abbey — and soon were going westward across tawny fields, where the farm-hands, lads and lasses, were laughing as they plied mattock or sickle; over little brooks which ran in full current cheerily, until the towers of Pontoise château were far behind, and before them spread the shaggy deeps of the great forest of Montmorenci. Here amongst the stately pines and cedars they soon knew that the wood was tenanted. For at the first turn in the road half a dozen green-clad men leaped out of the coppice, and ran to Ambroise, kneeling, kissing his hands and beseeching his blessing in the same uncouth speech as Ogier's. A kind of huge dog they seemed to Louis, with teeth very sharp, although just now they did not use them; and they had no scruples in pelting their new guest with questions, as they led him and Ambroise by winding paths, deeper and deeper into the heart of the virgin wood.

"So you are with the priest and vouched for by him. He is true as steel and his guests are ours, but wherefore are you come? You are a strange bird for the trees of Montmorenci."

"I come," said Louis, meekly, "because I know you are men in sore misfortune, and as a penance for my sins I have resolved to succor all in misfortune that I can."

"'All that I can,'" snorted the man with the longest beard; "but how if you cannot, not of course being the king. And how if we would not be succored, if one could?"

"Then," replied Louis, gravely, "I would gladly dwell with the men who wish for nothing better."

The gravity of his speech and something else made all the others laugh like horses, and the first speaker, Aimerel they called him, began to make sly sallies at their new friend's soft hands and lily skin. Ambroise turned and his rebuke was ready; but Louis was ready with something better yet. He cast his coat upon the grass in one trice, and ere great Aimerel had finished his guffaw, out from beneath him spun his legs, and down his huge body crashed into a thorn bush. De Joinville's wrestling trick, and Louis had never done it better. It scared the squirrels overhead just to hear the other outlaws laugh. And Aimerel rose up from the bush to pick the thorns out of his hose, then to grasp Louis' hand with his own broad paw.

T

"You are better than a knight, my master, you are a *man*. So take Aimerel the bandit's grip here for a friend's."

After that, speech was easy. And the more Louis talked, and saw that he was treated with honor not because he was "his Grace," but because he had thrown a giant into a thorn bush, he grew vastly pleased with himself, and presently found himself joining with all the others when they began a catch and a chorus that made the high boughs ring.

> " Easter-time in April,
> Hear them blithely carol,
> Every song-bird gentle.
> ' *Zo! fricandès! zo! zo!*
> *Zo! fricandès! zo!* '"

I fear the fact that Renart their comrade was dying did not weigh overheavily on the hearts of these broad-shouldered men. Every dog must have his final day, and whether that day was hastened through a sword, a rope, or only a stag, what was the difference? Renart was entitled to have the good priest anoint him, absolve him, and the band would contribute each a silver sou to pay for his masses. But that was no reason why one should not romp and sing.

By and by they came to the huts of sweet pine branches where the band was idling away the spring time, after the winter in a stronghold in the forest deeps. Ambroise went in to Renart, and, indeed, that free rover needed nothing but medicine for the spirit, for no salves or elixirs could have saved his sinful body now. His comrades hung about outside making a decent show of commiserating his hard fortune, but far more intent on talking with their stranger guest; and Louis, for his part, looking upon these men, and knowing that every one of them had deserved to be hanged more times than he had fingers, was yet amazed to see that they were not devils with horns, nor monsters of the deep, but beings much like himself.

Having won their confidence, they replied with childlike guilelessness when he asked them for their stories, and why they were free rovers and outside his Grace the king's high peace. Many of the replies made their questioner's ears burn.

"I," said big Aimerel, "was a tenant-farmer in Herblay. The seigneur's eldest son wronged my only daughter. His father laughed when I pleaded 'justice.' Therefore I sent an arrow into the ribs of both, and came here to the forest."

"I," said Ogier, the messenger, "was a weaver in St. Lieu and dwelt with my mother. One day the king's provost comes to her while I am away and demands three Tours deniers, because she had gathered a few sticks on the royal lands and 'she must pay her *banalité* or away to prison.'

"When I came in she lay on the floor, and the provost over her. He had beaten her till she was dead. I caught a great crock and dashed it at him. He never spoke again. But I saw he wore the king's livery, so I kissed my dead mother and thenceforth lived in the forest."

"And I," said Sugier, a lad younger than Louis' self, "went with my brother from my father's farm at Franconville into the royal wood. There we saw a hart wounded unto death. She had escaped the hunt the day before, but now was dying. We cut her throat, and were bearing her away, when we met the master of the king's foresters. He took my brother, and the crows picked his bones on the Pontoise gibbet. But I was swift of foot and therefore I fled into the forest."

All the stories were like these, save that one man said bluntly that he loved the rover's life, and did not mind a goodly chance of hanging. When they had all been told, Louis asked, "And what think you of the king?" Whereupon great Aimerel answered for the rest:—

"As for the king, fair master, we think very little of him, for were he a good man, he would have Christian laws and Christian officers; and were he a bad man he would be strong enough to chase down us merry folk and end our dancing. But since he is neither good nor bad, only a girl under a doublet, and led by the nose by his mother, we think very little of him at all."

When he had said that, the outlaws noticed that their guest smiled and smiled, but said nothing. Then after a long time he asked again the names of the evil seigneurs of Herblay, of the cruel provost, and of the relentless master forester, and he seemed trying to remember all three of them. After that some one came out of the hut, saying that Renart was exceeding near his end and would take leave of his comrades; so they went in one by one, yet Louis marvelled how little ado they made over their companion.

Renart had been six years in the forest; and six years is a good generation in Montmorenci wood. "We will miss him; but he did well to die dry-eyed; and surely Father Ambroise anointed and absolved him beautifully."

That was Ogier's wisdom, and the others said amen! Then came a feast on venison killed in the face of all law in the king's particular domain land. And after the feast was over "Sir Roland" took Aimerel's crossbow and knocked a squirrel from the tallest tree,—a feat which

made the giant more his friend than ever. And their
guest saw how these great unkempt men were very human
and very willing to be led by any who seemed better in
strength or wits than they. In fact Aimerel even clapped
his new friend upon the shoulder and vowed that "it were a
pity the knight must needs go back to a sleepy castle. Why
could he not stay in Montmorenci and lead them like royal
rangers, come provost, come forester, come king?" To
which appeal Louis only smiled again, and again kept
silence.

But after Ambroise had done all he might for Renart,
had promised to say masses in St. Maclou, and to carry a
little message to a sister in Argenteuil, the priest began
to talk of the return to Pontoise before nightfall, when lo!
there came a cracking step over the dead boughs in the
thickets, and a lithe, lean man, one Garic, whom Louis had
not seen, came breaking in among them to fall down panting. Ogier poured some strong waters down his throat,
and at last he could speak.

"Pontoise château, — last night something has befallen.
I was watching the road by Pierrelaye and met old pedler
Benoit, who brings us arrow-heads and news. The gates
are locked and guarded, but not by the king's yeomen.
De Ormoy's band left Conflans last night. They are in
Pontoise château now — or Benoit's mother bore a liar."

"De Ormoy in Pontoise château? Good friends, have
this fellow's wits scattered out at his ears?" So Louis,
who stared around to see if the forest was not reeling.

"Why, it is a queersome tale," admitted Aimerel; "yet
Garic is better at cutting throats than cooking lies. But
you have not shot off all — go on, man."

"The townspeople are barred from the château; but
Pontoise is like a buzzing hive, and every beldame's tongue

wags like a lamb's tail. And then they prate of 'Margaret, called the queen.'"

"'Called' the queen?" Louis cried out again, but no
one listened; all gaped at Garic.

"That she is no queen at all, by some trick of the priest.
That she has dishonored herself by trying to flee with a
lover. That my Lord de Coucy nipped her nice plot in
the bud, and last night in the great hall of the château
showed the pretty pair to all the court, to proclaim their
infamy. She is in an oubliette now."

"You are ill, my son." Thus spoke Ambroise, when
he saw Louis totter on his feet; but the young man shook
the priest off. He was fearfully pale, but he did not
stagger again; he did not even groan. On ran Garic.

"After that it seems that De Ormoy's men were let into
the castle. The yeomen, they say, have never struck a
blow. As to what has truly happened, Benoit says there
are as many guesses in Pontoise as there are heads.
But some plot there was doubtless to cast down the queen
mother, and put the king in other leading strings."

"Ay — but where *was* the king?" thrust in Ogier, with
his mouth wide open.

"You've landed your arrow there. The king, the wind
blows, was not in Pontoise château, but gone on a pilgrimage last evening to the shrine in the forest."

"That lies this way," quoth Sugier.

"And my Lord de Coucy, Benoit told, was riding thither
in force to fetch him. Because of that I ran, that we
might be prepared."

"Not to stop my Lord Chamberlain's company?"

"Ei, no; only not to have too many guests surprise
us."

"And the king?" said Ogier, his hand on his dagger;

"we are all loyal folk, and this is no taking deer, but black treason."

"Hush, rascal," ordered Aimerel, "the king is only a bolt for some other crossbow. We'll not spill a drop for that. If only we had a young king who *was* a king, a keen wrestler like Sir Roland!"

But Sir Roland at this strode straight up to Aimerel and put his hand on the giant's. Perhaps his face was still pale, perhaps his voice shook, but it was only a little.

"Hark you, good friend, will you pleasure me?"

"Yes, by St. Maclou; though it were to fight four men."

"I will not ask that. Take me to a spot in the wood where I may overlook the road and see truly whether this Garic is walking in his dreams, where I can see my Lord de Coucy and his band if he is riding to the pilgrimage shrine."

"And wherefore?" asked Sugier, the most impertinent of the band; but Louis' form seemed to take on two fingers when he flashed the answer back.

"Because such is my wish." Then every outlaw looking in his eye thought, "Here stands my master," and no one durst another question. I think Father Ambroise wondered most, for he had watched Louis all the time, and not Garic like the rest.

As for Aimerel, he made no more ado, but bade his guest straightway follow him, while the rest scattered among the trees, so that a foe raiding them would find only dead Renart and the empty tents. Aimerel led down a dark glade where the foot sank into the mould of last summer's leaves, over a brook, through a young pine grove, where the black trunks pressed so close there was scarce passing for two men, and then came out upon a hillock. Clear before Louis spread the broad royal highroad from Pontoise to St. Denis, and even as he stood and stared, this way and that, Aimerel touched him and pointed to the west.

"Look!" And Louis saw something like twenty moving sunbeams rising from a cloud of dust, men-at-arms spurring rapidly. Above them fluttered two pennons among the bristling lances. Louis did not wait for the bandit to lead the way, as he ran close to the road, and flung himself face down on the grass behind a thicket. The horsemen were still far off. While the click-click of their swift hoofs neared, he twitched the grass up piece by piece, and felt the hot blood in his forehead. Now they swept past, and out of the cloud of dust Louis beheld two figures riding side by side. They were in full armor, but unvizored. De Coucy — he would know that smooth face among a thousand! The other, he guessed, was the *routier* De Ormoy, and the pennons bore the Coucy arms and those of the free-lance. Come, gone; and now the dust closed over them. Now their thunder grew dim behind a distant hill.

Louis leaped to his feet and almost dragged Aimerel to his.

"As you fear God, lead me back to the huts and to Father Ambroise. Haste! haste! haste!"

The bandit was too far beneath the other's spell to even scratch his own head and wonder. By long strides they had gone to the highway; by longer leaps they sped back. And all the time Louis' brain swirled until he thought once that he was mad. Margaret in the oubliette, after being branded with infamy before the court, his mother perchance deposed, De Ormoy's ruffians guarding Pontoise château, and De Coucy riding at that free-lance's side in quest of him — him, the king of France! But at this all

Louis' muscles tightened, he felt his brow grow cool, and power passed through him. "I am a king!" he thought, "I am a king!"

At the huts he made plain to Ambroise that they two must haste back to Pontoise, as swiftly as two legs could carry them. Aimerel's friendship had so far advanced that he offered to bring the band along with "Sir Roland," if that gallant knight was intent on striking a blow to blast De Coucy's plots; or could they waylay the chamberlain, when he rode back with the king a prisoner? "For it was better to let blood in behalf of even a caitiff king than in breaking his peace, save when they had to."

But "Sir Roland" only thanked his zeal, and said none of the band should be the worse for his coming to them that day. And when out upon the homeward path, Louis made a request of the good priest.

"Dear father, as we go, let us both pray; first that wisdom and strength be given to the king, but still more let us pray that no grief touch ever his most dear wife."

CHAPTER XXIV

THE BLIND CAN SEE THE BEST

ONE dares not write all the unchristian things that the usually pious seigneur, Enguerraud de Coucy, thought and said when Pons, his squire, was missing in the morning. Sunrise and no Pons; matins and no Pons; it was drawing on toward noon and no Pons yet. The chamberlain himself went down to the château gate and asked De Ormoy's sentries; he clambered up a tower; he sent twenty varlets running twenty ways. All to fetch back the same — the squire had vanished. As for Pons himself, if De Coucy had been told, "Your faithful squire is now meeting deserts in hell," the good man would have answered, "He deserves it," and never have muttered a prayer. But back of Pons loomed another — the king; yes, the king. How the chamberlain had rubbed his hands when his liege lord had said, "I go with De Joinville to St. Romain's pilgrimage chapel in Montmorenci wood; do you keep the castle." It had given De Coucy control of the yeomen, and made De Ormoy's deed ten times easier. It had taken out of the way that most disagreeably vigilant and incorruptible officer, De Joinville. The chamberlain had doubted whether the king was really going to the pilgrimage shrine, because he took no horses. But all the better: he would not wander far; the easier to send out with Pons to guide, to lead back the king, to show him De Ormoy's *routiers* all over the castle; then to bend the knee, saying,

"Sire, be pleased to sign these few parchments sending your mother to a convent, accepting your humble chamberlain as lord-chancellor, and summoning Margaret of Provence, your so-called wife, and Gui, her paramour, before your court of peers." Then the king would weep and wring his hands, and weep again, but sign the parchments in the end; and after that, *gloria Deo!* every star would shine like a sun to Enguerraud and his fair daughter.

That had been the dream. But at noon the reality was this: the castle gates locked; De Ormoy's sentries on every battlement, and others standing guard over the disarmed yeomen; Pontoise quiet, but full of rumors; Pontoise château also quiet, but all its courtly folk putting their heads together, grumbling, and asking ever louder, "The king! what has befallen the king?" And De Coucy knew fairweather friends were already quietly asking, "Who knew if his Grace was not privily murdered by De Ormoy the night before?" It was one thing to depose the queen mother and dishonor her daughter-in-law, another to drag down the house of Capet and set up that of Coucy. Let the muttered rumors once become live fears, and no band like De Ormoy's could stand between the chamberlain and outraged France.

So at noon Enguerraud took the free-lance himself and twenty picked men, and went at a foaming gallop to Montmorenci wood. They found the pilgrimage chapel, and frightened its simple priest with a storm of questions.

The Holy Mother and St. Romain knew — he swore it on his soul — that no two such gentlemen as their lordships mentioned had been near the chapel, either last night or that morning.

Then back to the château went the troop, leaving behind them a curse for every stone in the road, their horses almost foundered as the sole reward for their pains. Still no Pons — and the masters of the château gathered in the great hall for a council of war.

Half the afternoon was wasted and no man had set eyes on the king since he had vanished into the gloom outside the gate in the evening. Cautious inquiries in the town for "two gentlemen — one stalwart, one slender" drew out that such men had been seen together watching one of the dances, but not afterwards, and "who could remember all one saw at an evening fête?" Peter of Brittany whistled through his teeth as De Coucy laid bare their situation; De Ormoy smiled more hideously than ever, and Theobald twisted his little beard.

"So the keystone is missing," hinted that last count, broadly, "and our arch is like to come a-crashing round our ears."

"That is an overgloomy dread, my dear seigneur," soothed the chamberlain. "True, this unfortunate absence of his Grace will have the effect of rendering our design slightly more difficult, but —"

"But where *is* the king?" probed Theobald, viciously.

"The ways of God and of His saints are inscrutable," suggested De Coucy, folding his lank hands.

"The ways of God are no riddle to me," frowned the count; "we have all been bulls with your rings in our noses, my Lord Enguerraud, and now we must not bellow at the butcher's knife. But what has happened I will tell you —"

"What?"

"Be the king the numbest head in France, Simon de Joinville is the sagest. The commandant of the guards has sniffed our pretty plot, and has whisked his master away up hill and down dale to Beaumont."

"*Agnus Dei, miserere nobis!*" began Bishop Godfrey, who had been listening dumbly all this time, but Theobald did not heed him.

"What is at Beaumont we know well enough. La Girard is there with five hundred men-at-arms, — tough dogs who have been in every foray from Flanders to Gascony since the days of old King Philip. And La Girard, we know too, will cut off his head with his own hand, if it be to serve or save the king of France. Now if he and De Joinville lay their two wits together against us, I begin to think I am nearer purgatory than to my pretty county-town of Troyes."

"The king is not at Beaumont!" The chamberlain almost snarled it, and began to grow red.

"I would give a thousand marks to know it," rejoined Theobald, with sarcastic urbanity. "I only say these things to make plain to your sage lordship that the king should be speedily found."

"Found, found! The devil seize you, Theobald," cried De Coucy, losing his temper. "Did you ride to the forest or I?"

"Did you cook this plot or I?" The count banged his clenched fist, and began to bristle like a cat.

"Peace, peace, fair seigneurs," put in the bishop, stretching forth his hands. "Says not the Apostle '*Carissimi, deligamus nos invicem, quia caritas ex Deo est,*' which is, being interpreted, —

"That we must cease catching at each other's throats, and give more heed to saving them, and by saving them I mean finding the king." The advice was from Peter of Brittany, and his words were good. So the others listened while he ran through with his questions.

"We have searched the town?"

"All that is safe," said De Ormoy. "My men are not so many that we can hold down the château and Pontoise too. Let the cry once spread, 'They wish to seize the king,' and we'll have a thousand brawny weavers howling at the gate and much ado to keep them out. City folk are always devilishly loyal."

"And questioned the queen mother?"

"The Castilian" — it was Alithe's turn now — "has not spoken since we found her with the blind maid. The doctors are still with her. But even if she knows whither her son is gone, wild horses or racks could hardly wring the secret out. I know her well enough for that."

"And who else can know?"

There was a long silence, broken by the guttural voice of De Ormoy: "That wench you call the Provençal? Have you asked her?"

"Her?" echoed Peter, incredulously. "You surely would not have us question that Margaret?"

"And wherefore not?" rejoined the free-lance, stoutly. "How can we know what passed betwixt her and her husband that last time they shot back and forth so amiably? Ten deniers to one he blurted out, 'I'll go here or there!' or 'I'll do this!' before he cursed and left her. At least I see no harm in trying."

"The Sire de Ormoy is very right." Alithe said it, and since that lady seldom spoke save to the purpose they listened to her readily.

"Good, then," commanded her father; "we'll have her from the oubliette. No doubt she'll gladly talk, if once we show her sunshine."

But Alithe shook her head.

"Wrong again. Trust a woman to know a woman. If we bring Margaret of Provence up into the hall, and fling

at her questions and threats, I see her straightening her
back and either closing her lips or giving us plain lies.   For
I tell you this — she loves the king and loves him still ! "

"Then we are all lost devils ! " muttered Theobald,
blackly, " and you the foulest ! "

"When I need a confessor for my soul, I choose not
you, but Monseigneur the bishop," retorted Alithe, with
a toss of her glorious head ; " and as for Margaret, I have a
better way than that."

" No torturing ! " warned Theobald, sternly.

" You are overanxious, fair sir," quoth Alithe, tartly.
" I propose to go alone to the oubliette, to visit our two
maiden prisoners in their cell, to speak them fair, to show
myself their friend ; in short, by a few pleasant words to
draw forth what you will not wring out by a thousand
sharp threats.   Even the blind girl may speak somewhat
to the purpose, for the Provençal plainly had her hidden
in her chamber all the evening long."

De Coucy held down his head and meditated.   For
himself, he thought threats and even stripes more to the
purpose than such an embassy.   But Alithe was very sure
that her way was the best.   She had a delicate dislike for
cruel scenes, and Theobald clearly agreed with her.   So
the chamberlain was persuaded.   He put in her hand
the little white baton of his office.   It was a talisman
every turnkey and all De Ormoy's men-at-arms would
respect.   Then the company dissolved ; the *routier* chief
and the chamberlain to go to the walls, the bishop to his
prayers, and Peter and Theobald to meditate darkly on the
folly of letting other wiseacres plot for them.

*   *   *   *   *   *   *

Alithe set down her lamp and looked about her.   Truth
to tell, even she did not like the feeling of so much stone

crushing down upon her head.   The bare, windowless cell, naked, dark rock for floor, wall, and roof, the whole barely lighted by her one weak lamp — that was all she saw save the two women.   Margaret had grown white, and stood back with her arm pressed about Falaise; but the blind girl remained motionless and silent, with the same calm look upon her face that was always there.   Alithe faced the two one moment, then mustered her courage and sent the turnkey away.

"You are not to lurk within earshot.   Neither you, nor any one else.   Do you understand?" with a wave of the white baton.

"Yes, my lady," growled the fellow, with a cringing nod; and they heard his shuffling steps down the gallery. Alithe turned and closed the door, as if doubly anxious against eavesdroppers.   Then across her bright and mobile features spread a pitying smile.   Ignoring Falaise, she addressed Margaret.

"Holy Mother of Christ!   Dear Lady, how is this I see you?   They told me you were in the oubliette; yet I did not think they dared do this!"

"It is your good father's handiwork," said Margaret, sullenly, never meeting her eye to eye.

"My father's, — well, praise God, my father's conscience is not mine!   You do not know how I have sought to turn him back; how I have knelt to him, wrung his hands, and prayed that he would not dip his fingers in those black plots — "

"You have prayed that?" echoed the Provençal.

"Why, yes; you see the Bishop of Beauvais and the Counts of Champagne and Brittany, — they have been hounding him on so long to overthrow the queen mother — and at last, do what I might, he yielded."

"What you say is not true." Falaise's voice was calm, but very firm also, and Alithe did not like it.

"Not true? And who are you to call me liar, mistress?" cried she, with a flash from her eyes which made Margaret whisper, "Silence, silence, dear Falaise. She is angry."

"What you say is not true," repeated the blind girl in the same measured tone. "I know what you said to your father when Boso hid at the feast. I know what I heard you say to the chamberlain when you came to find the queen mother, and talked loudly and wickedly before you discovered me. I have told Margaret already how you and your father sowed hate between her and the king and his mother, how too I know that Gui has been your tool in a trick befitting the great Master Devil. I have put my hand upon your face and mouth, and all your smiles are false and hard. Therefore lady, I bid you cease to tell any more lies, but speak out plainly — wherefore have you come?"

If Falaise had grown angry, had flared, screamed, I think Alithe would have answered with a laugh. But to have all this thrown calmly in her teeth, with never a tinge of rage, sent all the bad blood leaping through the De Coucy's veins.

"You will be silent, sightless hussy," she commanded, "or I'll have you whipped — yes, whipped until you cannot even howl with pain."

"Can you do that?" asked Falaise, never lifting her voice, and almost incredulously.

"Can I? Look — no, curse you, you cannot look; but understand that if I show this white chamberlain's wand to any of De Ormoy's men-at-arms, they will do my will even to the wringing of your wretched neck. Therefore, again — be still!"

u

As she stormed, Alithe moved impulsively away from the door and across the cell, and silently Falaise took her place, but the others never marked it then.

"Then you will not tell truly why you have come?" asked Falaise again; and not waiting for reply, she swept on with her own answer: "Then I will tell — for it is this. The king is missing. Oh! do not ask how it is I know it. I will never tell. God has many ways of speech to those who love Him, as you do not. You have the queen consort. You have the queen mother. You have Pontoise. You have De Ormoy and his wolves. You have all else — but you have not the king. Poor, weak, and helpless king — you did not think of missing him. I heard your talk. No; do not start and rage. It will do no good. You think by coming to Margaret with soft and glozing words to win from her some tidings of the king. 'Where is he? What does he? When is he back at Pontoise?' You would ask that; and I answer for both — we do not know. But we know the king is in the good God's hands to be kept safely. We know the good God is wiser and stronger than the prince-bishop or your father, or your beautiful, sinful self. Therefore, we do not fear for the king. We do not fear your wrath."

"Hush! hush!" again adjured Margaret, "you cannot see how terrible her face is. She has power over us. Oh, she will harm you cruelly! You will be dragged away, and I be left alone in the horrible dark."

"I rejoice, my Lady of Provence," ventured Alithe, her voice shaking, though she strove to control it, "that you have wisdom for this mad woman. I promise that you will aid yourself if you answer swiftly and to the point. Whither has gone the king? And understand that silence or lies will serve you in very ill stead."

The instant she let the mask drop Alithe might have known what would be Margaret's answer. Why could not the devils have burned that blind fool's tongue out of her throat?

"Margaret of Provence has no confidences with traitors," she said at full height, and making Alithe sevenfold angrier. The De Coucy knew that she ought to cajole, but it was far easier to threaten.

"Will you not speak? Not if I have you lashed?"

"I will neither confirm anything, nor deny anything. Are you commanded by the king's *Curia* to judge me?" returned the prisoner, scornfully.

"I face two fools," menaced Alithe; "take care, they will howl like whipped hounds in an hour."

"Those are courtly words for a great lady of France," rejoined Margaret.

Then before Alithe could return the arrow Falaise spoke boldly.

"Dear Margaret, where is the lamp?"

"The lamp! the lamp! Here at my side; what do you mean!" And the Provençal and her tormentor stared at the blind girl, wondering.

"Blow it out, blow it out, for the love of Christ!" ordered Falaise.

"Blow it out? I do not understand — the awful dark!" said Margaret; but Falaise's voice now was shrill.

"No questions; blow it out in the name of the king!" And thus conjured, Margaret did it while Alithe stood too much dazed to hinder her. The dark shut down instantly. The De Coucy only gathered her wits after a long silence.

"Fools! fools both of you!" she began at last; "what have you done?"

Her answer was in the voice of Falaise, tense and shrill.

"Now, bad and too-wise woman, think how God has punished you. Think how He has led you into this oubliette all alone, planning to work us harm, only that all your evil deeds may crash upon your head, while we, your foes, escape. In whose power are you now?"

"Now!" echoed Alithe, but the dark — the numbing, rayless, all-enfolding dark — was crushing the boldness out of her. Her own voice rang weak and hollow.

"Now!" spoke Falaise, for the first time in a wondrous kind of pride, "now *you* are helpless; *you* are blind; but *I with my hands can see*, and you are mine!"

"What is this?" Margaret cried, for even she thought her friend was turned quite mad, but Falaise bade her, "Stand still, and let me do the desire of God."

"Help! Rescue! Help!" Alithe's voice seemed dying in her throat, and in that little cell her cries were hurled back into her mouth, yet still she called.

"You gain nothing by this," said Falaise, almost gently; "the door is very thick; besides, you know you have sent the turnkey far away. No help will come."

But now Alithe felt two hands, small but tight, about her throat. She wrestled, strove, and beat the air as does a man when blindfolded. She felt herself grow ever weaker, and all the time the dark was pressing on her like a mountain. Then at last she was upon her knees, she was gasping, she felt a cloth being tightened around her neck, and she was upon the hard floor.

"Pity! Mercy! You would not have me die! There is no priest, I have done many evil things! Pity! Mercy!" she gasped it out word by word, and at the last lay on her back helpless.

"No," said Falaise's voice very near her ear, "you are not going to die. You are an exceeding wicked woman, and if I took your life, I do not think God would ever let you pass even to purgatory, much less to heaven. Therefore I will not kill you, but it shall be beyond your power to do us any more ill."

Margaret, who had stood and listened as bidden, heard a rending as of a kirtle, while Alithe still struggled feebly, but soon ceased to groan. Then she heard Falaise coming toward her, and pressing a mantle over her shoulders.

"What have you done? where is Alithe? are you grown wild, Falaise?" asked the Provençal, but the blind girl only tore her bliaut away, to replace it with a strange one, then answered between her quick gasps: —

"Where is Alithe? why, yonder. I have bound her hands and feet, and thrust a rag into her mouth. It was easy. She is not very strong, and it was like mastering a child. She will lie here on the floor and think of her sinful deeds until they make a great search of the castle."

"And we? we? What is this now? You are drawing the mantle around me close, and pulling the hood about my head? And why is this little wand thrust into my hand?"

"Because we will fly together, Margaret," — Falaise laughed as she spoke it; "because you are about the same height as this Lady de Coucy, because the turnkeys doubtless have not met her enough to remember her voice, or her face, because you will show the Lord Chamberlain's wand to all the sentries, and they will salute and bid you freely pass, and because if they make questions over me you will say, 'My father bids me take this blind girl out of the oubliette to question her privately.' And once out of the galleries — "

"Ah, yes, in the full bright daytime, when fifty will know us! Poor blind Falaise, you do not realize that."

"I do! Oh, the dear God just now makes me think so fast! Remember this is Pontoise, that I know every stone, every window, every hidden sally-port, remember that I can find Boso. Now be brave, and let us hasten before any one wonders 'Why is Alithe dallying?' Be brave — for Louis' sake!"

And to Margaret the oubliette seemed, I think, a dance with great glorious suns, as she kissed the blind girl's lips.

"For Louis' sake! for Louis' sake!" she said, "I will be brave."

CHAPTER XXV

GOOD AMBROISE IS ASTONISHED

THE dark gallery and Falaise leading her; a turn in the inky corridor; a light flashing out to dazzle in her face. It seemed to Margaret that she was treading on in some quick dissolving dream, a dream made real by the rasping voice of the turnkey.

"Ei! Noble lady, you come on me like a ghost. Your lamp is out."

"A draught down your gallery quenched it as I left the cell."

"But what is this you are leading?"

"This blind girl; I desire to examine her out of the Provençal's presence. The Provençal is happiest alone."

The warder, I have said, had no heart, but I was wrong —he had a very little one. He made one faint effort to do a kindly deed.

"Ah, but she takes it so piteously! The gloom is so terrible. She is just as safe in an upper cell. Do not separate her from this blind maid, and leave her in the oubliette."

He was answered by a nod, and a little shake of the white baton that made him repent his boldness.

"The Provençal is best alone. That is my opinion and not yours. So do you heed it. I have barred her cell, and she is in no pressing need of company. You will go at once to my father, and say to him that I have been unable to gain anything by examining the prisoners together; therefore I have taken this blind maid away, and will come to my father presently."

"Has your ladyship any other commands?" quoth the fellow, with a scrape and a twist.

"None others, so obey me quickly. Lead us up to daylight. I am perishing in this stifling oubliette."

The lamp went on before up stairways: Margaret's heart gave a great leap, something beautiful was springing forth to greet her — the light of a glorious afternoon in May. The little ray in the air-shaft had been a diamond; the myriad rays that fell about her now were as the treasure house of God himself. And now the turnkey was opening a great door, and he never looked to scan her face, for was not his crooked form bent low to do her reverence as she passed? And then, in the guard-room outside the prison door, Margaret saw the flash of steel, and her grip on Falaise's arm tightened.

"Look, Falaise — guardsmen! De Ormoy's men on sentry! What shall I do?"

"Do nothing; hold out the wand and go straight forward."

Clatter, clash, went the pikes and partizans as the free-lance's troopers presented arms at sight of the white baton. The clashing hid all the loud beats of Margaret's heart; the zeal of the sergeant in command to see that all his pikes were aligned aright prevented him from being overcurious, even from ogling at so famous a beauty as my Lady de Coucy.

There were one or two looks sent after Falaise — that was all. But now Margaret almost fell on her knees in thanksgiving. They were in an open court; the sunlight panelled the flagging, and overhead, cloudless, sinless,

stretched God's infinite blue, most beautiful thing in all
the beautiful world.

A little court and empty. All was silent save the voice
of a sentry tramping a distant rampart, and they could hear
him trolling a southern campaign song.

> "Peace delights me not.
> War — be thou my lot!
> Law — I do not know,
> Save a right good blow !"

But Margaret was not suffered even to stand and make
love to the sunlight and the sky. Falaise had taken her
arm, and she suffered herself to be guided. Now it was
under a great gray arch ; now up a winding stair to a little
flanking tower ; now between the parapets of the steep
wall overhanging the running Oise below. Once Falaise
put her ear to the stones and listened, took it up again,
saying, "One is coming," and drew Margaret into the re-
treat of another flanking tower. The Provençal held her
breath as the heavy-footed guardsman jangled past. "My
ears were better than your eyes !" laughed Falaise, and
again drew Margaret onward when all was safe. "How
well I know Pontoise ! "

Falaise glided along the parapet. It shut them in on
either hand, so that Margaret could see neither the castle
court nor the valley. The blind girl was counting off the
joinings of the stones with her hands, till she halted at a
small door let into the inner parapet.

"Is no one watching? You are very sure ?" she asked,
herself listening carefully.

"No one, I am sure."

Falaise knocked softly four times ; waited, then again four
times ; when they heard feet within and the door opened

to show a rudely furnished and dimly lighted chamber, but straight before them stood dwarfish Boso, who at sight of the blind girl began to howl with animal delight, and to hug and kiss her many times before she could draw Margaret into the little room and make the barrier fast.

"They told me you were in the oubliette! they told me you were soon dead! Oh, are you truly my Falaise and not her ghost?" He squeezed his comrade all over to make sure that she was real flesh and blood, while Margaret looked about and saw that this was clearly the lad's chamber — a straw truckle-bed, a bench, a chest. In one corner a narrow stairway wound down and out of sight.

"I am truly Falaise," said the blind girl, with her trilling laugh, "and the dear God does not think me good enough for heaven yet. But now you must help us, Boso, and help us well; I knew I could find you here."

At this point, however, Boso began to survey Margaret up and down as well as he might, for the light was only through a narrow loophole.

"And who is this woman?" said he, letting his jaw drop.

"This," said Falaise, a little proudly, "is my sister, and therefore yours."

"She is very pretty," confessed Boso, boldly, "but I never knew you had a sister. Well, if she is your sister, she will prove it by giving me a kiss."

I do not know what Margaret would have said two days before, had any one bidden her to kiss a grimy little dwarf who favored as much a demon as a man; but I know that at this moment she bent down without one thought and touched her lips to the cheek of Boso.

"Yes," said she, "I am Falaise's sister, and all her friends are mine."

"And what is your name?" asked he, now smiling mightily.

"My name is Margaret."

"A very good name, sister Margaret; my name is Boso, and my father is Huon the castellan; now who is yours?"

But Falaise did not suffer his curiosity to run further. Moments were dearer than gold. She put her lips to Boso's ear and said something; whereupon the boy turned with the spryness of a frightened rat.

"Come! come! come! I can lead you out of Pontoise château while you count twoscore on your fingers!"

"Follow him swiftly," commanded Falaise, again seizing Margaret's hand. "For if Gabriel could lead good St. Peter out of the prison-house, so can Boso, and God goes with us in His power this day."

Margaret never remembered all that came after that. For Boso guided them down the stairway, blind, dark, sinuous, like the one in the high donjon. Presently the queen knew that they were in a long store-room — lighted by little slits — with vast heaps of meal bags, tierces of salted butter, mountains of cured hams, but all as silent as the grave. Then through an armory, winding their way among chests of bolts for crossbows, grim battering engines and catapults, heaps of dust-covered and mouldering shields. All these deserted, too, but when they came to the next room Margaret's heart beat faster. They heard loud voices and singing through a narrow partition.

"This noise? Is there no danger?" said she, drawing back, but Boso only chuckled.

"The wine room, of course, sister Margaret. De Ormoy's men-at-arms have been swimming in Burgundy since morning, but they will not see us. Swift!"

And on he went, till the Provençal forgot to count the

great dim chambers through which they passed. Once again they heard voices that seemed following after them, but Boso suddenly wheeled in his labyrinth and the pursuers never came. Presently Margaret knew that the light was leaving her, that she was plunging downward. Their path turned and turned. Around them crept a damp and earthy smell such as had not been even in the oubliette. And once the Provençal's heart began to fail her.

"I am afraid. This is so like the prison."

"A little dark!" sniffed Boso, contemptuously. "I should not think Falaise's sister would fear that."

Then she found herself on a stair so steep that it needed both hands to keep herself steady, though Boso clambered down before with marvellous swiftness. The way was over bare rock, slippery with moss and weeds. Again returned the light — little cracks of sunshine it seemed, far away, now broader and brighter, through fissures pierced in the thick barrier of stone, but partly hidden by clinging grass and shrubs outside. Then at last Margaret knew what they did. They were descending to the bed of the Oise by a passage hewn through the heart of the rock.

"Perhaps Charlemagne made these stairs," said Falaise, as she clambered after Margaret, "perhaps holy St. Maclou; but barring the angels and blessed saints I think no one knows anything about them now save Huon, Jean of the Mill, and Boso, and I."

Now they heard the brawling of the river, and its swift splashing over rocks. Now the stairs ended in a little pool which rose to Margaret's ankles; they were in a dark cavern just high enough to let them stand upright. The floor was in water, but straight before them spread a panel of glistering brightness — a piercing in the rock so low that to pass under it one must bend quite double.

Margaret clasped her hands tight as she went beneath, with Boso aiding her. Would not her dream soon end? Would she not wake again in the sightless oubliette? But she was through, Falaise was through, Boso was through. Guiding hands led her through the shimmering, dancing water. She felt the warm touch of the May wind; all around her played the afternoon sunlight. She saw the rocks and the river, the fair green plain beyond the Oise. She could turn her head, and far above, at a dizzy height, rose the bristling battlements of strong Pontoise château. No alarm, no pursuit, no danger. Then all the castle, river, plain, seemed swaying and jarring together, and she put her hands to her face.

"Oh, catch me quick, Falaise; I am surely about to die! It is all so beautiful, too beautiful for earth and so like heaven! Ah, could I but see Louis first!"

The blind girl took her in her arms, and, with the help of Boso, got her to the bank and laid her on a bed of clover. After that Falaise bade the lad run with speed to the house of Jean of the Mill, which was not far away.

     *   *   *   *   *   *   *

Blanche had swooned out of terror, and her waking came hard; Margaret out of joy, and she awoke more swiftly. When she opened her eyes it was in a place she had never seen before — a thatched room all piled with meal bags and smelling of grist and flour. Through an open lattice poured the gold of the sinking sun. Overhead a great elm was whispering, and she heard two birds, arguing no doubt about the building of a nest. She heard the whir, whir, of a mill-wheel, and the lulling melody of gushing water. She lay on a bed of sweet fresh hay. It was contentment at first to lie, to listen, to know that Pontoise château and its dark oubliette God had taken away. Then curiosity surged back. "Where am I?" She rose on her elbow, and looked — started. Across the floor came Louis the king. . . . What Margaret first said, what Louis said, no pen has written, unless it be the pen of all-wise Raphael, who keeps the holy book of God from which no pure and loving thought or word shall ever be lost. Yet after the first gladness had passed, Margaret rose up, and, white as she was, made to kneel at her husband's feet.

"Lord, dear heart for whom I would so gladly die, hear, hear before a thousand others tell you. I have brought dishonor on your name. It is true I fled with Gui — "

But Louis lifted her up and kissed her pale forehead, nor might she say another word.

"Dear life," he cried, and would not let her go. "I know it all, and how you are still my true and blameless wife that none may take away. What you did, you did because God gave the devil power over me to kindle me to mad anger. Nor will I forgive you — who need no forgiveness, but might stand blameless before the highest saint — until you say you have forgiven me."

"Ah, Louis, that I have long hours ago! My love was all so great that it seemed my heart would burn away in my breast. We have been terribly deceived. But the Blessed Mother has opened our eyes and all is well — "

"And all is well?" There came a spark out of the king's eye that she had never seen before. She trembled, not with dread, but because the king stood up above her so tall and splendid.

"All is well?" spoke Louis, "you say all is well?"

"Why, yes, — but I forget; there is still danger. And doubtless France is lost!"

And then the king seemed grander to her than ever.

"I am king over Louis of Poissy," he spoke, with upraised hand. "What matter, then, if I am king over France?"

"You are grown taller," she cried out, "and your voice is like a trumpet, and your mien is not as yesterday, but as of a terrible and righteous king — a Charlemagne. What has happened? I am afraid of you; yet I love you all the more."

"I have been crowned; crowned not at Reims, but in some fairer shrine than that — I think by a spirit from God himself, for He has been good to me, and heard my prayer. Margaret," — and here he whispered, — "I am a king!"

Then while she wondered, he bent down again in his right noble pride and kissed her lips, and she looking up at him saw that it was even so.

"You are a king, Louis," said she, with glad sobbing. "You are my king."

Gently he comforted her, but at last returned to his first words, "And you say that all is well? Were you not held up in the great hall before all the court while Enguerraud de Coucy put dishonor upon you?"

"Yes; what matter? You have forgiven me. I care not now for the tongues and hatred of all France."

"But I care very much," said he, almost sternly. "And what is this foul tale that we are not wedded husband and wife? I do not understand."

His brow was dark, but Margaret saw the anger was not for her and answered, "Bless God, then, your mother was right! You do not know! The bishop has lied! You thought there was no flaw in our marriage."

"What bishop?" demanded Louis, his face like a thunder-cloud.

So she told him everything that Gui had said, and

Monseigneur of Beauvais had said, and Blanche had said.
When she was finished, Louis sat on the great corn-sack
by her bed and twisted and untwisted his fingers in a stillness only broken by the rushing of the mill. After a time
he asked : —

"Margaret, is it not commanded, ' Honor thy parents ' ? "
She nodded.

"It is well it is commanded, yet in this hour it is an
ordinance right hard to keep. It is also well that my
mother is so saintly; it will take a store of her alms-deeds
to cancel off this sin. So it has been proclaimed to the
court that not only had you fled with Gui, but that you
were very doubtfully my queen."

"Yes," — then she started, and caught his hand. "Oh,
dearest lord, why is your face so knit and hard ? "

"Because," he said gently, "I see that the world is
very full of sin, and that even with all my strength I can
redress only a little of it. But I know what I shall do for
this."

"What thing ? "

"Trust me; you shall soon see. Are you feeling more
strong ? "

"Much stronger," and again she rose, this time enough
to glance up through the lattice, and lo ! above her head
were the steep heights of Pontoise château. The color
began to leave her face once more. "The castle ! Oh, I
thought we were leagues away ! So near enemies who
seek you ! your danger is so great ! "

"I think not," he smiled confidently. "The castle is
both near and far. Near as the stone falls, far as through
the streets of the town. For the Pontoise burgher folk are
in a stormy mood just now, and I do not think De Ormoy
will send his ruffians riding down those narrow streets with

all the women tumbling roof tiles on their heads and the
hulking weavers swinging axes and bawling 'St. Maclou
and the king!'"

"Then you have declared yourself, the city has risen,
De Coucy is besieged!"

Louis shook his head and smiled again.

"I am 'Sir Roland of Poissy,' a plain captain, who in
the king's name has sent messengers to the royal men-at-
arms at Beaumont to come down at speed, and in the
meantime has promised the maîtres, echevins, and syndics
of the city that if their trained bands contain the rebels
in the castle, he will mention their loyal action to his
Grace, and beseech him to enlarge their charter."

"And where am I?" asked Margaret, feeling very safe.

"You are in the granary of the mill of one Jean, who
with his wife Brigite and child Nicole are honest folk
whom the good God loves. Falaise is near by with the
others; but barring Falaise they know only that you are a
great court lady who has escaped from the rebels, and
whom Sir Roland will protect. Yet, I think it is best to
tell the truth to another."

So he went to the door, and called softly, "Ambroise!"
The priest came instantly, and the first sight of his kindly
face was a joy to Margaret. Then Louis took her hand
in one of his, Ambroise's hand in the other, saying simply:
"Dear father, we are both in such a state that you must
know all the truth. This is the lady I deemed my wife,
about whom I came to you in such sore trouble, and all is
now well between us."

"I am very happy, sweet children," said Ambroise,
wondering.

"But now we are in sore doubts whether we are truly
married, and to resolve these doubts first I tell you who we

x

are. I am Louis of Poissy, called the king, and this lady's name is Margaret of Provence."

Ambroise grew as white as his own best alb. His teeth chattered. "*Salvator mundi, salva nos omnes!*" was all he could think to mutter in that supreme moment. Then his eyes grew wider till they almost started from his head. He had never spoken before with a greater man than the Vidame of Chauvry, who had been pompous enough for the Holy Father. At last he began sinking to his knees.

"Oh, *domine!* I am only a miserable, uncourtly, unlettered priest! What have I done? what have I said? Do eagles consort with sparrows? does the lion take counsel of mice? Pity me—I am undone!"

Louis' laugh was as clear as Falaise's when he lifted the curé up, and would not let him kiss his hand.

"Dear father, because it has pleased God to make us rich in this world's honor, He does not, alas, make us also so rich in the grace of heaven that you cannot give true aid. And in truth I would never have told you had there been any other way. Now rise up, hearken to all that I shall say to you, and give fair answer without favor, without fear."

Whereupon the king related all the infamy of the bishop, and of the sinful command of the queen mother at Sens. After which he looked straight at Ambroise and asked him flatly.

"Tell now, whether this lady is as much my lawful wedded wife as we are forever wedded in spirit and in love."

Ambroise grew terribly pale again, and shook with a palsy. It was some time before he could stammer—

"I am an unlearned man. It is a thing for canonists. I would send to Rome. The Pope must answer it. Has

your Grace no wise bishops and Paris schoolmen to
consult ? "

"None here," rejoined Louis, fixedly, "and yet to-night
this lady goes back to the château, and I hold her up before
all the court as my undoubted queen and wife.   And yet
you say there is much doubt."

"Oh, much!   Do not press me, *domine*.   I have no
wisdom," groaned Ambroise, wringing his hands.

"There is grave doubt," cried Margaret, close to tears.
"What we did before we did in innocency; but now we
must no more call ourselves husband and wife until the
Holy Father has spoken.   It is cruel, when we never
loved so much as now ! "

But the king only smiled serenely, and clasped her hand.

"Dear heart," he said, "do not fear.   There is an easy
way out of this last pain."

More he was about to say, when Jean's voice broke in
upon them.

"Your worship's pardon, but there is a tall knight
demanding to see you and will take no 'nay.' "

The king looked up and laughed gladly.

"De Joinville at last!   How he will marvel to see all I
have done and dared alone ! "

But the gladdest shout was from the guardsman, when
he saw his lady and lord together and love alight in their
eyes.

CHAPTER XXVI

A MARRIAGE IN ST. MACLOU

WHERE had De Joinville been? I fear he made awkward work relating it to his confessor. Truth to tell, after he had quitted Louis he wandered back to the merrymakers, and then — being no white-gloved warrior — into Jaufre's wine shop, where amid the clanking of cups, and songs from Florette and Eglantine, not overprudish maidens, he fell asleep. He woke about noon under the vintner's table, for the kind man had never disturbed his snoring. Next, after Simon's headache had passed a little, Jaufre began to pour into his ears, not Saintonge, but rumors from the château, when lo! St. George's dragon seemed raging in the wine shop.

"The king! What had befallen the king! To the devil with all the spawn of the house of Coucy!"

Simon raged down to Ambroise's house, and scared the old housekeeper into whimpering that "Sir Roland had gone with his Reverence the night before, and now was off with the priest to Montmorenci wood to visit a dying bandit."

"Thunder of God! It is France herself that is dying!"

Then De Joinville cursed himself for ever parting from the king, and for touching Jaufre's liquor, and started on a hired carter's nag for Montmorenci, but on the road, up behind him raced the chamberlain himself and an armed band, at so brisk a gallop that they never noticed whom they overtook. Clearly a pursuit of the king. Simon gave up his lord for lost, and fell back on a recourse he never tried save in dire extremity — prayer, I am not very sure whether to God or to the devil.

Nevertheless he followed doggedly, grinding his teeth and making mad resolves. At last he chose a convenient place in the road whence he could watch the return of the band. When it came in sight he would charge out, and send at least the sleek chamberlain to his reward before the others rode him down. Two mortal hours he waited, and comforted himself by muttered oaths. Then when the click and roar of the troopers was on him he made ready to spur straight out at De Coucy; then reined in and rubbed his eyes. The king was not in the band. The very droop of the horses' tails told of an unsuccessful hunting. So De Joinville scratched his head again, marvelling, and soon after the troopers had passed he met a peasant lad who ended his doubts.

"Yes, he had seen Father Ambroise returning a long time ago, and with him a comely young gentleman. They were walking fast."

"By which road?"

"Oh, along a by-path across the fields."

Simon breathed easier. Let the king keep off the road and he would never meet De Coucy. The guardsman cantered back, but the more haste proved the less speed. His sorry beast was soon winded, and the shadows were long when he neared Pontoise. To his amazement he saw the gate guarded by armed burghers, and peasants were trooping from the villages with scythes and hunting spears. At the bridge four fat constables stopped him.

"You will serve for the king against the rebels?" was their demand.

"That I will, by every saint! But who is the captain that has put Pontoise in this most brave array?"

"Sir Roland of Poissy, to be sure. We do not know whence he came, but two hours since, a gallant young knight strides into the Hôtel de Ville, where the syndics and echevins wagged their heads. 'Order out the *ban* and the *arrière-ban*, in the king's name, and besiege the rebels,' ordered he, and stood and spoke so masterfully and grandly, that their worships never asked 'your warrant?' So the bells began to ring, the commune ran to arms, and now the great folk in the château are sealed up like wine in the bottle."

"A wondrous leader is Sir Roland," answered Simon, smiling. "I know him well. But where may he be found?"

"At Jean's mill. When we came out to guard the bridge, he had gone to a noble lady, who had escaped from the château and lay there sick."

Thus it came to pass that Simon rode on to the mill, filled with surpassing wonder. The town in arms, the conspirators already half beaten! Was this the deed of a lad who but yesterday would weep twice a day for his mother?

Into the granary tramped Simon and made stiff, soldierly obeisance to the king; but I have told of his shout of gladness when he saw Margaret, still white, but safe and sound.

"O *damoiseau*, O little madame, tell me the saint who saved you both, and I —" Here he stopped, for he knew his prayers were not of the kind to be answered, and pilgrimages and fasts were seldom to his liking.

"The saint, good Simon," said the king, smiling, "has not the fair fortune yet to be in heaven, but, more fortunate than the martyrs, she shall not lack for friends on earth."

Then he called Falaise. The blind girl entered, and Louis said : —

"This is the saint who saved the queen of France from the oubliette of Pontoise château, and who, please God, shall evermore be my good sister."

Down on his knees went the iron form of the commandant. He held Falaise's hand to his lips reverently, and I think a tear fell on her fingers. It was a tribute more precious than gold. Falaise might not see, yet she could feel, the picture, and in her beautiful, sightless eyes there were bright tears also. Twice De Joinville tried to thank her, twice he coughed, then owned himself beaten, and was silent. After a while he mustered courage to fling at the king gruff questions.

"So you returned from the forest to Pontoise after learning of the plot?"

"You see me here, sirrah," said Louis, meekly.

"Imprudent, very; your duty was to lie safe, and let your vassals fight for you."

"My duty was to my captive wife and mother. My mother is still in the château." The king's voice broke a little.

"And so you roused the echevins and syndics; the town is armed; De Coucy and his cage of snakes besieged?"

"You are very right."

"As I'm a Christian sinner," swore the guardsman, "you answer like one of old King Philip's captains. Ah, but one thing is forgot, and it is well that I've come! The men-at-arms at Beaumont!"

"I have sent messengers to La Girard long since. He should be here soon after nightfall. Then *I* storm Pontoise."

"You! you! you!" and the guardsman's jaw sunk lower and lower. "You are but a raw lad. *damoiseau.* You

have never struck a blow in anger. You would faint at
sight of blood. Leave the storming to tough dogs like
La Girard and old Simon de Joinville. What would your
lady mother say?" And he slapped the king familiarly
upon the shoulders. He never did it to Louis again, for
under that stroke the king's form seemed to heighten with
pride.

"Good Simon de Joinville," Louis said quietly, "to-day
and henceforth I will ever bear you all gratitude and love,
but when I have spoken I have spoken, and who save God
shall say me nay?"

All the blood leaped into the guardsman's face. He
fell back a step, then bowed, in his manner, stiffly.

"My lord is right," he muttered; "my business is only
to obey."

"Ah, Simon," cried Louis, with his clear laugh, "now
I am glad; for now even you confess that I am in mien,
as well as name, a king!"

Then out he went to the worthy echevins, who were
come down to wait on his Grace's great captain, and to
tell him that thanks to the resolute front of the Pontoise
burgesses a sortie from the castle had retreated without
shooting an arrow. And they all wondered, but most of
all De Joinville, at his sureness of word and will, and the
flash of his eye, which silenced all their arguments. The
courage of the gallant magistrates had so risen that they
had to be restrained from trying to storm the château.
Therefore, Louis sent them away with his last orders, before the coming of La Girard's company, and never listened
to good Maitre Bourget's broad hint, "that his own house
was somewhat more fitting to harbor gentle dames than
the cottage of this honest miller."

After the echevins were gone, the king went back to

Margaret. She was no longer in the granary. Strength had returned and desire for food. The king found her in the house on a bench by Nicole's bed. In her lap was a huge wooden bowl full of rich milk and bits of the famous bread of Brigite, and her wooden spoon plied with a zest which did his soul good. Falaise sat on the floor by Nicole's cot, where he had knelt and had seen the vision. And as the blind girl sang to the little maid, who was still weak and wan, the king closed his eyes, and asked if heaven were not near in very deed. If only his mother were present also, his cup would be full!

The sun was low behind the town when Margaret finished her feasting and Falaise her songs. The long, gray shadows of the château and its rock went creeping out by stealthy marches across the river and Aumône beyond. As the light died the water seemed to run on in softer and softer plash and music. Bird whistled to bird in the tall elm. The evening was all peaceful and still, and it scarce seemed possible that the night it covered must see deeds of violence and doubtless of blood. De Joinville — fidgeting old war-horse — would tramp out into the road and squint toward Beaumont, tramp back again, clatter his scabbard, and gnaw at his mustachios, although he knew La Girard would not come for two good hours. Nicole's head had sunk in slumber when Louis called Margaret and Ambroise one side.

"Now you must take us to the church," he said to the priest.

"I do not understand; for what?" asked Ambroise, blankly.

"To marry us, to be sure. Have I not sworn that I will enter Pontoise château this night and that this night also Margaret of Provence reënters it as my wife?"

Ambroise was marvellously confounded.

"Oh, your Grace, how is this possible? It may be this lady is your wife; it may be she is not! A matter for learned canonists! A sacrament cannot be repeated. I pray you to wait. No bans are published, no — "

Louis silenced him with one fine sweep of his hand.

"Since it must be so, I, as your king, command you 'marry us.' For if we are not man and wife, in God's name make us so! And if we are, let all the sin of a double marriage rest upon me; and he that calls you to account shall answer to the sovereign of France, who will defend you — yes, against the Holy Father."

And after that, what more could Ambroise say?

If Margaret and Louis never forgot their marriage in stately Sens, still less did they forget their second marriage in St. Maclou. They had told Jean and Brigite that they had been long betrothed, and since "Sir Roland" must lead the attack that night, it was not well to remain unwedded. The miller, his wife, and Falaise — for an old woman watched Nicole — went up the steep way with them to the church, whither Ambroise had gone before. And short as was the time, he could not suffer such a pair to be married without a little state. There was a glorious array of tapers on the altar shining down the black nave, when they entered it, and Monsieur Tabal was rumbling the little organ. The dying twilight filtering through the flowery tracery of the windows spread the church out to a cathedral grandeur. And when Monsieur Tabal struck up a hymn Falaise's voice rose with it higher, higher, till all the hidden gargoyles seemed opening larks' throats, and from the roof there pealed out silver bells.

So they went up to the altar, where Ambroise met them in his fairest embroidered cope and surplice.

"But we have no ring!" said Margaret; and grew red and sad, thinking how she had cast her wedding ring away, while as for Louis', it was safely locked in the strong box of the Jew. But Brigite felt on her fingers and twisted off the silver ring Jean had set there on a wedding day in St. Maclou years before. How proud she was to lend it to a great knight for his lady! Then this small trouble being ended, Louis and Margaret stood side by side, whilst Ambroise made them man and wife. And clear and strong through the length and height of the church sounded the great words, "*Ego jungo vos!*"

After the wedding came the wedding mass. The married pair knelt down with the miller, the miller's wife, Falaise, and gruff De Joinville, and together they received the body of our Lord. After which the king rose up and kissed his wife upon her lips.

"Ah, Margaret," whispered he, "is this not fairer than great Sens? For we were children then, scared at the throng, and fearsome of each other. But to-night we are strong in love, you to me, and I to you, and to the dear God. So that I feel that I dare go forth to win for you the world."

Margaret did not answer him then; her voice was choked with tears, but they were only tears of joy. Hand in hand they went down the steep to the gate. The streets were dark; over them shone the best of marriage torches, all the stars, and that shimmering veil, "The Way of St. Jacques"—by some men called the Milky Way—spread out for Margaret's bridal. There was no lily in her hand or on her head. But she and the king cared not for that!

"A strange blunder you made," said Jean to Ambroise;

"you said 'Louis' in the service when it should have been 'Roland.'"

"Did I?" answered Ambroise, innocently; "well, it shall all stand right on the parish record."

At the miller's house there was already gathered a little band of armed burghers, with lanterns, pikes, and partizans, and not a few of them wondered why his worship the king's captain was absent from his watch at a portentous hour like this, and wondered still more that he chose to honor the house of Jean with his high company rather than to sit at ease in the Hôtel de Ville. But Louis was less interested in their scrapes and bows than in the sudden appearance of Boso, who came out of the darkness, darting like a cat, seized the king's hand, and dragged him away into a corner.

"I have it. I have been there," he announced unceremoniously.

"Been in the château?"

"Oh, yes, just as you bade me! De Ormoy's men are all lined upon the wall like blackbirds on a fence. They think you are going to batter in the gate."

"But inside the donjons?"

"You can count those guarding there on your fingers. And I have something else — the watchword. I crouched in the dark while the sentries passed it."

"You have it? are you sure?"

"Very sure; it was easy to remember, 'Alithe.'"

The king said nothing, but blew through his lips for a moment, and Boso knew that he was very well pleased. Then he called De Joinville, and the two together put to Boso more questions about the château and the ways of entering it than he had ever answered before in all his life. By the time they were ended, there was a distant

roar and rumble—a great band of men-at-arms approach-
ing through the night—and De Joinville started to give
a cheer.

"The Beaumont dogs at last!" But the king clapped
his hand across his mouth.

"The child is still weak. We must not wake her," he
said gravely. "Let us go out into the road and meet La
Girard and his men."

CHAPTER XXVII

THE TEETH OF ALITHE THE CAT

They found Alithe, as Falaise had said, "after a great search of the castle." Enguerraud de Coucy had fumed and raged when she did not come. How rage had given room to suspicion and suspicion to fear — you must be dull of wit if you cannot guess. The turnkey who had told the chamberlain that his daughter had taken the blind girl forth to question her was himself nigh tortured to see if he spoke the truth, and I presume only the word of the guard's sergeant that my Lady de Coucy had gone past him with her head high and the white baton outstretched saved the poor jailer from having a cord knotted around his forehead and duly twisted with a stick. Next the search; the high donjons, gate-houses, flanking towers, store-rooms, barbicans, galleries, cabinets, and baileys, — but last of all, and none too soon for Alithe, the oubliette. And there they found her.

She was a sorry sight. Falaise had stripped away her cloak to fling it over Margaret, and torn up half of her kirtle to bind her hands and feet and make the gag. The blind girl had drawn the knots unmercifully tight. Around Alithe's wrists were great red seams where she had struggled against the cords. A deep mark stretched from her lips like a scar. Her hair was dishevelled. When her father caught the first glimpse of her, the torch almost fell from his hand.

"Oh, Holy Trinity, is this my daughter?"

318

"Water!" gasped Alithe — they had just released her. "Water! my throat burns! Cover the light, it is like needles in my eyes!"

"But the Provençal, the blind girl, where, where?" was all De Coucy could stammer, his composure at an end.

"Gone. The blind she-fiend has eyes in her finger-tips. She blew out the lamp and bound me. She is strong as Beelzebub. Then they both fled."

"And the wand — my baton?" demanded the chamberlain, groping around the cell.

"They took it."

"The devil you say they did," and away raged her father after De Ormoy, to set the castle in pandemonium. Not a sentry but was almost racked with questions. Not a sentry but swore, — some piously, some impiously, — "I have never seen those women." The chamberlain could only vent his spleen by flinging the offending turnkey himself into the oubliette, and vowing that he would be hanged before he was one day older.

But all this mended matters little. A knot of angry spirits met in the great hall when De Coucy reassembled his council. The conspirators' faces were long and black, all save De Ormoy, who grinned and swore more hideously than ever.

"We would do well," the chamberlain warned him, "to refrain from profane jests at this hour, when we may sorely need the infinite compassion of heaven."

"Compassion of the king, you mean? His Grace's mercy is better than God's just now. I have just led out fifty of my stoutest lads to try the temper of these whelps of the commune. And as I am a sinful man every street is barricaded with paving stones and chains. Women stand at upper windows with kettles of hot water, and a

thousand strapping varlets with pikes, axes, and crossbows
stand behind the barriers. So back we rode like fifty
frightened fools and never swung a sword."

"Your paladins are very gallant," sneered the chamberlain, "to turn tail at a pack of the Pontoise canaille with
all their master syndics to boot."

De Ormoy did not deign to answer; he only gave a
yet more horrible grin.

"Well," thrust in Theobald, peevishly, "I am waiting to
learn wherefore I am summoned."

"To save our skins; the plot is blasted," announced Peter,
candidly, then lapsed into his former silence.

"You speak the truth," confessed De Ormoy, hands on
his hips, and eyes leering at Alithe. "I would curse your
soul, Enguerraud, for fetching me hither, if it would do
any good. However, since it is damned already, I am
listening."

Alithe put out her hand, and touched her father, as if
bidding him be calm, and said aloud : —

"My father, you would do well to state exactly how the
matter stands. We are not children who shut our eyes."

"Dear friends," began her father, the old winsomeness
returned, "we should neither too greatly hope nor too
greatly dread. True, God has deemed best to let his
Grace slip out of our hand; also a masterful enemy has
aroused the town. It is also heaven's will" — De Coucy
bowed like the Christian that he was — "to suffer the Provençal to escape our custody. Yet, that is the least of
our ills. I greatly fear that we must sustain attack by
La Girard. But Pontoise is strong. We have gallant
friends in the outlying baronies, who, hearing of our brave
stand, will rise against the king; besides, we have a hostage."

"A hostage?" quoth Peter.

"An incomparable hostage. For Blanche of Castile has not yet fled, nor indeed does she so much as know we have the castle. Will his Grace press the siege too hard"— how soft and gliding grew De Coucy's voice— "if once he knows 'Your foes can sadly inconvenience your dear mother, if you do fail to humor them'?"

Theobald looked half ready for an outbreak, but he only pressed his lips together. Nevertheless the chamberlain's wisdom was cut short by the entrance of two barons who, like almost all the court, had submitted to the conspirators, being not unfriendly to their aim; but now one of these seigneurs stated their business briefly.

"My lord, we are sent in behalf of the noblemen and knights now in the château. We have applauded your displacement of the queen mother, but what you did we presumed you did with the king's consent. And now we demand, where is his Grace vanished? For the rumor spreads that he has been foully dealt with. Also we would ask whether this Henri de Ormoy would hold Pontoise even against his Grace's precise command? For if it be thus, he cannot count upon our swords."

The chamberlain puffed himself up, and pointed down the hall.

"And this is the answer, sirs: He who says we seek the king's death, I brand as a liar, and to the dread lest we hold Pontoise against the king's will, I tell you we do not so much as know where now is the king, nor what his will may be. But assuredly, on our honor, we will not yield the château to the kites and crows of the Pontoise burgesses, until we learn they have at least a knightly leader. Does that suffice you?"

"Excellently well," announced the messenger; "we thank your lordship."

Y

So away went the twain, but when they were gone the others had turned a little whiter, and Alithe voiced the thoughts of all the rest.

"As I feared."

"No," snarled Peter. "De Ormoy's *routiers* cannot hold at bay the town, La Girard, and half the castle too."

Whereat De Coucy turned to the bishop. "Is the queen mother recovered enough to converse with us? You were with her last."

"I think so, *mulier miserrima et regina infelix!* She is still where she fainted, in that room in the main donjon once occupied by the likewise unfortunate Margaret."

The chamberlain, without more adieu, gathered up parchment, pen, and ink from the table by which he had been standing, and beckoned to the others to follow. The sign wrung out of Theobald his first speech in a long time.

"What are you going to do?"

"You shall see, my dear seigneur, you shall see."

"Nothing against knightly honor!"

"Honor is an excellent dame. I would always have her for wife, if I could," added De Coucy, enigmatically.

Theobald's frown grew darker than ever, but he went out with the rest, and let the chamberlain lead them up into the great donjon. It was night by this time. From the innumerable casements and loopholes of the château streamed the torch-light. Bands of De Ormoy's men-at-arms were parading the courtyards, bawling low songs, and banging their pikestaves, many much the worse for drink. They were an uncourtly crew, and their chief had been put to pains to keep them from plundering the castle. The knights and fine ladies, little pleased at this company, were keeping to their chambers, and even

Alithe winced at the base leers some of the rogues tossed to her. But her father, without a word, marshalled the others up the winding stair, and in the antechamber they were met by one of the queen mother's ladies-in-waiting, a confidante of Alithe.

"How goes it with her Grace?" asked De Coucy.

"Oh, she is nigh recovered. She can sit in the arm-chair and converse. She asks unceasingly for the king, and I do not know what to say, or how to tell what has befallen the castle."

"I will make haste to enlighten her," said the chamberlain, with his most courtly bow. And with that he went straight in to Blanche.

The Castilian sat in the high chair, propped with bright silk pillows, which made her white dress and the ghastliness of her cheeks intenser. Only a single lamp burned on the table, but near her feet smouldered a brass pot of charcoal — she had complained of being cold. When the others entered, she stirred, and fastened on them her great eyes. They had lost nothing of their brightness, but she was clearly weak, and her cheeks seemed sunken and old. She showed a little wonder when she saw how many followed the chamberlain, but she held out her hand for him, Theobald, and Peter to kiss, then looked sternly on the bishop.

"I do not give my hand to you, Monseigneur of Beauvais," she said coldly; "your life, sir, has shed little credit of late on your diocese."

"We are not here to discuss the fitness of my lord bishop for holy orders," rejoined the chamberlain, abruptly, before the prelate could even redden. "Our business, please your Grace, is more important."

Blanche suddenly sat upright, and the color surged back

to her forehead. Never had the decorous chamberlain used such a tone to her before, and all her pride rose up to resist him.

"Important, indeed," spoke she, "if you would press it thus and never beg 'permission.' I trust it concerns the welfare of his Grace the king."

"Madam," replied De Coucy, regarding her steadily, "it concerns not the king's safety, but a thing just now of far greater moment."

"Your meaning, sir?" Blanche was growing angry, more at his manner than at his words.

"The welfare of you and of ourselves. I am going to require you to sign a paper which I shall straightway write."

"Require!" The proud Castilian all but leaped from her chair.

"If your Grace prefers it, I will say that I command."

At that Blanche uprose in all her outraged queenliness. Her Spanish hauteur never became her better.

"Command? Little man, little man, 'command' is not a word to princes. Keep your distance, sir. It is a thing like this which brings great seigneurs' heads down to the block."

But De Coucy, with a pressure courteous but firm, forced her down upon the chair, and stood directly facing her. Another woman would have screamed and attempted flight, but Blanche's inexorable pride locked her fast. She sat silent all the time that he was speaking. Clearly, rapidly, striving neither to excuse nor to conceal, the chamberlain told what had befallen since Blanche had fainted when Gui had snatched off Margaret. Only when he told how they had sought for the king and sought in vain, Blanche interrupted.

"Say that again, sir!" And all the others saw by the

change of her face that a mighty burden had been lifted from her mind. At last De Coucy stopped, and he and the queen remained eyeing one another in stillness, like two lions each poising for the final spring.

"Is that all, sir?" asked Blanche at last, gently enough.

"All, except to observe most humbly to your Grace that we are desperate men, and cannot be over-tender in womanish gallantries."

"I thank you for saying it. I had presumed that even conspirators and traitors kept at least a few vestiges of chivalrous nicety." She was looking at Theobald, who turned away, his face on fire. "It is a small matter. You are rebels to your king; now what may his lady mother be happy to expect?"

The chamberlain laid his parchment on the table. His pen scratched furiously for a moment, and he arose with a writing which he held forth to Blanche.

"A very little thing, madam, and thereafter you need expect only our most tender courtesies. Your hand and seal to this." Then he read the lines aloud:—

"To his Grace the most Christian King, or to any and all of his captains, to whom these may come.

"Out of love for me you will refrain from pressing the attack on Pontoise château, or doing any harm to the Sire Enguerraud de Coucy, the Counts of Champagne and Brittany, the Sire de Ormoy, the Bishop of Beauvais, or their friends. To do otherwise will place your mother and queen in most grievous sorrow and jeopardy."

The chamberlain came close to the chair, looked at the White Queen, never relaxing his gaze, and all the time held out the pen.

"Madam," said he, "be so gracious as to sign."

Blanche simply returned his gaze. Not a muscle stirred,
not an eyelash. She did not deign to answer him a word.

"Madam," repeated De Coucy, "I say that we are
desperate men; be wise and sign."

Still not a word, and again De Coucy.

"Madam, if you hesitate, you drive us to a deed we
shall regret, yet nevertheless execute."

Blanche reached forth, took the pen, but before he could
pass the parchment, snapped the reed with both hands
and flung it on the floor.

"The Sire de Coucy has my full reply," she said.

The chamberlain, without even a muttered curse, took
another pen from the table, and offered again.

"Madam, sign quickly, or, by the Blessed Trinity, I
swear that we will hold a bright coal from this brazier
against your cheek. You are in our power. The king has
slipped through our hands — the fiends know why! La
Girard and De Joinville will soon be thundering under
the walls. Men dare do anything to save their heads;
yes, even damn their souls if needs be. Therefore, sign
this — or carry the scars on your fair cheeks down to your
dying bed."

Then it was a sight to see Blanche put on yet other
pride. Up she rose, and it needed no gold or jewels on
her beautiful white head to make her splendid as a pagan
goddess. Her eyes went round that little company like
two sharp darts thrusting deep into the hearts of all.

"And who will do this gallant deed?" cried she, with
the least hint of a laugh. "Who will do it, this rare
courtesy to the queen mother, to the first lady of France?
Ah, you, my Lord Theobald? We have long been friends;
once you sung my praise like an amorous jongleur. You
will do the deed?"

"God's death; no! I am not Satan's brother."

"Or you, my brave Lord of Brittany?" Peter only turned his back in silence, and he too grew red.

"Or you, Monsieur of the Handsome Mouth? I have not the honor of your name." Whereat De Ormoy turned his back and blasphemed inwardly.

"Or you, Monseigneur? A right clerical and holy office." At which the bishop groaned, "God forbid!" and looked more miserable than ever.

"Who, then?" cried Blanche, her hands upraised in triumph. "Who, then? For I am not so mild a lamb that my Lord de Coucy can do his pleasant deed alone."

"Madam, sign, or I will aid my father!"

But even as Alithe spoke, Theobald of Champagne smote her with one blow to the floor. The count was almost foaming with rage.

"Lie there, and let the fiends all seize you!" Then he whipped out his sword. "Your beauty is foul as death. Lie there, while I kill you — not 'Alithe of the Bright Face,' but 'of the Devil's Mask,' — that is your name!"

Alithe struggled from under his feet, while the others dragged back his sword. When he saw his prey glide away from him, he dashed the useless weapon at the queen mother's feet, then knelt down before her, and tears ran down his face.

"Your Grace," — he spoke thickly, — "I am a traitor to my king and to you. I have basely consented to the wronging of that innocent and noble princess Margaret of Provence. My life is forfeit by the law of God and by the law of France. But when I lay down my head at the Place de Grêve to make the 'honorable amend,' I will do it as a knight who has not wholly pawned his soul.

Come life, come death, I'll have no more of this De Coucy and his plot."

"Away, fellow," bawled De Ormoy. "Are you turned stark mad?"

The *routier* and De Coucy dragged Theobald to his feet; yet he shook them off as a stag does the hounds.

"Go to perdition by your chosen road," he shot back from the door. "Your road is no more mine. When Pontoise falls, I'll face the doom, and none shall see me wince."

"There goes a madman," spoke De Ormoy.

"A madman who raves aright," answered Peter.

But what De Coucy would have said will never be told, for at this instant a wide-eyed sergeant burst in without announcement.

"Haste, Lords — a great force of men-at-arms before the gates! Arrows are buzzing — an attack!"

"La Girard at last," proclaimed De Coucy, turning a little paler. "Well, we must beat him back. And then" — he winged a last sinister glance at Blanche, who yet stood facing him in her splendor — "we will resume the argument with your Grace."

A moment later, and Blanche of Castile found herself alone in the room of the high donjon, while far below, like echoes drifting from another world, uprose the shout and roar of combat!

CHAPTER XXVIII

DE COUCY FINDS THE KING

The sound of attack and defence rose and fell fitfully. Now all the dark seemed springing to life, so fierce were the war cries, so loud the jar and clash of arms; then, like thunder dying off among the hills, all would grow silent, till Blanche could catch only the creeping of the May-time wind, and the sweet hush of the warm night. Of a sudden belched the hoarse yell of De Ormoy's men, the *routiers'* war shout:—

"A lion! A lion! Lay on! lay on!" to be answered by the deep "*Montjoie St. Denis!*" the battle-cry of the royal house of France, and the rasping of ropes and a great crashing and snapping.

"They are working catapults," said the White Queen in her heart, for she had seen her share of battles and of leaguers, woman that she was, and knew their sounds too well. Then as the next moment of stillness came, a great wave of helplessness and sorrow swept over the Castilian. Other crises she had faced, but never one when she, the masterful and strong, sat helpless. She had two sorrows — fear, not for herself, but for Louis: pride — the wounded pride of self-righteousness proved in sinful error. How terribly she had been deceived in De Coucy and Alithe, how terribly in Margaret! And there was more than that; Blanche was face to face with her own transgressions. She was doing what for a truly good woman is hard enough — confessing her great sins. Not an over-worldly love for pearls and white samite, — for which Father Foulque had always an unctuous absolution, — but her real sins, — pride, wilful blindness, selfish love. She had treated Margaret with a wanton lack of charity. She had read in her deeds and words "guilt," where God had doubtless written "innocence." Inexorable to all others, the Castilian was inexorable to herself, and when she looked at her own sins she bowed her head in shame as well as grief.

" *Mea culpa ; mea maxima culpa !* If France is lost, and Louis, and Margaret, the fault is mine ! O dear Lord, I see all plainly now. I cannot bear this guilt upon my soul ! "

The answer to her prayer was a renewed bursting of the storm of battle. From the donjon windows she could see the lights dancing hither and thither in the open space before the château. Now came the clash of steel, and hand-to-hand fighting before the gate, while a loud voice — Peter of Brittany's, perchance — trumpeted to the defenders to "Fling La Girard's villains into the moat ! " But the " *Montjoie St. Denis !* " of the enemy sounded clearly back ; and soon the sortie — if sortie there had been — was driven behind the walls, and again came stillness.

Blanche shivered, and went back into the room. She tried the door. Bolted from without — the chamberlain had seen to that ere leaving her. In the courts below men went backward and forward with ringing steps.

"Every knave of you on the walls ! Another attack is mustering ! " thundered an officer. Blanche knelt down to pray for the souls of those dying in the fight. Dying — she told herself, with unspeakable bitterness, because of her own blind trust and folly. La Girard could never storm

Pontoise. She knew enough of the siege of castles to be sure of that. His attack would fail. The friends of Peter of Brittany, Monseigneur of Beauvais, and the De Coucys were half of the nobility and would rise all over France. There would be devastating war, the whole realm endangered, and the one strong heart and hand that had guided the kingdom through so many straits — her own — must stay a prisoner, a useful hostage in the rebels' hands. One comfort was hers — a great one. Louis had escaped. Doubtless he was now with La Girard, but who was he to be cast adrift in this fierce crisis — he who, in all his life — till yesterday — had never done a manly deed till his mother bade it. And Blanche bit her lips till they almost bled, as she realized the fateful use De Coucy would make of her as his prisoner. She could defy threats, tortures, death. But mere knowledge that the rebels held his mother, let her break a thousand pens, would make the king content to sign an abject peace, the ruin of the kingdom. Let her speak to him but once. "They shall murder me with tortures; these are nothing if you never yield;" and Blanche would have had her dearest wish.

Again the attack and fiercer. She was at the casement, saw dark masses of men crossing the open betwixt the town and the château. Next came the shattering blows of a great beam on the gate; but the Castilian shook her head. "They can never take Pontoise thus."

Then silence, broken by cheers from the defenders. The attack had failed. Blanche turned away sick and weary at heart. Her captors did not give her even the poor company of a keeper. All her high dignity had vanished. She was no longer young. Her youth had sped stormily, and now in her gathering evening God had sent her this great sorrow. She lay on the couch, the same couch on which Margaret had tossed in her own bitterness, and every vengeful thought would have left the Provençal — had it not already — could she have seen her husband's mother, trembling, sobbing in her lonely pain.

* * * * * * *

How long the White Queen lay there I can hardly tell. She was very weak. Perhaps a kind of drowse spread over her, lulling her to unhealthful rest. But after a time she awoke with a start. The lamp was burning low, yet over her spread the shadow of a man, — the shadow of Louis the king.

" My mother," and then, while yet she wondered whether an angel in his likeness had not flitted down from heaven, he knelt and laid his head within her lap.

" Louis, my son, and best beloved ! " for at the touch of his hand she ceased to tremble, and pressed him to her breast, nor did either say anything more for long. But Blanche was the first to wake from the ecstasy. A mother's fears are keen. " Oh, dearest and best ! " cried she, in yet new agony, " why are you here ? The castle is not taken ? A prisoner, too, and in De Coucy's clutch ? "

" No," he answered, with a grave, calm smile, which gave her joy, a smile she had not seen before. " I am no prisoner of De Coucy. Of my own will I entered Pontoise château. Do not be fearful ; we are wholly safe."

" Safe ? We ? " Blanche dropped his hands and stared about her, but he took them up again.

" Very safe, mother mine. Yet do not ask me why and wherefore, for in good time you shall see."

" And the repulsed attack ? "

" Was even as I ordered it."

"*You ?* Did you, and not De Joinville or La Girard, lead the fight ? "

"My mother," said Louis, sweetly and reverently, "last night God made me king. And sometime, not now, I will tell you all, that you may understand."

"Kneel down, Louis," she commanded, "here, where the lamp-light falls on you. Now look into my eyes." And then she scanned his face. She saw all the lines of drooping weakness gone, and strength and calm written there, — the high, pure strength that might not fail. "Louis," she said at last, "you are indeed a king."

"My mother," he answered, while she kissed his forehead, "I would rather hear you say that, than have all Spain and England added to my crown of France."

He rose and stood with her head against his breast, and stroked her beautiful white hair.

"Mother mine," he said, "Margaret has told me everything. She is innocent."

"I know it."

"Also, my mother, when you caused that flaw to be cast on our marriage at Sens, do you know that for the first time in your life you committed deadly sin?"

"I know it. I did it all in love for you and for France. I would not have you yoked unhappily. But can you and Margaret ever forgive? Can God ever forgive?"

"Margaret and I have forgiven you already. And if we who are human and sinful can forgive, is the dear Lord God more harsh?"

He moved from her toward the door, but she drew him back with both her hands.

"You will not leave me all alone?" she pleaded, almost like a child, yet he put her by most gently.

"I will not leave you. I would only summon De Coucy."

"De Coucy? Do I hear aright?"

"Most surely. Do not fear. Though the things I say

and do seem strange and perilous, be not troubled. For
God is with me this night and makes me sage and strong."

Then she heard the clinking of a ring shirt beneath his
cloak, and was a little comforted. He took the dagger
from his belt and pried through the crack, pushing the
clumsy bolt until the door sprang open. Outside no one
was watching, but a little down the stairs was crouched a
serving varlet, a clownish scoundrel, who had taken a
monstrous fright at the din of the onslaught and had
hidden himself in the donjon. If he feared the attackers
greatly, I think he feared the sudden advent of the king
about as much as he would the coming of the devil. But
at last he got over his trembling and whimpering enough
to rush away with strict orders "to find the Sire de Coucy,
and tell him his Grace the king awaited him in the queen
mother's chamber." Whereupon his lord deliberately
returned to the White Queen. She saw that he arranged
his dress carefully to conceal the ring shirt, and also that
he drew the thick curtains, covering the inner bedroom,
tightly together. But Blanche was growing wise that
night; she never asked a question.

One moment, two, three, and into the room strode
Enguerraud de Coucy. The chamberlain was flushed and
almost panting. Across his forehead was a red gash, the
wound of a passing arrow; he wore a helmet and a cuirass.
When he came face to face with the king, the two stood
looking upon one another in tense silence an instant, till
habit sent the newcomer down upon one knee. "Your
Grace, this is a sudden advent amongst us. We have
searched for you. We feared some evil had befallen —"

"I thank you for your solicitude," said the king, quietly,
nigh unconcernedly; "you see I am exceeding well. At
the pilgrimage shrine I visited, it pleased God to show my

spirit great mercy and resolve all my fears; therefore I returned to the château."

The chamberlain was still eyeing the king to make sure here was no impostor or ghost. Louis stretched out his hand, De Coucy seized and kissed it, and the touch resolved the last doubt. Louis of Poissy, the keystone to the great arch of conspiracy, was truly in Pontoise and in the confederates' power! Anything, everything, was possible. The king could almost hear the "*gratias Deo*" murmured by the lips that pressed his fingers. Still the chamberlain could not cease from wonder.

"But, sire, may I make so bold to ask how your Grace entered Pontoise château, and by whose command is this attack launched on us if not by your orders? Is this not La Girard's company?"

"You are very right. This is surely the Beaumont garrison. But the king of France," Louis spoke with the least tinge of pride, "need not fear to trust himself in his own castle. It was at my command that La Girard drew off his men-at-arms. My mother was in your custody." He moved over beside her, and stood with his hand upon her shoulder. "Rather than suffer her to be tormented with fears in my absence, I presented myself alone before one of your sally-ports, and the watchers, recognizing, made haste to let me in. They said my lady mother was in the great donjon; therefore I went to her."

Louis had spoken naturally, winsomely; all the time his grave eyes seemed searching De Coucy through and through. He went on: —

"And I made haste to send for you, fair seigneur, because I knew they were wrong when they said to me that loyal and proven vassals, such as the De Coucys and their friends, could desire to possess themselves even of their

royal master's castle from any reason save love for his
kingly glory and the yet greater glory of God.   Therefore
I would ask of you — what is your wish, and wherefore
have you seized Pontoise château ?''

Enguerraud was a man of brisk and nimble wit, but
he had scarce prepared himself for this — for the king to
cast himself upon his mercy and his Christian honor.
Clearly Blanche had not told of the insults and the threat-
enings.   Then, with a rush of certainty, it came over De
Coucy that he had only to deal with a sweet-spoken fool,
who would barter his kingdom rather than have blood flow
or high words spoken.   *Carpe horam !* one must strike
while the iron was hot.

The chamberlain had never bowed more gracefully than
when he gave his answer.

"Let it please your Grace, the thing your loyal lieges
have done has been long maturing.   They have long rejoiced that your Grace, as befits a truly pious king, has
bestowed more attention upon the deeds of the spirit than
those of the body.   Nevertheless they observed that the
government of this realm was falling into an unhappy and
disordered state.   It accordingly seemed good to them to
remove from around your Grace such influences as might
prevent them from making effectual petitions as to the
betterment of the kingdom."

"I understand," spoke the king.

"It has, perchance, come to your Grace, how it has
pleased God to make manifest the sinful folly of Margaret
of Provence and Gui of Avignon, and also to cast grave
doubts upon the validity of your marriage."

"I have heard everything.   You know in what manner
we parted."

The king seemed submissive and guileless as of old.   His

mother gazed up at him, and began to tremble. As for
De Coucy, he was striving against too broad a smile. Mirth
did not become one who might soon be the virtual potentate
of the kingdom with its cares.

"If it will please your Grace," said the chamberlain,
"your humble lieges made bold to set on parchment certain reformations which they conceive will be for the honor
of your throne and the vast welfare of France."

"I would gladly see them," and Louis bowed almost
obsequiously, "since a trusted friend like you, fair sir,
assures me they are for my kingly honor. But your
friends — my other vassals — who united with you in this
enterprise?"

"If my lord will be so good, I will summon them."

"Do so, without delay."

The varlet, who had run once as messenger, was still
hanging without the door, and ten words from the De
Coucy sped him on a second errand. The chamberlain
himself did not dare to quit his precious prisoner, but
killed the time in glib talk about the infinite mercies of
God and of Our Blessed Lady; of how the kings of France
had ever been the favored sons of heaven; how the De
Coucys had performed infinite service for their suzerains;
to all of which Louis smiled gravely, answering, "True,
most true," until the appearance of the other confederates
gave other things to think of.

Peter of Brittany was there, Monseigneur, De Ormoy,
Alithe, and Theobald of Champagne, but he came almost
perforce, for Peter and De Ormoy stood behind him, and
the *routier* kept his heavy hand on the count's shoulder.
Low was the reverence; Alithe's courtesy had never been
more graceful. The pallor of her imprisonment had passed.
Her father said in his heart. "She was never more beauti-

ful; see how the king looks at her with desire." And truly
Louis looked at her, but not — it may be — as the Sire de
Coucy thought. When the White Queen saw Alithe, her
lips curled. I think she would have spoken bitterly, but
the king touched her shoulder. She kept silence, and let
Louis work his will.

"Are these the loyal friends who have undertaken the
better ordering of my realm?" asked the king, facing
them.

"We are, please your Grace," spoke Peter, though even
he was nervous and still a little pale.

"This is a strange manner of loyalty, gentlemen." Louis'
gaze seemed wandering, and his voice had the least un-
steadiness. "If it were not that my mother is in your
hands — "

"Think not of me, not of me, I pray it! Oh, let them
wreak their worst! Think of your kingship! Think of
France!" Thus Blanche. Again the firm touch, and she
was silent. Louis stood over her, his arm cast round her
neck, and sheltered thus she grew confident and calm.

"I am at your mercy, gentlemen," said Louis, with almost a quiver; "holding my mother, you hold everything.
I can only beseech you to state your terms speedily, that
I may deliver her from this evil plight. I must take your
professions of sincere loyalty as true coin."

"If your Grace is willing — read." It was Alithe who
held out the parchment, and presented it with another
inimitable courtesy. The king unfolded it slowly, rattling
the stiff sheet. And now Blanche dared a whisper.
"What is this? sounds from behind? did I hear harness
clank?"

"Hush, my mother. Fear nothing; pray to God and all
is very well."

Then he held up the parchment, and began in a voice needlessly loud and shrill.

"The text of a proclamation—and in your own writing, my Sire de Coucy. It only lacks my hand and seal, which doubtless you desire?"

"Your Grace is right," smiled the chamberlain.

"To begin then, '*Louis, by the Grace of God King of France, Duke of Normandy, Count of Paris, Lay Abbot of St. Martin of Tours, to all our faithful lieges do will and ordain:*

"'*First—that we may not be distracted from the eternal and inestimable profiting of our soul by the transient and temporal cares of this sinful and carnal world, we do appoint our trusty vassal, Enguerraud de Coucy, as our actual regent and governor in all our realms.*'

"This is no common office, fair sirs," said the king, without a frown. "Are you agreed in intrusting so great discretion even to so sage and Christian a lord as the Sire de Coucy?"

"We are agreed," spoke Peter and Monseigneur, but Theobald kept his sullen silence.

"I do not debate it," continued the king; "but now to the next.

"'*Second, we are pleased to grant to our noble vassals and prelates hereinunder named the following fiefs, seigneuries, presentations, jurisdictions, pensions, and immunities.*'

"My loyal vassals are not modest in requests. But let the list pass, and again what do I read?

"'*Third, we command her Grace the queen mother of France to withdraw from our court to the Abbey of Mont-lhéry, there to remain, and not to pass beyond the confines of its domain land.*'"

The king frowned and looked twice at the confederates.

He saw Theobald of Champagne struggling forward, and Peter and Monseigneur thrusting him back, but De Coucy spoke up firmly.

"We are resolved on this, your Grace : the queen mother must depart from court, or she abides our prisoner."

"Let me read the next," spoke the king, without discussion. "Ah ! what is this?

"'Fourth, we command that Margaret of Provence— hitherto esteemed our wife — be brought before the High Court of Peers for the grave and capital crime'" — he would not speak the words that came next — "'and if, as is too probable, she shall be found guilty, we accept, as our true and honored bride, the noble lady Alithe de Coucy, to be our queen consort of France.'"

The king lowered the parchment and looked straight at Alithe. She flushed, fluttered, fell upon her knees, and held down her head, but sent forth shy and dovelike glances.

"So *this* is the lady you would have me take to wife?" That was all the king said. De Coucy answered with a sweeping bow, and all the time the beautiful Alithe blushed and blushed, while Louis looked on her in a manner that rejoiced her father's heart. A right royal queen for France !

"You would have me sign and seal this parchment?" asked Louis, his voice again with the slightest quiver.

"Yes, if it pleasure you," replied the chamberlain.

"The great seal of the realm — "

"Is in our custody; we will affix it as soon as you have added your name."

"And how shall I sign?"

"See how the fish smacks as he takes the hook," quoth Peter in Monseigneur's ear. "The sight of that kneeling Dame Venus is enough to fire an anchorite."

"Silence!" commanded the bishop, "the chamberlain is answering."

"The manner of your signature, lord," said Enguerraud, "should be thus, '*Jubeo, Ludovicus Rex.*'"

"Give me the pen." De Coucy presented it on his knees. He saw that the king's hand shook as he held the reed. He looked at the queen mother. She was pale, but did not stir. Alithe was gazing upward with wide, glad eyes. Dead silence — then the scratching of the pen on the parchment, the king handing the writing to De Coucy.

"Read!" he commanded, his voice rising; but the paper seemed dropping from the chamberlain's hands. The bishop caught it up, glanced, and gasped, "The writing is '*nego*'!"

They gazed at the king. Could Charlemagne have reared himself with higher, nobler mien? Could St. Michael's self have shot more majestic lightnings out of enkindling eyes? The king stretched out his hands.

"And why not *nego*, traitors? Shall I pawn my power at the nod of such as you, and you, and you?" His finger swept around the circle, then rested on Alithe: "Who are you, woman, whose white skin covers loathsomeness, to sit on the throne of my pure and beauteous wife? Away with you! I will not endure your sight!"

Alithe shrank back against the wall, pallid, quivering. Peter of Brittany blenched, the bishop also, but Theobald of Champagne leaped forward.

"I have no part with them, Lord, yet traitor I own myself, and cry your mercy. Your words are just."

He stretched his arms out to the king. But the chamberlain and De Ormoy stood their ground.

"Sire," said De Coucy through his gritted teeth, "as I

told your lady mother, we are men pushed to bay. Do not rave too rashly."

The king took the dagger from his belt, cast it on the table, and stood with folded arms, an image of power.

"See," he proclaimed, with a toss, " I am unarmed. I speak to you. I, your king, to whom you have bowed down and sworn, in Heaven's name, fealty. Will you thrust on me this great wickedness, this outrage on my mother, this crime against my wife, this spoiling of my realm, to serve your selfish ends? How will you justify this deed on God's Great Day?"

"We are resolved."

" Resolved on perjury, cruelty, and treason? It cannot be. This is some monstrous jest. Confess it, ere all be too late, and I will freely pardon."

" We are resolved," from the chamberlain again.

The king shot his gaze around the room.

"Whoso is on the side of right and God, now let him stand by me."

Whereat Theobald sprang toward him, and as he did so De Ormoy, whose sword was bare, leaped at the count.

But as he leaped, the king leaped also. The *routier* struck Louis fairly on the breast, when lo! his weapon sprang back, turned. The king reeled, stood up scatheless, and looked into the ring of hostile eyes.

" Would you dare murder?" was all he said.

"We dare anything," cried the chamberlain, drawing also, while Theobald dragged Louis back.

" They are desperate men, Sire, yet they shall kill me the first,"—but the king shook him off.

"One last time—will you repent?"

" No!"   De Ormoy, De Coucy, Peter, cried it together.

" Then let God judge!"

The king leaped back as they sprang on him; sprang and stood still like waves frozen in the storm. A jangling of arms; the curtains of the inner chamber pushed aside; great De Joinville reared in full armor with uplifted partizan.

"*Voilà*, messieurs!" rang out his voice. "I do ever love a noble stage-play!" And looking into the faces of the rest were twelve crossbows, levelled by good men and true. The king drew his mother aside, and stood before, his mailed body covering her, while under the menace of the pointing bolts down sank the upraised swords, their dumb bearers recoiling to the wall. Not a word spoke De Joinville as he advanced to the table, took the lamp, and waved it through the casement, when a shout and crash from the courts below made all the castle shake.

"*Montjoie St. Denis!* For God and for king!"
Louis pointed toward the wretches facing him.

"Advance, Simon; do your office!" And I think De Joinville's mouth wore the grimmest smile in all his life, as he knotted the cord around the hands of Alithe of the Bright Face.

CHAPTER XXIX

"THE QUEEN OF FRANCE"

THUS it was that with Boso's help La Girard and De Joinville won back Pontoise château. How half the Beaumont men-at-arms went up the hidden passage in the rock, whilst the rest of them pressed their noisy feint outside, how Boso guided the king and after him the crossbowmen by the blind staircase to the queen's room, — I leave that for some one else, if he wills, to tell. Enough that as Pontoise had fallen with hardly a blow, it was retaken with hardly a blow; for De Ormoy's crew — bereft of leaders, and assailed from within and without — proved chicken-hearted rebels indeed. They threw down their swords and howled for "mercy!" almost before their veteran enemies had begun the merry game of killing them. And mercy they received, because the king would have it so, though De Joinville and La Girard scowled, and felt cheated of their sport; for they loved a pleasant massacre a little better than a feast. As for the fine court dames and cavaliers, they had rushed from their chambers at the first clatter of pikes in the baileys, only to be met by stern sentinels at every door and a bidding to stay in their quarters, for they were prisoners of his Grace !

After a long time the king went down from the donjon, and La Girard, the commandant of Beaumont — a huge bony man, a boon comrade of De Joinville, came with his report.

"Sire, the castle is your own."

"I thank your valor; have you lost any men?"

"Not one, praise St. Anne! And what shall I do now? Begin to hang the traitors?"

"By no means. Let the great hall be cleared, and all the court folk brought into it; not one shall be away, great or small. The rest I will devise with De Joinville. Make haste. It is close to midnight."

So once more the torches and lamps flared, the black shadows wavered over the dim rafters of the hall of Pontoise château. Seigneurs, pages, noble ladies and their maids, all stood therein. But their lips were whiter and more silent now than when the weapons had flashed and all had thirsted for the Provençal's blood. At every entrance the Beaumont men-at-arms stood with lowered pikes and axes, while in every heart was the same thought: "We all consented to the treason; we all cried '*Mort!*' Now is the vengeance."

They stood close and silent, men and women, while La Girard's spearmen pressed around the doors with files of steel. Then a door behind the dais opened, and all beheld the king.

He walked between Margaret and his mother. The Provençal carried her head high and looked at no one, but the calm, searching gaze of the White Queen sent fear through the boldest baron. "The king was her tool; she would be merciless." And after these came another more dreadful yet — a gigantic man with a brutish face. He wore a tight suit of plain yellow, and bore a long two-handed sword. This was "The King's Sworn Tormentor" or the public executioner of France. Behind him walked

De Joinville and between a file of guards the rebel chiefs, all pinioned and pale as death. Only Theobald's arms hung free. In stillness the king advanced to the edge of the dais. He stood above them, tall as an archangel. At the sweep of his hand, with one impulse, men and women, the noblest in the realm, fell on their knees, while some held out their hands, silently entreating mercy. Then their lord's voice rang like a clarion down the hall. Their king in form and face, but when had their mild king's words burned through their guilty hearts as now?

He told first how France had dwelt in glad peace under the gracious rule of his mother; next, growing terrible, he told how he knew that they were one and all well-wishers of De Coucy's plot; and as he spoke the Beaumont men clashed their weapons horribly.

"It was not my lady mother's misrule, my masters, that made her yoke so heavy to bear, and made you partners in this crime to man and God. It was your selfish lust to oppress the weak, and wage your unholy private wars, to grow rich and wanton as you would; to grow fat upon the blood you would suck from the poor of France. It is that which made you smile upon this crime. What hinders you from meeting your just reward?"

"Mercy, seigneur, mercy!" Men breathed it rather than cried it, and all stretched out their hands. But Louis turned his back on them, and shot his lightnings over the Sire de Coucy.

"Fair lord!" his voice was lower now, but how hard, "you have outwitted my mother and my guards; you have corrupted my court; you have prepared strong friends in France; only *the king* you deemed it safe to neglect. And God, through me, your despised king, arises to your undoing. Thank God — if indeed you can truly pray at all

—that you were spared the completion of your sin, for that were enough to blast the merits of a saint."

Then taking Margaret by the hand again he faced the hall.

"Gallant knights and loyal seigneurs, your swords flew out swiftly to strike a defenceless woman down. Where were those swords to defend your liege-lord's castle, to save his honor from these worse than rebels, who desired to strip him, not of power only, but of his dearest wife's true love?"

"We have sinned! We are disloyal knights! Mercy, kind Lord, mercy!" The groans came from all over the hall, whereupon the king drew Margaret closer. "Look on them all," he whispered in rightful pride, "they kneel to you, to me!" Then he spoke aloud.

"Wherefore, in this public place, I declare that Margaret of Provence is my pure, blameless, and lawful queen. What she did she did because of her husband's sinful blindness and the plottings of these traitors. Yet, for the resolving of all doubts, I have this night again been wedded to her, of which thing the Sire de Joinville stands as witness; and whosoever by word or deed or thought casts shadow on her womanly innocence or royal title shall answer on his life to Louis of France!"

Whereat upon that dais, with the red light over them, the myriad eyes upon them, he took Margaret in his arms and kissed her face, while all the time the multitude knelt, and kept tense silence.

The door behind the dais parted. There entered two pikemen, betwixt them a small man in a dapper dress sadly awry. The manacles were still upon his wrists. He blinked about painfully, unaccustomed to the light. It was Gui of Avignon just from the oubliette. When

Margaret saw him, she flinched a little; but the king, for the first moment since he had entered the great hall, smiled.

"Strike off those fetters," he ordered De Joinville, and by the time that they had fallen the troubadour had gathered his scattered wits and saw how the country lay. He made his fairest reverence to the king, and his hands flew again in their airy gestures.

"Oh, noble, wise, puissant, and ever victorious Lord! valiant as Cœur-de-Lion, magnanimous as Saladin, victorious as Philip Augustus, courteous as Simon de Montfort, potent as Charlemagne, pious as his imperial son styled Louis, whose name you also justly bear —"

But here the king would have no more.

"Spare your praises, if you would pleasure me!" he ordered, part sternly, part in laughter; and Gui had sense enough to grow grave and silent, while De Joinville thrust him back, as Louis looked upon the file of prisoners.

"And now, my masters," spoke he hardly, half to the hall and half to the captives, "what — what shall be the lot of these, — of these who plotted, who drew swords against their king, who threatened his mother with torment, his wife with black dishonor?"

Down went Brittany upon his knees, down Monseigneur, grovelling with his tonsured head, down Theobald, down Enguerraud, down Alithe — and she did not blush and glance shyly now.

"Mercy! mercy! mercy!" They bleated it all together, and the chamberlain was so abject as to shuffle nearer, that he might kiss the king's feet.

"Mercy?" echoed Louis, in a tone like beaten steel. "Did you show mercy when my wife stood on this dais one night ago?"

He drew himself back that the chamberlain might not touch him. Then his eye lit on Theobald. "Rise up, my Lord of Champagne. You have sinned like a man, and repented like a man. Fear nothing. You shielded my wife and mother. The king forgets the rest. Rise up, and let your first treason be your last."

Then as the count arose, the whole hall rose up with him. A load was falling from three hundred hearts; it must vent itself in a cry.

"Long live Louis! Louis the merciful king!"

But their lord beckoned "silence," and turned on the other prisoners.

"Traitors you are! I will not hear you! Not though you plead a thousand years. But plead to the queen of France, and if she pity, let her ask your lives. For I will only hark to *her!*"

I cannot tell all that they said to Margaret as they cowered upon their knees. I think the Provençal was not too little a woman and too much an angel to feel some joy at their agony. Peter the Breton was the calmest, the bishop raved, Enguerraud almost kissed the planks before her feet, but when Alithe pressed near to touch the hem of her dress, the king's voice rang sharper than ever.

"No nearer; who are you to breathe the same air that my wife breathes?"

Only De Ormoy, sullen, desperate, stood like marble and worked his long mustachios. Once he looked at the cringing Coucys, and grinned in violent contempt. He had played his game, and like a true gamester would not weep to save lost stakes.

But now Margaret courtesied daintily to the king, and her voice was winsome and mild.

"Dear lord and husband, I know these folk have grievously sinned, yet let their lives be given them that they may not perish in their guilt and pass from your wrath to the keener wrath of God.   For as He has this night showed us mercy, so let us do likewise."

The king bowed his head, beckoned, bidding the prisoners rise, and spoke while yet they trembled.

"You have heard the queen.   Her wish is law; I give you back your lives.   As Louis of Poissy the man, I pardon you, for Our Lord commands us 'pardon.'   But Louis of France, the shepherd of the realm that you would plunge in bloody strife, must take sureties for the quiet of the Christian folk whom he would guard.   Peter of Brittany," the count hung down his head, "you may go to your own lands, when you have yielded to our captains all your castles. Monseigneur of Beauvais," the bishop's scared eyes ceased rolling, as the king pointed at him, "get you to Rome, where our ambassador shall make such presentations of your unchurchly life as will give you much to answer to the Holy Father.   Enguerraud de Coucy," the chamberlain's ghastly features flushed, "return to your château, and while you live pass not your private bounds, and cease from every plot, or, as I wear my crown, you die.   Henri de Ormoy," the free-lance only stared, and grinned out of his toothless jaws, "you have not sought pardon.   Nevertheless, for your deeds in Pontoise, I give it.   But you shall go to Paris, and at our provost's courts make your defence for all the former crimes wherewith you stand attainted."

Then the king looked on Alithe.   He was silent a moment.   He was wondering how only yesterday this ghostly, palsied woman had almost stolen Margaret out of his heart.   He drew his wife aside that all the hundreds might see the De Coucy standing there in her unlovely agony. It was one of the few deliberately cruel deeds in all his life.

"Alithe de Coucy, you shall go to the Montlhéry, where you would send my mother, and take the vows and veil in that strict convent; there you shall beseech God to have mercy upon a soul which for me it is hard to forgive."

"I — thank — your — Grace!" whispered Alithe; then staggered speechless into the pikemen's arms, and they made haste to carry her away. But Louis had turned to the last of his prisoners, Gui. Again he smiled.

"My Lord of Avignon, I do declare you what I think many here know you full well to be, to wit, one part knight, one part knave, but ten parts fool. At dawn I will despatch you homeward to Provence, and beseech my good father to send to me an older and graver ambassador." To which word, Gui made the wisest answer in his life — he said nothing, and let De Joinville lead him thence.

Then at the end the king bowed to his mother.

"Madame mother," said he, in his clearest voice, "may I ever owe you duty, obedience, and love, may I ever be guided by your counsel, but let these good vassals know, what we ourselves know already, that henceforth I am the lord of France!"

Whereupon a shout went up that made the black beams shake in their shadows.

"Long live Louis the king! Long live the noble queens! Long live they all!"

Louis answered with his smile and pointed to the doors. La Girard's guards were withdrawn already.

"Brave knights and noble ladies, we have had two passing strange days here in Pontoise; forget them if you may, and do not let too many monks inscribe them in their books.

Your king will forget them the first.   And now good night, and may God's peace be with you all.   Farewell."

* * * * * * *

After the rest had left them, Louis took his wife and Blanche and led them each into the other's arms, beautiful youth to age as beautiful.

" My daughter, my daughter, my sweet child," cried the White Queen through her tears. "I have been jealous, and stubborn, and hard.   God has not dealt with me after my sins.   Can you still call me mother ? "

" Yes, mother mine ! " said Margaret, with Louis' own word ; "for even when you were cruel to me I tried to love you, for I knew it was out of surpassing love to him that you seemed so harsh to me."

The king laid a hand on the shoulder of each.   " Henceforth I have three kingdoms, and I will not tell which one I prize and long to serve the best — for they are France, my wife, and my mother ! "

CHAPTER XXX

WHEN THE LARK SINGS

ONLY one morning more and then I and my tale will leave you. It was the day which dawned after the retaking of Pontoise château, a morn when the gold springs out of the sky, the warm sweet smell from the ground, and one wonders whether the blooming fields of heaven have a fairer green than the fields of pleasant earth. After the sun had banished the last clouds, forth from the castle rode Louis the king and Margaret his true wife. They rode in state, on high-stepping white palfreys whose bits were silver. They did not spare the scarlet, ermine, silks, and lace of gold. Before them ran trumpeters who blew their long, clear tubes with merry glee. Behind, in their best and brightest, rode twenty great lords and dames, with twice as many of La Girard's men-at-arms, each one in silvered harness. They cantered down the streets, and all the honest burgher folk ran to the windows to cheer them. First they rode to the Hôtel de Ville, where the worthy syndics and echevins scraped and bowed to their liege lord when he handed them the precious charter giving Pontoise liberties freer than any other commune in France.

"And whither now?" asked De Joinville, who led the troop.

"Whither indeed," answered his master, "except to the manse of St. Maclou?"

And thither they went. It took all of Ambroise's cour-

age to stand at his own door and greet his one-time penitent, what with the arms and scarlet flashing round, and
the city folk thrusting in, rejoicing to see "their father"
was so honored.   The king leaned down in his saddle, and
Ambroise made to kiss Louis' hand, but the king thrust it
into the priest's palm.

"Am I so changed, so dreadful, because I wear a cendal
bliaut?" asked Louis, merrily, and set the curé at his ease
in a twinkling.   "But now," spoke the king in louder
voice, "what shall be your reward? you who gave true
friendship and counsel to the lord of France in his hour
of extremity and grief?   Ask what you will, for I know
you will only ask aright."

"Grovel to this priest," enjoined a listening baron to a
friend.   "His Grace will make him Bishop of Beauvais."

But as they waited, Ambroise thoughtfully and humbly
scratched his head, devising a great petition surely.

"Gracious lord," spoke he, in the expectant hush, "if
my small service may call for any reward at all, and I be
not waxed overbold, give me twenty marks for the poor
of Pontoise."

And he had them — augmented to two hundred; for
nothing that Louis, nothing that Margaret, might plead
could induce him to take anything for himself.   A bishop-
ric? a fat canonry at Paris merely?   The priest was rent
with grief.

"Oh, sweet lord, I am only a simple peasant's son.
My life is all around St. Maclou, and my children here who
love me.   *Nolo episcopare!*   Spare me, in mercy, spare!"

As the king and queen rode from the manse, I think
royal lips reëchoed another shout from the burghers.

"God bless Ambroise, the father of Pontoise!"

But Margaret and Louis rode down through the Beau-

mont Gate to the cottage of Jean of the Mill. When
Brigite had seen them coming, she had called her husband
to watch their Graces pass by; but when the tall palfreys
halted, when the little house was beleaguered with spruce
pages and jingling men-at-arms, when a young man, all in
silks and ermine, leaped down and swung from her saddle
the fairest, most splendid lady of them all, and when at
last the miller's wife saw the faces of these twain, — what
shall I say, — for Brigite and Jean stood on their threshold
like two dumb statues, far too scared to courtesy, much
less to speak, while Louis and Margaret went up to the
cottage door, and all the rest waited in silence.

"A fair morning, Brigite," said Louis, lifting the gem-set
cap. "Does Nicole still mend? And is Falaise now here?"

But she could not speak. The king and queen went
straight past her into the cottage, where Falaise was just
rising from beside the bed.

"Margaret," cried the blind girl, blessed again in her
blindness; no sheen of samite and no flashing coronet
could dazzle her. She ran into the queen's glad arms.
And while she rested there the king went beside Nicole,
who raised herself on the pillow.

"Sir Roland! Roland the kind knight! Good morning,
dearest Roland, you see I fast grow well!"

"Saints in heaven, what raves the child!" groaned
Brigite, her speech returned at last. Louis answered with
his gladdest laugh: —

"Let me be what you will in the castle; in this cottage
I am Sir Roland of Poissy, never more!"

Then he took from his belt a bright gold piece.

"See, Nicole; this is the coin I promised you when you
lay so very sick — a bezant."

"Gold!" cried the little maid, clutching eagerly, "it is

pure gold! Oh, next to God, my father, mother, and Falaise, I think I love you most!"

"If the price of love were a bezant!" spoke the king, a little wistfully; but Nicole did not hear, whereat he took both of her little hands. "Yes, pure gold; and on the word of a king, I promise it shall be a royal decree and registered at Paris, 'To Nicole, daughter of Jean the Miller of Pontoise, so long as she lives, every month from the privy exchequer, a bezant.'"

"Do you hear, child?" demanded Brigite, covering her tremblings under fuss and noise; "a syndic's daughter's fortune. Out of bed, down on your knees, and thank the too-generous king!"

"King?" said Nicole, staring round. "I see only dear Sir Roland of Poissy, but he is beautifully dressed."

Louis made her lie down on the bed. "Dear child," he said, "you are very right. This is only Sir Roland of Poissy. Your mother must not frighten you. Another day I will speak to your father, and make it plain to him that come famine, come harvest, he and his shall never suffer want."

Then he let go her hand and went over to Falaise.

"You are Louis, and you are Margaret," spoke the blind girl; "and all your doubts are cleared away and you are very happy, therefore I am happy too!"

"And next to God," the king answered her, "you have given us back all joy. We must part now, but to-night at the château you shall learn how much my mother loves you for our sake."

Margaret kissed her; the king, while his wife nodded sweetly, kissed her also. They went to the door, but did not open. Falaise had knelt down by the bedside. Perhaps she thought them gone. She began to sing : —

" The babe in the cradle, the bird in the nest
  Are rocking, are sleeping, well cherished and blest.
  The mother guards one, and the oak tree the other —
  The winds are their friends, and the wide world their brother.

" Lord Jesu, shall I wake and tremble with fear
  When thou and thine own blessed angels watch near ?
  The oak tree may shatter, the mother may die, —
  But safe in Thy hands I will dream as I lie.

" And I ask but to feel the soft beat of the wings
  When Thy spirits come close for my heart's pleasurings —
  Hear them murmur and move as my anxious thoughts cease —
  To awake when Thou wilt, in the love of Thy peace."

. . . The king and queen came out of the cottage, with
a glow in their faces brighter than all the gold on Margaret's hair. They mounted their palfreys and rode at a merry
canter toward Montmorenci wood. At a tall beech they
halted, and De Joinville, taught of Ambroise, blew a shrill
whistle thrice, whereupon strange, bearded men seemed
springing out of the brakes of the forest — Aimerel, Sugier,
and the rest. It took not a little coaxing to make them
drop their bows and draw nigh to the splendid lords on
horseback. But when they saw the knight who had cast
giant Aimerel down, they crowded up to him gladly, and
perhaps were not so much amazed as Jean when they
knew who it was that Ambroise had led with him to the
wood.

"We are your loyal vassals, sire," spoke Aimerel, bluntly,
"first because you are the king, but chiefly because you
are a *man*." Nor could he have said anything to please
his liege lord more.

"My friends," Louis told them, "go you to Pontoise.
My clerks are drawing up your pardons. Quit the wood-
land. It is a merry life, but not for Christian men. I

will see that you never lack honest bread. Also that you shall stand before my judges without fear, to accuse my evil seigneurs and officers, for your own king will be your advocate."

Then the band cantered forward until they came to the heart of the great wood. There Louis turned to the others.

"Fair friends," said he, "wait for us a while. We two would go on alone."

Down a green-hung avenue the king and queen rode. None but heaven's eyes watched them. The fresh boughs whipped softly in their faces. They heard the crickets chirp, the purling and gushing of a little brook, whose crystals flashed fairer than the crown-jewels of France. They joined hands and rode slowly, laughed, talked of an hundred nothings, while overhead — an invisible escort in the tree-hid blue — a lark sang their new marriage hymn. Around them breathed the perfume of uncounted wild flowers, the offering of spring to the bursting summer.

"How good it all is," said Margaret, while the wise palfreys stepped slower; "trees, flowers, cricket, lark, they are speaking one word 'Joy!' 'Joy!'"

"Yes," answered Louis, putting out his arm and drawing her face near, "to-morrow we belong to France; but to-day we are not king and queen: we are a lad and a lass being glad together, and the Dear God over us all."

*   *   *   *   *   *   *

So far I have wandered with you through the paths of old romance. Now the mists of years are closing; the way grows dim; I can lead on no farther. Only once or twice afterward I see the gray mists lighten; I see flashes here, there, yonder, of those who walked and talked, who laughed and wept, in old Pontoise two days in a certain May long ago.

I see a blind abbess at Maubuisson, who goes through her own dark world, but, everywhere she treads, sheds heavenly light, and sinful men and women cease from their sins when she sings to them, and despairing hearts take hope when they look on the joy in her face. "Sister," so the king and queen call her, and she is often with them. Also when the great and good Blanche of Castile lies on her death-bed at Melun, with her children in far Palestine, you can read in the old books how this abbess closes her eyes and sets the last kiss on her forehead. But what Louis and Margaret did is not written in one book, but in ten thousand; why then need I write another? For God fulfilled all that He promised through the archangel, when Louis was crowned in the cottage. "Thou shalt rule many years and do and suffer great things for Him, and men shall call thee blessed."

When the great life was ended, this is what one who mourned for his king wrote: "In his day France was like the sun amongst the other kingdoms. In his day was righteousness and peace. He loved God and Holy Church, and we know he is ever with the saints in light."

NOTE

The flaw in the wedding-service of Louis and Margaret, herein described, is simply an illustration of what was too often deliberately practised in the Middle Ages, to leave a loophole for an annulment of a marriage, when by church law no regular divorce was admissible.

Of the various verses in this book the majority are translations by the author from the Old French and Latin.

For assistance on several historical and literary details I am deeply indebted to my friend, Dr. Walter Lichtenstein, and to my sister, Miss Fannie Stearns Davis; also to Professor Justin H. Smith's valuable work, "The Troubadours at Home," for two brief songs.

W. S. D.

HARVARD UNIVERSITY, *June* 1, 1904.